THE
CABINET OF
DR. LENG

A Pendergast Novel

DOUGLAS PRESTON &
LINCOLN CHILD

GRAND
CENTRAL

New York   Boston

ALSO BY DOUGLAS PRESTON AND LINCOLN CHILD

AGENT PENDERGAST NOVELS

Bloodless • Crooked River • Verses for the Dead • City of Endless Night • The Obsidian Chamber • Crimson Shore • Blue Labyrinth • White Fire • Two Graves* • Cold Vengeance* • Fever Dream* • Cemetery Dance • The Wheel of Darkness • The Book of the Dead** • Dance of Death** • Brimstone** • Still Life with Crows • The Cabinet of Curiosities • Reliquary† • Relic†

*The Helen Trilogy **The Diogenes Trilogy
†*Relic* and *Reliquary* are ideally read in sequence

NORA KELLY NOVELS

Diablo Mesa • The Scorpion's Tail • Old Bones

GIDEON CREW NOVELS

The Pharaoh Key • Beyond the Ice Limit • The Lost Island • Gideon's Corpse • Gideon's Sword

OTHER NOVELS

The Ice Limit • Thunderhead • Riptide • Mount Dragon

BY DOUGLAS PRESTON

The Lost City of the Monkey God • *The Kraken Project* • *Impact*
• *The Monster of Florence* (with Mario Spezi) • *Blasphemy*
• *Tyrannosaur Canyon* • *The Codex* • *Ribbons of Time* • *The Royal
Road* • *Talking to the Ground* • *Jennie* • *Cities of Gold* • *Dinosaurs
in the Attic*

BY LINCOLN CHILD

Chrysalis • *Full Wolf Moon* • *The Forgotten Room* • *The Third
Gate* • *Terminal Freeze* • *Deep Storm* • *Death Match* • *Lethal
Velocity* (formerly *Utopia*) • *Tales of the Dark 1–3* • *Dark Banquet*
• *Dark Company*

THE CABINET OF
DR. LENG

Copyright © 2023 by Splendide Mendax, Inc. and Lincoln Child

Cover design by Flag. Cover photographs by Getty Images. Cover copyright © 2023 by Hachette Book Group, Inc.

Grand Central Publishing
Hachette Book Group
1290 Avenue of the Americas, New York, NY 10104
grandcentralpublishing.com
twitter.com/grandcentralpub

First Edition: January 2023

Grand Central Publishing is a division of Hachette Book Group, Inc. The Grand Central Publishing name and logo is a trademark of Hachette Book Group, Inc.

The publisher is not responsible for websites (or their content) that are not owned by the publisher.

The Hachette Speakers Bureau provides a wide range of authors for speaking events. To find out more, go to www.hachettespeakersbureau.com or call (866) 376-6591.

Grand Central Publishing books may be purchased in bulk for business, educational, or promotional use. For information, please contact your local bookseller or the Hachette Book Group Special Markets Department at special.markets@hbgusa.com.

Library of Congress Cataloging-in-Publication Data has been applied for.

ISBNs: 9781538736777 (hardcover), 9781538736807 (ebook), 9781538742662 (int'l edition), 9781538742822 (Canadian edition), 9781538741559 (large print), 9781538742808 (B&N signed edition), 9781538742785 (signed edition)

Printed in the United States of America

LSC-C

Printing 1, 2022

THE CABINET OF
DR. LENG

DOCTOR LENG WILL SEE YOU NOW…

I

THE MORNING SUN, FILTERED through a veil of dust and smoke, fell feebly upon the intersection where Broadway crossed Seventh Avenue. The thoroughfare was made of dirt, its potholed surface packed so hard from an infinitude of horses and wagons it seemed as impermeable as cement, except in the muddy areas surrounding the grooves of the cable car tracks and the hitching posts, sunk in manure.

The intersection was called Longacre. It was the center of the carriage trade, an outlying district of the rapidly growing city where horses were stabled and buggy makers toiled.

On this particular chilly morning, Longacre and the avenues and streets leading from it were quiet save for the occasional pedestrian or horse cart passing by, and nobody paid much attention to the young woman with short dark hair, dressed in a purple gown of an unusual cut and fabric, who stepped out from an alleyway and looked around, squinting and wrinkling her nose.

Constance Greene paused, letting the initial flood of sensations sink in, careful not to betray any sign of the upswell of emotions that threatened to overwhelm her. The sights, noises, and odors unexpectedly brought back a thousand memories of her childhood, memories so distant that she scarcely knew she still retained them. The smell of the city hit her first and most viscerally: a mixture of earth, sweat, horse dung, coal smoke, urine, leather, fried meat, and the ammoniac tang of lye. Next were sights she'd once taken for granted but now looked strange—the telegraph poles, invariably listing; the gaslights on various corners; the numerous carriages, parked upon or next to sidewalks; the ubiquitous shabbiness. Everything spoke of a city growing so fast it could scarcely keep up with itself. Most strangely, the white-noise susurrus of modern Manhattan was missing: the growl of car traffic; the honking of taxis; the hum of compressors, turbines, HVAC systems; the underground rumble of subway trains. In its place was a relative quiet: hoofbeats of horses, shouts, calls, and laughter; the occasional crack of a whip; and, from a nearby saloon, the tinny, off-key strains of an upright piano. She had grown so used to seeing the boulevards of Manhattan as vertical steel canyons it was hard to process this scene, where the tallest buildings, as far as the eye could see, were no greater than three or four stories.

After a few minutes, Constance took a deep breath. Then she turned south.

She walked past a frowzy restaurant offering a choice of oxtail goulash, potted veal chop, or pigs' feet with kraut for five cents. Outside stood a busy newsboy with an armful of papers, his clear piping voice announcing the headlines of the day. She passed slowly, staring, as he held one out hopefully. She shook her head and walked on, but not before noting the date: Tuesday, November 27, 1880.

November 1880. Her sister, Mary, nineteen years old, was currently being worked half to death in the Five Points House of Industry. And her brother, Joseph, twelve, would be completing his sentence on Blackwell's Island.

And a certain doctor had recently begun his ghastly, murderous experiments.

She felt her heart quicken at the thought of them still alive. She might yet be in time.

Reaching into the smock of her dress, she felt the reassuring heft of her antique stiletto, along with eight hundred and fifty dollars in period money. She went on at a brisker pace, heading in the direction of Herald Square and a better part of town.

A dozen blocks to the south, she found a couturier that, in addition to tailored dresses, also sold prêt-à-porter outfits. An hour later she emerged, with a shop's assistant holding a hatbox and two large bags in tow. Instead of the purple gown, Constance was now wearing an elegant bustle dress of peacock-blue silk and white ruffles, with a matching bonnet and heavy Eton jacket. As she walked briskly to the curb, the gazes she attracted were admiring rather than curious. Constance waited while the assistant flagged a hansom cab.

The driver began to get down from his seat, but Constance opened the door herself and—putting a high-buttoned shoe on the running board—sprang up easily into the compartment.

The driver raised his eyebrows, then mounted his seat as the shop assistant put the bags and the hatbox inside the cab. "Where to, ma'am?" he asked as he drew in the reins.

"The Fifth Avenue Hotel," Constance said, proffering a dollar bill.

"Yes, *ma'am*," the driver said as he pocketed it. Without another word, he urged his horse forward, and in moments the cab had merged smoothly into the ebb and flow of the noonday traffic.

It was another dozen blocks to her destination: the opulent palace of marble and brick, six stories high, that occupied the entire block of Fifth Avenue across from Madison Square. The cab came to a stop at the hotel's entrance portico. "Whoa, Rascal," the driver said.

Constance opened the small trap door in the rear of the roof. "Would you wait for me, please?" she asked.

He glanced down from his sprung seat behind and above the compartment. "Certainly, mum." He released the door lever and she stepped out. Immediately, two doormen rushed forward to take possession of the bags and hatbox. Not pausing to wait, Constance walked swiftly beneath the rows of Corinthian columns and across the white-and-crimson marble flooring of the entrance hall.

Past a barber shop, telegraph office, and restaurant, she found the large front desk of carved wood, polished to a brilliant hue. Behind the desk were several men, dressed in similar livery. One of them approached her.

"Are you looking for the ladies' reception room, madam?" he asked deferentially. "You will find it one flight up."

Constance shook her head. "I would like to take a room, please."

The man raised his eyebrows. "For you and your husband?"

"I'm traveling alone."

The eyebrows went back down discreetly. "I see. I'm afraid, madam, that almost all of our standard rooms are taken—"

"A suite, then," Constance said.

The central lobby of the hotel was a large space with a high, vaulted ceiling, and the constant procession of chattering guests, their footfalls echoing on the diamond-patterned marble, made it difficult for her to hear.

"Very good, madam." The man turned to a row of niches built into the wall behind him, withdrew a leatherbound book from one, and opened it. "We have two suites available on the fourth floor, and several on the second, if you are not inclined to use the perpendicular railway."

"The what?"

"The perpendicular railway. It has intersections on each story of the hotel."

He was, Constance realized, talking about the elevator. "Very well. The second floor will be fine."

"Would you care for a view of—"

"Just give me the best available, if you'd be so kind." Constance felt like screaming. *November 27.* Now that she knew she was in time to save her sister, every minute spent on such trivialities seemed an age.

The hotel manager was too well trained to remark on her impatience. He turned over a heavy leaf in the ledger, dipped a pen into a nearby inkwell. "Very good, madam. There is an excellent corner suite available, complete with parlor, chamber, dressing room, and bath." He raised the pen. "The rate is six dollars per night, or thirty dollars for the week. How long will you be with us?"

"A week."

"Maids?"

"I'm sorry?"

"Your maids? How many are traveling with you, madam?"

"None. Two."

"Two. Very good. We can accommodate them in the servants' quarters. With meals, of course?"

Constance, fidgeting, nodded.

"May I have your name?"

"Mary Ulcisor," she said after the briefest of pauses.

He scribbled in the ledger. "That will amount to thirty-five dollars and fifty cents."

She handed him four ten-dollar bills. Turning, she saw two porters waiting patiently behind with her modest shop bags.

"Will you have those taken up to my suite?" she asked the manager as he returned her change. "I'll follow later... along, ah, with my maids."

"Of course."

Constance gave each of the porters a quarter, and the manager a dollar. His eyes widened in surprise and he took it gratefully. She left the lobby and returned to the entrance, pausing just long enough at the literary depot to pick up a street guide to Manhattan.

She found her driver and hansom cab waiting outside the portico in the dust and noise of the avenue. As Constance approached, she took a closer look at the man. He was perhaps in his mid-forties and heavy-set, but his build was muscular rather than stocky. His cold-weather uniform was clean and his manners were good, but something about the square cut of his jaw and crooked bridge of his nose told her he knew how to take care of himself.

She walked up to his seat. "Would you be interested in making some more money?"

"Always ready for business, mum." He had more than a trace of an Irish accent—County Cork, she guessed; something else that would be useful.

"I need transportation downtown."

"How far downtown, mum?"

She opened the street guide she had just purchased, located an intersection, and showed it to him.

"Lor', mum," he said. "Sure, there must be some mistake."

"No mistake. I'm going to pick up someone and bring her back here."

The cabbie had an expression on his face somewhere between bewilderment and apprehension. "It's no place for a lady down there, mum."

"That's why I need somebody who knows how to handle himself. And who's equipped with—" she mentally dug into her knowledge of Gaelic— "*liathróidí cruach.*"

The man opened his mouth in surprise, but he remained silent when she reached into her purse, took out two five-dollar bills, and held them out to him—making no effort to hide her stiletto in the process. "There's another ten waiting when you bring us back here safely."

He whistled. "Not afraid of the sight of blood, then?"

"Not after breakfast."

"Well, I'll be..." He laughed as he took the money. "Climb aboard, then. Willy Murphy never ran from anything in his life." He winked at her a trifle saucily. "If I'm headed for the hereafter, missus, I'd rather they found me with a tenner in me pocket."

"If that's indeed where you're headed," Constance replied as one of the doormen helped her into the cab, "I'll keep you company on the journey."

The cabbie laughed again; shook his head in disbelief; pulled the lever to close the carriage door; then raised his whip, cracking the air above Rascal's head, and they went trotting off.

2

As the coach made its way down Broadway, Constance sat back in the small compartment. The leather of the seat was worn and cracked, and with every jolt she could feel the lumpy springs of the cushion dig into her.

She estimated she'd arrived about two and a half hours ago. That would make it early afternoon. Good: where they were going, the earlier in the day, the less dangerous it might be.

She had made it safely to this time and place. In half an hour, maybe less, she'd be reunited with Mary and spiriting her away from a miserable existence of overwork and ultimate death. At the thought of death, Constance became aware of her pounding heart. She almost couldn't process all that had happened in the last twenty-four hours— and if she allowed herself to dwell on it, the thoughts would quickly overwhelm her. She had to concentrate on one thing only: rescuing her sister. As the coach made a brief jog along Fourteenth Street before heading southeast once more, she closed her eyes and, with long practice, let the sounds and sensations around her grow dim, purging herself of all unnecessary thoughts. When she opened her eyes again, the cab had just crossed East Houston Street, and Fourth Avenue had become the Bowery. Putting two fingers to her wrist, she felt her pulse: sixty-four.

That would suffice.

Now once again she let in the external world. The landscape had changed dramatically from the upscale neighborhood of the Fifth Avenue Hotel. Here there were more wagons than cabs, with battered wheels and goods covered in stained oilcloths. The pedestrians that thronged both sidewalk and street wore vests and jackets of coarser material. There were few women visible. Every man, no matter how disheveled, wore some kind of hat or cap. The broad pavers of Fifth Avenue had given way to cobblestones.

She felt the cab begin to slow. A moment later, there was a rap on the door in the compartment's roof.

She reached up and opened it. "Yes?"

The head of Murphy, the cabbie, appeared above the trap door. He had pulled the flaps of his cap down around his ears. "Begging your pardon, missus, but I'd rather not be taking her directly through the Points."

"Of course. Please pull over a moment."

While the cab waited, she consulted the city map she'd purchased. "I would suggest turning west on Canal, then south on Center."

"And then...left on Worth?"

"Exactly. Can you manage it?"

"I'll pull in at the corner."

"Very good. And Mr. Murphy?"

"Yes, mum?"

"If there's any trouble, you don't need to return us to the hotel. Union Square will do. I would not want you getting involved in anything that might cause...difficulties for yourself. I just need to get my friend safely away from that place."

"Begging your pardon, mum, but if she's confined in the workhouse, there must be a reason."

"She had the bad luck to be out after dark and was swept up in a raid by police looking for streetwalkers."

"They may not be in a bloody great rush to release her." It seemed the closer he came to becoming a partner in crime, the more familiar—or at least pragmatic—the coachman became.

"I'll persuade them the same way I persuaded you. Two raps when we arrive, please." And Constance closed the trap door.

As the cab started up and she sat back once again, Constance knew her voice had been steady. However, inside she felt anything but calm. With each clop of its hooves, the nag was bringing her deeper into her own distant memory. And as their surroundings grew increasingly dirty and impoverished, Constance was assaulted by smells she'd long forgotten: the scent of penny pies and sheep's trotters and steamed oysters; the odor of printer's dye being readied for inking the next day's broadsides; acrid coal smoke. And the sounds: the call of the street vendors shouting "Buy! What'll you buy?"; the singing of children playing hopscotch or skipping long rope, blithely ignorant of their poverty:

Johnny gave me cherries,
Johnny gave me pears.
Johnny gave me sixpence
To kiss him on the stairs.

And then—as the cab turned down Center toward Worth—came another change, for the worse. Constance felt as if she had just parted the forbidden veil of Isis and passed into the unnatural world beyond. The air now grew thick with greasy fumes from the illegal tanneries that infested the area. The singing of children, the cries of merchants, vanished. As a premature dusk descended from the thickening atmosphere, Constance began to make out new sounds: whimpers of despair and pain; grunts and curses; the cackling and screeching of streetwalkers; the sickening sound of brickbats hitting flesh. These, too, came back as memories, but memories she had long suppressed.

The carriage turned a corner, then came to a lurching stop. Two raps, and the trap door opened slightly. "Let me just put the blinders on Rascal, mum," said Murphy, his voice tight.

Constance readied herself, sliding one hand into the pocket that contained both money and stiletto. A moment later, there was a rattling sound, then the door to the carriage opened and Murphy extended one hand to help her out. In the other hand he held a long wooden cudgel, with a spine of metal, that he had partially drawn out of one coat pocket.

"No fears, mum," he said. "It's just me ugly stick." But his attempt at a lighthearted tone failed, and his eyes were constantly in motion. Constance noted his posture was that of a man ready to repel a threat at a moment's notice. No doubt he was wishing he'd stayed uptown. But it was just as obvious that, having escorted a lady to such a place, he would not abandon her.

With this thought, Constance moved forward one step, another— and then, raising her eyes to look ahead, stopped with an involuntary gasp.

3

THEY HAD STEPPED OUT at a corner. Ahead, at the far end of the
block, lay a confusing intersection of muddy streets. Four of its five
approaches were dense with buildings of decaying brick, their upper
stories leaning perilously over the sidewalks below. The fifth held a
small square, with nothing more than a well handle for public water,
surrounded by a fetid pig wallow into which all manner of garbage
and filth had been tossed. A few ancient wooden structures from the
previous century were visible here and there—squat and in ruinous
condition. Chickens and pigs wandered unchecked, pecking and root-
ing. Windows everywhere were broken; some mended with waxed
paper, others boarded over, still others open to the elements. No
signage protruded above the blackened shopfronts: what commerce
had once been eked out here had long since been given over to
grogshops, tippling houses, and dens of prostitution. Men lolled in
doorways, drinking, expectorating gobs of phlegm or yellow ropes of
chewing tobacco; women, too, were on the street, sprawled drunken
and senseless or calling out to potential customers, lifting a skirt or exposing a breast to advertise their wares. A group of young boys played
in the gutter with a paper boat folded from a piece of newspaper.

This was the Five Points—the worst crossroads in the worst slum in
all of New York. To Constance the spectacle was doubly traumatizing,
because she recognized it in the most personal of ways. Nearly a

century and a half before, she herself had scurried along these same streets and seen these same sights as a little girl, hungry, freezing, dressed in rags.

"Mum," she heard the coachman say, while giving her elbow the slightest pressure. "We'd best be about it." He turned to the boys nearby, took a silver dollar from his pocket and flipped it, then slipped it back in, leaving them staring with longing. "That's for you if me horse and carriage are here when we get back."

Once again, Constance pushed down hard on the whirlwind of memories this sight stirred so violently. She had to be strong, for Mary's sake—later, in safety, she could deal with the emotional aftermath.

Murphy guided her forward. She went along, ignoring the muck and filth that spilled over the curbside and onto the sidewalk, eyes fixed ahead, shutting out the hoots and lecherous catcalls, along with the curses of other women who—seeing the fine cut of her clothes and the clear complexion of her skin—took her for unfair competition. She refused to glance down the dark and narrow lanes that led back from the street—crooked alleyways calf-deep in mud, sky obscured by clotheslines, lined by men in bowler hats guarding the hidden entrances to underground dens. These alleys exhaled smells of their own, much harder to shut out because of their vileness: sepsis; rotting meat; sewage.

She stumbled on a cobble and felt the steadying hand of Murphy on her elbow. They were halfway down the block now, and the ancient structure of the House of Industry rose up on their left, its soot-streaked façade cracked, its windows barred.

Mary was inside. *Mary.* Constance began to say the name over and over to herself, like a mantra.

She glanced across the street at another large structure in better condition than its neighbors. This had once been the site of the Old Brewery, the most notorious tenement building in New York, so large and airless that most of its interior spaces had no windows. Its entrances had been given nicknames—the Den of Thieves, Murderers' Alley, Sudden Death. But a ladies' missionary society had it torn down and replaced it with the Five Points Mission, dedicated to helping indigent women and children. Constance knew the building well; many times, as a young orphan, she had begged bread from its kitchen entrance off Baxter Street. Mary was supposed to be quartered and fed in the Mission. But corrupt interests had transferred her and so many others across the street to the House of Industry instead, to get the benefit of cheap labor. She spent all her time locked within the House of Industry, working sixteen-hour days in crowded, lice-infested quarters.

Steeling herself with this thought, she glanced over at Murphy, who nodded in readiness. Raising his hand to the worn brass doorknob, he turned it to no avail.

"Oi!" he said. "Locked." He started to knock, but Constance stayed his hand.

She pulled a hairpin from her bonnet, bent toward the lock, and inserted it. Within a few moments, a click sounded. She stepped back again from the scuffed and dented knob.

"Lord blind me!" the coachman said.

"Surprise is important. Would you agree?"

Murphy nodded.

"In that case: after you."

The coachman grasped the knob again, holding his cudgel firm in the other hand. Then in one swift move he opened the door, stepped inside, and Constance followed. He closed it behind her.

Constance glanced around quickly. The entry room was bisected by a hinged wooden counter, which could be lifted for passage through, much in the manner of a bank. Doors to the left and right led into other, larger rooms, with high ceilings of pressed tin. She could smell the tang of urine and lye in the air. Chicken feathers and oyster shells were piled in the corners.

A man sat behind the divider, visible only from his chest up. He wore a worn coat and a white shirt with a filthy collar, unbuttoned at his neck. A pair of crepe armbands adorned his arms just above the elbows, and his fingernails were black with accumulated grime.

He pushed an ink-stained cap back from his forehead and looked from one to the other. "What's this? Who are you lot, then?"

"We're here for Mary Greene," Constance said, stepping forward.

"Are you now?" said the man, seemingly unfazed by her prosperous appearance and ability to bypass the lock. "And what might your business be with her?"

"My business is no concern of yours. I wish to see her—now."

"Oh, indeed? You 'wish to see her.' What do you think this is—a zoo?"

"It smells like one," said Murphy.

Quickly as possible. Quickly as possible. Constance reached into her pocket. "Let me explain. You are in a position to make yourself a good deal of money for very little work. Go find Mary Greene. Bring her here. And in return you'll receive twenty dollars." She showed him the money.

The man's eyes widened in his soot-smeared face. "Nellie Greene, is it? By God, you should have told me this involved an exchange of currency. Give me the money, and I'll go get her." And he reached over the desktop.

Constance returned the money to her pocket. "It's Mary. Not Nellie."

Murphy moved toward the clerk-*cum*-jailer. "Money later," he said, brandishing the cudgel.

"No, no, my friend," said the man, holding out his hand with a coaxing motion. "*Now.*"

"Give us the girl," Murphy said in a threatening tone.

A silence ensued. Finally, the man behind the counter replied: "I wouldn't give you the steam off my piss."

"Bloody gombeen!" Murphy cried as he lunged to the counter and grabbed the man's shirt in his fist, literally pulling him up and over. But the man, shouting at the top of his lungs, had gotten his hands on a butcher's knife from beneath the desk and went to slash at Murphy.

Taking advantage of the brawl, Constance ducked into the room on the left. It must have originally been a chapel, but now the windows were barred, and instead of pews there was row upon row of cots, straw scattered across the floor among them. It was brutally cold. The mattresses were so thin she could see the outline of the metal grilles beneath. Rags and bits of clothing lay beneath the beds, worn and dirty. Where plaster had fallen from the walls, the exposed laths had been patched with newsprint and oiled paper.

Almost mad with the need to find her sister, she ran to the next room, full of dirty clothes and scullery equipment, and into the next, where a clacking, humming sound filled the air. There, in a vast, dim space, were two rows of girls and women. They sat on what looked like milking stools, and were dressed in dirty, one-piece shifts. Before each of them was a foot-pedal-operated mechanical loom.

Slowly, the hum subsided. One after another, they stopped their work and looked silently in her direction.

As Constance approached, desperately searching the faces for her sister, a uniformed man came striding over from the far end of the room, a truncheon in his belt, his hobnail boots loud on the wooden floor. "What's this? Who are you?"

Constance skipped back and exited, running toward the entrance, pulling out her stiletto as she ran. When she entered, she found that Murphy had the attendant in a hammerlock, the knife on the floor, the man begging and whining.

At that moment, the door at the far end of the entryway banged open and a woman strode in.

"Cease and desist!" she cried as she came storming over, her voice cutting the air.

She was tall and thin, almost skeletal, and wore a long brown dress with buttons that ran from her waist to her neck. Her eyes were sharp and intelligent, and she had such an air of chill authority that the two men ceased to struggle.

"What is the meaning of this disturbance?" she said, looking at the three occupants of the room in turn, fixing on Constance.

Constance felt the sharp gaze freeze her blood. "We're here for Mary Greene," she said, still gripping the stiletto. "And we'll be leaving with her—one way or another."

The woman gave a mirthless laugh. "There is no need for dramatics, young lady." She turned back to the two men, who had released each other and were standing, disheveled and panting. "Royds," she snapped, "get about your business."

As the man skulked away, giving them a final leer over his shoulder, the woman went to a nearby shelf and drew from it a large ledger book, put it on the counter, flipped the pages until she found one marked with a ribbon, then smoothed it down. "As I thought. She was taken from here yesterday."

"*Taken?*"

"To the sanatorium. The doctor found her ill and condescended to favor her with special attention." The woman paused. "What is your interest in the matter?"

"She is a friend of the family," Constance said.

"Then you should be grateful. Very few of our residents are lucky enough to come under the care of Dr. Leng."

"Dr. Leng," Constance repeated. For a moment, it felt like the floor was burning away beneath her and she was about to fall into the earth.

"Yes. His arrival here last summer was the greatest blessing. Already, five of our young ladies have been sent to recover at his private sanatorium."

Constance could hardly speak. The woman continued to look at her dubiously, one eyebrow raised.

"Where...is this sanatorium?" Constance asked.

"It would be above my station to question the doctor. I am sure it is a fine place." The woman spoke primly, yet with a voice of iron. "For the safety of its patients, the location is kept strictly private."

Moving as if in a nightmare, Constance pulled the book toward her. The page had roughly a dozen entries—several new arrivals, one released with time served, another dead from typhus and removed by hearse...and two others marked TRANSFERRED TO SANATORIUM FOR CLOSER OBSERVATION. The most recent entry was for Mary. She had been signed out on Monday, November 26. Yesterday. And beside the entry, written in ink that had not yet completely lost its gloss, was a signature: E. LENG.

Yesterday. Constance staggered, raising the hand holding the stiletto as she did so.

Mistaking the movement for aggression, the lady said: "Do your worst. I am ready to meet Him as made me." And she stared at Constance with defiant scorn.

"We're leaving now," said Murphy, as the clerk reached for the alarm bell. He took Constance's arm and urged her toward the door. She went unresisting. Just before it closed, he yelled back at the man within: *"Buinneach dhearg go dtigidh ort!"*

The walk back to the coach was more of a stagger, Constance oblivious to the jeers of the onlookers and the stench of the street. When she came fully back to herself, they were once again on Canal Street, heading for the hotel.

The trap door opened slightly. "I'm very sorry, mum, that we couldn't have done more."

"Thank you, Mr. Murphy," she managed to say. "You did all you could."

As the cab pulled up at the hotel's porte cochere, and the doormen rushed out to open the carriage door and assist, Constance rapped on the trap. Murphy opened it. She handed ten dollars up to him through the opening. "Mr. Murphy? I wonder if I might hire you exclusively for the next week or so."

"As you wish, mum—and thank you kindly."

"Very good. Please be here tomorrow morning at nine and wait in the cabbie queue for me."

"Yes, mum."

"And Mr. Murphy? Perhaps you might use this sunny afternoon to do me a small kindness."

"And what would that be, mum?"

"Fix this lumpy seat."

He touched his hat with a grin. "Sure it will be done, mum."

As the trap door closed, she descended from the cab, walked up the marble steps through bronze doors and into the great lobby, finishing under her breath the children's rhyme she'd heard an hour earlier, when she'd been so full of hope:

I gave him back his cherries,
I gave him back his pears.
I gave him back his sixpence
And I kicked him down the stairs.

4

CONSTANCE STOOD BEFORE THE bow window of her parlor, watching as lamplighters lit the gaslights, one by one, along Fifth Avenue. She remained there, motionless, for some time as night crept over the city and a winter fog rolled in from the harbor, turning the lamps on the passing coaches into fireflies and the lights of Madison Square into a constellation of soft globes.

A blackness had settled over her and, for a while, rational thinking was extinguished. Slowly—as she looked into the dark—emotion and reason reasserted themselves. First came anger: blind, useless anger at the quirk that had brought her back one day, *one day*, too late to rescue her sister. Dr. Leng now had Mary in his "sanatorium"—and Constance had good reason to believe the woman at the House of Industry when she professed ignorance of its location. That was not something Leng would want known, because his sanatorium was not a place from where people emerged cured—or even emerged at all.

Constance knew Leng had begun donating his "services" to the House of Industry that summer. Before returning here, she'd already known she might be too late. She could take some comfort—cold though it was—in knowing her sister was relatively safe for the next few weeks. Leng would put her through a period of special nourishment and observation before he performed his surgery…and made his harvest from her body.

The more urgent problem involved her brother, Joseph, who had just turned twelve and was imprisoned on Blackwell's Island. Constance knew he would be released on Christmas Eve. She also knew that he would be beaten to death the following day—Christmas—during a pickpocketing attempt gone bad. She knew, because she had witnessed the horrifying event herself.

The traumatic and brutal six-month stay on Blackwell's Island would change Joe: upon his release he would have become a different person, skilled—but not skilled enough—in the criminal arts that so quickly led to his death. Every day he was incarcerated, she knew, was damaging him further, making him less like his former innocent, trusting self.

And then she had to consider her own doppelganger. In this parallel reality, there was another Constance Greene out there: aged nine, cold and hungry, roaming the streets of the Five Points. That was the strangest caprice of time and the multiverse: that she also had to find and save her own younger self. Now that Mary had been taken, young Constance could not even rely on the crusts of bread her older sister had been able to toss to her from the barred windows of the House of Industry. But the young Constance of this era, this parallel world, would survive. Constance knew this—because she herself had survived.

She needed to collect herself and devise a plan. She knew now she could not remain Mary Ulcisor. A young, single woman, traveling alone, would attract attention of the wrong kind. She regretted she had caused a scene at the House of Industry—she should have been more careful. Luckily, she had not given her name, but what had happened there would not soon be forgotten by that iron-fisted woman.

Turning from the window, she walked over to a nearby writing desk and took a seat. Several items lay upon it: an afternoon newspaper, her atlas of New York, the stiletto—and the bag of gemstones and two folded parchment sheets that had never been far from her side during the last few years.

The Fifth Avenue Hotel would be an acceptable abode—for her and her two nonexistent maids—over the coming week. But for what she had in mind, she needed a secure base of operations, a place she could retreat to, where she would have privacy and security for herself and others. She also needed a persona and a history that would explain her presence and allow her to be accepted in New York society without stirring up unseemly gossip. And she needed accomplices she could trust. Murphy was a good start. But she would need others to carry out various assignments and to help her navigate her way through this strange, barely remembered time.

Money would make all this possible. An intriguing young woman of great wealth and beauty, with a mysterious past, could enter society—if she was clever and careful.

A mysterious past. She opened the newspaper, leafed through it quickly until she found the article she'd noticed earlier about a tragic shipwreck. Dipping a pen into the inkwell, she circled it. As she put the pen back, she drew the bag and parchment sheets closer.

Mary would be safe for now. Her own younger self, Constance, would be easy enough to find and was in no immediate danger. It was Joe who was her priority: Joe, who right now was being brutalized at Blackwell's Island in ways she could only imagine.

But even before that, she had to create her own rebirth. She had to rise phoenix-like from the ashes of her future. Such a curious transformation required a plan of great subtlety—one that, in fact, she had already anticipated.

5

November 29, 1880
Thursday

GEORGE FREDERICK KUNZ SAT in his private office on the second floor of Tiffany & Company. The noise and bustle of Union Square were muted by the thick stone of the building, and tall, narrow windows—north-facing, of course—cast an indirect light over a row of glass-fronted display cases. The cases were filled, not with diamonds, emeralds, and sapphires like those on extravagant display in the showroom below, but instead with dull, ugly minerals. Not a single gleam shone in any of the gray, brown, and beige-colored chunks of rock behind the glass. The brilliance of precious stones passed through Kunz's fingers every day, like water. The trophies within the case, by comparison, were his and his alone. Nobody save Charles Lewis Tiffany himself had ever inquired about them, and the customers who entered his office were too preoccupied with their own business to pay much attention to their surroundings. But Kunz himself knew their true worth, because he had discovered them, had dug them out of the gneiss of New Hampshire mountains and the igneous rock of the North Dakota batholiths. Each one had its special place in his self-taught mastery of mineralogy, and the accumulated field research they represented had been sufficient to make him, at twenty-three, a vice president at Tiffany—and its Chief Gemologist.

Now Kunz shot his cuffs and opened his appointment book. Most of his late mornings and early afternoons were given over to gem examinations and acquisitions, and today was no exception. It had proven rather a boring morning: an uncut black opal of 7 carats—Kunz was a strong proponent of the new decimal metric system of gem grading, and frequently made private use of it in his work—and a group of inferior freshwater pearls that he had turned away, unpurchased. The only item of interest was an unfaceted ruby of twelve grams, brought in from Ceylon by a Belgian ship's captain. Although Kunz had not challenged the captain's insistence it was a ruby, its isometric crystallization as well as other factors made Kunz fairly certain it was in fact an example of the variant known as a spinel. Quite rare, and of a beautiful pigeon's-blood color, so deep it reminded him almost of Tyrian purple.

He smiled to himself, his thoughts returning to the showroom on the first floor and those who worked there. Under Charles Tiffany, the establishment had gone from being a "fancy goods" store to the most fashionable emporium of jewelry in the country. The cream of society came here to purchase rings, timepieces, bracelets, and rare jewels; the salespeople who waited on them were the best in the business and were paid accordingly. But—although they were peddling diamonds—at the end of the day they were still just peddlers. When he passed them in the mornings and evenings, on his way to and from his office in this "Palace of Jewels" situated at 15 Union Square West, they nodded and smiled at him as they tended their counters. But Kunz doubted it ever entered their minds that this young man was responsible for the merchandise they displayed. He purchased it, sourced it, and—on particularly gratifying occasions—designed and created it.

Just six weeks after he was taken on as the store's gemologist, he sailed to Paris, where a stone was awaiting him—a huge, rough, yellow pebble from the Kimberley diamond mines of South Africa. Charles Tiffany, who had an understandable weakness for yellow diamonds, had purchased it for a monumental sum, and it was his new gemologist's job to ensure that Mr. Tiffany had made a good investment.

It was the responsibility of a lifetime. Perhaps his youth allowed him to make choices an older, more experienced man would have

considered reckless. Mesmerized by the stone's unique color saturation, he decided to cut it to maximize not size but radiance. Instead of
employing the fifty-eight facets of the traditional "brilliant" cut, Kunz
called for an unheard-of eighty-two facets. This daring decision had
resulted in the Tiffany Diamond: a canary-yellow gemstone unique in
size and depth of color. It cemented Tiffany as a brand—and it made
Kunz's career.

Kunz knew that he might well never top this early success. His
skills were now in great demand, and he knew he could make more
money doing appraisals at Sotheby's or even Lloyd's of London. But
Charles Tiffany had a dream he'd shared with Kunz. He wanted to
become known as the King of Diamonds—not just by hoarding the
most stones, but by discovering the most interesting and most rare.
And he was not afraid to risk enormous amounts of money to do it.
So, although Kunz knew that foundational work of some sort lay in
his future—perhaps a consulting position at the American Museum—
Tiffany's dream was one he eagerly wished to be part of.

With a sigh, he turned to his book. One last appointment for
the day—just moments away, in fact. It promised to be interesting: a
woman of noble birth, from an eastern European duchy, or fiefdom,
or the Lord knew what—territorial wars broke out there so often,
and countries changed names so frequently, Kunz had no interest
in keeping up with it all. Of course, such places were good at
spawning fraudulent princesses and counts, eager to sell their equally
imitation gems of paste or inferior stone. However, Kunz had a
capable, discreet assistant named Gruber who, in addition to keeping
his schedule, acted as a gatekeeper—or perhaps *gold panner* was a
more apt metaphor, sieving nuggets from ordinary mud. Gruber had
recommended he see this woman, pronouncing her to be the genuine
article, although a bit of a mystery. He'd even gone so far as to say that
he thought Kunz would find her "remarkably interesting." Coming
from the phlegmatic Gruber, this was a favorable introduction indeed.
Given that—and given the lady was offering fine diamonds, among
other gems—Kunz had made the appointment for one o'clock: any

later, and the quality of daylight coming in the north windows would be insufficiently white for accurate evaluation.

As if summoned by his thoughts, Gruber gave his distinctive knock on the rippled glass front of his office door. "The lady is here, sir."

"Please show her in," said Kunz.

Gruber opened the door, and after a few moments a woman stepped into the office. Immediately, Kunz stood up—compelled by instinct more than courtesy. Her overall appearance was striking. She was of average height, slender, with a fur wrap across her shoulders, of which Gruber relieved her. Beneath, she wore a stylish dress of pink silk—that year's color—with basque bodice sleeves edged in Mechlin lace. Despite the exquisite fit and style of the dress, it was unlike most Kunz saw passing in and out of Tiffany's. It had no bustle and showed rather more of the woman's figure than was customary. Overall, it was a little...*daring* might be too strong a word, but certainly more commonly seen in the salons of Paris than New York. She was a very beautiful woman.

Gruber cleared his throat. "Her Grace, the Duchess of Inow... Inow..."

"Inowroclaw," the woman finished for him. She had a low but pleasantly modulated voice.

Kunz stepped around his desk and pulled out an overstuffed chair. "Please, Your Grace. Be my guest."

She thanked him, came forward, and took a seat with a movement that managed to be both demure and lithe. Gruber closed the door, then quietly took a seat beside it. In addition to being Kunz's secretary and gatekeeper, he was also his bodyguard, with pistol at the ready should anyone be of a mind to attempt a robbery. Kunz himself carried a two-shot derringer in his coat pocket; it was almost a requirement of working at the Palace of Jewels.

Kunz offered her refreshment—which she declined—and returned to his place behind the desk. He smiled and engaged in a few pleasantries, which also served as a subtle test of authenticity. The woman spoke very good English, with just a trace of accent, and there was nothing in her manner, bearing, or behavior to suggest she was not nobility. And yet, there were certain irregularities that gave him pause. She lacked the usual retinue. Her address was that of a hotel—admittedly the finest in the city—and Gruber suspected she had employed an alias in taking those rooms. All this might require further investigation. Of course, the greatest proof of all would lie with the remarkable jewels she claimed to have on her person.

Now he smiled again, nodded, and placed his hands palm down on the desk. "I understand, Your Grace, that you have in your possession certain gemstones you are interested in proffering to us."

The woman inclined her head.

"Very good. This being the case, I wonder if you'd be so kind as to describe their background, and how they came to be in your possession."

There was a pause. This moment was often awkward.

"You understand," he continued, "that as the preeminent purveyor of gemstones, we are required to take the most complete measures to ensure the quality and provenance of what we sell—and thus, what we buy."

"I understand," the duchess replied. "And I shall be happy to grant your request to the best of my ability. However, I would like a favor in return: to speak to you in confidence, which should not only satisfy your curiosity, but also help assure the safety of my person."

Kunz considered this a moment, then nodded discreetly to Gruber, indicating he should leave. It was certainly proper to be alone with this woman in a place of business. As for her motives, what devilry could she hope to accomplish: leap upon him, perhaps, a dagger gleaming in her hand? Preposterous: this was New York of the 1880s, not some penny dreadful. Nevertheless, he pressed his right elbow against his side as Gruber left, confirming the presence of his derringer.

Kunz caught his breath involuntarily when his eyes met the noblewoman's: a most unusual shade of violet, and with a depth that gave an indelible impression of intelligence, experience, and self-confidence. This was a woman who had seen more than her age would imply.

"I will tell you my story," she said. "I must ask you to keep this in the strictest confidence, because by telling you this I, quite literally, place my life in your hands. And I do it only so that, when you see the gemstones, you will understand."

When she paused, Kunz gestured for her to continue. "Please, milady."

"My name is Katalyn," she began. "I come most recently from the former Principality of Transylvania, where my family was in hiding, but my ancestral home is the duchy of Inowroclaw in Galicia. I am of the house of Piast, and trace my lineage back to Casimir IV, Duke of Pomerania. He died, supposedly childless, in 1377 whilst in battle against Wladyslaw the White, and was succeeded by Wladislaus II, who was excommunicated in 1380—apparently, the last duke of Ino-wroclaw. However, unbeknownst to the territory-hungry Wladislaus, Casimir had a son—Casimir V—who, in return for aiding Louis I of Hungary during the turbulence that followed Wladislaus's death, was allowed to claim his rightful duchy, lands, and jewels. Louis demanded unwavering fealty, and my family survived and gained wealth by keeping faith with our kings and valuing loyalty over ambition: *a băga mâna în foc pentru cineva*. However, this tradition was interrupted when the territory was annexed to Prussia in 1772. My ancestor, then duke of Inowroclaw, fled to Transylvania. Unfortunately, unrest followed: my grandfather died in 1848 during the Hungarian Revolution, and my father in the *Ausgleich* of the Seven Weeks' War, thirteen years ago. Only my mother and I remained, the last of the once-proud duchy of Inowroclaw. Our title remained intact—transferred down from my father through the female line—as did our considerable fortune. How-ever, when my mother died last year, my existence became known to certain other members of the old house of Piast, a line stemming from the adopted son of Boleslaw V the Chaste. If I were to die without heir, their line would inherit my title and my wealth." She paused. "I knew that, if I stayed in Transylvania, my life would not be worth a guilder. And so after my mother's death, I secretly left Europe, travel-ing alone and under an assumed name. My household, with all my possessions, were to follow me to America six months later—at which time I would make my existence, and my birthright, known."

Now she fell silent, having apparently concluded her tale.

"And have those six months passed?" Kunz asked. He had gotten totally lost in this tangle of titles and events.

She nodded.

"May I be so bold as to ask: why this need for secrecy?"

"Because my eight servants, along with all my household goods and family possessions, sailed from Liverpool earlier this month...on the SS *City of London*. It took much of my fortune to the bottom, with the exception of my jewels."

It took a moment for Kunz to make the connection: a passenger steamship of that name, he remembered, had vanished a few weeks ago while en route to New York. Forty-one souls had perished.

"Dear God," he murmured. "I'm so sorry."

Instead of replying, the young duchess reached into a large hand-bag, took out a soiled leather envelope, and handed it across the desk. Just as wordlessly, Kunz took it, opened it, and withdrew a folded piece of parchment from within. He laid it on his desk, then unfolded it with great care.

He had seen any number of similar letters patent, real and forged. Across its top were three crests, illuminated, with heavy gilt shading, now as crazed as ancient porcelain. The rest of the document was in black ink, beginning with the words *Louis Király Nevében* in large calligraphic letters of the Roman Rustic style. At the bottom was a tricolored ribbon, attached with a large wax seal, itself cracked across the middle. Kunz examined the parchment, the crests, and the wax, employing a powerful magnifying glass that he took from his desk—after securing the permission of the duchess to take such a liberty. Although he didn't understand a word of what he assumed was Hungarian, or perhaps Ro-manian, he was expert enough in patents of nobility to have no doubt this was genuine. Any qualms Kunz had harbored about this lady, her history, or the provenance of her family treasures were now satisfied.

He folded the document carefully and replaced it in the envelope, which he handed to the duchess. "Thank you, milady. With your permission, we shall continue?"

"I wait upon your pleasure," came the reply. "I understand that, in these matters, you speak for Tiffany and Company. For reasons I hope are obvious, I require a line of credit from a banking house as soon as possible to cover my expenses. Assuming that we come to terms on the gemstones, I would ask you to provide me with a letter of credit, drawn against Tiffany's, made out to the Wall Street branch of the Bank of New York, effective today. That will serve as partial payment. No doubt you or Mr. Tiffany will wish to bring in your firm's personal banker to complete the transfer of the full sum; we can also draw up the legal paperwork to set a date for this, convenient to both you and myself."

While Kunz understood the first stipulation, the second left him amused. Being a foreigner, she evidently didn't know that Tiffany's, the city's greatest jeweler, had in its basement vault many thousands in ready cash, sufficient, he was sure, to cover the cost of her gemstones.

"I believe you may rest easy, milady," he replied. "No doubt we can reach an agreement on disbursements—if our, ah, appraisal merits such a step—without difficulty."

The woman nodded.

"In that case, shall we proceed? I hope you'll understand that bright natural light is required."

"I understand," the duchess replied.

Kunz called out to Gruber, who came back, locked the door behind him, raised the window blinds to their highest extent, then took up his earlier position. Putting the magnifying glass to one side, Kunz opened his desk again and brought out a variety of tools, a beaker of mineral oil, a loupe, and two large squares of the finest black felt, which he laid next to each other on the center of his desktop. Then, pulling on a pair of fine white gloves and smoothing the lapels of his vest, he turned to the woman sitting across from him.

"Your Grace," he said with a deferential nod. "Shall we begin?"

6

THE DUCHESS REACHED INTO her bag with a gloved hand. Kunz and Gruber exchanged glances. Despite the hundreds, if not thousands of times he'd gone through this exercise before, it was a moment that, for Kunz, never got old.

"I shall tell you what I know of each stone," she said, taking out a small satin bag closed with a thread of the thinnest gold.

Kunz nodded his understanding, eyes on the satin bag, which the woman now handed to him. Carefully, he undid the gold thread with his white-gloved fingers and eased the stone within onto a piece of felt.

He had made it a rule never to display any emotion, or even facial expressions, at moments such as these, and he did not break that rule now. Nevertheless, he felt disappointed. On the felt lay a good-size emerald of an octagonal, step-cut shape. It was a pastel green, to be sure— but not the darker, almost seaweed shade frequently found among the best stones. Rather, it was of a light-chartreuse hue: lovely, but not of the most desirable saturation. Somehow, he had expected better.

"This stone went by the Greek name of Elysion," the woman told him. "I believe that is rendered in English as 'Elysian Fields.' It came originally from New Granada—I should say, the United States of Colombia."

Kunz murmured his understanding while he fixed the jeweler's loupe to one eye, raised the stone gently between a pair of padded forceps, and examined it closely, turning it this way and that in the light. Most emeralds, especially larger emeralds, had inclusions, but this stone was almost free of imperfections.

He was all too aware that the field of gemology, always turbulent, was currently in a particular state of flux. The rules for grading gems—their clarity, color, and particularly size—were given different terms by proponents of this theory or that, and were proving slow to stabilize. Just three years earlier, the Syndical Chamber, a most influential group of Parisian jewelers, had standardized on the proposed "international carat" of 205 milligrams. Kunz preferred a metric carat of 200 milligrams—a fifth of a gram precisely—and used it in his personal evaluations. Of course, anything was better than the days when carat size had been determined by weighing gemstones against the seeds of a carob tree. He estimated this stone to be about 1900 points, and weighing confirmed this approximation: 18.9 carats.

After several minutes, Kunz returned the stone to the felt. He knew that emeralds of this size were rarely flawless—and, if a colored stone displayed no visible inclusions to the naked eye, it would be considered eye-flawless. But this was not such a stone; its tiny flaws were just visible to the eye, and more so under magnification. In clarity and color, it was nevertheless a fine specimen, certainly deserving of a spot in Tiffany's primary display case.

He cleared his throat. "This is a most beautiful emerald, milady. The hue is lovely. Only in its transparency is it of the second water." He sat back. "We would be willing to pay a very good price indeed. As much as $3,500, in fact."

It had been several weeks since he'd offered this much money for a stone, and he waited for the gratifying display of delight from his client. He was quickly disappointed.

"Sir," the woman replied, "if you are implying that the stone is essentially byewater, I would with all respect have to disagree. Its diaphaneity is obvious, and I would ask you to please take another look, particularly in regard to how the proportion and cut of the stone enhances the reflection and refraction of light."

Kunz raised the emerald again, not so much to examine it as to hide any sign of embarrassment. This duchess knew something about gemstones—at least, the one he was now examining. Diaphaneity: while the use of this term was more common to mineralogists than gemologists, it was apt, as was the rest of what she had said. And her inference that grading a gem by first, second, or third "water" was obsolete hit him in a most tender spot.

"Of course," the woman said, intruding on his thoughts, "you are the expert, not I. And in the end, experts will be the judges. It was, and is, my hope that I could conduct all my business here with you, rather than risking the time and exposure required to visit those who do business on Maiden Lane."

This reference to what was then known as Diamond Row was a threat, although a politely worded one. Kunz, too, would rather transact this lady's business—and he was increasingly curious to see what else might be in her handbag.

She had not held out her hand to request the stone be returned.

"You are quite right," he said, returning the emerald to the felt. "I believe on closer inspection that we might be able to raise our offer to $4,500."

"It was my grandmother's favorite stone. I would be willing to part with it for no less than six thousand."

"We, ah, will have to think about that," Kunz said after a moment. It all depended on what was in the rest of that handbag. He replaced the emerald in its satin pouch and put it aside. "May we see the next gemstone, milady?"

The woman handed a second pouch to Kunz. He opened it and eased the stone out—and found himself staring at an amazing specimen of red diamond—the rarest color on earth. Because truly "fancy" diamonds—diamonds with color—were so uncommon, intensity was more important than clarity. This specimen had been cut in an unusual triangular brilliant type that he'd never seen before, but that had the effect of bringing forward the red hue perfectly.

"That is the Napnyugta," the woman told him. "The Sunset Diamond. It was presented to my grandfather by the king for his personal valor in the opening days of the Hungarian Revolution."

Kunz barely heard. He was still staring at the diamond. He had seen very few red diamonds in his career, and certainly none this large—he estimated it at 25 carats, or perhaps even more.

Once again, he raised the loupe to his eye and peered into its depths. Internally flawless, with just the slightest bit of feathering. There was no red diamond in the world as large or as perfect as this. It took a moment for him to find his voice.

"A most beautiful diamond, milady," he said.

"Thank you."

What was it worth? The lady was waiting. This was a stone that he simply could not let get away.

"I would be content, sir, with $100,000," the duchess said.

Kunz swallowed. He had never paid so much for a stone. "Would you consider seventy five?"

"No, thank you, I would not."

Kunz put the stone back in its pouch and handed it to Gruber. "We will take it at your price, milady."

A new satin bag was opened. And out came the next stone: a deep violet cabochon sapphire that sported twinned stars—asterisms—forming a total of twelve points instead of the usual six. Even at a glance, Kunz could tell it was the equal of the Midnight Star at the American Museum.

"It is from Mogok, Burma," said the duchess, as he examined it with the loupe.

Kunz decided he'd better state his price before she did. "We can offer $40,000 for this stone, milady."

"Fifty thousand—with the emerald."

"Absolutely."

They went back into their pouches and were turned over to Gruber.

Kunz turned to her for the next stone, but found she was simply looking back at him, hands atop her bag. "These next—and last—

two stones are of particular value. I mean as...world treasures." She seemed to be struggling with some kind of emotional difficulty.

"I understand, Your Grace." World treasures? He found his heart accelerating.

"They are inseparable from my family history, and thus of infinite value to me. If your firm does not have the resources to purchase them, I..." She paused to collect herself. "I will understand. I am not sure I have the heart to part with them."

And with this, she reached into her handbag, withdrew another silk pouch, and offered it to Kunz.

He took it very gently from her hand. What could she mean by Tiffany's not having the resources?

He tipped the bag and the stone rolled out. He froze.

There is a moment in every jeweler's life when they see the one gem that represents a divine ideal. In that moment, Kunz knew for sure that, as long as he lived, he would never again see a diamond as beautiful as the one that lay before him now. It was the distillation of perfection.

Gently, so gently, he picked it up with his jeweler's tweezers and—trying to keep his hands from trembling—fixed the loupe to his eye and held the gem up to the light. He turned it this way and that, examining it not only facedown—normally the only way to determine the body color through a colorless diamond—but from across its table and underneath, from the culet as well.

"The stone has been in my family for centuries," the duchess told him. "It is called Athena's Tear, because only the eye of a god could produce something so perfect. Beyond that, little is known. Supposedly it came from Burma during the chaos following the fall of the Pagan Empire. I have heard that ten thousand Buddhist temples were sacked in that time."

Kunz nodded, but barely heard. He put down the stone only long enough to scribble a note and hand it to Gruber, who immediately left the office. Then Kunz picked up the stone again.

It was large—not as large as the Tiffany Diamond—but it was perfect. Absolutely perfect and infinitely colorless, glittering like ice with a heart of fire. He had no idea how large it had been as a rough stone, but the cut—always the primary factor in a diamond's quality—was a paradigm of symmetry, with a girdle that was not too thick and a ratio chosen to bring out its incredible, scintillating brilliance. But more than that, it was flawless. Utterly, completely flawless: under the loupe, he could detect not even the slightest sign of crystals, clouds, knots, or cavities. In his short but highly active career, Kunz had never seen a stone as perfect.

For centuries, diamonds of more than a dozen carats without inclusion were known as paragons. This diamond was, without any doubt, a paragon. A paragon of close to 100 carats.

At that moment, Gruber returned, slightly out of breath, with a reply to the message he'd sent. Quickly, Kunz read it over, then he turned to the lady. "Your Grace," he said, almost forgetting to return the gemstone to its enclosure while he spoke, "would you please excuse me for a minute? I would like to bring down Mr. Tiffany. May we take him into your confidence?"

"Of course."

Charles Lewis Tiffany's office was two floors above, at the north corner like Kunz's; not much larger but far more sumptuous. The man was sitting behind his desk, wearing his usual uniform of charcoal frock coat, black vest, brushed cotton trousers, high collar, and a tiepin featuring his favorite pearl. He rose when he saw the look on Kunz's face.

"George, are you ill?" he asked.

"I should like you to come down and view a gemstone," said Kunz.

A moment later, Kunz was standing beside Gruber, while Tiffany himself took the chair at the gemologist's desk. He examined Athena's Tear for a long time, stretching into minutes. When he was done, Kunz quickly summarized the history of the duchess and her gems, showed him the patent of nobility and the gems he had just purchased.

Tiffany was silent again, his brow furrowed, head slightly bowed. And then he raised it: "Your Grace, Tiffany's is prepared to offer you $300,000 for this diamond. I might just mention that is the largest sum paid to date for any gemstone."

The duchess returned his look with a cool expression. "Let us defer negotiations on the final price until you see my last stone."

"Of course, milady," said Tiffany.

"This one is dearest to me and my bloodline." She turned toward Kurz. "I almost hope you cannot acquire it... Parting with it would be like a small death to me."

Hearing this, Tiffany looked at Kurz. Then he turned to Gruber. "Get Mr. Thompson, please. Bring him here: we will need his services shortly."

Once again, Gruber left—this time, to fetch the founder of Chase National Bank, whose office was nearby.

There was a brief, fraught silence. Tiffany cleared his throat. "If you would care to show us the stone, milady, we are most anxious to see it."

The woman gave a faint smile and reached into her handbag.

Kunz watched, back to the wall, as his employer took the satin pouch she removed, hefted it in his hand—and opened it. He was secretly glad the firm's owner was now in charge of the proceedings. He felt dazed, spent.

At first, nothing emerged from the pouch. Tiffany gently tapped the satin, as if to urge forward a timid creature. Suddenly, with a flash of yellow, the gem appeared, almost tumbling out under its own weight.

There was a moment of stasis. And then, almost in unison, Tiffany and Kunz reflexively uttered the same expression of amazement as they both recognized it.

Of course, neither had seen the gemstone before. Nobody living had seen it—not in many hundreds of years. Most gemologists had dismissed it as myth. Yet there it was, on Kunz's desk, flashing as if challenging the sun's own brilliance: deep yellow, with a unique orange inclusion at its center.

Kunz found his voice first. "Is that..." he began. "Is that the Sol Gelida?"

"My family knew it as the Novotney Terra. But, yes, even when the sovereign Louis I gave it to my ancestor Casimir V, half a millennium ago, it had already acquired the sobriquet of Frozen Sun."

No picture of the gem existed, Kunz knew, but the enraptured descriptions of the ancients made it unmistakable.

She continued. "For obvious reasons, this was my family's most prized gem. We were told it was mined in Muscovy, then made its way through a dozen owners, conquerors, thieves, and murderers with the Golden Horde into Lithuania."

Kunz, a purist, had always preferred colorless diamonds, but he could see that Tiffany, with his weakness for fancy diamonds, was fixated by the Sol Gelida. There was an almost unearthly yellow glow emanating from the stone, deeper and richer than even the Tiffany Diamond, with a cloudy whirl of deep sunset orange in the center. The mythic status of this stone meant there could be no encumbrances to its sale. In addition to everything else, it was remarkably large; perhaps 160 carats. Kunz could not quite bring himself to look at it through the loupe, at least not yet: he was overwhelmed by the beauty of perfection.

A knock came on the door and Gruber returned with Tiffany & Company's head banker in tow. The banker nodded a greeting and then looked at the noblewoman, waiting for an introduction.

"Her Grace, the Duchess of…Inow…Inor…Ironclaw," Gruber said.

"*Inowroclaw*," Kunz corrected, glaring at his assistant.

The woman laughed mildly. "Please," she said. "I find 'Ironclaw' quite satisfactory. In fact, I think that is what I shall call myself in America from now on: the Duchess of Ironclaw. The other is too hard to pronounce."

And half an hour later—once a price of $1 million had been agreed upon for the Sol Gelida, the Frozen Sun—the Duchess of Ironclaw left the store, the jewels locked safely in Tiffany's vault and a letter of credit for a most remarkable sum tucked in her handbag.

7

Fitzhugh Ernest Moseley, assistant physician, carefully descended the wide staircase of Blackwell's Island Asylum, the steps slippery with grease and urine. It was half past four, and the inmates on cleaning detail would not arrive for another half hour. He had finished his rounds for the day, which thankfully had been confined to what the asylum labeled Class Two patients: those diagnosed as ordinary idiots and defectives. It was tomorrow he dreaded: the weekly visit to the Class Five patients, deemed mild in temperament but "given over to bad habits" such as self-mutilation, masturbation, and a fascination with their own fecal matter. The doctor found these cases the most troubling of all, even more than the violent, bellowing creatures assigned to Class One. All the medical literature deemed them incurable and prescribed ice-water baths, purgatives, and restraints. But the assistant doctor's observations over the years convinced him that more time spent talking with them and tending to their comfort, rather than binding them in straitjackets and dousing them in freezing water, yielded more promising results. But all his attempts to make changes were rebuffed by the physician in charge. When he'd pressed the matter, he was reminded—in no uncertain terms—that he had not completed medical school and was not a fully accredited physician; that his opinions carried no authority; and that he had a regimented set of duties to carry out without question or comment.

As he continued to descend, the shrieks and weeping grew fainter until, by the time he reached the bottom of the octagonal tower, peace and calm had arrived. Thanks to a strong breeze out of the north, even the stench of the cesspool was cleared away.

He threaded a labyrinth of passages and emerged into the chill afternoon light. He looked around a moment, breathing in the fresh air and letting the heavy pall of oppression and misery that engulfed him during his rounds disperse.

When he'd first arrived, his job "treating" the insane men had been discouraging enough, but over the years it had become a plague on his soul, forcing him to constantly resist the beckoning oblivion of laudanum—a habit he'd picked up in medical school that had, ultimately, been the chief instrument of his failure to complete his degree.

As he glanced toward the city, he noticed a private yacht had docked at the jetty reserved for important visitors. Looking more closely, he spied its passengers: a small party of well-dressed men and women, with walking sticks and parasols, out for an afternoon's entertainment visiting the lunatics. It was no better than a human zoo. They'd be taken to Hall 3, he knew, where a "suitable class of patients" was kept especially for such occasions, and where conditions of cleanliness and calm were carefully enforced.

He wondered what the visitors would say if they were taken instead to—say—the Lodge...

He washed his hands at a nearby pump handle, then turned south along the walkway toward the workhouse, passing various institutional structures large and small. The dark expanse of the East River flowed to his right, and beyond it rose the buildings of Manhattan—this far uptown, around Fortieth Street, still mostly private homes and fashionable town houses.

As he approached the workhouse, he began to see various labor crews at work: some in the stables, some making shoes, and others doing repairs to the paths and roads. They looked up as he passed.

"Evening, *Dr.* Moseley," said the orderly on guard duty, an insolent fellow he had once reprimanded for striking a female inmate. He walked on, ignoring the titters of the prisoners. He was used to it: not completing his medical degree somehow put him on a lower rung than if he were simply an aide. Even some of the nurses had the cheek to give him advice.

Now the grim stone façade of the workhouse loomed over him. Dinner for the staff didn't start until six, but he rarely bothered to join them. However, he'd missed breakfast that day. He'd have time to grab a roll from the kitchen while still making the Department of Public Charities and Corrections steamboat leaving the island in fifteen minutes. He walked into the cold shadow of the building, passed the guard station, and took the stairs down into the basement kitchen.

As he made his way along the damp passageway, he could hear a familiar voice ahead—Paddy, the loutish head cook—raised in a storm of swearing. Turning the corner into the kitchen, Moseley stepped into a chaotic scene: Paddy, who weighed at least three hundred pounds, was looming over a yellow-haired workhouse boy a quarter of his size, who was holding a tray on which were balanced several crockpots of stew.

"At it again, are you?" Paddy snarled, grabbing the boy by the collar and yanking him roughly. The tray fell to the floor with a loud clatter and an explosion of crockery.

Immediately, Moseley understood what was happening. He recognized the youth: an introverted, sensitive lad who—though quiet— had a way of standing up to authority that got him into trouble more than once. Paddy was infamous for ladling out meager portions, and the boy had just been caught in the act of sneaking out more food for himself and his mates.

"Playing Father Christmas behind my back, eh?" Paddy said, lifting the youth bodily off the ground with one fist. "I've a mind to give you a holiday present of my own." And then he hauled off with the other fist and smashed the boy in the face, sending the figure flying across the kitchen and tumbling onto the rough floor.

"And I've got a knuckle sandwich for your dinner, too!" Paddy said, lumbering forward.

Instinctively, Moseley stepped forward, interposing himself between the boy sprawled on the floor and the cook. "That's enough!" he said angrily. "Get back to work!"

"Who are you to be telling me what do to?" the cook cried, raising his fist again.

"I *am* telling you. Come on, back away now!"

"What's going on?" asked a new voice.

Turning, Moseley felt his heart sink. It was Cropper, the workhouse superintendent.

"What's going on?" Cropper repeated as he stepped into the room. His office was down the passage, and he must have been roused by the noise.

Moseley pointed at the cook. "He assaulted this boy for no reason."

"That's a lie!" Paddy said. "That there's a bad 'un, always causing trouble. Look: he dropped a whole tray of my good stew, on purpose, just to get my goat!"

Cropper looked down at the vile, watery "stew" that lay in puddles on the floor, then at the half-stunned boy, struggling to sit up. "Always causing trouble, is he? Well, I'll have a talk with that new warden at the penitentiary. I hear a cot's freeing up there by the end of the week. We'll see how much trouble he can stir up behind bars."

"You can't put him there!" Moseley said, aghast, outrage overcoming his better judgment. "He was only transferred from the Octagon last month. The penitentiary will be the death of him!"

"Paddy, back to your cooking," Cropper said. Then he stepped closer to Moseley. "And you, wet nurse," he said. "You mind your own damned business—unless you'd like me to talk to the head surgeon and get your wages docked for you. Can't put him in the penitentiary? You just watch."

Moseley opened his mouth to protest, then realized there was nothing he could say to change anything. He turned toward the boy sprawled on the floor.

"Be on your way!" Cropper said.

At this, Moseley held his ground. "I need to check him for injuries."

"Is that a fact?" Cropper said, surprised at this rebellion in minia-ture. His eyes narrowed. "You been at the pipe again?" He grabbed a kerosene lamp, then held it close to Moseley, examining his eyes. Moseley squinted but did not look away. After a moment, Cropper hung the lamp back on its peg.

"Be quick about it," he said, then turned and exited the kitchen.

Moseley knelt and helped the boy to a sitting position. Quickly and expertly, he felt the boy's limbs and skull, checking for fractures or a concussion. Then he peered at the boy's face. A nasty ecchymosis—black eye—was already forming. He gently palpated the orbit, then examined the eyeball itself. No serious damage—thankfully.

"You'll be all right," he said in a voice too low for the cook to hear. He grabbed an underdone, dough-heavy dinner roll off a nearby table, then another, and stuffed them into the boy's pockets. "Get upstairs now. Try to keep your head raised overnight—it will help with the swelling."

Moseley assisted the boy to his feet, watching until he had safely left the kitchen—he had remained remarkably quiet, even taciturn, throughout the confrontation. Then he took a roll for himself and began to make his own way out. He'd missed the ferry, but Otto wouldn't mind his being late.

As he passed by the cook, Paddy cackled. "Wet nurse," he repeated, leering. "That's a good 'un."

8

MOSELEY SAT IN HIS usual shabby booth near the steps leading up from the St. Mark's Place Rathskeller. To his left, where the wall met the ceiling beams, stood a window—the only window in the room—showing a pavement-level view of horses' hooves and broken vegetable crates. The eatery was lit by flickering gaslight. To his right was the long bar, sticky from spilled beer, busy with customers at this time of the evening. Beyond were tables and booths of patrons—tradesmen, deckhands, soldiers, roustabouts—drinking, laughing, and talking loudly. The stuffy basement air was thick with the smell of cigar smoke and yeast.

Now Hilda, the wife of Otto—proprietor of the Rathskeller—approached to refill his glass of brandy and take away his empty plate. *"Der Eintopf schmeckt sehr lecker, danke,"* he told her. She shrugged at the compliment and walked away, as stout as a barrel of lager and at least twice as heavy.

Moseley didn't make much money, but he had struck an arrangement with Otto to have a booth he could call his own and be served whatever the family was eating that evening. The Rathskeller was much warmer than his furnished room around the corner on Third Avenue, and Otto didn't mind if he stayed in the booth, reading, until closing time. He'd chosen the booth closest to the stairs up to the street because—though the Rathskeller was a tranquil establishment by local standards—brawls nevertheless broke out with regularity.

The neighborhood was a two-mile walk from the ferry to Black-well's Island, but it suited his budget and was safer than the cheaper neighborhoods farther south. The wealthy had lived here earlier in the century, building palaces along Second Avenue and Albion Place, but now they had moved northward again, leaving behind row houses and "Old Law" tenements. Even though it was one of the more densely populated areas of the city, it was peaceful: a condition Moseley prized above all else, since there was no peace at his place of employment.

Moseley downed the second of the two brandies Otto served him each evening. The barely potable spirit seared his esophagus, but it was sufficient to stave off other, more insidious cravings. Instinctively he pulled out his tattered copy of the *Corpus Hippocratus*, to continue an article concerning urinary stone formation, but he couldn't concentrate and eventually shoved it back into his coat pocket.

Wet nurse. That's a good 'un.

He would never finish medical school; he would never be a doctor—and continuing the pretense of study was risible, fooling nobody but himself. Medicine didn't even interest him particularly: his tastes were drawn more to the study of art and architecture. But here he was, hired as a surgeon's associate but doing work barely suited to a carnival mentalist... with the meager salary to match. Already at thirty-five, his life was taking on a diurnal cycle of distressing regularity—one that would only hasten his acceleration toward old age.

This gloomy meditation was interrupted by somebody sliding into the other side of the booth. Moseley was used to this. His claim on the booth was contingent on how busy the beerhouse was, and tonight it was full to bursting: some ships had docked along the East River that day, and two dozen or more seamen were now packing the bar, drunk when they'd come in, filling the smoky air with raucous curses and shouts: "That's mine, you geebag!" "Good God, the head on ya!"

Moseley looked over at the newcomer, mostly to make sure he didn't appear dangerous. He was short, and despite the heavy pea coat he wore and the oversize cap cocked rakishly on his head, looked little more than a boy. The arrival stared back at Moseley with eyes unusual not only for their color, but their expression—secretive yet disinterested: the eyes of someone who already knows how the story ends. The youth raised his hand and touched the brim of his stained cap, and Moseley nodded in return. With this slight, fine-featured young man as a boothmate, it seemed his evening would remain as peaceful as the noisy surroundings permitted.

This assumption was proven premature a minute later, when the booth groaned under the weight of another arrival—an acquaintance, apparently, of the young man—who sat down and bid a gruff good evening to Moseley. Now, this was a different character altogether: as Black Irish as they came, with the ruddy skin and Cork accent to match. He was heavyset, but it didn't require Moseley's anatomical training to see that the bulk was made up of muscle rather than blubber.

Hilda came up and the heavyset man ordered a pint of their best; his young companion indicated silently he'd have the same. This was followed by a strange moment of stasis amid the riot of the beer hall, as the two new arrivals looked silently at Moseley and the medical practitioner considered whether—under the circumstances—he should go back to his row house earlier than planned. Then Hilda banged two steins on the table and the young man leaned forward to speak.

"I need your help," he said. "And before I explain why, I'd like your promise that you'll hear me out before you leave."

Moseley was surprised, even alarmed, that they had sought him out. He had to strain to hear the words over the din, but he immediately realized this person was not only educated, but cultivated, speaking in a cool, elevated tone. He considered his options. The heavyset Irish fellow could stop him from departing if he chose. And if the truth be told, he was curious as to why these two fellows would go to such trouble to seek him out.

He nodded his agreement.

"Thank you," came the reply. "I require your assistance in freeing someone from Blackwell's Island. This person is a boy, incarcerated despite being innocent of any wrongdoing, and though I have no proof to offer, I can furnish one or two references as to his upstanding moral character—if necessary. You of all people must know how many innocents end up in that Gehenna, and how many supposedly brief terms become lengthy incarcerations—or sentences of death. This boy is as unmarked as the blank of a coin. But he is also impressionable, and before his sentence is finished, the confinement he's subjected to will stamp him for life."

Moseley listened in growing disbelief and suspicion. Could these be Pinkerton agents, running some kind of flimflammery? Perhaps they were in the employ of some wealthy person currently locked up on Blackwell's—but that seemed improbable, because poverty was the essential requirement for imprisonment on the island. Wealthy inmates were kept in Manhattan's House of Detention, better known as the Tombs—or, more frequently, acquitted in exchange for a suitable consideration.

"Why are you asking this of me?" he ventured.

"Because, Mr. Moseley, you have knowledge and access—and the good character to right an injustice. I also believe that a handsome sum of money would not go unappreciated."

Moseley, stunned to hear his own name, was about to protest when he suffered an even greater surprise. The large Irishman had already finished his pint and shouted for another. As he did so, the speaker pushed his own untouched stein toward his companion—and Moseley caught a brief glance of a slender, graceful wrist and forearm, covered with the merest trace of downy hair, before it disappeared once again into the pea coat.

Moseley looked into the fine, regular features of the speaker. No male past puberty had a delicate bone structure and smooth skin like that. "You—you're a girl!"

Instantly, the Irishman seized Moseley's wrist in a grip of iron.

"It's all right, Mr. Murphy," the girl told him. "Our friend will be careful to keep his expression neutral and his voice low from now on."

The grip on his wrist eased. Moseley pulled it free and rubbed it absently, feeling great confusion.

"Calm yourself, Mr. Moseley. It's true I am a woman, but that makes no difference to our transaction. I merely wanted to speak to you without causing any distraction."

Moseley realized this made sense: no woman, even a wagtail, would set foot in an establishment such as the Rathskeller.

The young woman rummaged in the heavy coat, pulled out a small leather satchel tied with a heavy lace, and dropped it on the table. It made a faint chinking noise against the wood.

"Mr. Murphy," she said over the din, "would you mind opening that and showing our friend here the contents?"

The heavyset man scooped the pouch into his palm, untied it, and angled it toward Moseley. Inside were at least half a dozen $20 double eagles.

The woman took the pouch into her own hand, dipped her glove inside, and removed a single coin. She put the pouch back in her pocket and extended her hand—palm facing the wall, away from prying eyes—toward Moseley.

Moseley stared at the gold coin, for the moment mesmerized. He finally took his eyes away.

"That's for you," said the woman. "Please take it."

He took it and slipped it in his pocket. "Who is the boy?" he asked.

"Given your position, you must know him. He's twelve, rather short for his age, and goes by the name of Joe Greene. He has blond hair and an early-onset cataract—cloudy left eye—a byproduct of congenital rubella. Ah! I see you are familiar with him."

Moseley nodded. "I know the boy." The cloudy left eye she referred to was, at the moment, black and puffy, and no doubt painful as well.

"Here's what you must do. Arrange to work a night shift, and then— when all is quiet—let us into the Octagon and point out which bed is his. We'll then reward you further." She indicated the pocket with the leather satchel. "We'll also allow you time to get away and establish an alibi of your choosing; and then we will let ourselves out—with the boy."

The woman spoke of it with as much ease as if she were planning a bathing outing at Coney Island.

"You'll be noticed," said Moseley. "As soon as you enter."

"We will not. Let that be my concern."

"How do you plan to get to and from the island without alerting anyone?"

"Again, my concern. You select the evening, and we will meet you at the time and place of your choosing."

The woman spoke about the place with the familiarity of first-hand knowledge. "There's a problem," said Moseley. "The boy's no longer housed in the Octagon. He's being held in the workhouse and is scheduled for transfer to the penitentiary."

For the first time, an emotion—surprise, concern—flickered in the young woman's eyes. "When?"

"They need to clear out a cell. Three days, maybe four."

"How do you know this?"

An instinct for self-preservation warned Moseley it was better not to mention that the cell waiting to be "cleared out" was, in fact, currently undergoing sanitization—of a sort—after its most recent occupant died of smallpox.

He took hold of the double eagle and squeezed it tightly, as if to assure himself all this was real. "I, ah, receive a copy of the schedule."

"The workhouse consists of three floors, does it not?"

"It does."

"Which floor is the boy housed on?"

"The first."

"The floor with the smallest cells."

"Yes."

The woman paused a moment, evidently collecting her thoughts. "I had hoped to give you at least a few days to consider my request. But this development requires more urgency. Have you access to keys?"

"For the Octagon, yes. I could perhaps get my hands on a master key for the workhouse—temporarily. Obtaining any keys for the penitentiary would be impossible—for me, at least."

She nodded. "Very well. We will meet again tomorrow night in your chambers. To discuss the specific plan."

Moseley's jaw worked silently for a moment. "I can't be found with a workhouse key on my person when you put your plan in motion. They'll search me."

"Can you arrange to bring the master key to our meeting tomorrow night?"

Moseley nodded.

"We'll take an impression of it and you can return it, the following evening, before the escape takes place. It will appear as if no ordinary keys were used in this...liberation. So, then: Tomorrow night? Midnight?"

"Tomorrow night," Moseley heard himself say. "Yes. Yes."

"The coin is yours to keep, whatever your decision, but I feel certain you *will* make the only humane choice and provide us your assistance...and that we *will* proceed at tomorrow's meeting to finalize plans for freeing the youth on the next evening—before he can be moved. Will that work, Mr. Moseley?"

Reassured by the solidity of the gold coin, and intimidated by the presence of the Irishman, Moseley nodded. "If you do your part with success, it will work."

"Then I ask only one other favor."

"Yes?"

"It's my understanding you have a weakness for *zhuī lóng*—chasing the dragon. Will you pledge to stay away from laudanum until we complete our rescue?"

Moseley looked from this strange woman to her companion and back again. They'd given him half a year's pay, free and clear—just like that, with much more to come.

He nodded.

"Most excellent. Until tomorrow, then." Another tip of the cap, then Moseley's new acquaintances exited the booth, ascended the stairs, and vanished into the night—leaving behind only two empty pint glasses as proof the last twenty minutes had not been a figment of his imagination.

9

Sunday, May 21
Present Day

Sᴘᴇᴄɪᴀʟ Aɢᴇɴᴛ Aʀᴍsᴛʀᴏɴɢ Cᴏʟᴅᴍᴏᴏɴ walked down the second-floor hallway of what had been, until ten days ago, the Chandler House. Now it was more a construction project than a building. The damaged structure was surrounded by cranes, metal scaffolding, and bracing to stabilize it while the upper two stories were being rebuilt behind screens. Even as he walked, Coldmoon could hear the faint snap of nail guns, feel the vibrations as pieces of roofing were dropped into place. The whole city was being repaired, 24/7.

The hallway was dimly lit and empty. Besides a skeleton staff camped out in the employees' quarters in a far corner of the first floor, the entire hotel was deserted. Save, that is, for one most unusual lodger—Special Agent Pendergast—who had essentially refused to leave.

Coldmoon hadn't known Pendergast all that long—Christ, was it really just three months since he'd first met the man?—but over the trio of cases they'd worked since, he felt he'd come to understand this enigmatic, intensely private person better than most did. He was aware the man had suffered a deeply emotional trauma when his young companion, Constance, had abandoned him and used the machine to launch herself back in time. *Companion* didn't quite describe their connection; in point of fact, Coldmoon had no idea what their true relationship was. *Ward* was obviously a title of convenience. There was more between them than some quaint legal formality.

Coldmoon had read the goodbye note she'd left, and while he found it more confusing than informative, it suggested why Pendergast would feel devastated.

Directly ahead of him now, a chair had been placed against one wall of the corridor: a wooden ladder-back Shaker chair with a seat of woven jute. Coldmoon could attest to its lack of comfort: he had spent time in it every afternoon now for the past five days.

Reaching the chair, he picked it up, placed it in front of the nearby door marked 222, then took a seat with something closer to a groan than a sigh. He cleared his throat.

"Hey, Pendergast," he said. "Aloysius. It's Coldmoon. Again."

He told himself not to bother trying the handle. He did anyway. Locked as usual.

"Pendergast," he said to the door, "I thought you should know that I got Dr. Quincy back onto a bus headed west. Just this morning. He kept asking about you, even as he was boarding. I didn't say anything. But I think you owe him a phone call, at least. And you owe me a couple of hundred bucks in beer money—that old guy was like a sponge."

He was answered by the usual silence.

"Look," he said after a minute. "I know I've said this before. But I really mean it. You can't stay in there forever. I know what you're going through—that is, I don't know from your perspective, but... hell, it's wrong to just stew in there, like...like a potato in a bank of honey-locust embers. At least *talk* to me. It would help me to, you know...hear from my partner."

He fell silent, waiting, but no sound came from within. Up above on the roof, the noise of construction faded as the workers paused for Sunday lunch.

He took a deep breath. "You know, speaking of heading west, I got another call last night from the SAC of the Denver Field Office. Dudek. He's been pressing me pretty hard, and I finally had to tell him I couldn't take on any cases until—"

The door opened with such speed it was all Coldmoon could do not to fall out of his chair. In the entryway stood Agent Pendergast. Cold-moon stood up, blinking away his surprise. Instead of the devastated man with mussed hair, a rumpled shirt, and a week's worth of beard that Coldmoon imagined, Pendergast looked as immaculate as the day they'd first met. The obligatory black suit, white shirt, and elegant, muted tie—Hermès today; Coldmoon had never seen him wear the same one twice—looked as crisp as if they'd come off a tailor's dummy. His face was as pale, smooth, cool and chiseled as marble. Coldmoon ticked off these observations instinctively, one after the other, with both relief and surprise.

"Agent Coldmoon," Pendergast said. There was a slight rasp in his voice, as if from long silence, but the tone was neutral, the accent as smooth as the molasses in dark rum. "Please come in." He indicated a set of chairs in the front room. "Have a seat."

Coldmoon took the opportunity to look around. The suite was neat as a pin. Through the open door leading to Pendergast's bed-room, he could see the bed was made up. Who, he wondered, was taking care of that? The door to Constance's bedroom, on the other hand, was shut.

Pendergast took the chair across from him. He moved gingerly, a mark of his earlier injuries, but without obvious signs of pain or frailty. Coldmoon was relieved—he looked almost recovered from the severe blood loss he'd suffered. His true state of mind, Coldmoon knew, lay behind Pendergast's ice-blue eyes...and that was territory he could not hope to traverse.

"I apologize for my rudeness," Pendergast said. "There really is no excuse I can offer."

"No worries," Coldmoon replied. "And no need to explain. I only wish I could have been of help."

"You can help now," Pendergast said.

"Anything."

"Excellent. Then please take out your phone and make another call to SAC Dudek."

Coldmoon frowned. "I'm not sure—"

"Just call him, if you please. You can tell him you'll be there late this afternoon."

Coldmoon began to protest but saw from Pendergast's expression it would be useless. He pulled out the phone and made the call—all the time under the senior agent's watchful eye. As he put his phone away, it occurred to him that Pendergast had opened the door because he mentioned he was, essentially, beginning to put his new assignment in jeopardy.

"You'll need to leave shortly," Pendergast said, "but I believe there's time for a drink." He stood up. "What will you have?"

Coldmoon glanced at his watch. It was quarter past noon. There was no use asking for a beer; Pendergast would have none. He glanced at the row of bottles on a shelf. "Um, just a little dry vermouth, please. On the rocks."

"Very well." Pendergast made his way over to the serving cart. Coldmoon watched him splash some vermouth into a tumbler, toss in some ice. Taking a highball glass, he poured in a generous measure of Belvedere vodka, followed by ice, fruit-infused Italian sparkling water, and a jigger of some unctuous purple liquid from a large, medicinal-looking bottle. He dropped in a glass stir rod, then returned. Coldmoon watched the agent's movements more carefully now. They were a trifle unsteady, but he nevertheless put down the drinks without spilling a drop.

Pendergast seated himself once again and reached for a small tin of blackcurrant-flavored pastilles, removed one, and dropped it into his glass. He stirred the mixture slowly with the crystal stirrer and lifted the highball glass to his lips.

"That's 'lean,'" Coldmoon said.

Pendergast raised his eyebrows as he took a sip. "I'm sorry?"

"What you're drinking."

"This? It's a concoction favored by a friend of mine from the French Quarter of New Orleans. Now sadly deceased, alas." Pendergast raised the glass again and took another deep sip. "There's one more thing you can do," he said. "To help."

"Anything." Coldmoon sat forward.

"Please listen to what I have to tell you, without interruption, and while suspending your disbelief. I would caution you to never tell a living soul what you are about to hear—but that won't be necessary, since no one would believe you anyway."

Coldmoon hesitated a moment. And then he nodded. "Okay."

10

Pᴇɴᴅᴇʀɢᴀꜱᴛ ᴡᴀꜱ ꜱɪʟᴇɴᴛ ꜰᴏʀ ꜱᴏ long, Coldmoon began to wonder if he'd drifted off under the influence of the opioid in his drink. Finally, he spoke. "I know you read the note Constance left me—and of course you are puzzled."

Now it was Coldmoon's turn to say nothing.

"You know that the machine we discovered during the case that just concluded had the ability to see into the future—not *our* future, but a parallel future. Initially, it could see only a few minutes ahead. Ultimately, with adjustments, it could see much farther ... into a multiplicity of parallel universes, recognizable and strange, future and—*past*."

Coldmoon nodded. He remembered only too well.

"If you can accept the bizarre nature of that machine, you should also be able to accept what I'm going to tell you now—about Constance." He paused to take a sip of his periwinkle-colored beverage. "She was born in 1871, on Water Street in lower Manhattan. Her parents died while she was still very young. Constance and her two siblings became street children. In 1878, her sister, Mary, then seventeen, was arrested for solicitation and sentenced to a period of labor at the Five Points House of Industry. The Five Points neighborhood was the most dangerous, pestilential, and squalid slum that New York ever knew—before or since."

He sat forward, observing Coldmoon as if to gauge what reaction his words were provoking. Coldmoon was careful to keep his expression opaque.

"In 1880, Constance's brother Joseph was sentenced for a period of time to the prison on Blackwell's Island. It changed him. Not long after his release, he was murdered."

He took another sip. "During these events, a certain Dr. Enoch Leng offered his medical and psychiatric services to the House of Industry. He did not charge for his services, and he had a diabolical motive. He was attempting to create an elixir to significantly prolong the life of a human being—his own. A necessary ingredient for this elixir, he discovered, was the cauda equina—the bundle of nerves at the base of the human spine—vivisected from girls."

"Jesus," Coldmoon could not help but mutter.

"The House of Industry proved a good source for the experimental victims he needed. No questions were asked when he took them away to his 'sanatorium,' and no interest was taken in them afterwards. Some he would put under the knife to remove the cauda equina, while others would be the guinea pigs to administer the latest elixir to test. He would keep these latter experimental subjects in his own mansion. Unfortunately, the elixir was imperfect and the various combinations of it were powerfully fatal. When a guinea pig died, he would dissect her to see what went wrong.

"Constance's older sister, Mary, was taken not as a guinea pig, but as a provider of the essential ingredient. She fell under the knife of Dr. Leng shortly after her brother was killed. It occurred in January 1881. Constance herself was only nine at the time."

Now—slowly—Pendergast sat back.

"Under normal circumstances, Constance—a guttersnipe without family—would have died from hunger, disease, or exposure. But fate intervened. Dr. Leng noticed her presence in the vicinity of the House of Industry. Around early summer 1881, after the death of her sister, Constance became the last young person to be taken under the wing of Dr. Leng. He administered to her the elixir prepared from her sister's own body. This time, the elixir worked."

Pendergast reached for the highball glass. Coldmoon remained silent, hardly able to process what he was hearing.

"Constance became Dr. Leng's ward. She grew up in his mansion. Although, of course, 'growing up' is a relative term, because with the elixir her body aged so slowly that, a century later, she had only reached the physical form of a twenty-year-old. Leng also partook of the elixir and remained youthful as well, so he could continue his scientific work toward an ultimate goal of immeasurable importance to him—which there is no need to go into now. Leng later perfected a synthetic substitute for the cauda equina, and then no more unfortunates were sacrificed.

"I don't know when or how, but Constance learned that she herself was kept unnaturally young by the sacrifice of her own sister. You can imagine the effect on her psyche. In any case, Dr. Leng was killed a few years ago. Constance, no longer under his influence, stopped taking the elixir. And she became my ward."

Coldmoon stared. "But how?"

"Enoch Leng was my great-great uncle. I inherited his mansion on Riverside Drive, and in it, I found Constance. She had lived there for the past hundred years."

"What?" Coldmoon cried.

Pendergast merely waved a hand.

Coldmoon shook his head. It was impossible...and yet it was in keeping with Constance's eccentric manner and her old-fashioned speech and dress. An ancient woman in the body of a girl...No wonder she knew so much, could speak so many languages. It boggled the mind.

"You can guess the rest," Pendergast said. "That infernal machine opened up a kaleidoscope of alternate worlds, including New York City, circa 1880. I saw it myself. No doubt Constance did, too, when she rescued me." He cradled his drink. "She saw an opportunity to return to an alternate past and save both her sister and brother from death. I can only hope she succeeds."

Pendergast fell silent. Coldmoon shakily drained his drink and Pendergast refilled it. "I'm no physicist," Coldmoon said, "but...doesn't that mess things up? I mean, Constance going back to..." He fell silent again, still mentally sorting the potential consequences. "What if she meets herself?"

"She will certainly meet herself. That is not, however, the paradox it might seem. I remind you that all that is happening in an alternate, parallel universe, almost but not quite identical to ours. Anything that happens there will not affect us—especially since the machine that created the gateway has been destroyed. That door is now shut."

Pendergast's voice broke during these last words. As for the complex relationship between Pendergast and Constance...*Na da ma y azan*, Coldmoon thought to himself. "What are you going to do?" he asked.

Pendergast looked surprised at the question. "I'm going to return to New York."

"And what about Constance?"

A change came over Pendergast's features, and he turned away slightly while draining his glass. "Constance has made her choice."

"That's really it? She's gone?"

"Where she has gone, I can't follow. Nor would I want to. Letting Constance put those ancient ghosts to rest without my interference is all I can do for her now. I shall never see her again."

He put the highball glass down on the table with a sharp rap.

"So what about you? Just one day at a time?"

"One *day* at a time?" Now, at last, Pendergast's lips twitched in a ghost of a smile. "Would that I had such luxury. No, my friend: my agony is measured not in days but in seconds. Even less. Not unlike a hummingbird."

"I'm sorry?" Coldmoon wondered if the drink was messing with his reason.

As if on cue, the senior agent got up, went over to the drinks cabinet, and made himself another. "How much do you know about humming-birds, Armstrong?" he asked as he settled into his chair again.

"Not much." This was turning more bizarre by the minute. "They float in the air. They're iridescent."

"A hummingbird is perpetually starving," Pendergast said. "They couldn't even survive a single night without food if they didn't enter a kind of nocturnal hibernation. Did you know that?"

"No."

"As you said: they float in the air. That feat requires an incredibly fast metabolism. Their hearts beat sixty thousand times an hour. And their wings—" he paused to pick up his glass— "beat a hundred times a second. A *hundred* times a second. If I'm to have any peace of mind, I cannot live day by day, only moment by moment. I live in the space of time between the beat of a hummingbird's wings. Taking life at longer intervals...would be unendurable."

He raised his glass again and drank deeply.

"And now I've kept you long enough. Thank you, my friend, for all your kindnesses—large and small. It is time we parted—for good."

Coldmoon, feeling an odd lump in his throat, demurred.

"I never asked for a partner," Pendergast said, "but in retrospect, I couldn't have asked for a better one. *Vale.*"

There had to be something else to say before he left that darkened suite of rooms, but Coldmoon couldn't think what it might be. "*Tókša akhe,*" he replied.

And then, as Coldmoon turned away, Pendergast laughed. This was so uncharacteristic Coldmoon turned back.

"What?"

"I was thinking of something you said, outside the door. You com-pared me to a potato, cooking in a bank of honey-locust embers."

"That's right."

"The expression is new to me. Are they particularly good?"

"If you know what you're doing, there's nothing better. The embers of the honey locust emit just the right amount of heat to crisp the potato jackets, puffing them out like the skin of a Peking duck. And the potato itself is soft as butter."

"Thank you for that gem of rural wisdom, Armstrong. Mind how you go."

And as Coldmoon closed the door behind him, he could still hear the faint sound of Pendergast's laughter—dulcet, melodious, yet infinitely sad—as he maintained his sanity by skipping from one tiny sliver of time to another, between the beat of a hummingbird's wings.

II

THE FIRST THING COLDMOON noticed on entering the Denver Field Office was the smell: for a fleeting moment, he was reminded of home. It was, he realized, an odor very similar to that of the long-boiled coffee that he favored. However, he soon learned the smell had nothing to do with coffee: it came from a mass of half-incinerated evidence hauled out of a counterfeiter's shop in a raid and recently brought into the evidence storage room.

Denver was all he remembered it to be: the western vibe, the distant peaks, the bracing air. The Field Office itself was a long, low building with a façade of glass squares in shades of blue—unusual but attractive, like a mosaic. Even though it was Sunday, the government never slept, and he'd assumed someone from HR would be waiting to guide him through the red tape that came with a transfer, but to his surprise he was taken directly to the office of the Special Agent in Charge, Randall Dudek.

Dudek was on the phone when an assistant ushered Coldmoon in. The office looked toward the dun-colored suburbs rather than down-town. It was a smaller version of Assistant Director Walter Pickett's office—down to the photos of the Capitol, Lincoln Memorial, and the FBI headquarters on Pennsylvania Avenue, as well as the obligatory portraits of the president and vice president.

Dudek gave him a brief nod and swiveled his chair around so he was facing the trophy cases on the rear wall. This had the effect of leaving Coldmoon standing, bags in hand, staring at Dudek's broad shoulders and closely shorn scalp. The call went on for several minutes. Finally, Dudek rang off, turned around, placed the handset on his polished desk, and folded his hands.

"Agent Coldmoon," he said. "Have a seat."

Coldmoon approached, put down his luggage, then sat in one of three identical chairs facing the desk.

"So," Dudek said, "at last. The prodigal son returns."

"Prodigal son, sir?" Coldmoon asked.

"Did you neglect your Bible studies?" He laughed at what was evidently meant as a joke.

"I'm not a Christian, sir."

"Oh. I see." There was a silence just long enough to make Coldmoon wonder if he'd failed some secret exam. "In any case, welcome. I don't normally make a habit of greeting new agents the moment they arrive—especially on a Sunday evening—but we're changing your assignment to a new case that's developing quickly. SA Pologna was already in the starting gate, so to speak. This is a murder that just took place up north on the Rosebud Rez. Normally, that's handled out of the South Dakota Field Office, but they seem to think they needed an agent that speaks Lakota."

"Thank you, sir," Coldmoon said.

"Don't thank me yet." Dudek pulled a file toward him, opened it, and leafed through the contents. "The acting director has really sung your praises here. You've been partnering with that Agent Pendergast—the one whose perps all seem to buy the ranch before trial. Lot of rumors about that fellow."

Coldmoon said nothing. He didn't like to make premature judgments, but there was an air about Dudek he recalled from a drill instructor at the academy: impatient, intolerant, inflexible—and a gossip.

Dudek was still looking through Coldmoon's file. "I knew it was Agent Pendergast who held you up, but I hadn't realized how long he'd been at it. So you worked with him on two cases, start to finish?"

"Three, actually, sir," Coldmoon said. "Two in Florida, one in Georgia."

"Well, from what I've heard of the guy, you're well rid of him." Dudek palmed the file closed with a slapping motion. "Are the rumors true?"

"Rumors?" asked Coldmoon, wondering if he should continue appending "sir" to everything he said and deciding not to.

"You know, those stories about him driving a Rolls, living in a . . . well, never mind. The important thing is you're here now, and you escaped with your reputation intact. Not only intact, but elevated, it seems." Dudek shook his head.

Coldmoon resisted the impulse to inform his new superior that the improvement in his professional reputation was due to Pendergast.

Dudek looked up from his desk, meeting Coldmoon's eyes. "You grew up on Pine Ridge Reservation, correct?"

"Yes, sir."

"How many years?"

"Seventeen."

"Much interaction with your pals over in Rosebud?"

The residents of the next reservation over were hardly pals of Coldmoon's, and he wasn't sure why Dudek assumed they might be. "No."

"Good. And your undercover operation in Philly last year—were you native?"

At first, Coldmoon didn't understand. "I was undercover as a terrorist."

Dudek blew a little air out from his cheeks, as if surprised Coldmoon couldn't keep up. "I mean: were you in character as your own ethnicity?"

"Oh." Coldmoon paused. "No. Sir."

Dudek pushed the file toward him. It was not clear whether or not this was a gesture of dismissal.

"And will there be a briefing on the case, sir?"

"Briefing? Your role is to solve the homicide of a prominent Lakota artist. It's straightforward. Pologna will brief you once you've been onboarded." He glanced from the office door to Coldmoon and back again. "I asked you here because I wanted to have a look at you first."

As in, like, a side of beef? That's what Coldmoon would have said to Pendergast after such a remark. But somehow he didn't think Dudek would appreciate it. And speaking of appreciation, he squashed a twinge of doubt about SA Pologna. He carried the Lakota principle that he would render no judgments on anyone except through direct experience.

At that moment Dudek's phone rang again, and Coldmoon—hoisting his bags—left to find his own way to the Human Resources department.

12

December 1, 1880
Saturday

Hugh Moseley waited in the darkness of the small point of land jutting out from Blackwell's Island, directly across the river from the coal pier of Murray Hill. It was quarter past eleven according to his pocket watch, and traffic on the East River was light. This section of Blackwell's, far from any buildings and sheltered by a thick stand of chestnut trees, had been agreed upon the night before as the place he should meet his strange new employer and the Irishman she'd referred to as Murphy. But they were late, and his agitation was increasing. He had arranged to take the night shift this evening—an easy enough task, given all the nocturnal vices that beckoned the workers from across the river—but he had only forty-five minutes left until he had to report. Instinctively, his hand reached for the vest pocket that usually contained a small vial of laudanum. But the pocket was empty, and foreswearing the tincture—at least for now—was one promise he didn't dare break.

For maybe the thousandth time, he wondered who the young woman was that he'd met, first in the Rathskeller and then, the following night, in his own lodgings. On both occasions she'd been dressed in male clothing, but even so, her beauty could not be concealed. Despite her youth and stature, she displayed a calmness of mind and singleness of purpose that was nothing short of remarkable. Her eyes had sparkled with keen intelligence as well as determination.

It was obvious she was extremely wealthy: she treated money with something close to indifference. He could almost believe she was a figure out of some Gothic romance, a noblewoman or even a princess in disguise...were it not for this urchin she was bent on saving.

His thoughts were interrupted by the low crunch of a keel upon the shingle beach. Looking upriver, he made out the dim form of a rowboat, two figures emerging from it. Clouds covered the moon, and the vessel had made use of the darkness to approach almost invisibly. As he began walking toward it, he saw the brawny silhouette of Murphy, quietly pulling the boat up and shipping the oars. The mysterious woman came toward Moseley, and he received a fresh surprise: she was dressed from head to toe in a close-fitting black garment, attire more appropriate for an acrobat or trapeze artist than for a woman of means. A leather belt such as a soldier might use had been fitted around her waist, and from it hung a variety of pouches and an antique dagger with a hilt of gold. As he stared, she removed the dagger for a brief inspection, and as she tested its readiness he realized it was a stiletto, its razor-sharp blade gleaming faintly in a brief patch of moonlight.

Now Murphy came up. He, too, appeared ready for bloodshed: he held a policeman's lead-spined billy club in one hand, a dark lantern in the other, and in his belt he'd stuck a foot-long, bayonet-like blade known as an "Arkansas toothpick."

"Calm yourself, Mr. Moseley," the woman said in her curious low tone. A black knitted cap was pulled low over her forehead. "These weapons are for persuasion only."

"Aye," said Murphy, pulling his massive blade free with the singing sound of steel. "I won't tickle anybody with this unless necessary."

Moseley watched him brandish it. For some reason, the young woman's stiletto, so much smaller and more elegant, was what made him most uneasy. Had he been deceived in their true purpose? If the boy was innocent, why these preparations for violence? It was not the first time he'd considered this possibility—and he'd come prepared.

"If there's bloodshed, it will go the worse for me," he said. "So

I took the liberty of obtaining this." He pulled a large vial from his battered satchel—not laudanum, more's the pity. "Chloroform. You can use it to incapacitate the keepers."

The woman took the proffered vial. "Thoughtful and clever of you," she said. "But unnecessarily dangerous. Chloroform can all too easily cause airway collapse and death." She handed it to Murphy, who pitched it out into the river. "I've come with my own admixture." And she patted one of the pouches on her belt.

"You have?"

She nodded. "A variant of ACE."

"I...I see." Moseley had heard of this drug, which had recently come into favor among anesthetists. What surprised him more was that she would be familiar with it.

"Let's proceed," she said. "Last night, you told us the basement entrance beside the south wing affords the quickest and quietest access to the workhouse cells. We'll go in through there."

He nodded.

"Before we do that, please repeat for me the plan."

"I'll report to work as usual. The cook, chaplain, and physician should all be off-island. There is a guard outpost at the Octagon, and a barracks at the penitentiary, but at night there's usually only a keeper or two in the south wing of the workhouse—along with the handful of resident employees which, as I said, are likely to be off-island. At twelve thirty, I'll unlock the basement door, then distract the superintendent with something that will require his presence in the women's wing to the north. That should leave you with the one keeper on the first floor of the south cell block, and perhaps another on the second or third floors, to deal with. The key you made from the wax impression should open all the cells. Joe Greene is in the first cell, first floor right. As far as I know, there haven't been any new inmates transferred to that cell."

The young woman listened to this recitation, then nodded. "Very good." She reached into another pouch, drew out a short stack of double eagles, and held them out to him.

"Begging your pardon, but I can't take those at present," he said. "If I'm found with them on my person, once the alarm is raised..."

"Of course. I admire your trusting nature—I'd assumed you would simply bury them somewhere." She returned them to the pouch. "We'll get them to you later."

"Just...*please*, no violence." And with that, Moseley turned and hurried off into the darkness, toward the grim institutional buildings that lay to the south.

Half an hour later, he'd covertly returned the passkey the woman had made an impression of and made sure his presence was noted. To his great dismay, the cook was not off the island, as anticipated, but rather in his foul-smelling chambers, snoring, face flat on the table beside an empty bottle of gin. Moseley's heart sank: much as he hated the man, he couldn't countenance being party to his death.

At quarter past twelve, he made a cursory round of the north wing, where the women were housed. Keepers weren't assigned to this wing, and he'd hoped and expected to find something amiss. He was not disappointed: a brawl was underway in a cell near the far end of the second floor. One streetwalker had accused another of thievery, it seemed, and the argument had spread to all six occupants, now shrieking and cursing at blows both given and received.

After making a cursory attempt to stop it, Moseley retreated to the administrative building between the two wings. Slipping into the basement and ensuring his movements weren't detected, he unlocked the door to the outside. Then he glanced at his pocket watch again: twelve twenty-five.

He returned to the first floor and knocked on the superintendent's door.

"Yes?" came the voice from within.

"It's Moseley, sir."

A sound of shuffling, and then the door opened. Bottle in one hand and glass in the other, Cropper looked him up and down. "What in the living hell do you want?"

"I'm sorry to disturb you, sir, but there's a fracas taking place in the north wing."

"A what?"

"Fight, sir."

"Well, why the devil didn't you take care of it?"

"All the inmates in that cell are involved. It's riling the rest of the block, and I fear the agitation might spread."

The superintendent delivered a brief, blistering critique of would-be surgeons who lacked the oysters to break up a fight among a group of slatterns. Then he put on his coat, picked up a truncheon and his keys, and began to make his way down the passage.

"Grab that," he said, pointing to a large chamber pot sitting by the entrance to the north wing. "If they won't leave off, we'll give them a proper bath." And he laughed.

Gingerly, Moseley picked up the overflowing bucket and followed the superintendent up the stairs, then down the length of the second-floor corridor. As they drew closer, it was clear the fight showed no signs of abating. This was good: it was now half past twelve, and he'd brought the superintendent as far from the south wing as he possibly could. Except for the presence of the cook, everything was going to plan.

It was only then he realized that—from this moment onward—he had not been told what that plan consisted of.

13

As THE SECOND HAND swept past the topmost mark on the subdial of her pocket watch—marking twelve thirty-one precisely—Constance quietly snapped the hunter case shut over the Patek Philippe, tucked it away, and nodded to Murphy.

They emerged from the bushes onto a roughly paved path that led to the basement entrance, not a dozen feet away. The black bulk of the workhouse loomed above them, enshrouded by dark clouds over the moon. Constance glanced around quickly. Except for a few distant voices, all was quiet.

She crept up to the metal door, verified it was unlocked, then glanced around once again. She would have preferred to blacken her face for the undertaking, but she didn't dare present such a frightful visage to her brother Joe: she knew only too well that opening the door to his cell was a beginning, not an end, to readjusting him to civilization—and her success from that point on would require his cooperation.

She glanced at Murphy. "All good?"

"Any finer and I'd be China—begging your ladyship's pardon."

"Remember: the single most important thing is the safety of the boy."

He nodded.

"The second most important thing is: no violence unless absolutely necessary."

"No?" said Murphy, a note of disappointment in his voice.

"Leaving bodies behind would only attract attention." Reaching into a pouch, she pulled out a stoppered glass vial wrapped in thick gauze and handed it to him. "Just in case," she said. "If you need to use it, remember to place the body in a sitting position, against a wall. Be careful not to breathe in any fumes or, God forbid, drop the vial— I'd never be able to lug your bulk back to the rowboat."

The man took the gauze-wrapped bottle with a chuckle. It contained, as Constance had told the surgeon's assistant, the admixture known as ACE: more specifically, alcohol, chloroform, and ether. She retained a second bottle for her own use.

Now she stepped aside, letting Murphy ease the door open. A dark hallway lay beyond, dressed in damp stone. Slipping behind the coachman, she closed the door, then looked around. To the right was the stairway leading up to the south wing. To the left was a narrow passage, punctuated by three doors, provisional residences for the chaplain, physician, and cook. The first two were closed, with no sign of light underneath: they were off the island, as Moseley had predicted. The third, however, was open, and from it emanated the flicker of a lantern and a low, rhythmic sound of snoring.

Damn.

Nodding to the coachman, she crept up the chill passageway to the open door. A fat man wearing a greasy cook's smock and apron was half-draped across a table, insensible.

This was a problem. One or perhaps two keepers they were prepared to deal with, but this ogre of a man was an unexpected variable. If he roused himself and went for help, he'd betray their plan. Having to confront him in a drunken rage was equally undesirable.

She inched closer to the doorframe, pondering what to do. Then she noticed the door. It was steel, banded and riveted, thick as all the other doors in the prison. Silently, she mimed a plan of action to Murphy, who nodded his understanding but took hold of his truncheon nevertheless.

With consummate stealth, she took a step into the room, then another, all the time keeping a close watch on the cook. Grasping the handle of the door, she paused a second, then began stepping back in the direction she'd come, drawing closed the heavy door with the faintest whisper of the latch sliding past the strike plate. Pulling a set of lockpicks from a pouch on her belt, she inserted first a short hook, then a gem hook, into the mechanism, working by feel. After a moment she nodded to Murphy, who pulled a metal shim out of his own pocket and shoved it forcefully, but quietly, into the gap left between her picks. She withdrew her tools, and the coachman used his bull-like strength to bend and break off the shim, rendering the lock unopenable. They waited a minute, making sure the snoring continued. Once the cells were opened, they would use similar shims to damage the locks to cover up evidence that a skeleton key had been used.

They crept back down the stone passage, passing the exit and pausing again at the bottom of the stairway. Constance could see it spiraling up like a corkscrew into the dark void above. Mentally, she sketched out a plan of what awaited them. The stairs were set into the northernmost wall of the south wing of the workhouse. They opened onto three landings, all vertically aligned, corresponding to the three tiers of cells. Moseley had told them that a keeper was always posted in a rude pillbox near the first-floor landing. From there the guard could, by simply walking out into the hollow core of the building, gaze up and across all three cell blocks, stacked one upon another, with a gallery running around the doors of each level. From the vantage point of this "great hall," anything amiss could be immediately spotted. Moseley had warned them that sometimes a second keeper was stationed on one of the floors above—and there was no knowing when this would happen.

Satisfying herself again that no one was aware of their presence, she led the way cautiously up the winding staircase to the first floor. As she did, the nocturnal coughs, sighs, groans, and imprecations of imprisoned humanity—as well as the stench of unwashed bodies— became more evident.

They paused in the darkness of the first-floor landing. Beyond, a narrow tunnel, illuminated at its far end by a kerosene lantern, revealed a small wooden hutch, bolted in place against one of the walls and reinforced with cords of iron. The lantern hung inside a barred window, and Constance could make out a shadowy form within: the keeper. The foul, chill air exhaling from the passage confirmed that a large space, invisible in the darkness, lay ahead.

Suddenly, a sharp, hacking cough sounded almost directly above them, followed by a disgustingly extravagant expectoration. They froze. The noise was too close to the staircase to have come from a prisoner: it could only mean that a second keeper was on duty that evening on one of the floors above.

In the faint glow of Murphy's dark lantern, the two exchanged glances. The coachman nodded his understanding of how this complication fit into their plans. He shut the hinge of the lantern, hung it on his belt, then gingerly drew out the vial Constance had given him. He unwound the gauze until the glass stopper was visible, and began creeping up the stairs.

Constance followed him, slipping her stiletto from its sheath. It was not her plan to kill anyone, but if anything went wrong upstairs and their presence became known, she'd do whatever was necessary to free Joe and get him out of this odious place.

She waited on the steps, senses hyperacute. For a minute, all was silent. Then a faint noise filtered down—a lurching groan, as if someone had just had the wind knocked out of them. Another minute passed, and Constance heard a faint scratching sound—twice.

That was the signal: Murphy had successfully overcome the second keeper and would now be on his way up to the third floor, where the largest cells housed up to twenty-four men each.

It was Constance's turn. She slipped back down to the first-floor landing and flitted along the passage, her form black on black, effectively invisible.

She crouched beneath the window of the pillbox and glanced at her pocket watch. She had five minutes until Murphy would start opening the cell doors, triggering a stampede.

The problem was, the keeper near her appeared quite comfortable in his miniature guardhouse and showed no signs of wanting to leave. She needed to get him to step out—without causing a premature alarm. She wanted Joe safely out of his cell and down the stairs before the riot commenced.

From her crouching position, she took a deep breath; let it out; then took in another, drawing in as much air as she could manage. She raised the tip of her tongue so it just touched the soft palate of her throat. Then, bringing the wind up from deep within her diaphragm, she lowered her tongue and forced air across the roof of her mouth. A sound very much like the droning of a bee seemed to emanate...from the far side of the keeper's pillbox.

Remaining crouched in the darkness, Constance did it again. This time, she heard a rasp of a chair being pushed back as the keeper stood up. He'd heard it, too.

Constance's father had been a poet, a prankster, and a dreamer. One of his more impractical ideas had taken him from London to New York just before the outbreak of the Civil War. He'd never truly been able to find his footing in America, but he never lost his fondness for carnival tricks, picked up as a youth at Lambeth Fair, and he'd delighted his children with exhibitions of ventriloquism before his death from cholera in 1877.

She lowered her chin, contracting her larynx as much as possible, and forced more air from her lungs. This had the effect of lowering the drone from high in the air to someplace near the ground: in the parlance of the carnival trade, exchanging the "sky technique" for the "ground technique."

The keeper, mystified at the thought of a bee in the workhouse on a chill winter night, unlocked his window and stuck his head out inquiringly. Immediately, a piece of sopping cotton gauze was pressed into his nose and mouth, and seconds later his inert form was propped against the inside wall of his pillbox, Constance rifling his pockets.

There was no key: this was not unexpected, as Moseley had said the keys were normally kept on the basement level, out of harm's way. Standing, she checked her pocket watch again: three minutes had passed. She could imagine Murphy in much the same position: two flights above, waiting in the darkness of the vestibule, ready to unleash mayhem upon the restless island.

She hurried forward until she stood on the verge of the great hall itself. She could just make out the tiers of cellblocks, could hear the susurrus of night sounds that drifted about the enclosed space.

Sudden footsteps sounded from above. It was Murphy, moving quickly toward the last cell on the third floor, ready to unleash the hounds of hell. Spurred into action, Constance ran to the cell door and inserted one of the two skeleton keys they had made. A murmur of voices was beginning to rise around and above her—sleepy, curious, annoyed. She slid the key into the lock, turned it, pulled the door open. In the dimness, she could see a single figure inside, sitting upright on what appeared to be a filthy pallet, motionless. Motionless, but alert: he, too, had heard her ventriloqual drone. She took a step toward the little figure, all alone, her heart abruptly pounding, the mephitic air so full of tension it was as if she were surrounded by an electrical field paralyzing in its power.

The figure inside jumped to his feet, staring at her and backing up. Above, there was a clang of iron as Murphy opened the farthest cell on the third floor.

In the dim light, she could not make out the boy very clearly. She took a step forward into the cell, and the boy retreated again.

"Joe," she said. "I'm not going to hurt you. I'm here to take you away from this place."

The boy didn't move. Above, a second cell door banged open, and she heard Murphy's voice cry out: "All out, boyos! Run for it!"

Now, on all three levels, prisoners were waking up, the noise escalating dramatically.

Constance stepped closer. The boy was like a wild animal, tense, ready to fly. Realizing how she must look in her catsuit, she pulled the cap from her head and shook out her hair. As she did, she got a better look at the boy's face.

"Who did that to you?" she said, pointing at Joe's bruised and swollen eye.

For a moment, he didn't answer. Then: "Cook is what done it," came the voice...

...A voice out of the uttermost limits of her memory.

She stood, paralyzed, a few seconds longer. Then—as the clatter of footsteps echoed down the stairwell and the voices swelled to a roar— she reached out and grasped Joe's hand. "Come on!" she cried, pulling him toward the basement door ahead of the mob that was gathering behind them.

14

CONSTANCE RACED DOWN THE stone stairway, clutching Joe's hand. As they reached the bottom landing, she could hear from above the boom of iron and cries of men, along with the thunder of trampling feet. Meanwhile, from down the basement passage, she could also hear a muffled pounding and shouting: the cook, who had been roused and was beating on his locked door. She glanced again at Joe's face, bruised and ashen in the lamplight, and thought for a brief moment of exacting revenge on the cook. But there was no time for that now. She grasped Joe's hand tighter and rushed out the door into the night.

At first, Joe had resisted her, pulling back against her headlong charge, but once outside he willingly followed her across the lawn into a stand of laurels, where they stopped and hid, waiting. Moments later, a stream of men burst out of the doorway. Some were stumbling in leg irons, others running free, many shouting at this unexpected deliverance.

A siren began a mournful wailing from the direction of the Octagon. Immediately, the knot of third-floor prisoners cramming through the door grew frantic, inmates pushing each other aside in their hurry to escape.

Constance spied Murphy among the crowd. She rose and beckoned him to their hiding place. He slipped into the laurels, breathing hard.

"That was a sight I'm not likely to forget," he said, a grin of excitement on his face. "All them gobshites streaming from their cells like hornets from a kicked nest—pardon the liberty, ma'am."

Constance turned to Joe. "This is Paddy Murphy," she told her brother. "He's helping me get you off the island." She paused, uncharacteristically struggling for words. "I know how strange all this must seem. But please—trust me. Once you're safely away from this awful place, I'll explain everything."

Joe had instinctively shrunk back at the appearance of the burly coachman, but now he allowed Constance to again take his hand as they pushed their way through the thicket of laurels to the other side, then ran toward the lonely shore where they'd hidden the boat.

Keeping to the darkest patches, they hurried along. Joe remained silent. Constance could now see guards running toward the work-house from both the penitentiary and the Octagon. As the guards and keepers began grabbing and tackling stray prisoners, sounds of scuffling, shouts, and curses reached her ears. The Octagon siren kept up its wail, and kerosene torches began to grow more numerous, fireflies in a velvet night.

They descended a small bluff to the spot where the boat was hidden. Now, the sound of baying dogs added a new note to the confusion of noise.

"Hurry," Constance said to Joe. "The boat's right here." She released his hand, expecting him to jump in—but instead, he whirled around and began running northward along the shore, into the darkness. With a curse, Murphy dropped the oars back into the rowboat and took up the chase. Constance, much fleeter, ran after the boy as well, and with her superior speed made a looping circuit to cut him off between the shore and the bluffs. She quickly gained distance on the undernourished and underexercised youth, overtook him, and turned back to face him.

Joe, a look of surprise on his face, halted and tried to veer inland, but Murphy anticipated the move and blocked his way. Joe stopped and looked around with desperation. A rotting dock jutted into the river, sagging over the black water. He sprinted onto it, leaping over broken pilings and yawning holes, until he reached its end. There he stopped.

Constance was terrified he might jump. But he didn't. She indicated to Murphy he was to stay back.

"Joe," she called to him down the ruined dock. "Come back. Let us take you away from here. I'm...your aunt. I'm here to help Mary and Constance, as well. I've gone to a lot of trouble to free you, out of respect for your dead parents. If you stay here, this place will kill you. Please, Joe, trust me long enough to get you to safety. If you still want to leave then, I won't stop you."

If this made any impression on the youth, it didn't show—just as he'd shown no obvious recognition of any family resemblance in her face. He glanced over her shoulder in the direction of the institutional buildings, gas lights coming on. Then he turned toward the water, edging up to the very last plank of the dock.

"Joe, *don't!*" Constance shouted. "The current is strong. If you jump, you'll force me to come after you. I know you can't swim."

Now the boy turned back. Constance took a step away from the base of the dock, and another. Slowly at first, Joe walked down the ruined dock. Once again, Constance held out her hand. Another hesitation. Then—as a desperate person might commit himself, for better or worse, to the only option still left—he grabbed her hand and held firm.

A few minutes later, they were back at the boat, the sounds of baying dogs growing closer. Shortly thereafter, they were a mere dot on the East River, heading for Manhattan under cover of darkness.

15

December 2, 1880
Sunday

The eminent surgeon walked down the stone hallways of Bellevue Hospital, the familiar smell of bleach, ammonia, and fecal discharge enveloping him. He moved at a stately pace, being passed by many people in a greater hurry—nurses, orderlies, residents from the Columbia University College of Physicians and Surgeons, maintenance workers. The surgeon, who held a distinguished consulting position, displayed no such urgency, satisfied to drink in at leisure the atmosphere of suffering and sickness that surrounded him.

Other hospitals and famous clinics had vied for his attentions, but the eminent surgeon had chosen Bellevue. The fact that it was the oldest public hospital in the United States, or that it led the way in such progressive developments as sanitary codes and vaccination regimens, mattered little to him. What had been most important was its size—providing him with an almost limitless variety of the human specimen in all its variations of illness. He moved down the corridor with purpose, not unlike a cook strolling through a greengrocery, mind open to the many possibilities at hand.

The surgeon had spent years learning his profession at schools of medicine in both Heidelberg and Oxford. He had initially specialized in general surgery before being drawn to problems of the mind. These, he felt, were riddles worthy of his curiosity—for it was the mystery of insanity that most captivated him. At Heidelberg he had focused on the diagnosis and treatment of mental alienation, recently re-classified as "psychiatry." His special interest was surgery of the brain, to ameliorate symptoms of madness, sexual deviance, and psychosis. During his extended period of education and clinical practice, he had developed certain private ideas about the human nervous system and how it related to mental health and, especially, the aging process.

And so it was toward Bellevue's asylum that he was headed. From the first floor, he descended a series of steps to an iron door, which opened to him, and then a second door, deeper down. Here, in the subterranean levels of Bellevue, the odors and noise were far more intrusive. He passed an orderly's office and guard post and entered the most fortified wing of the hospital, home to the violent and dangerous.

As he started down another corridor, lined with barred doors not unlike a prison, a medical student addressed him. "Good morning, Doctor," he said. "Here to make your Sunday rounds?"

"Just looking in on the results of last week's procedures, Norcross. Would you care to join me?"

The medical student, flushing with pleasure at being singled out, led the way down the hall, stopping at several locked doors. Without going in, the surgeon listened while Norcross updated him on the patients strapped or manacled within—how they were recovering from surgery, the state of their vital signs, and whether or not there had been any improvement in their condition. Two cases in particular showed improvement. The surgeon recommended continuing the hydrotherapy with ice water for one and a mixture of ergot and ferrous iodide *bis in die* for the other. A third inmate was deemed unchanged, while a fourth was clearly expiring. The surgeon gave the student orders to have the body removed immediately upon death and taken to the college; corpses for the anatomy classes were always in short supply.

"Now then, Norcross," the surgeon said. "Any new arrivals you think might be of interest?"

"Only one, Doctor," came the reply. "The night before last. If you don't mind my taking the liberty, I fear this one might be beyond even your curative powers." He paused a moment. "You can hear for yourself, Doctor."

The doctor paused, listening to the larynx-shredding yells and shrieks that were sounding from the end of the passageway, muffled by thick walls.

"Put that way, Norcross, you present me with a challenge," the surgeon said. "We must always hold out hope for *mens sana in corpore sano*. Please, lead on."

They went down the hall, past whimpering skeletal figures crouching semicatatonic against the walls, or struggling wildly against straitjackets. And always the yelling increased in volume until they came to the final cell. A man dressed in tatters raged against the cuffs and chains that held him fast between two walls. The two medical men stood well back from the iron bars so that the spit, sweat, and bloody phlegm flung out from the cage did not reach them.

"Engage him in conversation," the surgeon told the student dryly.

"I'm sorry?"

"Humor me."

The student cleared his throat and then asked the raging man a series of questions, all of which elicited more incoherent screaming.

"Thank you, Norcross," the surgeon said, as the student stepped back again. "What is your diagnosis?"

Norcross grew nervous. "Ah...unrelievedly delusional, fulminating psychosis...total mental alienation from the norms of society."

The surgeon smiled slightly, recognizing the textbook passage. "Of society—or indeed of civilization. Your recitation reeks slightly of the lamp, Norcross, but well put nevertheless. Treatment?"

"I would deem the patient incurable."

"Incurable or not, do any surgical procedures recommend themselves to you?"

The student exhaled with private relief. "Leucotomy?" he said with the slightest of hesitations.

"Excellent. Prefrontal leucotomy—and the sooner we relieve this creature of his suffering, the better. Please speak to Dr. Cawley about scheduling."

This was Bellevue's chief of psychiatry, in charge of the mental asylum. "Of course. Shall I suggest a time to him?"

The surgeon pulled out a pocket watch. "Tomorrow morning should be suitable. I'm lunching at one, so tell Dr. Cawley to have the operating room ready and the patient prepped at half past eleven."

"Yes, Doctor." Norcross hesitated. "May I ask—will this be a burr-pattern procedure?"

"No, Norcross, I don't believe we'll need to go to such trouble in this case. A single trephine hole through the skull with a crown saw, followed by excising and debriding using…" He thought a moment. "A nine-inch spoon curette." Noting the student's interest, his eyebrows shot up. "Would you care to view the procedure?"

"Very much, sir!"

"Excellent." The surgeon preferred working with advanced students rather than newly minted doctors—they were more malleable, more open to new ideas. "You'll take care of the details with Dr. Cawley?"

"Immediately."

"Thank you. In that case, I'll take my leave. Until tomorrow, then."

"Until tomorrow. And thank you again, Dr. Leng!"

The surgeon dismissed this with a polite wave and then—cape briefly encircling his slender form as he turned—walked back down the stone passageway at a somewhat brisker pace than he'd entered with.

16

May 23
Tuesday

LIEUTENANT COMMANDER VINCENT D'AGOSTA stepped out of the squad car on Central Park West and looked up at the pillared entrance to the New York Museum of Natural History. So many memories in this giant building, he mused: the good, the bad, and the ugly. Despite all the crazy things that had happened inside, he was still fond of the old pile.

The Crime Scene Unit van pulled up behind him and Johnny Caruso, head of CSU, got out with his team. They began unloading their equipment, preparing to haul it up the stairs and into the museum.

"I loved this place as a kid," Caruso said, coming up alongside D'Agosta, a small duffel bag slung over his shoulder. "My babysitter used to take us here so she could fool around with her boyfriend behind a totem pole in the old Indian Hall, while my sister and I ran around loose."

"When I was a kid," D'Agosta said, "I got yelled at by a guard while trying to climb onto the elephants in the African Hall. I guess every New Yorker has memories of this place."

Caruso chuckled. "Yeah. And weren't you involved in that really bizarre case about a dozen years ago? The museum murders?"

D'Agosta shook his head, neither agreeing nor disagreeing. "It's a calmer place these days."

It was true: it *did* feel a lot calmer. But at least it was different

from the numbingly similar, depressingly pointless parade of shoot-
ings, stabbings, and rape-homicides he'd investigated over the past
few years, as crime had risen under the previous administration—
thanks to which he was now feeling burnt out to the point of
carbonization.

A couple of borough homicide squad cars pulled in behind the CSU
van. Everybody, it seemed, wanted in on this case. D'Agosta looked
around. The team was complete.

"Okay, people, let's go," he said.

They climbed the stairs and passed through the great bronze
doors. It was two o'clock in the afternoon and the Rotunda thronged
with visitors, voices of excited children echoing in the vaulted space.
D'Agosta saw the museum's director, Lowell Cartwright, hustling
around the tail of a large brontosaurus skeleton, trailed by several
others. He was tall and lanky as a scarecrow, with a stride so long the
others had to trot to keep up with him.

"Incoming," D'Agosta murmured to Caruso as the director
rushed up.

"So glad you could come," Cartwright said. "I'd like to introduce
Martin Archer, our director of security, and Louise Pettini, Public
Relations."

Public relations. At least one thing about the museum hadn't
changed, D'Agosta thought—its obsession with public image.

"The accident took place up in Mammalogy," said Archer. "We'll
go there directly."

D'Agosta let the "accident" comment slide. A naked curator locked
in a freezer didn't sound much like an accident to him. For a moment
he felt a pang of regret that his old pal Pendergast wasn't there. He'd
gone down to Florida in early March on what was supposed to be
a brief trip, but that had been almost three months ago. What he
wouldn't do to have that FBI agent's cynical, cryptic presence at his
side. God, he was fed up with the same old, same old.

Cartwright glanced around at the assembled team. "You really need
so many, Lieutenant?"

"NYPD standard operating procedure for this kind of situation," D'Agosta said.

Cartwright led them out of the Rotunda to a nondescript locked door and, beyond that, to a huge service elevator, which rose with ponderous slowness to the fifth floor. It opened into a broad area with numerous branching corridors. There was a strong smell of death in the air—far too strong to be from the one curator—and besides, he was supposed to be frozen.

"The maceration area is just down the hall," said Cartwright. "Hence the smell."

The maceration area. That, D'Agosta recalled, was where they reduced animal corpses to skeletons by placing them in warm water and letting the flesh liquefy off the bones. Lovely.

"The freezer is this way," Cartwright added.

They turned left, then right, and D'Agosta was almost instantly lost. They were under the eaves of the great museum, and the rooflines slanted this way and that overhead, creating a confusing labyrinth of beams and arches.

At last they came to a gigantic door, perhaps ten feet high and ten wide, made of gray painted metal, dented, scratched, and old. A group of people were gathered outside, standing around nervously.

"The body is still in there?" D'Agosta asked.

"We haven't moved it. He was frozen solid."

"What's the temperature in there?" Caruso asked.

"Twenty degrees below zero."

"Oops," said Caruso. "Forgot my parka."

"We have coats for you here," the director said without breaking a smile. He made a gesture, and one of the people with him opened a closet holding a rack of ancient, greasy coats. Next to the rack was a bin of equally questionable gloves.

"Nice collection of fossils you got here," Caruso said, fingering one of the coats. "But I think we're going to have a problem wearing these over our monkey suits."

His team looked at D'Agosta, waiting for some sort of solution.

D'Agosta tried to conceal his irritation: he should have thought of this ahead of time. The interior might be a crime scene—but how were they going to collect evidence while freezing their asses?

"What's in there that needs to be kept frozen?" D'Agosta asked.

"Animals and animal parts," said Cartwright. "We have frozen elephant skins, collected by Teddy Roosevelt, to replace the ones in the African Hall when the time comes. We have a gorilla in there that just died up at the Bronx Zoo, awaiting maceration. Things like that."

"A gorilla," D'Agosta said slowly. "Okay...Here's what we're going to do. We'll go in by teams. The door will be left open. No coats. Each team will work as long as they can safely, then the next team will go in. Rotate until the job is done."

"We can't leave the doors open too long," warned the director.

"We'll be in and out as quickly as possible. If necessary, we can always shut the door and let it cool off again. That work for you? I mean, how long does it take for a gorilla to thaw out?"

Cartwright didn't look too pleased. "The freezer is equipped with a heat alarm."

"Great. That will be the signal for us to shut the door and take a break." D'Agosta turned to Caruso and the rest. "Let's go."

The Crime Scene Unit team put on their protective suits. Archer, the security chief, unlatched the door and swung it open on massive hinges, releasing a gust of bitterly cold air that filled the hallway with clouds of vapor.

D'Agosta gasped involuntarily. The curator was sprawled grotesquely on the floor of the freezer, on his back, head raised, mouth open in a frozen grimace, eyes wide and covered with frost—dressed in only his underwear and one sock. The rest of his clothes lay scattered around—suit jacket, pants, vest, shoes. But no coat.

The first team went in, D'Agosta standing at the door watching. The photographer began taking pictures, and the trace evidence collection team started in with tweezers and ultraviolet light. The coroner leaned over the body, examining it closely from head to toe.

D'Agosta turned to the director. "What's his name?"

"Eugene Mancow."

"Why didn't he have a coat?"

"I don't know."

"Any idea what he was doing in here?"

"That's a mystery. This freezer belongs to Mammalogy, but he's from Anthropology. We know he wasn't in here at close of day, so whatever happened must've happened overnight. A lot of curators work late, and there's no special security up here beyond the usual locked doors, to which he'd have a key."

"Are there any anthropological items in this freezer?"

"No, they have their own storage areas."

D'Agosta pulled out his flashlight and examined the open freezer door. It was clearly of vintage make, massive, dented, and greasy. There was a latch on the inside marked EMERGENCY RELEASE. It was pulled into the upmost position.

"That's what you use," Cartwright said, "if you're accidentally locked in there."

"Looks like it didn't work." D'Agosta examined it closely with the flashlight and turned to Caruso. "We're going to need to pull some latents off this."

Caruso nodded.

"Did you bring a firearm and tool guy? I want someone to examine this mechanism."

"That would be Paul Nguyen. Hey, Paul!"

One of the CSU guys came over.

"Will you take a look at that emergency release," D'Agosta asked, "and see why it didn't work?"

"Sure thing." The man immediately got to work, unscrewing the covering plate and peering in with a headlamp, poking around.

The coroner emerged, shivering. "Done and ready to be bagged."

"Time of death?"

"I would guess fairly early in the evening, given he's frozen all the way through. I'll have to do some calculations back at the lab."

"What's with the strip-down? Who did that?"

"He did," said the coroner, peeling off his gloves and rubbing his hands together.

"*He* did? How do you know?"

"It's called 'hypothermic undressing.' Very common in such circumstances. A person freezing to death eventually starts to feel unbearably hot, and they often tear off their clothes."

D'Agosta winced. Weird shit.

"Um, Lieutenant?" It was Nguyen, peering into the release mechanism with his light. "Take a look." He backed away and shone his light on a small brass lever inside the hollow door. It had been filed through, the cut fresh and gleaming.

"That confirms it," said D'Agosta. "Homicide."

17

THE SOUTH DAKOTA SUN shone indifferently on the bloodstain that remained after the body had been taken away. Special Agent Coldmoon stood at the base of the cliffs, Agent Bob Pologna next to him, along with Jason LaPointe, commander of Rosebud Sioux Tribe Law Enforcement Services, and RPD Homicide Detective Susannah Wilcox. The wind blew skeins of dust across the floor of the canyon, rattling the saltbush and clumps of parched ricegrass. It was late May, but the wind still had a raw bite to it that reminded him powerfully he was back in South Dakota. He inhaled deeply of the air smelling of dust and stone. God, he loved it.

"This is where we found him," said LaPointe. "He was shot once in the back with a .223 round."

Pologna, bored, scuffed the dirt with his foot. Coldmoon wanted to say something about not disturbing a live crime scene, but held his tongue.

LaPointe went on. "See that layer of red rock up there?" He pointed to the cliff above. "That's a kind of rock called pipestone. He was up there collecting it when he was shot."

"No ropes? Climbing gear?" Coldmoon asked, looking up at the steep rocks.

LaPointe shook his head. "Grayson Twoeagle was a strict traditionalist. Lakota have been collecting pipestone from that outcrop for centuries without ropes, and that was the way he wanted to do it."

"What did he do with the stone?"

"He made pipes," said LaPointe. "Sacred pipes. And other things. He was famous for his replicas of traditional artifacts— lances, parfleches, knapped arrowheads and spearpoints, tomahawks, beadwork."

Coldmoon nodded. "So tell me what happened, who investigated— the full story."

LaPointe turned. "Susannah responded to the call."

Susannah Wilcox was young and serious, with long black hair and almond-shaped onyx eyes. She had a tablet in one hand and consulted it. "On May twenty-first, at 4:10 PM, the RPD got a call from Margaret Twoeagle, Grayson's wife, who said he'd left to gather pipestone several hours previously and hadn't returned. She was worried he might have fallen. We dispatched an officer, who found him at the base of the cliff with a gunshot wound. I arrived at 6:16, at the same time as the paramedics. But he was deceased— killed instantly by a bullet through the heart, which entered from the back and came out the front. We sent an officer up the cliff and he found the round lodged in the stone. So we initiated an investigation."

"Good," said Coldmoon. "We'll run ballistics on that round at the lab. Along with any other evidence that needs analyzing. Agent Pologna and I can go over that back at headquarters."

"Thank you."

This was two days ago, Coldmoon thought, rather a long time when a murder investigation was involved. Selfishly, he was glad they hadn't moved more quickly—he hadn't been able to sort out all the HR red tape and get his final clearance until Monday.

"Let me just add," said LaPointe, "that Mr. Twoeagle was a prom- inent member of the community." He hesitated. "We're glad to have the FBI assisting, but we'd appreciate it if you kept a low profile."

Coldmoon nodded. It was a shame the body had been removed

before the coroner had a chance to examine it. "Tell me about your investigation so far."

LaPointe continued his narrative. "To make a long story short, we've focused on Mr. Twoeagle's business dealings and background. He didn't seem to have any enemies, and we didn't find any evidence of wrongdoing or business disputes—except one. It was substantial. He owed money to a dealer in silver, shells, and stones. Name of Clayton Running. It seems Twoeagle was having trouble paying what he owed and Running cut him off. They had a fight."

"You mean an argument?"

"No, a real fight. Fists and all. Running started it, but Twoeagle got the better of him, pummeled him pretty good. He was a big strong man, didn't drink or smoke, ran five miles a day."

"You interviewed Running?"

"We did. He doesn't have a good alibi for the hours in question—just his wife saying he was around the house all that time."

"How much money did Twoeagle owe him?"

"About three thousand dollars."

Coldmoon considered this pretty thin so far. A lot of people were owed money and got into fights, but they didn't kill over it. "Did you get a warrant to search his house?"

"Not yet."

"Okay, let's get the paperwork underway. And search for that .223 rifle. Did you find the shooter's location?"

"No."

Coldmoon wondered why not. He got an odd impression that, for some reason, they weren't too keen on the idea of searching for it. Was this whole investigation being slow-walked?

"People knew he came here to gather pipestone, so it wouldn't be hard to ambush him from a sniper-style perch." Coldmoon looked around. "That canyon rim is a good place to look. An even better place would be that bench about halfway down, where the caves are. Has it rained?"

"No."

"There should be footprints. Let's go."

"Now?" asked Pologna. "Shouldn't we get an ERT out here?"

Coldmoon looked at him. Getting an FBI Evidence Response Team out there would take days, red tape, and all kinds of hassles, while whatever evidence existed would be blowing away.

"Yes. Now. Meanwhile, that bench is accessible on the right—there's an easy route up."

Coldmoon led the way, the others following reluctantly. Very reluctantly. Coldmoon was starting to get irritated. When they reached the base of the opposite cliffs, where a ridge led up to the bench from the canyon floor, LaPointe said, "I've got a heart condition. Mind if I stay here?"

Coldmoon looked at him. He didn't look like a guy with a heart condition. "Fine." He glanced at Wilcox. "You good with this?"

She, too, looked uneasy. "I might stay here with Commander LaPointe. That looks a little dangerous."

Coldmoon glanced up the broad, gentle slope to the bench. He shook his head. "Suit yourself. Pologna?"

"I'm good."

They started up and quickly reached a sandy area, where human footprints were clearly visible, softened by two days of wind. A single person. Too blurred to be worth casting. Coldmoon took a series of photos. As they continued climbing, the outcrop of pipestone slowly became more exposed until they reached a large fallen rock. Behind it was a sandy area with a cluster of confused prints. Coldmoon took more photos. He crouched behind the rock and peered at the outcrop on the opposite side of the canyon—a perfect vantage point.

"This is where the shooter was," he said, examining the rock for any trace evidence: hairs, fibers, a cigarette butt.

"No doubt." Pologna was looking around, too. "Hey!"

Coldmoon turned. Pologna was reaching down to collect something wedged in the sand.

"Whoa, there," said Coldmoon, coming over. And there it was: a shell casing. "Let's photograph that sucker first."

"Right."

Coldmoon took a series of photos from every angle, then picked up the shell with rubber tweezers and dropped it into a test tube.

"Good work, partner," he said, glad that Pologna had made the discovery. Maybe this would draw him into caring more about the case than he seemed to. At least he appreciated the guy's silence. A partner who talked nonstop was a nightmare.

"Thanks."

"Where does this Running guy live?"

Pologna chewed his lip for a moment. "Let's find out."

18

D'Agosta took a tentative sniff. It was true: somehow, he'd grown accustomed to the stink of the museum.

"We've got to remove that whole thing," D'Agosta said to Cartwright, indicating the freezer door. "It's evidence."

"Impossible!" Cartwright said. "We can't let things unfreeze in there. Those elephant skins have been frozen for over a century!"

"I'm sorry," said D'Agosta, "we have to establish chain of custody for this door, and right away. Can you move the stuff to another freezer?"

"Those elephant skins weigh over a ton apiece." Cartwright turned toward a man standing across the corridor with the others—evidently museum employees. "Ivan, can you come here, please?"

Ivan was short and round, with mussed hair, a rumpled suit, thick glasses, and a high, domed forehead as smooth as polished ivory.

"This is Dr. Ivan Mussorgsky," said Cartwright, "chairman of the Mammalogy Department. The lieutenant," Cartwright continued, "wants to remove this door. I'm trying to explain how important it is that we maintain the freezer's integrity."

Mussorgsky turned his bespectacled eyes, magnified alarmingly, in D'Agosta's direction. When he spoke, the voice was startlingly deep and carried quiet authority. "Not a problem. I'm sure our staff can jury-rig a temporary door in an hour or two. That should suffice until I can order another."

D'Agosta felt a surge of gratitude for this small, disheveled man who actually seemed willing to be helpful. "Thank you," he said. "That's much appreciated."

Cartwright was suddenly nodding vigorously. "There, there, an excellent solution! We're doing all we can to assist, Lieutenant."

"Dr. Mussorgsky," said D'Agosta, "could I ask you a few questions while you're here? We're going to want a formal interview later, but there are a few things that perhaps we can clear up right now."

"Of course."

D'Agosta nodded him aside. Cartwright made a move to accompany them, but D'Agosta shook his head.

As they moved around a corner and away from the group, D'Agosta held up his cell phone. "Mind if I record?"

"Be my guest."

"Did you know the decedent?" D'Agosta asked. A large body bag was now being toted past the intersection, containing the contorted, frozen shape of the victim inside.

"I do." He pushed his glasses back up on his face. "Or rather did. Dr. Mancow was a curator in the Anthropology Department."

"What was he like?"

"Affable. I didn't know him well, really, but he seemed to get along with everyone just fine."

"Any idea what he was doing here?"

"None."

"Was it something he did regularly?"

"As far as I know, he never came up to the mammal preparation area. This isn't a popular place, on account of the smell. The only people here regularly are technicians and curatorial assistants—and they're rarely around at night."

"He seems to have gone in without a coat, and the door mechanism was sabotaged to prevent him getting out. That all points to homicide. Any idea why?"

"None at all. It's a terrible shock."

"Was he particular friends with anyone in the Mammalogy Department?"

"Not that I know of, but you can certainly ask around."

"What was his field of study?"

"North American ethnology, I think—but you'd best talk to the Anthro Department about specifics like that."

"Anything else you can think of that might be useful?"

The man hesitated. "If I might offer a little conjecture?"

"Please."

"This was a bizarre way to kill someone. Why not just shoot them in a street or restaurant, or some dark corner of a subway station? Risk was involved in getting Dr. Mancow up here and into the freezer. Unless he was drugged, he would have been pounding on the door before he succumbed to the cold. There are people around the museum all night—curators, night guards, and so forth. So my conjecture is that this was done to send a message."

D'Agosta was surprised to see Mussorgsky riding the very train of thought that had been running through his own brain. He was careful not to show it. "Interesting... What sort of message?"

"I don't know. But of course, when this gets out to the press— if it hasn't already—I'm afraid the museum is going to be very embarrassed."

D'Agosta slid a card out of his pocket and gave it to the curator. "Feel free to call me with any fresh information. Day or night. Oh, and one final question: in addition to being head of the department, do you have a particular area of study?"

"The evolution of the genus *Rattus*."

"Rattus?"

"Rats."

"Right. Thanks." Made as much sense as anything else, D'Agosta thought: rats had been around before Homo sapiens; sooner or later, they'd be the dominant species once again. These days, it was feeling more like sooner.

* * *

Ninety minutes later, the Crime Scene Unit had finished their work. The freezer door had been removed and sealed as evidence, and a group of museum workers was installing a temporary covering made of two-by-sixes and plywood, heavily insulated.

"Ready to face the ravening wolves out there?" Caruso said as the group returned to the main floor, leaning toward D'Agosta's ear and speaking in an undertone.

News of the murder had indeed leaked, and Central Park West was now crammed with media vans and reporters bristling with boom mikes and cameras.

"No worries, my friend," said D'Agosta. "I've escaped from this place before. Mr. Archer?"

The security director came over.

"Could you please have one of your men escort us out the basement security exit to staff parking? We'd rather not run the gauntlet."

"Gladly," said Archer, turning to a guard.

A different elevator took them to the basement, and they followed the guard through dim, labyrinthine stone passageways, some with small stalactites growing from the ceiling.

"Christ," said Caruso, "this is like something out of a horror film."

"It once was," D'Agosta replied dryly, the memory of his terrified escape through these basement and sub-basement tunnels still fresh, years later.

As they turned a corner, a strange mass of closely placed steel pillars partially blocked the corridor. "See those columns?" D'Agosta said to Caruso. "The way they come out of the floor and go up through the ceiling? Know what they're holding up?"

"The fossilized dick of a T. rex?"

D'Agosta laughed. "The largest meteorite in the world. It was found in Greenland by Robert E. Peary, on one of his expeditions to reach the North Pole."

"You're not shitting me, are you?"

"Would I shit you, Caruso?"

The guard led them to a door that opened into a small parking area amid the jumble of interconnected museum buildings. From there they walked along a driveway, past a guard station, and onto Columbus Avenue.

"What now?" Caruso asked as they emerged. "We still have to go around front to our vehicles."

"Since we're not in uniform, they won't know who we are until it's too late."

As they walked along Eighty-First Street, the evening light streamed eastward down the streets leading from the Hudson River, striking the tops of the trees in Central Park. D'Agosta's phone rang. He slid it out to see, to his surprise, that the caller ID indicated Pendergast's landline.

"Whoa, I gotta take this." He answered. "Pendergast?"

"Hello, is this Lieutenant Vincent D'Agosta?" a breathless, warbling voice asked.

D'Agosta recognized it as belonging to Pendergast's cook. His heart went into his throat: she had never called him before. Ever.

"Mrs. Trask? Is something the matter?"

"I'm—I'm afraid so."

"Is it Agent Pendergast? Is he back?"

"Yes, he is, and... well, I'm sorry to call you. I'm just *so* worried."

"Is he all right?"

"I don't think so. He returned home without Constance. He's not himself."

D'Agosta felt a surge of relief. At least he wasn't dead, or injecting drugs again.

"Not himself. How, exactly?"

A hesitation. "I'd be grateful if you could pay us a little visit. Just a social call, to say hello. Please don't tell him I spoke to you. But you know him better than almost anyone—perhaps I'm just imagining things, and you can set my mind at rest."

"Of course. When?"

Another brief silence, then the tremulous voice asked: "Would tomorrow be too soon?"

19

P<small>ARMELEE WAS A WINDSWEPT</small> intersection in the middle of nowhere, dotted with trailers and shotgun houses. A cold wind rattled the weeds and shook the branches of the only tree in sight, dead. A few horses grazed in a fallow field.

Running lived in a typical HUD house, a low, rectangular prefab in gray siding with a Pro-Panel roof and a large pile of wood in front. A reedy stream of smoke issued from the chimney.

"Butt-fuck nowhere," said Pologna, looking around.

Coldmoon said nothing. It reminded him strongly of the village of Porcupine, where he grew up—and not necessarily in a bad way. People on the Rez were poor, and there was misery and addiction, but there was also warmth and family and a pot of coffee on the wood stove, ready for any guest. And there were horses: that sacred connection to the past. Just to see them around made him feel good.

They went up a dirt walkway and Coldmoon rang the doorbell. A moment later a woman answered, heavyset but with a bright, wrinkled face.

"*Hau*. I'm Special Agent Coldmoon, FBI—" he showed his badge— "and this is my partner, Agent Pologna. We'd like to talk to your husband, ask a few questions."

She hesitated, and replied, "*Tanyán yahí*." She turned. "Clayton? Some cops to see you."

Coldmoon heard a grunt from the back. "Okay, bring 'em in."

She stood aside and they stepped in. Entering the living room, Coldmoon saw it also doubled as a workshop, with a long table down the center. In various open boxes he could see chunks of turquoise and azurite and onyx; sheets and rods of silver; a stack of abalone shells; a bundle of feathers; and beads and polished sticks of red coral. A wood stove, radiating heat, stood in the middle of the room, and—sure enough—there was a speckled blue enameled coffee pot sitting on it.

At the table was a wiry man with a classic Lakota face, wearing a fringed buckskin shirt finely decorated with beads and a red bandanna tied around his head, holding long gray hair in place. He was the very picture of a traditional elder, so much so that Coldmoon was once again momentarily transported back to his own childhood.

The man's eyes narrowed, looking at Coldmoon. "You Lakota?"

Coldmoon nodded. "Pine Ridge. *Wíyuškiŋyaŋ waŋčhíŋyaŋke ló.*"

The man rose slowly and extended his hand, returning the greeting in beautifully formal Lakota, and then led them into the sitting part of the room. "Please take a seat." He gestured. "Coffee?"

"Oh, yeah," said Coldmoon.

"Sure," said Pologna doubtfully.

Running picked up the pot as his wife brought in some chipped mugs and set them down on a plywood coffee table. She poured the steaming liquid into both cups. "Cream, sugar?"

"No thanks." Coldmoon took it and sipped, the burnt taste bringing back still more memories. Just as he liked it. He glanced at Pologna, who was looking with a distaste bordering on horror at the mug he was just handed. Poverty required everything be stretched to the limit, and coffee, one of the most important staples on the Rez, was no exception. Those grounds might have been simmering in that pot for a week, with water and additional fistfuls of grounds added periodically. Dump the grounds once a week and start over—that was the Lakota way.

"Mr. Running," Coldmoon began, "we're here to ask you a few questions about Grayson Twoeagle. Voluntarily."

"Do I need a lawyer?"

"You have that right, of course." Coldmoon waited. It was not yet time to read him his rights, and he didn't want to spook the guy.

"Go ahead."

"I'm told Mr. Twoeagle owed you money."

"Damn right."

"How much?"

"Three thousand two hundred and four dollars."

"What for?"

"He's been buying silver, shells, feathers, and stones from me for years. I've always had trouble getting him to pay. He makes, or rather made, beautiful things, but he doesn't sell them for enough money. A lot of the time he wouldn't sell them at all."

"So you cut him off?"

"Yes, sir."

"When?"

"Two weeks ago. I have to pay my suppliers. You see all that stuff over there? Cost me hundreds of dollars. I supply all the artists and jewelers in this section of the Rez."

"And you had a fight with him?"

"Yes, sir. I went over there to collect at least some of what was owed. My wife has diabetes and she can't work anymore. I need the money. So I went there and he spoke to me disrespectfully and we had a tussle."

"I see you still have a black eye."

"He threw the first punch."

"People say you threw it."

"They can go to hell."

"They also say you lost the fight."

"They can go to hell two times over. No one got the better of me. I whupped his ass."

Coldmoon thought. "That buckskin jacket you're wearing? Beautiful."

He grunted.

"Is that the work of Mr. Twoeagle?"

"Payment in kind."

Coldmoon nodded. "Mr. Running, Mr. Twoeagle was murdered between noon and four on Sunday. May I ask where you were during that time?"

"Right here. With Mrs. Running."

"That's right," said his wife loudly from another room, where she had apparently been listening.

"What were you doing?"

"What do *you* do, sittin' around the house? Drink coffee. Listen to music. Catch up on work."

"Do you own a rifle, Mr. Running?"

"Yes."

"What kind?"

"Browning."

"Browning what?"

".223 caliber, lever action, twenty-inch barrel, stainless."

"Can I see it?"

He didn't move out of his chair. "You thinking I shot Twoeagle with a varmint rifle?"

"I wouldn't exactly call your Browning a varmint rifle."

"It was stolen a week ago."

At this, Coldmoon felt a prickle of suspicion. "Did you report it to the police?"

"I'm reporting it now. You're cops, aren't you?"

"Why didn't you report it before?"

Running shifted uneasily. "Maybe I need that lawyer after all. Maybe you should leave."

Coldmoon rose. "Fine. We'll see ourselves out."

They climbed back in the car and Coldmoon exhaled. "We'd better get that warrant ASAP."

"Yup," said Pologna. "I think we found our man."

That was a little premature, Coldmoon thought as he started the car and eased onto the road, but then he couldn't really disagree.

20

He'd like to speak with you. In the library."

Proctor, staring moodily into a cup of black coffee in the back kitchen of the mansion on Riverside Drive, did not immediately realize this statement was directed at him. After a moment, he looked up to see Mrs. Trask staring in his direction.

"Me?" Proctor said. The question sounded stupid even as he asked it, but somehow he needed confirmation.

Since his employer had returned from Savannah, he had not spoken once to Proctor: his driver, bodyguard, and Keeper of Particular Secrets. A few others had passed in and out of the house—doctors or scientists, a two-star general, and another person who stood out because he was so utterly banal in appearance Proctor figured he must be an undercover agent of some kind—but still Pendergast had not spoken with him.

Proctor considered that if he had feelings to be hurt, they would be. Fortunately, he did not.

Two days ago, Pendergast had suddenly arrived, without Constance. He had deactivated the security system and walked in, leaving his suitcases in the refectory. He had glided up the stairs and locked himself in his private chambers almost before Proctor knew he was in the house. Since then, Mrs. Trask had seen him several times—she'd served him spartan meals in the library, along with afternoon tea—but whenever she entered his private chambers, there'd been something in her expression that told Proctor she knew as little as he did...and warned him not to make any inquiries.

This late-evening summons, therefore, had come as a surprise. Proctor stood up, smoothed his jacket, drained his coffee, and made his way toward the front rooms of the mansion.

He arrived at the marble reception hall and the double doors leading into the library. He paused before the doors to practice some box breathing. Strange he should feel more anxious now than when slipping into the bedroom of a snoring dictator armed only with a garrote, or while being ambushed by enfilading fire in Yemen.

He rapped on the door.

"Come in," came the familiar voice. Proctor entered the library and closed the doors behind him.

Agent Pendergast was standing by the tall windows at the far end of the room, hands behind his back. He looked exactly as if he was taking in the view, which of course was impossible, since the library's shutters were, as usual, closed.

"Ah, Proctor," he said. "Please join me." And he indicated the wing chair on one side of the fireplace.

This was a most unusual request. But then, everything had taken on a touch of unreality in the last few days, and Proctor saw no reason to question his employer. He came forward and sat down. As he did so, he noticed the library appeared unused: there were no piles of books or old papers spread about as was often the case, and the polished wood surfaces were dust-free and gleaming. Also, unusually, no fire flickered in the grate. The harpsichord sitting in a far corner— its painted lid closed—caught his eye, reminding him of Constance's absence.

Pendergast took a seat in the chair opposite him. "I apologize, old friend, for not greeting you earlier," he said. "I'm not myself."

"Unnecessary, sir." Proctor took the opportunity to observe Pendergast carefully. The man was paler than usual, and his movements indicated to Proctor's keen eye that he was recovering from an injury to his left shoulder. Most startling were his eyes, which stared out at the world with a kind of desperate ferocity that belied his easy, courtly manner. He was, indeed, not his normal self.

But Proctor prided himself on his lack of imagination, and he knew Pendergast would notice signs of curiosity, so he was careful to maintain an impassive expression.

"I'm afraid it is necessary," Pendergast replied. "Especially since I'm going to be asking a lot of you in the coming days."

"I'll assist however I can, sir."

"I know that. Just as I know I can rely on your complete discretion. I have a project for you of the greatest importance—and delicacy."

He nodded.

"Naturally, money won't be an issue; spend what you need. Nobody is to know who you are, whom you work for, what you are doing, or why you're doing it. You will need to devise a cover for your activities. What that is, I will leave up to you."

Proctor nodded again.

"You know, of course, the former ice room in the basement? The one lined with zinc?"

"Certainly."

"What is its current condition?"

"I believe it's empty."

"Excellent. Please make sure it is not only empty, but immaculately clean."

"Yes, sir."

"Tomorrow you will be going to Savannah. As you've heard, the city was recently attacked."

"So I understand." The disaster had been all over the news, but with no clarity as to what had happened. Proctor knew Pendergast had been involved, one way or another, but exactly how was equally murky.

"I want you to retrieve a machine and bring it back here." Pendergast indicated some rolled-up blueprints on the table between them. "Here are the relevant diagrams. It is in the basement of a hotel, in a hidden room, and it is badly damaged. Comprehensiveness is critical—

one missing chip, one overlooked transistor, could be catastrophic."
Pendergast fixed Proctor with eyes that pinned him to the sofa. "How
do you read, Chief Warrant Officer?"

"Your signal is five by five, sir."

"Very good. Then let us proceed: we have a great deal to cover."

Pendergast held Proctor's eyes a moment longer before turning his
attention to the closest blueprint, which he now unrolled on the table
and secured with glass ornaments. And then he began to speak in a
low but rapid voice.

21

May 24
Wednesday

T HE SEARCH WARRANT CAME through the next morning. Coldmoon and Pologna arrived back at Running's place with LaPointe, Wilcox, and two officers. The sun was still rising in the sky and the wind had picked up, blowing skeins of dust across the bare ground.

They knocked on the door, and Mrs. Running opened it. It was a no-knock warrant, but there would be no breaking down of doors while Coldmoon was in charge.

"Warrant," said Coldmoon, showing it to her. "To search the premises, outbuildings, and grounds for firearms and ammo."

"Is that those damn cops again?" came a voice from inside.

Coldmoon said, "I'd like to ask you and Mr. Running to go into the kitchen and remain seated at the table while we conduct the search."

She stared at him with naked hostility and then said loudly to her husband, "We gotta go into the kitchen!"

Running appeared, his face red.

Coldmoon held out the warrant. "If you'd please cooperate, we'll finish as quickly as possible."

Running snatched the warrant from Coldmoon and looked at it for a long time, frowning, his hand trembling.

Coldmoon gently took it back. "Make yourself comfortable in the kitchen. Detective Wilcox will stay with you."

Wilcox ushered them into the kitchen and shut the door.

"Okay," said Coldmoon to the team. "Let's get to work. No damaging anything without me or the commander expressly authorizing it."

The officers began a methodical search of the front hallway and closets, while Coldmoon took notes and made occasional suggestions. The cheap HUD construction made it easy to search. Pologna ran a special weapons-calibrated metal detector over walls and floors, periodically stopping to rap on the wallboard.

Coldmoon was about 90 percent sure they wouldn't find the rifle. Running was no dope, and if the rifle was indeed the murder weapon he would have hurled it in Eagle Feather Lake or buried it in some distant pasture.

Coldmoon and Pologna went out to search the yard while the officers finished up in the house and inspected the crawl space underneath. The yard contained a hay shed, a corral, and a half-ruined shack of indeterminate function.

"I still wonder why the South Dakota FO wouldn't handle this case," said Pologna, staring around at the endless horizon and shabby trailers. "I mean, this is a long way to go for a simple homicide."

"I guess they don't have any Lakota agents in the South Dakota FO." Coldmoon had wondered about that, too: why a Lakota agent was specifically called for. It wasn't as if there was a language issue. He had a sneaking suspicion that Dudek wanted to get him out of the way for some reason, and that Pologna, with his less-than-charming personality and lackadaisical record, had been assigned as junior agent for similar reasons. The two of them had essentially been packed off to nowhere.

Commander LaPointe joined them in the yard with the two officers.

"Why don't you search the shack," Coldmoon told them. "Agent Pologna and I will check out the corral and hay shed."

The hay shed was constructed of sawmill slab-sides. A partial stack of moldy alfalfa sat inside, baled with string.

"Nothing in here," said Pologna, glancing around and kicking over an empty feed bucket.

One of the bales on top was a little askew. Coldmoon grasped the string and heaved the bale off the pile. A Browning .223 and ziplock bag full of loose ammo fell to the ground with them.

"Bingo," Coldmoon said.

22

D'Agosta got out of the cab in front of 891 Riverside Drive and paused in front of the mansion with a degree of trepidation. Even in the afternoon sunlight, it didn't look exactly welcoming. He took a deep breath, walked up the drive and under the porte cochere, and—after a second pause—pressed the bell of the great oaken door.

Usually, it took ages for someone to answer the door, if it was answered at all. But today it took less than fifteen seconds before Mrs. Trask opened it. He felt relieved: he'd been preparing to deal with the stone-faced Proctor. D'Agosta wasn't easily intimidated, but he was just as happy to skip that particular formality.

"Thank you so much for coming," Mrs. Trask said, clutching his hands briefly but firmly. "I'll see you to the library."

D'Agosta followed the housekeeper through the refectory, the vast reception hall with its displays of fossils and gemstones, to the double doors that led into the library. "What can I get you?" Mrs. Trask asked as D'Agosta chose a sofa in the middle of the room. "Tea?"

D'Agosta had spent a long morning coordinating the investigation of the frozen curator; this was the first time he'd been able to get away, and he was in no mood for tea. "Any chance of a Bud Light?"

"Very good." She disappeared. A moment later, another figure appeared in the doorway.

"My dear Vincent!"

D'Agosta rose.

"Don't get up, please." Pendergast stepped inside and took a nearby chair. "I apologize for being out of touch, but I'm pleased that you've arrived in time to join me for a drop of preprandial refreshment. What brings you here?"

D'Agosta took a moment to consider his friend carefully. He was immediately struck by his gaunt appearance, the uncharacteristic garrulousness, the exaggerated drawl.

"I was just in the neighborhood and thought I'd drop in," said D'Agosta.

"Indeed?" One pale-blond eyebrow rose above Pendergast's ice-chip eyes.

D'Agosta was spared from responding by Mrs. Trask arriving with a silver salver, bearing drinks. She placed a beer and glass on D'Agosta's side table. By Pendergast she placed an arrangement that was more complex: a bottle filled with green liquid, labeled Vieux Pontarlier Absinthe; an oddly shaped stemware glass; a small flask of water; a slotted silver spoon; and sugar cubes.

D'Agosta poured his beer and took a deep draft. Both beer and glass were wonderfully frosty, just as he liked it. Mrs. Trask never failed. She'd been so quick about it, D'Agosta thought she might almost have had everything waiting.

Pendergast busied himself with his own bizarre cocktail. He laid the slotted spoon over the glass and placed a sugar cube in it. Then— opening a small, almost invisible drawer in the reading table beside his chair—he drew out a small bottle, topped with a black silicone bulb. Unscrewing this, Pendergast pulled off the bulb to reveal a glass dropper, complete with graduation marks. It was filled with a reddish-brown liquid a few shades darker than blood. Carefully, he held the pipette over the sugar cube and squeezed out several droplets: one, two, three.

An amber-like color began to suffuse the sugar cube.

Returning the dropper to the bottle and the bottle to the drawer, Pendergast then drizzled the absinthe slowly over the cube, allowing the effluent to run into the glass. He took a gold Dunhill lighter from one pocket and, with a practiced motion, lit the cube and spoon on fire. A blue flame flared up, the sugar melting, sizzling, and dissolving into the glass below. After a few moments, he picked up the flask and dribbled a little cold water over the remains of the cube, putting out the flame. Lastly, he stirred the concoction with the sugar-encrusted spoon. The liquid in the glass swirled with a cloudiness that was part ivory, part crimson.

He set aside the spoon, took the glass, and held it up. "Thank you for indulging my little rituals. Here's to you, my old friend." And he took a sip of the drink, placing it back on the side table and dabbing his lips with a silk napkin.

Little rituals, my ass. D'Agosta wasn't so concerned about the absinthe, though he'd read about the alarming effects of wormwood, its most controversial ingredient. It was the little brown bottle that worried him. Tincture of opium, probably: laudanum. But there were no needles this time, thank God.

"Let me make this easy for you," Pendergast said. "I'm exceedingly pleased you decided to 'drop in,' though I doubt it was a spontaneous act. I imagine Mrs. Trask is worried about me?"

D'Agosta hesitated just a moment. "Yes, if you must know. But now that I see you, I'm worried, too." He leaned forward. "You don't look good."

"And I am *not* good," said Pendergast. "But we shan't discuss that. I'd prefer to hear about you. For example, how is Captain Hayward?"

"She's fine," D'Agosta said. "Doing well, actually. She recently moved to the Film and Television Unit as assistant commander."

"Film and television?"

"She's in charge of assisting film productions with traffic control, shutting down streets, shooting on bridges and highways—making sure everything's done safely and nothing gets screwed up. Her unit also handles the permits, use of prop firearms, all that kind of stuff."

"I'd never heard of such a unit before."

"She loves it, gets to meet the stars and directors. They love her, too, it seems, and ask her advice on technical cop details. I'm happy for her—she's seen more than her share of violent crime."

"And your own career?"

"I don't know." D'Agosta shrugged. "I'm almost ready to quit. It's one shitty case after another. I've begun to think most human beings are just brainless, evil sons of bitches."

"Ah, you've got that wrong, my dear Vincent. We're accomplished at evil precisely *because* we have brains. I can assure you that if chimpanzees or lions or even lizards had our brains, they'd be just as creatively cruel as we are."

D'Agosta grunted, not wanting to get into a philosophical debate with Pendergast, which nobody in history would ever win.

"But surely your *new* case presents a level of interest above the commonplace?"

"You mean—the one at the museum?" How did Pendergast know about that? Just as quickly, D'Agosta answered his own question: as an FBI agent, Pendergast had access to police channels as well as more private ones. Besides, he should know better than to be surprised at anything Pendergast learned, did, or said.

"A frozen curator," Pendergast went on. "How intriguing!"

"Someone monkeyed with the freezer door to disable the emergency latch, and the victim was locked inside to freeze to death. But look, Pendergast, I really don't want to talk about the case. I want to know what's going on with *you*."

A vague, almost blank look briefly crossed Pendergast's face. "My ward, Constance, has departed."

"Constance? Where?"

Instead of answering, Pendergast took another sip of his drink.

"What're you doing about it?"

Pendergast put down his glass. "Another beer?"

D'Agosta drained what was left of the first. "Sure."

"Mrs. Trask?"

The housekeeper appeared almost too quickly with another beer and frosted glass, then bustled out again with a sidelong glance.

D'Agosta waited until her footsteps had receded into silence. "Okay, look," he said, turning back to Pendergast. "You and me, we've been friends and partners for a long time. We've fought Amazonian monsters, zombies, and mindless creatures living a mile beneath this city. We've been arrested, shot, stabbed, locked up in an Italian castle; we've stalked a madman through a burning asylum—and cheated death every time. All of that has remained just between us. Goddamn it, I hope you know you can tell me anything. I'd move heaven and earth to help you. So don't patronize me. Tell me what's really going on... and how I can help."

Pendergast slowly turned his gaze toward D'Agosta. "I apologize, Vincent, for appearing flippant. I deeply appreciate those sentiments. If there were *any way* you could help, I would ask. The simple truth is that I find myself, for want of a better description, at a crossroads of no return. I alone must choose my path forward—and yet I seem to be paralyzed and unable to act." He paused. "I truly welcome your companionship here in the library, *as long as* we speak of other things—reminiscences either good or bad." He reached for the bottle of absinthe. "Strange as it seems, even the zombies you refer to seem almost a nostalgic interlude to me now. But first: please tell me more about the frozen curator."

23

May 25
Thursday

WELL," SAID AGENT POLOGNA, returning to their motel room with the ballistics report in hand, "I guess that's it. The bullet and casing are from Running's gun, he's guilty, and now we can go back to Denver."

Coldmoon would have liked nothing more than to get back to Denver. Two nights spent in the White Feather Motel with Pologna were two nights too many. But he tossed the hard copy on his bed and said nothing.

Pologna looked at his watch. "If we take the perp into custody now and wrap this up with the RPD, I bet we could get out of here by noon and be back in Denver by six."

Coldmoon nodded. "Okay, let's go."

It was an easy morning's work. They arrived back at Running's place in Parmelee with LaPointe, Wilcox, and two other RPD officers. Coldmoon and Pologna remained in the car, so as not to cause a stir, as the four local officers knocked on the door and took Running into custody. After a few feeble protests while he was being cuffed, the man fell silent. Mrs. Running stood at the door cursing them in Lakota as they drove him off.

"You understand what that old biddy said?" Pologna asked as they followed the RPD van.

Coldmoon nodded. "She referred to certain anatomical parts of the arresting officers, saying that the creator had been drunk when they were conceived and gave them organs belonging, respectively, to a toad, a mud puppy, and a mosquito."

Pologna almost doubled over in laughter. "I love it."

At the police station in Mission, the prisoner was processed and locked up, awaiting a bail hearing. Coldmoon and Pologna filled out paperwork, and by eleven thirty were outside.

"Back to the motel, collect our shit, and we're out of here," said Pologna.

They got in the car and drove in silence for a minute. Then Coldmoon spoke. "Are you sure we got the right man?"

Pologna looked at him incredulously. "What do you mean?"

"I don't know."

"You don't *know*?"

Coldmoon wondered if he shouldn't just shut up and call it a day. But he felt uneasy and knew the right thing was to voice his concerns.

"It's just all a little too...pat."

"How so?"

"First of all, the gun."

"What about the gun?"

"We discussed this already, back before the search. Running must have known we were coming back with a warrant to search specifically for that rifle. Why'd he keep it on the premises? And you have to admit that hiding place was pretty lame."

"Most criminals aren't smart. You know that."

"He didn't strike me as dumb at all."

"And that bullshit story about the gun being stolen—and yet he didn't report it? You believed that?"

"No." The story was clearly bogus, and certainly a strike against Running. "But what about the shell casing out at the shooting post?"

"What about it?"

"It was just sitting there, for all to see." *Even you,* Coldmoon thought. "Why didn't he pick it up? He was careful not to leave any other clues. There were no latents on the casing, so he must've loaded it with gloves. Why take care with that and then leave the casing?"

"You don't think clearly when you've just killed someone."

"The ballistics report says the gun and ammo were also wiped clean."

"He wiped it all down before he hid the weapon."

"On his own property. In a stupid place."

Pologna looked at him. "You're not serious, are you? You think the rifle was planted?"

"Like I said, it's too pat."

"It's pat because it's the truth."

They drove for a while in silence, until the shabby outline of the roadside motel came into view. Coldmoon eased the car into the parking lot. He stopped, took a breath, then said: "I'm calling Dudek and asking for another couple of days."

Pologna began to laugh. "This is a joke, right? You want to spend a couple more days in this dump? I'm not sure we're even allowed to continue investigating, when the RPD are in charge on the Rez and they closed the case."

"The case isn't closed until the prisoner is arraigned."

Pologna shook his head. "Jesus, this is crazy."

Coldmoon hated to pull rank, but it was time. He tried to make it soft. "I'm just not satisfied, and as the senior agent I've got to go with my gut feeling here. The arraignment's two days from now."

Pologna continued shaking his head, saying nothing. Coldmoon took out his phone and called Dudek.

"Congratulations," the SAC said before Coldmoon had a chance to talk. "Just got word. Nice quick work."

Coldmoon cleared his throat. "Sir? There are a couple of loose ends I'd like to clear up." He quickly explained about the gun, the casing, and the rest of his doubts. When he was done, Dudek asked: "Is Pologna there?"

"Yes, sir."

"Put the phone on speaker so you can both hear."

Coldmoon laid the phone on the console between them.

"Pologna, what do you think?"

"Um, sir, with all due respect to my senior partner, I disagree. Like I was just telling him, this is an open-and-shut case. Running had the means, motive, and opportunity. He owned the murder weapon, and it was found hidden on his property. He lied about it being stolen. And as you know, sir, a wife is no alibi."

A short silence. "What's your response to that, Coldmoon?"

Coldmoon wondered if he was just being a stubborn asshole because he didn't exactly like Dudek or Pologna. But still... "Sir, I want to ask Running about the rifle—why he lied when he said it was stolen. I want to talk to Twoeagle's widow—we never interviewed her. And finally..." He hesitated because it sounded far-fetched, even to him. "It seems there was a certain reluctance on the part of the Rosebud Police to accompany us to the shooter's location. I'd like to find out what that was about."

A long silence, then a loud sigh right into the phone. "Christ. Coldmoon, this puts me and Pologna in an awkward position. I mean, you could be called up as a witness, and this conversation—and your doubts—could come out."

Coldmoon hadn't thought of that.

"So I'm pretty much obliged to let you pursue your feeble misgivings."

"Thank you, sir."

"Don't thank me, Coldmoon, because I'm seriously pissed. This is not a good start, and it's going to have repercussions. I'm giving you until noon tomorrow." He hesitated, then added: "Sorry, Pologna."

"Right, sir," said Pologna.

Coldmoon hung up the phone and looked at Pologna, who was staring back at him with a hostile expression.

"Okay, what now?" said Pologna.

"We talk to Mrs. Twoeagle."

24

Twoeagle's house lay some distance from Mission, near the banks of Rosebud Creek. Pologna had been silent on the long drive, which was fine with Coldmoon.

As they drove down a long dirt road, a small but neat battenboard house came into view, painted white and shaded by cottonwoods. Coldmoon parked the car in the driveway. They got out, walked up onto the porch, and Coldmoon knocked on the door.

It was quickly opened by a tall woman, clearly Mrs. Twoeagle, wearing jeans and a checked shirt, her long hair spilling over her shoulders. They introduced themselves and entered. As he stepped into the living room, Coldmoon saw the ubiquitous pot of coffee on a wood stove, near a table where a plate of freshly baked cookies had been laid out. He'd called ahead, and Coldmoon realized she had baked these cookies especially for them.

"Please sit down," Mrs. Twoeagle said, and they took their seats. "Coffee? Cookies?"

"Both," said Coldmoon.

Pologna also helped himself.

She waited expectantly, hands folded, saying nothing.

"I want to start out," Coldmoon began, "by saying how sorry I am for your loss."

"Thank you."

"And we appreciate your being willing to answer a few questions."

"Why now? I just heard about the arrest on the radio. What a surprise that was."

"We're just tying up a few loose ends."

"Very well."

Coldmoon hesitated, thinking about her comment. "So you were surprised by the arrest of Running?"

"Well," she said, "Grayson was about to pay Running what he owed. And he told him so."

Coldmoon was startled. "So Running *knew* he was about to get paid? In full?"

"In full."

"Do you still have the money he was going to use?"

"It's in the safe. He was going to take it from the ten thousand dollars you'll find in there."

"Ten thousand dollars?" Coldmoon said, incredulous. "Where'd all the money come from?"

"A big sale. Grayson made replicas of Lakota artifacts, and he was the finest artist on the entire Rez—his work is in the Lakota Museum, in fact." She didn't try to hide the pride in her voice. "You should go and see it if you have time. It's his legacy."

"What was the sale?" Coldmoon asked.

"It was ceremonial pipes. What they call 'peace pipes.' He'd been working on them for a while."

"Is that why he was collecting stone when he was shot?"

"Yes. Pipestone, or more properly catlinite, is only found in one place—that outcrop."

"Who did he make the sale to?"

"It was that curator from back east. Dr. Mancow."

"Mancow?"

"He's an anthropologist at the Natural History Museum in New York—an expert on the Lakota. Even speaks some. He's been coming here for years, doing research and such. He's an old friend of Grayson's."

"And he bought things from your husband?"

"Yes. He was a good customer. Buying for himself, I mean. Being a curator, Dr. Mancow's not allowed to collect genuine artifacts. That's one of the museum's rules, he explained. But he loves Lakota craft, and on his most recent visit, I remember he took a special interest in the ceremonial pipes my husband was working on. Grayson didn't usually discuss business with me, but he did mention he could pay off his debt because Dr. Mancow had just made a big purchase."

"I see." Coldmoon hesitated, then asked: "Is there any way these replicas could be faked up to look old, and sold that way?"

"Not a chance. My husband engraved or burned his initials into every piece. He didn't want anyone passing them off as real."

Coldmoon hesitated again, longer this time. "Do you think Running killed your husband?"

She folded her hands. "Running was always coming around here, pressing my husband on his debts. They had a fight and Grayson decked him. But..." She hesitated. "I wouldn't have thought him a murderer. And why kill someone who owes you money? It's a guarantee of never getting paid."

"You know of anyone else who might have killed your husband?"

"That's the thing—nobody. Grayson was a peaceable man: didn't drink, do drugs, or pick fights. He didn't have any enemies. Everyone liked him."

Coldmoon glanced over at Pologna, but the man's face expressed nothing beyond boredom.

"Can you show us his workshop?"

"Of course."

The studio was behind the house, closer to the creek, a small log building. There was a single room inside with a wood stove; worktable; various stone-cutting, grinding, and polishing equipment; several small looms for beadwork; and racks draped with tanned buckskins, strings of feathers, trays of stones and shells. In a corner, shelves held pieces of wood for carving, and on the floor was a stack of reddish stone blocks.

"Is that the stone?" Coldmoon asked.

"Yes."

"Mind if I take some pictures?"

"Go ahead."

Coldmoon wandered around the shop, taking pictures, while Pologna followed, doing nothing. As they exited, Coldmoon noticed a pile of debris behind the studio. He walked over to it, Mrs. Twoeagle following.

"What's all this?" There were dozens of broken pipes of the same reddish stone, along with many half-carved pipe stems.

"Anything that wasn't perfect got dumped out here."

"Why so many?"

"That's what he'd been working on for months before he died. He was making pipes."

"And throwing them away."

"Grayson was a perfectionist."

He thanked her and they got back into the car. Pologna had remained silent, and Coldmoon finally said, "She asked a good question: why kill a man who's about to pay you what he owes?"

"They're *always* about to pay what they owe," Pologna said wearily. "And they never do. People who owe money are always making promises."

Coldmoon had to admit there was more than a little truth to the observation.

Pologna looked at his watch. "Almost three. What next?"

"The jail."

The jail was in Mission, behind the Rosebud PD, a large, ugly, flat structure set in a vast expanse of prairie. They found Running in a holding cell by himself, dressed in prison gray, sitting on a cot and staring at the wall.

The warden unlocked the cell and led Running down the hall to a barren sitting area. Coldmoon and Pologna took seats opposite the prisoner, who looked dejected and listless. The warden remained standing at the door.

"Mr. Running," Coldmoon began, "may I ask you a question?"

The man shifted in his seat and didn't answer, avoiding Coldmoon's eyes.

"Why did you lie about your rifle being stolen?"

Again, he didn't answer.

"Is it because you killed Twoeagle with it? Or is there another reason?"

He finally looked up. "I didn't kill nobody."

"Then why did you lie about the rifle being stolen?"

Running shifted uneasily in his chair. "It *was* stolen."

"Look, Mr. Running, that was a lie when you first told it to us and it's still a lie. You would have reported it. That's an expensive rifle."

Another uneasy shift. "It was stolen," he repeated. Then, after a hesitation, he said, "I *thought* it was stolen by my nephew."

This revelation hit Coldmoon hard. "You didn't report it because you didn't want to get a relative into trouble?"

Running nodded. "He's my sister's kid, been in trouble all his life. But who reports their own family to the cops?"

Coldmoon nodded. "Did Twoeagle tell you he had the money to pay you?"

"Yeah, but he was always saying bullshit like that. Promising to pay."

Pologna scoffed quietly.

"So you didn't believe him?"

"No."

Coldmoon rose. "That's all I wanted to know. Thank you."

"You gonna get me out of here? I didn't do it."

Coldmoon didn't answer, unsure what to say.

25

THE WARDEN LED THEM back to the lobby, where Coldmoon noticed Sergeant Wilcox just coming in.

"Sergeant?" Coldmoon asked. "Do you have a moment?"

"Sure." She dropped off some paperwork at a nearby desk. "What is it? I'd invite you into my office, but it's just a cubicle."

"A quick question. When we were at the site of the murder, I noticed you and Commander LaPointe seemed reluctant to climb up with us to the shooter's location. Why was that?"

She lowered her voice. "As you may have noticed, the commander isn't in the best of shape."

"You're in good shape."

"I wanted to stay with him, so he wouldn't be embarrassed."

Coldmoon looked steadily into her eyes. "What's the real reason?"

"Is this important?"

"Yes."

Her eyes wavered. "You're Lakota, right?"

"Right." He decided not to mention he was half Italian.

"Well, it's like this... Those caves up there? There are old burials in those caves. To go up there... would be disrespectful."

"I see." And he did see, quite clearly. "Disrespectful, and possibly even risky?"

She nodded.

"Why, then, did Running go up there to shoot Twoeagle?"

"A lot of Lakota today don't care about tradition."

"But wasn't Running known for respecting tradition?"

Wilcox shrugged.

Coldmoon nodded. "Thanks."

He went back out to the car, where Pologna was already waiting. The man looked pointedly at his watch.

Coldmoon started the car but didn't drive off. Instead, he turned to Pologna. "What do you think now?"

"Still guilty as hell."

"Really? Let's review the facts. One: the rifle is hidden in a way that feels planted. Two: we now know why Running didn't report the gun stolen. Three: the shooter carelessly left the casing, and yet he took all kinds of care in wiping down the weapon and the unfired rounds. Four: Running is a traditionalist, yet he didn't seem troubled using a spiritually dangerous place for a sniper's roost. Five: Twoeagle had the money and was maybe about to pay."

When he was done, silence grew in the car. Finally, Pologna said, in a tired voice, "One: criminals are stupid when it comes to hiding evidence. Two: we only have Running's word—we don't know if it's true. Three: again, criminals do stupid things. Four: a guy committing murder is already in a spiritually dangerous place. And five: so what if Twoeagle had the money? A lot of people with money stiff their creditors and lie about promising to pay. Besides, we never *saw* it. His wife just *said* it was in the safe. You didn't ask her to open it."

Coldmoon was rather taken aback by this intelligent refutation and colored, thinking he should have asked her to open the safe. That was stupid of him.

Pologna went on. "And finally, let's back this up a little. If Running didn't do it, who did? What was the motive? There's zero evidence of anyone else being involved in this crime, and even Twoeagle's wife said he didn't have any enemies. Something else: the shooter obviously had local knowledge. He knew when and where Twoeagle would be collecting stone. He positioned himself and waited. That points strongly to Running. So what are you thinking? Some outsider stole the rifle, did the deed, and then planted it back at Running's place? And all this on an Indian reservation, where a stranger, probably white, would stand out like a sore thumb? You're talking about a sophisticated and well-planned operation—just to kill a harmless guy with no enemies."

Coldmoon shook his head. "Still..."

Pologna swore under his breath. "Look, Coldmoon, can't you accept that we solved the case? Let's get off the clock and go have a beer."

"You're forgetting," said Coldmoon, "we're on the Rez. No beer in fifty miles."

"Shit."

Coldmoon started the car. Part of him wanted to agree with Pologna—a large part of him, in fact—but he couldn't shake the fact he still had misgivings. He drove out of the RPD parking lot and started down the road toward their motel.

"There's the Lakota Museum," he said as they passed a low building. He slowed and put on his blinker.

"What are you doing?" Pologna asked.

"I want to have a look at Twoeagle's replicas. The ones his wife said were on display."

"Why?"

Coldmoon couldn't really come up with a reason why.

Pologna groaned loudly. "I feel like I'm in hell."

"Give me fifteen minutes."

He parked and they went toward the low, nondescript building. Entrance was free and the volunteer at the lobby desk said that a case of Twoeagle's replicas could be found in the back. Everything else in the museum was real.

Entering the museum proper, Coldmoon noticed they were the only people there. He was surprised at how nice the place was. The lighting looked professional, and the artifacts were amazing, if not incredible. Ghost Dance shirts, intricate bead- and quillwork, head-dresses, extraordinary ledger books filled with pictures, Sun Dance buffalo skulls painted and stuffed with sweetgrass... The richness of it was staggering.

Looking at the treasures of the past, Coldmoon suddenly felt like a dagger had been plunged into his heart. Here were the remains of a rich culture, locked away behind glass: fading echoes of a once-proud nation. He thought of everything that had been taken from his people—their culture, their land—and mentally contrasted it with where they were today, living in cheap HUD houses on impoverished reservations.

He almost wished he hadn't come in here. What was he thinking? He went to the back and looked at the case of Twoeagle's replicas. They were gorgeous and finely made; the man was a true artist. But what was he hoping to see? He shook his head at his own folly. Maybe Pologna was right and Running was guilty.

On his way out, he paused at a large case dominating the center of the hall. It displayed a single, extraordinary artifact, beautifully lit: Sitting Bull's famous peace pipe. Coldmoon recognized it instantly as the one with the twisted stem so prominently featured in the photograph of the Lakota chief. And nearby was that very photo, blown up, of Sitting Bull. He stared into the camera with a face full of sadness, the face of a man who had witnessed the destruction of his way of life.

Coldmoon stared at the renowned pipe with its wooden stem, the hanging bundle of beads and eagle feathers, the long, polished bowl carved out of red pipestone. He had just seen dozens of broken or imperfect examples of this same bowl design in the rubbish heap behind Twoeagle's studio, along with half-finished examples of that twisted wooden stem.

Twoeagle hadn't been making a copy of any old peace pipe: he'd been working on a replica of *this* one.

An idea came into Coldmoon's head, and he froze. Was it possible?

He raised his cell phone and took a series of pictures of the pipe through the glass, from every angle he could manage. When he was done, he looked around for Pologna. He found him on the far side of the room, staring at a wall of beaded baby cradles. "Okay, we can go now."

Pologna turned. There was a different look on his face than Coldmoon had seen before.

"There's some incredible stuff in here," he said.

Coldmoon nodded.

"It must be something for you to see this," Pologna said. "I mean, your history and all. It's probably like how I felt when I went to Rome and saw what *my* ancestors created."

Coldmoon thought it prudent not to mention that the ancestors on his mother's side, the Espositos, had come from Naples. But he was surprised at Pologna's sudden empathy. Maybe the guy wasn't such a dick after all.

They left the museum. It was five o'clock, and dark clouds were drifting across the sky.

They got in the car, Coldmoon once again behind the wheel. He sat for a moment, collecting his thoughts, then turned to Pologna.

"I think," he began slowly, "I've found the motive—the real motive—for the murder."

Pologna stared at him.

"Did you see Sitting Bull's peace pipe?"

"I sure did."

"It's a fake. Made by Twoeagle."

"How the hell do you know that?"

"All those broken pipe bowls behind Twoeagle's studio? They were all in that distinct shape. His wife said he was a perfectionist, but nobody's *that* anal without a damned good reason. And that twisted stem—there were a lot of those, too. He was trying to make a perfect replica of that pipe."

"But why?"

"Why? I can give you exactly ten thousand reasons. Twoeagle made it to be substituted for the real one, which was then stolen from the museum."

"Stolen?"

"Sitting Bull's peace pipe has got to be worth millions."

"And the motive for murder?"

"That's a little less obvious. Maybe the people who hired Twoeagle to replicate the pipe killed him to cover it up. Maybe Twoeagle wanted more money. Maybe he had misgivings and was going to confess."

Pologna stared at him. "Have you gone off the deep end?"

"What I've just told you can be proved. I took photographs of that pipe. I'm going to send them to the FBI image-analysis lab in Quantico and ask them to compare my photos to the pipe in Sitting Bull's photograph. They can tell us right away whether it's the same object—or not."

Pologna continued staring at him, and then he finally said: "Man, you are one tenacious son of a bitch."

And the way he said it, Coldmoon couldn't tell if it was a compliment—or the opposite.

26

December 5, 1880
Wednesday

SEVERAL DAYS PASSED WITHOUT Moseley hearing anything from the strange young woman. Not that it particularly mattered—he was kept busy enough with the aftermath of the escape.

A total of ninety-eight inmates had escaped the workhouse. The cook had finally broken out of his locked quarters, but it turned out not to have been a good idea, as he was set upon by some of the inmates and badly beaten. By dawn, fifty-six had been chased down and apprehended. Over the next two days, another twenty-one were discovered hiding in various island nooks. Another ten had been apprehended as they reached either Manhattan or Brooklyn by various means—on ferries, improvised rafts, a few even by swimming. It was presumed the remaining eleven had either drowned in the crossing or vanished in the great city.

Once the majority had been returned to their cells, the superintendent's attention shifted to the cause of the mass escape. The locks had been forced open and disabled in a way nobody could figure out. The two keepers who had been attacked couldn't explain what happened to them. Prisoners were interrogated, but in the general confusion of the escape nobody seemed to know how they had been freed, or by whom. Everyone had a different story. All the escapees were from the third floor—save one, a youth incarcerated on the first floor, who had disappeared, but he was scrawny and they presumed he'd drowned trying to swim the East River. The investigation was inconclusive and the superintendent ended up blaming the keepers, docking their pay and accusing them of sleeping on the job.

To his great relief, Moseley, who remained in the north wing with the superintendent at the time of the breakout, completely avoided attention. Once most of the prisoners were recaptured, the story dropped out of the newspapers, and the ephemeral attention of the public moved on to new subjects.

But four days later, on an early December evening as he was approaching his rooms, Moseley heard a sharp hiss from the street. There, in the flickering gaslight, he saw a coach—and the lamps bracketing the driver's seat illuminated the man he had come to know as Murphy.

The coachman gestured for Moseley to get in. After a brief hesitation, the surgeon's assistant put a foot on the carriage step and hoisted himself into the passenger seat. Almost before he'd closed the door, Murphy snapped the reins and they jostled out into traffic.

Murphy took a roundabout route to their destination, and it was half an hour before they pulled up in front of a house on the corner of Fifth Avenue and Forty-Eighth Street. Here the coach halted, and Moseley waited, unsure what was going to happen and nervous about their stopping in such a conspicuous neighborhood. This was the section of Fifth Avenue known as the "Gold Coast" or "Millionaires' Row," and while most of the buildings here were elegant brownstones— large and lavishly appointed, some double-width—others were vast, gaudy palaces. Among them were the mansion-fortresses owned by the Vanderbilts, and beyond was the as-yet-unfinished "Clark's Folly" being built by copper king William Clark, which when completed— the papers claimed—would boast several art galleries and an underground railroad for bringing in coal.

Still, the coach did not move.

"Are we waiting for someone?" Moseley finally asked the driver through the sliding panel. "If we linger here, Mr. Murphy, the police will surely be coming by, asking our business."

"Out with you," came the reply from above. "Up the main steps, bang the knocker. Be quick now."

"But...is the woman in service here? What should I say to the person who answers the door?" The building looked very grand, but Moseley somehow didn't think this woman would be a domestic.

"There ain't a need to say nothing."

Moseley stepped gingerly down from the carriage. Once on the pavement, he paused to take a closer look at the structure. Though big, it wasn't as absurdly lavish as some of the other grand palaces on the avenue. This mansion looked graceful, and the word *delicate* came to Moseley's mind. It had an unusual marble façade—a rich white that revealed hints of pink in the glow of gaslight. *Whimsical* might be a better word: the details of its façade had a sculptural quality, almost akin to calligraphy, that seemed to fuse the Byzantine and Gothic— quite unlike the neoclassical giants surrounding it. He was reminded of postcards he'd examined of certain buildings in France: the Palais du Trocadéro; the chapel of the Sorbonne. The mansion was, apparently, still in the process of final completion: a small section of a rear gable was exposed, and this revealed that, while the fabric was marble, its bones were of iron, brick, and concrete.

A muttered imprecation from Murphy, sitting atop the coach, served to propel Moseley up the flight of stairs to the ornate front door.

Within seconds of his nervous tapping, the door was opened by a maid, and he entered a hall framed in gilt—a remarkably long and beautiful space. Sheets hung over furniture and paintings, and un-opened wooden packing cases were stacked to one side, evidence the house was still being fitted out. Moseley had little time to examine the interior: the maid who answered the door led him—without asking his name or demanding a card—down the hall and then right, through a pair of open French doors with lights of pale jade, and into a study lined in dark wood. It, too, was only partially furnished, but neverthe-less the bookshelves were half-full of books, several paintings graced the walls, and an antique harpsichord stood in a corner, open, with music on the stand. The rich Persian carpeting and silk-upholstered sofas exuded warmth and intimacy. A fire crackled in the fireplace, and it—along with candles set upon tall wrought iron stands—furnished all the light.

"Mr. Moseley," came a voice from the dark recesses of the room. "Good of you to come."

He recognized the voice instantly, and saw it came from a dark figure seated at the far end. He began to approach, once again full of confusion, but the voice stopped him. "Before we speak, there's one item of business. Please go out the way you came in and descend the steps to the pavement. You'll see something familiar lying there. Please retrieve it—and return."

Mystified, Moseley followed these instructions. Back outside in the chill of the evening, he spotted a small leather pouch lying on the pavement that was, indeed, familiar. Glancing down the avenue, he saw the coach now parked some distance away, Murphy keeping a close eye on the proceedings.

He snatched the heavy pouch off the sidewalk and retreated back into the warmth of the mansion and its candlelit study.

"Please take a seat over here," came the voice again.

Moseley did as he was told and, as he approached, his eyes adjusting to the dim lighting, he could finally see the woman, perched on a tête-à-tête love seat of buttery leather, wearing a pale dress. Her left hand rested on two books on a tea table next to her.

He awkwardly took a seat in an armchair on the other side of the tea table.

The woman could now be seen clearly for the first time. He'd seen her dressed as a workman; he'd seen her dressed as something like a carnival artist. Now here she was, apparently a wealthy member of New York's most privileged class. But in his experience she had already shed two skins, and he had no confidence that the woman he saw before him was not merely another disguise. She was in her mid-twenties, strikingly beautiful, with violet eyes and a slender yet curvaceous figure. Her eyebrows were thin and arched in the French fashion, and her dark mahogany hair was straight and cut quite short—Moseley would be tempted to call it pixyish, save that nothing else about the woman's presence betrayed evidence of an ingenuous nature. Quite the opposite.

"Welcome," the woman said in her velvety contralto voice, lifting her hand from the books, which he could now see. One was a volume of Latin poetry. The other was *Francis's New Guide to the Cities of New-York and Brooklyn.*

She nodded at the pouch in his hand. "I see you found something lying in the street. Have you examined the contents?"

Moseley had not, but he knew well it was packed with gold double eagles. "Thank you," he managed to say. "You are most generous."

"Not me. But isn't it delightful you made such a lucky discovery on a public street?" The woman had a slight accent, which he didn't recognize.

Moseley nodded.

"You have a kind and charitable nature. You were sympathetic to my Joe. And you are trustworthy—uncommon traits in a city and age such as this. But fortune has dealt you a poor hand."

Moseley did not reply.

"I understand that my various disguises and activities must seem eccentric to you, or perhaps even criminal. And so before we continue, I'd like to give you the chance to ask me any questions you'd like. Although I must tell you it's quite possible I'll refuse to answer."

Moseley was still conscious of a dreamlike sensation, similar to that brought on by the first puff from a *yen tsiang*—as if everything was familiar and yet foreign at the same time. Nevertheless, he'd certainly banked up several questions over the last few days.

"Who are you?" he asked.

"You may refer to me as the Duchess of Ironclaw. Privately, you may call me Livia."

A duchess. Could it be true? She certainly acted like one. He nodded, wondering if he could ever bring himself to call this formidable woman Livia.

"The person you met in the Rathskeller only existed long enough to free Joe Greene from an unjust imprisonment." She paused. "The truth is, I come from far away—very far away. My history there, and my real name, are of no concern in this place."

Moseley took all this in. He had sensed from the beginning she was a person of fierce intelligence and strong will, a person with the confidence and self-possession to care little for what others thought.

"What are you doing here?" he said, feeling emboldened by her openness, and by the comforting weight of the gold coins inside the pouch.

"I'm here to rescue certain family members from a grave danger. I've just accomplished that with Joe."

"But...why did you choose such a method to free Joe? Surely someone with your money could have found an easier way."

"The situation is complicated. If I explain the reasons why, I'll be placing the safety of myself and those I care about in your hands— never forget that. Do I have your assurance of absolute discretion?"

Moseley realized that, for better or worse, he was about to enter a secret world...if he was willing to take what amounted to an oath of silence. He hesitated, then nodded.

The young woman continued. "One complication is that Joe and my other relatives do not know who I really am. Their parents died some years ago, and they have lived an impoverished existence in the streets ever since. They've learned through harsh experience to trust no one."

"They're your relatives? In what way?"

"Let us just say I'm their distant aunt, from Galicia by way of Transylvania, and have only recently learned of their desperate circumstances. My attempts to help them will be complicated by their ignorance of my relation to them."

Moseley nodded. "And the danger you alluded to?"

"There is a man, a brilliant and esteemed physician, living here in New York City. He is keenly interested in my relatives. His motives—" she paused, and for a moment Moseley saw a crack in her polished veneer— "are vile, inhuman, cruel beyond imagining.

If he learns of my existence—and my attempts to save my relations from his grasp—it will put all of us in danger. Including you."

"Why is he interested in them?"

"He is working on a medical experiment. But that is all I can say at the present time."

On that note she stopped. A long, thoughtful silence filled the room. It sounded melodramatic. *A medical experiment?* He wondered if the woman wasn't just a bit...touched.

"I had you brought here for two reasons. I wanted first to thank you for your help in freeing Joseph."

She stopped again.

"And the second reason?"

"To offer you employment."

Moseley had already begun to think this might be in the cards.

"You realize, of course, that you're wasting your life on Blackwell's Island. The reasons you didn't complete medical school can be rectified. You need to renounce opium, of course—and keep my confidences." She paused. "You are free to refuse my offer. The money you found on the street should be enough to see you through two years of existence—less if you take again to the pipe. But I'm offering a ladder out of the pit."

He took a deep breath. "What would be my responsibilities?"

"I need a tutor for Joe. You are the closest thing he knows to a trustworthy adult. Not only does he need a traditional education, but he also needs the trauma of his incarceration eased, and he must have the wrong type of education he'd begun to receive in the Octagon and the workhouse erased. You would have to leave your current employment in a way that raises no suspicions. I'm sure you could arrange for your dismissal."

Moseley nodded. "Anything else, Your Grace?"

"Yes. I, too, require education in...I suppose you could say the subtler customs of New York. I'm a foreigner. I am ignorant in matters of etiquette. I appear odd to people. I need you to help rid me of any behavior or habits that might bring unwanted attention. Things—" and here she gestured toward the guide lying on the table— "that can't be learned from a book."

Moseley inclined his head. He didn't dare ask about remuneration; the bag of gold was already two years' wages.

As if reading his thoughts, she said: "Your compensation will be two of those double eagles a week."

He was stunned and felt himself flush. "That's . . . absurdly generous."

"If you knew the risks to which I am putting you, you would realize the compensation is barely adequate."

This sent a chill down his spine. He wondered what else he might have to do. "So that's all there is: just advising you and tutoring Joe?"

The woman—the duchess, Livia, or whoever she was—suddenly smiled. "Mr. Moseley. If you're willing to enter this Masonic lodge of mine, let's see how those first two assignments work out. Then perhaps you can graduate from 'entered apprentice' to 'fellow of the craft.' Your time of employment will not be long—six weeks, perhaps. But if we're successful, and we survive, I'll see that your dreams of becoming a doctor reach fruition."

These words, spoken in that unusually low voice, were smooth and clear in enunciation, and it was only when the woman fell silent that Moseley noticed she had included survival as a codicil of employment. Again, he felt that chill. But he put it aside.

"How shall I begin?" he asked.

"Joe is upstairs. He's comfortable physically, but emotionally he is suspicious and in distress. You can help with that."

"In that case, please lead the way."

The woman smiled once again. Then she rose and, after waiting for him to do the same, led the way out of the candlelit study.

27

Back in the central hall, the duchess led Moseley toward a grand staircase leading to the upper floors of the mansion.

"I apologize, Mr. Moseley, for the condition of the house," she said. "I'm still in the process of moving in. Everything should be in order within a week or so."

"It's beautiful," he replied, truthfully. "I couldn't help but admire the marble exterior."

"Thank you," she said as they ascended. "It's one of the reasons I took the house."

"I'm no expert, but the stone has a pearlescent effect—as if it had depth as well as surface. And the pink color that the gaslight drew forth from it was extraordinary."

Sharing his aesthetic observations with others was quite unlike him. The woman appeared to be struck by them and she paused on the stairs. "I would certainly agree. The original owner was French, and was so attracted to that rare marble that he bought the only known quarry of it, outside Montluçon. I fear his good taste not only exhausted the quarry but also his finances, and he went bankrupt. He was forced to sell the house in the state you see at present. His loss was my gain."

"Evidently." Moseley wondered what a place like this would sell for. A fortune, of course, but from what little he knew of the Morgans and

Astors and Vanderbilts, he guessed they wouldn't like it—for the same qualities he found most intriguing. "You understand, Your Grace, I've never before been inside a house like this. But I've always taken a great interest in architecture..." He trailed off, thinking he had said too much.

She turned to him with an arch smile. "Your *Grace*? No, please. Livia."

He looked back at her.

"Say it," she coaxed. "Livia."

"Livia. The wife of Octavian."

"Yes." She turned and continued to ascend. "In France, this style is called *La Belle Époque*. It has yet to take much of a foothold on this side of the Atlantic."

Reaching the second floor, she led him down a carpeted hallway, decorated with side tables, vases, and paintings. Again, they appeared to Moseley to have been acquired for their beauty rather than pretense. This was a duchess with not only money, but an appreciation for art and architecture. Above, he could hear occasional hammering and the muffled voices of workmen putting the finishing touches on the roof. As they walked, he noticed that the maid who'd let him in—a short, slender woman about his own age—had quietly joined them.

"This is Féline, my *femme de chambre*," the Duchess explained. "She's a quick study, discreet and reliable."

As they walked, a troubled look crossed her face. She spoke quietly. "I'm hoping Joe's familiarity with you will help allay his anxiety. He seems comfortable here now—but he's hard to read. I'm worried he still harbors suspicions. Féline and I keep a careful eye on him, but it would be far preferable if we could rest easier, knowing that he stays of his own inclination."

As they paused at an ornately carved door, he said, "I'll do whatever I can."

"Thank you," she replied. "Féline will get you anything you need. Do you speak French?"

"Mais un peu."

The two women exchanged a glance that seemed to Moseley almost sly. "Her English is fair, but she prefers to speak French. You'll have free rein of the house. Bring any concerns directly to me. Would it be possible for you to stay away from your duties on Blackwell's Island a few days—some pretended malady or other, perhaps—and then arrange to get sacked when you return?"

Moseley nodded. Every Wednesday the superintendent took a dinner of ham with treacle, and accidentally spilling a pint of black-strap molasses down Cropper's frock coat was the first of several scenarios that came to mind.

"Very good. Once that is taken care of, shall we put your hours at, say, Monday through Saturday, ten to six? Your wages will be as mentioned, and you'll have room and board. It would in fact be preferable for you to confine your life mostly to this house and no longer visit the Rathskeller or mingle with your old friends."

He nodded. Nothing in his old life held any attraction to him.

The maid opened the door at a nod from the duchess, revealing a bedroom with tall windows looking onto the stable yard behind the mansion. Though dusk had fallen, the room, painted blue, was brilliantly lit by gaslight. There was a four-poster bed, a dresser, and shelves of books, toys, and games.

Joe was sitting on the floor, assembling a steam engine from pre-cut pieces of wood in a box. As he frowned in concentration, Moseley noticed the youth's black eye was healing nicely, and he'd already put a little weight on his skinny frame. He looked up—with sudden alarm in his eyes—but a smile quickly spread across his face as he recognized the new arrival.

"Hello, Joe," Moseley said, coming forward and kneeling beside him. "How are you feeling?"

"How'd you get here, Doctor?"

"Your, ah, the duchess brought me. What are you making?"

And as Joe began to explain—haltingly at first, then with greater ease—Moseley heard the door close softly behind him.

★ ★ ★

Constance waited outside the closed door for a moment, listening to the conversation within. Then, after a brief exchange in French with Féline, she made her way back down the corridor and into her own rooms fronting Fifth Avenue. She walked through the sitting room, and then slowly through the bedroom, until stopping before the spacious windows, framed by rich curtains and lightly rimed with frost.

To date, her plans had come off without a hitch. She had enough money to live in wealth and comfort, and had already made sure her funds were well invested. It was useful to know the future, and she had put a large amount of her fortune into a firm called the Standard Oil Company, run by a young fellow named Rockefeller, which sold kerosene for lamps but was destined, she knew, for far greater success with the arrival of the automobile.

She had assembled an excellent and trustworthy staff, starting with Murphy—who was now employed solely by her and had taken rooms beside the carriage house—as well as a footman, a cook, a cook's assistant, a parlormaid, an upstairs maid who doubled as a governess, a housekeeper, a ramrod-straight butler named Gosnold, and of course Féline. She had found them by frequenting, in disguise, rooming houses and eating places of the servant classes, listening in on conversations and making inquiries. In this way she was able to find people who were unencumbered by family, sober, efficient, and loyal. Most importantly, they were honorable and discreet. Féline had been an accidental but fortunate find: an educated woman with a clever mind and keen observation. She had been the victim of a marital fraud that left her in New York, penniless and ruined, far from her home in the 8th arrondissement. Féline in truth was more than a private maid; she was also something of a counselor. While Féline did not know Constance's real story, she understood that not all was quite as it seemed—and let it go at that. She was good with numbers and managed her mistress's spending and larder, smoking out the scams and cheats from tradesmen and others who sought to take advantage.

Constance thought that Moseley, too, with his sensitive nature and familiarity with Joe, seemed a good fit as tutor—as long as he kept clear of his laudanum habit.

Constance's eyes focused now on the gaslit avenue beyond the windowpanes, and the pedestrians and coaches passing by. Heavy flakes of snow were falling, swirling like cut paper doilies around the lampposts and settling gently onto the cobbles. Her feeling of satisfaction fell away as she recalled there was another sad and cold person out in that snow: that would be herself, nine years old. How strange to think of it. She cast her mind back, trying to remember that same snowy evening back in early December 1880, when the big flakes fell. The young Constance, known to her family as "Binky," was living on the streets, her older sister—who had smuggled food out to her whenever possible—recently taken from the Five Points House of Industry by Dr. Leng. For weeks afterward, she would go to the window where Mary handed her food, to find it shut and locked night after night. There were too many of those cold, snowy nights—when she was alone, shivering, and hungry—to discriminate between.

She wondered why she hadn't already called for Murphy and the carriage and rushed down to that dreadful slum in search of her own younger self. Was it because she knew she would survive, unlike her siblings? Or was it just the phenomenological terror of it all?

Once she'd made up her mind in Savannah to go back to the New York of 1880, she'd assumed that freeing her siblings would be her immediate, overriding goal. And indeed, she'd tried to liberate Mary with all possible haste, and had freed Joe with the same determination. But when it came to her own younger self—she felt a strange reluctance.

Abruptly, she turned from the window. She knew Leng; she knew he was preternaturally brilliant, suspicious, and intensely devious. She needed to proceed carefully, to take time to create a base from which she could operate. She had accomplished a great deal in just over a week—but there was much still to do.

The Constance of this parallel universe would spend one last night in the cold. Tomorrow, she would find her and bring her here to comfort and safety. Mary had become her chief concern: Mary, in the hands of Dr. Leng, scheduled to die on an operating table just one week after New Year's Day. She now had less than five weeks to find Leng's secret lab, penetrate it, and rescue her older sister.

To save her, she would do whatever it took, spend whatever it cost, and remove whoever stood in her way. And then, once Mary was back with her siblings, safe in this mansion-fortress, Constance would focus the power of her hatred on one remaining goal: turning Enoch Leng's earthly existence into a crescendo of agony and torment, ending in death.

28

May 26
Friday

S IR?"

Pendergast—who was sitting in an armchair, staring at the fireplace, still cold and dark—roused himself and looked toward Proctor, standing in the doorway.

"It's done."

"Excellent." Pendergast rose from the chair and turned to face his majordomo. "Lead the way."

He followed Proctor out of the library, through the echoing and vaulted reception hall with its cabinets of wonders, to a door that led into the private areas of the house. The two moved down the darkened passage beyond to another door, which Proctor unlocked. They descended a staircase into one of the stone passageways that honeycombed the mansion's basement. At length they stopped at a stout door in a section of the cellar that had fallen into desuetude. A keypad and scanning device had been installed in place of a lock, and they gleamed anachronistically against the stonework of the wall. Proctor handed Pendergast a piece of paper with the combination. Pendergast tapped in the sequence of numbers, and the door sprang open.

Beyond lay what, many years before, had been the mansion's large ice room, its walls insulated with cork and lined in zinc. Pendergast felt for the light switch and snapped it on. He caught his breath at the sight: the empty space beyond had been transformed.

It was now, in every detail, a simulacrum of the basement room in Savannah's Chandler House—a scorched hulk, as it had looked the last time he laid eyes on it, shortly after Constance left both him and the twenty-first century behind. Proctor had brought back every piece and reassembled it exactly: the gears, wheels, and belts blackened with soot, the melted wands of stainless steel and copper, the burnt cables and broken monitors. In the center was a large control knob, still twisted clockwise to its uttermost setting, just as Constance had left it when she undertook her final journey.

But it was not this alone that so powerfully affected Pendergast. It was the meticulous level of detail in re-creating the machine's wreckage, even to the bolts and clips scattered about the floor, sprung free by the machine's brutal shaking.

"Thank you, my friend," he managed to say. "This is...perfect."

Proctor nodded. Nothing else needed to be said: the vast amount of logistics, secrecy, and effort involved in this mission spoke to the great loyalty and respect he had for his employer—a feeling that was reciprocated in full.

"If there's nothing further you need for the moment," Proctor said, "I'll take my leave."

Pendergast extended his hand, grasped Proctor's for a moment, then let it fall away. He heard the heavy door whisper shut. The footfalls faded in the passage. Still he remained, leaning against the wall, as he surveyed the room.

Although the basement space of the Savannah hotel had been slightly larger, Proctor had carefully compensated, placing everything in proportions so exact even an architect would have been impressed. Everything from the Chandler House room was there, down to the old-fashioned electric light switch and the dusty chunks of rubble. All that was missing were the dead husks of the peculiar insects that had lain scattered on the floor, and the gaping hole in one wall.

Pendergast walked to the worktable with its notebooks. Like everything else, it was coated in dust—save for at one place, where a rectangle of its surface was clear.

Pendergast reached into his pocket, took out an unmarked envelope, and placed it upon the table with a hand that trembled. It fit the dust-free section of the table perfectly. He plucked it up again and—despite himself—opened the envelope and read, one more time, the handwritten note within.

I am going back to save my sister, Mary. I belong with her, anyway. This machine has given me that opportunity—and Miss Frost herself made it clear why I must take it. In her, I see my own lonely, loveless future. It is anything but pretty. And so I will return to my past—the destiny I was meant to have. I will make of it what I can—what I must. If I can't have you on my terms, I can't have you at all.

Goodbye, Aloysius. Thank you for everything—most particularly for not coming after me, even were it possible. That I could not endure; I'm sure you comprehend my meaning.

I love you.

Constance

Pendergast refolded the note, placed it back in the envelope, then set it down carefully within its dust shadow.

He turned to the ruin of the machine, approaching it slowly. Coming close, he reached out a hand—then drew it back with a reaction little short of galvanic. He stood, motionless, for a long time, staring at the device. And then, deliberately, he knelt before it, placing his elbows on the soot-darkened surface beside the keyboard, and let his forehead rest gently on his intertwined fingers.

There, in the deep and thoughtful silence of the basement, he remained, lips moving silently. He might have been praying, or meditating—or engaging in some secret, internal dialogue. Only three people on earth knew him well enough to hazard a guess: one was dead; another missing; and the third was now—in time, if not in distance—impossibly far away.

29

VINCENT D'AGOSTA SAT IN the banquette at Buongiorno, double-checking his to-do list for the day's investigation. Reports that were due and done, ingoing and outgoing; questioning of museum workers who'd stayed late the evening of the murder; review of the autopsy; filing into evidence the best CSU photos—check, check, and check.

Even though the circumstances in this particular homicide were bizarre, the usual mountain of paperwork, red tape, and procedures never varied. He'd thought, initially, that being back in the museum on a fresh case might be energizing. Instead it was proving to be the opposite: every hour he spent in that damned old pile increased the feeling that he'd lost the fire in the gut. The lieutenant of long ago, he mused, who had worked and fought inside those columned walls, was now treading water.

Tommaso, the waiter, appeared with a bottle of D'Agosta's favorite Chianti, opened it with a flourish, poured out a small glass, then set it, the bottle, and another empty glass on the table. D'Agosta picked the glass up by the stem and swirled its contents ruminatively, not bothering to taste it.

He'd felt a similar funk a decade before, during his bachelor years, when he'd taken leave from the force and gone to Canada, planning to write mystery novels under the name Campbell Dirk. That hadn't gone so well. Deep down, he knew he was a cop. He'd done it his whole life and he was good at it. He couldn't complain of a lack of recognition. He'd made lieutenant commander two years before. His wife, Laura, was a captain, one of the youngest women in the NYPD to achieve that rank, but he felt no jealousy about that...only pride.

All good. So what the *fuck* was going on with him?

The swish of cloth, a faint waft of perfume, and Laura seated herself across the table. As always upon first seeing her, he felt a limbic flush: this beautiful, accomplished, intensely desirable woman was his wife. Given her current assignment, she was out of uniform, and there was a glow on her face that betrayed hours spent outside in the sun and wind.

"Vinnie!" she said, leaning over the table to kiss him. "Hi!"

"Hi, sweet thing." He was biased, but she didn't look any older than the day he'd placed a ring on her finger. Hadn't put on any weight, either—unlike him. Sometimes he wondered what she saw in the guy she'd married.

"How was your day?" she asked as he poured some wine for her, then filled his own glass.

"Good, thanks," he said with a smile.

Buongiorno had become almost a home away from home for them. It was just around the corner from their Second Avenue apartment, only six tables, with no sign outside and a menu consisting of whatever Tullio—first generation, ancient, unrepentant *dal Piemonte*—felt like preparing. The Upper East Side had changed in the last decade, and now it felt more like a bedroom community than a vibrant Manhattan neighborhood. All their cop friends, it seemed, had headed for either White Plains or New Rochelle or way the hell out in Nassau County. But neither he nor Laura felt a similar urge. They were earning decent salaries, Laura especially; they'd made a smart real estate move, upsizing to a big two-bedroom in the same building when one became available during a dip in the market. They'd just as soon have dinner here at Buongiorno or at home as fight for bragging rights to reservations at places like Au Cheval or 4 Charles. Besides, Laura got invited to enough wrap parties to keep things interesting.

The waiter came by and recited the handful of available dishes. Laura ordered an appetizer of burrata, Cinta Senese prosciutto, and lardo di Colonnata, with heirloom tomatoes, basil, and pane tostato. How the hell did she stay so thin eating stuff like that? D'Agosta ordered fresh mafaldine pasta alla puttanesca—supposedly the pasta sauce favored by Italian prostitutes.

"And yours?" he asked, taking a sip of his wine.

"Great! It was the opening day of second-unit photography on that neo-noir they're filming down by the Battery."

"You mentioned it last night. What's it called again?"

"There's just a working title, but it's a remake of a 1950 crime film, *Side Street*. The original had a famous car chase in and around Wall Street, shot from choppers and the tops of buildings. This time, they're using drones, and we'll be closing half a dozen streets over the weekend for the shoot. I haven't met the director yet, just the DP and some assistants, but the lead was there—Leonardo DiCaprio! Can you believe it? We chatted—he was totally cool, told me to call him Leo. He's not like some of the other stars, prima donnas shut up in their trailers or method types out trying to rub shoulders with real crooks or wiseguys. But..."

The excited flow of words stopped abruptly as, for the first time, she took a close look at D'Agosta. "Vinnie, what is it?"

"Nothing, nothing. Go ahead." He forced his face into a bright smile.

She reached across the table, took his hand. "Here I am, blabbing on. Tell me more about your own day." Her index finger played slowly back and forth across his knuckles.

He shrugged. "Same old. No question it's a homicide, but still no witnesses or suspects. The killer was smart. No security footage caught a glimpse of him, can you believe it? In a museum overflowing with cameras. It was a day of asking questions, dragging the net around hoping to snag something." Eager to talk about something else, he said: "I went to see Pendergast."

The index finger went still. "Really? When?"

"Day before yesterday. At his place on Riverside Drive."

"Why didn't you tell me before?"

Because I knew you'd react like this. Aloud, he said: "Slipped my mind. I was there less than an hour. I only went because Mrs. Trask asked me to."

Laura's brow furrowed. "She *asked* you? Is something wrong?"

"Yeah. He's been away, you know, down south for several months." He paused for a sip of wine. "He told me Constance had left—I think that might be it."

"So? She's left before. That woman isn't exactly predictable."

"I know. But something happened. Something bad. All he said was he's at 'a crossroads of no return.'"

"Sounds like a line from the movie they're shooting. What does it mean?"

"No idea. You can never tell with Pendergast. He didn't look good." He shook his head. "He kept turning the conversation back to my own piece-of-shit case."

Laura looked at him more guardedly. "Vinnie, that is *not* a piece-of-shit case you're on. It's unusual. It's what you're best at. And the press is huge. There's a big opportunity for you here."

"I know." *Opportunity.* He realized he no longer gave a rat's ass about that. He didn't even want to talk about the case, to tell the truth.

He met her gaze for a moment, then took another sip from his glass. Laura knew him well enough to see when something was wrong. She was also shrewd enough to gauge how deep it ran—and whether there was anything she could do to help.

"You know, I'd hoped that being back at the museum would—"

"Would what? Be like Old Home Week? Bring back fond memories of decapitated bodies?" It had been his hope, as well—but hearing it from Laura somehow stung even more.

"No, of course not. I'd hoped...I don't know. That you'd find it reinvigorating. I know you've been in a bit of a funk."

She'd put her finger right on the problem—and it hurt even more than he'd expected. "It *is* exciting, okay? I *love* dealing with stiffs, day in and day out—and this one was stiffer than most. I know it's not as exciting as working with Cary Grant or...or *Leo*...but..."

Laura withdrew her hand. A moment later, the waiter appeared and placed their dishes in front of them.

"Laura, sweetheart," D'Agosta said quickly, "I didn't mean to sound like that. I'm happy about your assignment: it's got great visibility, and you're not putting yourself in danger anymore. You're right about my case, it's a good one, and being back at the museum reminds me of why I became a cop to begin with. I'm sorry that I just can't seem to, you know, get more enthusiastic."

"It's okay, Vinnie," Laura said. "It's okay."

They ate their meal in silence.

30

Gᴀsᴘᴀʀᴅ Fᴇʀᴇɴᴄ sᴛᴀʀᴇᴅ ᴏᴜᴛ the front door of his cabin deep in the Monongahela National Forest in Mingo County, West Virginia. In the dirt track leading to his cabin, he had installed motion and electro-magnetic sensors along with several hidden cameras, infrared as well as visible spectrum, so he could see who was coming long before they arrived. On that early, early morning he heard the warning chimes go off and went over to the matrix of screens in time to see a car easing its way along the track. It wasn't a car, actually, but an SUV—a black Escalade with smoked windows.

He'd always feared they might come for him, sooner or later.

Quickly, he spun the dial on his gun safe and removed a Walther PPK .32, which he tucked in the back of his belt. And then he went out onto the cabin porch and waited for the vehicle to appear.

Soon enough, it eased cautiously around the final bend, came to a stop in the grassy area in front, and sat there for a moment before the driver's door opened and a man got out.

The man's appearance immediately alarmed Ferenc. He was strongly built, his ripped frame draped in a dark serge suit. As he strolled toward him, he moved with an ease of motion, a cool, unhurried animal bearing, that was almost beautiful to see. His brown hair was cut in the high and tight military style, and his face was as serene and imperturbable as a Buddhist monk's.

He stopped a good ten yards from the porch.

"Dr. Ferenc?"

"Who's asking?"

"Proctor. May I approach?"

Ferenc felt his anxiety increase. A man like this, alone—it was not what he'd expected. What had he done wrong? Was this some unexpected blowback from NASA? Was it a kidnapping, or a black-bag operation with a one-way ticket to Guantanamo? The inscrutable person standing before him didn't look like standard law enforcement or even CIA. He looked like Special Forces.

His heart rate accelerated. "What do you want?" he called loudly.

"I'd like to speak to you privately."

"Not until I know what it's about."

"There's no reason for alarm." He held out his hands, palms up. "May I at least join you on the porch?"

"If you must."

The man strolled to the steps, mounted, and came up to Ferenc, hand extended.

Ferenc shook it reluctantly. "Have a seat," he said, indicating the shabby outdoor furniture.

"Thank you."

They sat down.

"Okay—how did you find me?" Ferenc asked.

"I didn't know you were hiding."

"I'm not," said Ferenc. "But I value my privacy, and I didn't tell anybody where I was."

The man named Proctor nodded pleasantly, giving him an easy smile. "Perseverance."

"That's how you found me?"

"No. That's why I'm here. You were instrumental in engineering the Mars rover, Perseverance."

"So?"

"You felt your work wasn't as appreciated as it should have been. So you resigned in anger and now you're out here, sulking—which suits you better, since you have a reputation for being meddlesome, difficult, and prickly."

Ferenc's heart slowed again. Whatever this was, it didn't include immediate danger—if that had been the case, he'd be on the way down the mountain already. His innate truculence reasserted itself. "Difficult and prickly? Fuck you."

Proctor chuckled indulgently. "But your own project is not going well, because the expense was far more than you anticipated and you're running out of money. Still, you won't consider investors because you don't want anyone telling you what to do. Again—difficult and prickly."

At this Ferenc felt a growing anger. Who was this son of a bitch telling him his own life story? He rose. "Get back in your vehicle and drive your ass out of here."

Another chuckle. "You, Dr. Ferenc, are the world's expert in self-sabotage—and you know it. Now, if I may continue?"

Ferenc continued staring at him.

"I've come because—*despite* the character flaws I've mentioned—you are possibly the most brilliant engineer alive today."

Ferenc couldn't help but be mollified by this. But only slightly.

"I'm not here to offer myself as an investor, or to interfere with your work. I'm here to offer you a large sum of money for a few weeks of your time. Then you can come back here and continue working on your project, flush with all the cash you need to complete it."

"So what's the work...and how much is the money?"

"It's a time machine. And the money is half a million dollars."

At this Ferenc stared and then, as the absurdity of it sank in, laughed harshly. "Time machine? Is this a joke? Who put you up to this? That's impossible—even theoretically."

"Possible, *if* you consider we're living in a multiverse with many parallel timelines. 'Time machine' is a misnomer, actually. The device punches through one universe to reach another, on a different timeline."

Ferenc shook his head as he sat down again. While this concept had been advanced theoretically, it had never gone beyond that, and he couldn't even imagine how to build such a device. "There's no way I'm going to waste my time with crazy shit like that."

"A quarter million up front, the other half in three weeks, whether we succeed or fail."

Ferenc couldn't believe what he was hearing. The man looked sane, but then a lot of people who looked sane turned out to be nuts.

"Dr. Ferenc, there is a benefit to you far beyond the money."

"Which is?"

"This project will absolutely and irrevocably blow your mind."

The way the man said it, so serenely confident, so coolly self-assured, led Ferenc—for just a moment—to almost believe it. And then he began to laugh, shaking his head again. "Wow, you almost had me there."

"May I show you a video?"

Without waiting for a response, Proctor took out his cell phone and tapped at it, then handed it over. Ferenc couldn't help but watch. What he saw could only be described as a flickering tunnel, apparently carved through time, at the end of which slowly materialized a view of a city square. It looked to be more than a century ago, with horse-drawn carriages coming and going and people in old-fashioned dress walking about, to a backdrop of low brick and stone buildings. Then the image wobbled and flickered into black.

He handed the phone back. "Nice bit of CG."

"Not CG. That view at the end of the tunnel was of Times Square, circa 1880. In a parallel universe, of course." He rose. "Dr. Ferenc, I won't waste any more of your time or mine. You now have the basic facts and must make a decision."

"A decision? I need a hell of a lot more information than this. Like who am I going to be working for, where is this machine now, who built it, what's its history, what are you going to do with it—and if you have the thing already, why do you need me?"

"I can offer no more information until you've agreed." He looked around. "I have a private jet waiting at Appalachian Regional Airport, and it's a forty-mile drive via mountainous peckerwood roads. You have thirty seconds."

"Thirty seconds? Are you kidding me?"

But the man was now looking at his watch. Ferenc waited, counting out the seconds in his head.

Sure enough, after thirty seconds passed, the man turned without another word and walked down the porch steps. Ferenc watched him stride toward the blacked-out SUV. He couldn't say why, or how, but he felt a sudden surge of regret. What if the man was not crazy? What if this was real? And even if it was bogus, how stupid was he to turn down half a million? He'd demand the upfront money in his bank account today. As a guarantee.

"Hey, hold it!"

The man paused at the door handle.

"All right, I'm in. But I want the first payment today."

The man calling himself Proctor smiled. "And you shall have it. Today. Now get in, please." He went to the rear door and opened it.

"I need to pack first."

"Absolutely everything you will need—from clothing and lodging to your migraine medication, to a laboratory with massive computing power and a high-tech machine shop—will be provided. And leave the gun. There will be better ones where you're going."

What the... "So, about the money?"

"It will be wired into your account before we arrive at our destination."

Ferenc turned back to his house, set the alarm, locked the door, and slid into the leather-perfumed interior of the SUV.

"What destination, exactly?"

"New York City."

31

THE FBI's FORENSIC IMAGING laboratory must have worked through the night, because their report reached Coldmoon's cell phone at six the next morning. They were certainly efficient, Coldmoon thought with appreciation. He was already up, preparing coffee on the hot plate in the sitting room of their White Feather Motel suite, Pologna still racked out in the bedroom.

He opened it eagerly. It was short and to the point: the ceremonial pipe in the original photograph of Sitting Bull was not the same as the object he'd photographed in the Rosebud museum. Forensic imaging technicians had taken both pipes and interposed one over the other: the grain in the wood of the twisted stem of the museum's pipe almost, but not quite, matched the grain in the sharp glass-plate photograph of Sitting Bull.

The results were conclusive beyond doubt.

Coldmoon's first impulse was to wake up Pologna and get his ass out of bed. Dudek had set a noon deadline for returning to Denver. But Coldmoon figured he could act more nimbly alone. He would finish his coffee and take off, leaving Pologna to wallow.

He forwarded a copy of the report to Dudek, who must have already received it but probably hadn't looked at it. Coldmoon added a note to the effect that this did indeed suggest another possible motive for Twoeagle's murder, and that he was looking into it with all possible speed.

His coffee wasn't quite ready, but he poured out a cup anyway and considered his course of action. It was six fifteen, which by Dudek's clock gave him a little less than six hours to identify a suspect. The Rosebud PD would be no help: they believed they had their guy and would resist him overturning that. Coldmoon would have to figure this out on his own. But it shouldn't be that hard, he thought, because he was convinced the killer was not Lakota—based on the natural reluctance of a Lakota to use the ledge near those old burial caves as a sniper's nest. Even a non-traditionalist would be wary, in case the spirits of the dead might jinx or otherwise interfere with the success of the killing. The killer had to be an outsider. Such a person would be noticed on the Rez—that was a given. Of course, there were many non-Lakotans living there: doctors, clinicians, teachers, missionaries, activists, wannabes. But the theft of Sitting Bull's peace pipe was a sophisticated crime requiring specialized knowledge and ability. He just couldn't see any of those types being involved.

Another curious thing: the pipe, while worth millions, wasn't an object that could be sold. It was like the *Mona Lisa*; it was too famous. So it must have been stolen to order by someone with connections. And whoever stole the pipe probably murdered Twoeagle, its maker, to cover up the crime or stop him from talking.

He gulped the last of his coffee and began to rise, when he suddenly realized he already *knew* who the thief must be. It was that curator Mrs. Twoeagle had mentioned: the old friend of her husband's from New York's Natural History Museum. What was his name?

Mancow.

Hell, yes. Mancow was the killer, or was at least deeply involved with the killer or killers. It was the obvious, the *only* answer. Mancow had all the necessary local knowledge. He knew where Twoeagle got his stone. He probably knew Running, knew about the debt, and realized Running could be framed. Mancow, a curator, surely had contacts on the other end who would buy the pipe—he'd know collectors who might pay millions for an artifact that could never be sold or publicly displayed. Mancow also knew that Twoeagle was the only person alive who could make a replica so exact the theft would never be discovered. One way or another, he was at the very heart of this crime—the theft *and* the murder.

Mancow. Was there a first name? Mrs. Twoeagle hadn't mentioned it. Thank God it was such a unique name.

He quickly logged into the FBI's Uniform Crime Reporting database to see if there was any crime data associated with someone named Mancow. It only took a moment for the UCR system to provide a hit. Coldmoon stared, hardly able to believe his eyes: a homicide had been reported to the UCR database just three days before by the NYPD. It had taken place in the New York Museum of Natural History, a curator named Eugene Mancow, Boaz Distinguished Curator of Ethnology in the Department of Anthropology.

Son of a bitch, Coldmoon thought. Twoeagle murdered, Mancow murdered—this had all the ingredients of a mopping-up operation.

He opened the bedroom door and looked upon the sprawled form of Pologna. He banged his fist on the wall, the agent abruptly bolting upright in bed.

"What the hell?"

"Get your clothes on, partner, looks like we're out of here."

"Christ, about time," Pologna said sleepily. "Back to Denver?"

"Only long enough to change planes and get me on a flight to New York."

32

December 6, 1880
Thursday

CONSTANCE STOOD AT THE second-floor window of the paper box factory, looking out over Mission Place and the junction of Worth and Park Streets, which comprised the heart of the Five Points slum. The window was filthy and fly-specked, but the grime helped conceal her presence.

Night was just falling, the cloak of darkness somehow heightening the squalor. At dusk, a shabby man had come by and lit the gas lamps along the streets—far fewer than in the wealthier districts to the north—and dull, flickering lights had also begun appearing in the windows of grogshops, brothels, gambling dens, flophouses. The feeble pinpoints of light daubed the shadowy doorways of the ramshackle lanes with additional menace. A light snow was falling again. Even in the enclosed space where she stood, the stench from beyond seemed to leak in—a vinegary admixture of decay, rot, and urine.

There was a soft sound behind her, the creaking of footsteps on wooden planks. Turning, Constance saw the heavyset man named Bainbridge, owner of the factory, along with a man she assumed must be the night watchman.

"Going to be here all night?" Bainbridge asked her in a rough voice.

She shook her head. "Just another hour, perhaps two."

Bainbridge spat a stream of brown tobacco juice onto the floor. "Keep an eye on her," he told the watchman, then—after muttering a few words under his breath—heaved his bulk down the stairway. More creaking of floorboards, then the slamming of the outer door. She stared down the watchman until at last he turned away to make his rounds, though not without glancing back suspiciously now and then in her direction.

Constance had realized she could not simply loiter around on the streets, looking for her younger self. She would immediately be taken for a streetwalker and annoyed, propositioned, or possibly even arrested. Instead she had chosen a different way to surveil the area. She had given Bainbridge a dollar in exchange for allowing her to take up a position overlooking the Points. She had dressed as a Bohemian, a painter, carrying a shabby portfolio with sketching carbon. She told him she wanted to observe the view before and after sunset. If she decided to proceed with a painting, she'd give him two dollars a week more. Bainbridge, a man who had no doubt been witness to every imaginable crime and deceptive practice, was naturally suspicious, but Constance had paid up front and—as she'd hoped—her story sounded just eccentric enough to be true. An hour earlier he'd set her up at the viewpoint she requested, warned her not to touch anything or speak to any of the workers, and left her to her vigil.

As the watchman's steps receded, and his form grew indistinct behind the stacks of paper and half-assembled boxes, Constance returned to the window. She could not have asked for a better vantage point. The factory ran the westward length of Mission Place, with entrances on both Worth and Park Streets. To the left was the House of Industry, where the week before she had missed her older sister by the narrowest of margins. It was here that, as a child, she'd come in the evenings, leaving one of the half-dozen hiding places where she waited out the days, braving the nights to visit Mary at a basement window to get some illicit nourishment—a few pieces of stale bread, a half-rotten apple, or a few dry carrots—and a word or two of comfort.

Young Constance did not know that Mary had been taken by Leng. Eleven days had passed since the nine-year-old Constance had last seen her older sister through the bars of the workhouse window, but still she went, with gradually failing hopes. Constance vividly recalled going night after night to the window—chilled, starving, and wondering why Mary was no longer answering her rap on the glass. For a week, two weeks, three weeks, she had come looking for Mary, until at last she'd given up. She never saw her sister again. She had felt she was going to die of loneliness, cold, and starvation, until...

Constance knew all this beyond any doubt—because she *remembered* it.

In this timeline, it would not be that way. Everything would change; and *she* would change it. Their lives would be utterly different.

Constance could not look for the child during the day. The girl had too many hiding places, too many nooks and filthy cubbyholes, and it was impossible to remember which one she used on which night. The better strategy would be to wait here at the window, overlooking a place where she knew her own younger self—gnawed by hunger, still clinging to hope—would be sure to appear.

Murphy had parked his carriage and was waiting, with Rascal, on White Street, a few blocks north near the Tombs.

All was silent. The building's night watchman was somewhere distant. Constance didn't bother pulling out her pocket watch; she sensed instinctually it was eight o'clock. Four hours to midnight. Tomorrow would be December 7. In thirty-one days, Mary would be laid out on the operating table in Leng's infernal laboratory and die, unless...

Suddenly she froze, her train of thought arrested by the sight of a girl who had just materialized from around the Baxter Street corner. Constance's heart accelerated and she felt herself flush with a strange, alien emotion—not unlike what she'd experienced when she first saw Joe in his filthy cell—as she watched the little girl scurrying along the street, avoiding the whores, drunks, and thieves. She managed almost to remain invisible as she flitted from one doorway to the next: frighteningly gaunt, a figure so small and wispy it seemed she might dissolve into the falling snow. Constance stared, her mind temporarily paralyzed by a dreadful mingling of memory, fear, and horror, past and yet still present...

Then she tore herself away from the window and ran toward the stairway. The thin, waiflike creature had nearly reached the workhouse, and now, having seen her, Constance could not bear the thought of the girl slipping away again.

"Here, where are you off to in such a hurry?" the watchman barked as he approached from the shadows, certain she was making off with something. Constance shoved him aside, flew down the steps, opened the factory door, and ran across the mephitic commons to the workhouse, where the little girl was now stooping before a window that looked down into the basement kitchen.

"Constance!" she cried before she could help herself.

Hearing her name, the little girl leapt up, with a swiftness honed by self-preservation, and turned to flee. But already Constance was there, nearly bowling them both over, her arms grasping the girl's terribly thin body.

"Constance," she said. "Don't be frightened."

The girl wasn't just frightened—she was terrified. She let forth a high keening screech of terror while Constance held fast, whispering.

"It's all right, Binky. It's all right."

The child, surprised to hear this family endearment, still struggled pitifully.

"I'm your friend, I won't hurt you... You're safe now..."

Constance tried to keep her voice calm, but she realized she was choking with emotion as the little girl finally stopped struggling and looked up at her. Her face was smeared with mud, the filth obscuring her expression, but the look in her wide, white eyes was unmistakable—the pathetic look of fear and resignation.

Constance took a long, deep breath, and another, then reached out a hand to smooth the matted hair away from the girl's forehead, careful to maintain her grip. Staring into that face, *her* face, temporarily took away her words. All she could do was look, and the little girl looked back.

Finally she found her voice. "Constance, dearest... I've been looking for you. Please don't run. I'm here to help you. Mary sent me."

At the mention of Mary, Constance could see a glimmer of hope in the terrified eyes.

"Mary?" came the little girl's first word.

"Yes, Mary. Your sister. She isn't here anymore—they took her away. But come with me and you'll be safe." A particularly garrulous gang of men went by, one of them staggering to a stop and reaching out to grope her, his companions thankfully hauling him away with derisive laughter.

She had to move quickly. "I knew your parents. I've been searching for you a long time. I have a house—a large house where you'll be warm and dry." It was all she could do not to squeeze the matchstick limbs too tightly. "Joe's there already. He's waiting for you. I got him out of Blackwell's. And now I'm here to bring you home, too."

The girl stared, confusion and hope mingling on her dirty face.

Constance rose to her feet, helping the girl stand but also keeping tight hold as she did so. "Come, now—we need to hurry. I have a carriage just a few blocks away."

It broke her heart to watch her younger self briefly consider crying out for help or running away, but then resign herself. Whatever this was, whatever fate might be in store for her, good or bad, she would have to go; and her shoulders drooped in submission as she let Constance lead her off into the dirty night.

33

A STORM HAD BROKEN over the city by the time the Rolls-Royce pulled up to a dark house on the west side of Manhattan, facing the river. Flashes of lightning forked the night sky. Ferenc stared up at it, in his mind the very picture of a haunted mansion. What had he gotten himself into? But there was no turning back now.

The Rolls slid under the porte cochere, and almost immediately a stout oaken door was opened by an equally stout elderly woman.

"Mr. Proctor, do come in," she said, "and get yourself and your guest out of that nasty weather!"

As they entered, the woman closed, locked, and bolted the door behind her. "I am Mrs. Trask, the housekeeper," the woman said to Ferenc, stepping back to let him pass.

Proctor swept past her, not bothering to introduce Ferenc.

Ferenc couldn't help but feel he'd entered some sort of strange horror film, directed by Wes Craven or, more likely, Herk Harvey. They'd flown back to New York, Proctor saying nothing beyond ordering Ferenc to put on his seat belt when the weather turned bad. They had landed at Teterboro Airport, the jet taxiing off to some remote corner, where a vintage Rolls-Royce sat on the tarmac, as serenely as if at some Hollywood premiere. And now their journey had ended at a mansion the Addams Family would have been proud to own. The sensation of unreality and menace only grew as he followed Proctor through a dim passageway and into a huge, vaulted room that was more like a museum than a private residence, with case after case full of rocks, bones, fossils, and gemstones.

"What is this place?" he asked Proctor, receiving no answer.

They came to the entrance of what was apparently a library, where Proctor halted. "Dr. Ferenc," he announced to the occupant, seated by the fire, then abruptly turned and left.

Ferenc stood on the threshold of a most elegantly appointed room. A gaunt figure, remarkably pale, rose from a wing chair.

"How good of you to come, Dr. Ferenc," the figure said in a honeyed southern accent, extending his hand. "My name is Pendergast."

Ferenc took the hand, put off by its marble-like coolness.

"Please sit down," the man said, indicating a chair. "Mrs. Trask will bring you something. What would you like? I'm having absinthe, but that is not to everyone's taste."

Ferenc gathered his wits. Everything had happened so fast. Just this morning, he'd been in a zip code where the lone dentist barely had sufficient teeth to work on. He eyed the pearly green liquid on the inlaid table beside the man, and it brought back the memory of his grandfather drinking the same during his childhood in Budapest.

Aloud, he said: "James Joyce thought absinthe rendered you impotent."

Pendergast glanced at him with a bemused expression. "Indeed?"

"Well, so I read." *Funny. If that was the case, how could I be here? Herecouldbe, I? No.*

"I'll have one anyway," Ferenc said, as he settled into the chair, which was exceedingly comfortable, enjoying the warmth of the fire. Occasional flashes of lightning and rumbles of thunder barely penetrated the deep, shuttered windows. It was all so strange, so marvelous, so Old World. These people, whoever they were, might be crazy—in fact, he was sure they were—but he might as well enjoy the ride. If they meant him harm, he'd be dead by now. Or maybe he was in a movie, with hidden cameras all around, recording his reaction.

"First things first," said the man named Pendergast, handing him an envelope sitting next to his drink. Ferenc took it, opened it, and pulled out a slip of paper. It was a SWIFT wire transfer of $250,000, made several hours ago, into his own bank account. He stared. Could this be fake?

"It's quite real," said Pendergast. "You're welcome to check."

"I will." Ferenc pulled out his cell phone, logged into his bank account. "Holy shit," he said as he stared at the new balance.

"Now, Dr. Ferenc—" Pendergast began.

"Call me Gaspard," he said.

"We're on a formal basis here," came the cool reply. "After we enjoy our cocktail, would you care to be taken to your rooms to freshen up? You'll find clothes and toiletries already provided. It's just past seven. Dinner is in an hour, and you've had a busy day."

"I want to see the machine," Ferenc said. "Is it here?"

"It's in the basement," said Pendergast, and Ferenc could see he was not displeased by the request. "I'll take you there after our drink."

"I want to see it now."

"Excellent." Pendergast rose just as the woman, Mrs. Trask, came in carrying a tray.

"Mrs. Trask," Pendergast said, "we're going down to the basement for a moment. You can leave that for our return."

Once she left, Pendergast spoke again. "I understand you are afflicted by migraines with aura. My sympathies. Forgive me, but I must ask: are there any specific conditions that trigger an attack? Bright lights, stress, certain foods, lack of sleep?"

"Bright lights aren't so great. But none of those other things act as precipitators, and in any case my medication keeps things under control."

"I'm very glad to hear it. Now, if you'd come this way?"

Ferenc followed Pendergast along corridors and down a staircase into a space that was, if anything, even more reminiscent of a horror film: a labyrinth of ancient, stone passageways that branched out in multiple directions. A short walk through dusty spaces brought them to an old door that, he saw, had been recently retrofitted with an electronic keypad and fingerprint scanner. Pendergast tapped in a code on the keypad, then opened the door and turned on the light.

Ferenc could hardly believe his eyes. One half of the room was filled with the burnt, blasted remains of what had once been a machine—a very peculiar machine. It seemed to combine modern computer switches and chips with old-fashioned components like vacuum tubes, semiconductor diodes, crystal oscillators, Fleming valves, transducers: like some nightmare steampunk fantasy. But one thing it obviously wasn't was random: the various components seemed ganged together in a logical way. This was not some ginned-up fake; it once served a real purpose. But was that purpose actually to pierce the veil of the multiverse?

Gazing at it, he felt a delicious sense of mystery and discovery ahead. It might not have been a time machine, but it had once done something extraordinary.

A trestle table made of soapstone stood alongside the far wall, on which were laid photographs of the machine as it must have originally appeared, as well as half a dozen thick binders, messy with scribbles and Post-it notes.

Pendergast waited for him to take it all in, then spoke. "This device was originally in the basement of an old building in Georgia, where it was ultimately stressed beyond its capabilities—resulting in the damage you see. Every wire, nut, bolt, circuit, and chip has been transported here and arranged in the exact location it was found in Georgia."

Ferenc nodded. What a job *that* must have been. Even slivers of shattered glass had been placed on the floor, presumably as found originally.

"Those binders," Pendergast went on, "contain the notes, operating diagrams, layouts, specs, and everything we could recover associated with the original machine. Your job, Dr. Ferenc, is to restore it to working order. In three weeks or less."

"Three weeks?" Proctor, he now recalled, had alluded to this.

"Hence my question about how stress, or lack of sleep, might be a concern for you."

"Why three weeks?"

A silence. "That is a question that falls into my sphere of business. One thing, Dr. Ferenc, must be clarified: Your sphere of business is to get this machine operational again. My sphere of business involves the question of *why*. That sphere is mine, and mine alone, and no curiosity or inquiries in that direction will be entertained. Are we clear?"

This remark, or more to the point its peremptory nature, annoyed Ferenc. He reminded himself to keep cool, not repeat the mistakes of the past. The thought of the quarter of a million dollars, still cooling off from its transfer to his bank account, helped. "Fine. Enjoy your sphere."

The faintest fleeting trace of a smile. "Now, then: before dinner is ready, shall we return to the library and worship at the altar of absinthe—chaste acolytes though it may render us?"

Ferenc stepped back. "Lead the way."

34

H. P. Munck examined the dingy cuff of his frock coat, the edge of which was heavily soiled, and plucked off a bit of flesh clinging to the fabric. He flicked it away with a muttered curse in his native Circassian language. He then turned his attention back to his wooden barrow, grasping the handles in his rough hands. The bundle inside the barrow was not heavy, certainly less than six stone. Munck was relieved it had not started ripening. The professor had left the last bundle too long, and in the heat of the Indian summer, in the close air of the tunnels, it had begun to turn. With the coming of December, the tunnels were nearly as cold as winter's clay, and the professor's bundles would not turn as quickly. For that, Munck was grateful.

Munck wheeled the barrow along the damp corridor, the wooden wheel creaking with each rotation. At regular intervals, guttering torches set into wrought iron sconces in the brick walls cast feeble yellow light, illuminating the streaks of niter, black mold, and damp that stained the walls. These tunnels lay under what had been a foul alley known as Cow Bay, previously home to an ancient subterranean pumping station dating back to the Collect Pond, during the days of the early Dutch settlers. The waterworks had been shut down and sealed a year ago. This, as the professor had told him, had been a great stroke of good fortune. The professor had had him break through the back wall of a disused coal tunnel that once serviced the building above: Shottum's Cabinet of Natural Productions and Curiosities, a popular museum of oddities and freaks of nature. That breakthrough gained access to a maze of maintenance tunnels, passageways, and catwalks that had once served the old pumping station, now sealed off from the world above. He had then helped the professor move his laboratory and surgery from the third floor of Shottum's Cabinet of Curiosities into the reclaimed tunnels.

He turned a corner with the barrow, walking slowly. A cluster of wolf spiders scurried away, their eyes pinpoints of light on the dark walls. Munck ignored them and continued pushing the barrow, turning the final corner. Here he passed through the short tunnel he had excavated connecting the coal tunnel to the waterworks, walls and ceiling freshly bricked and vaulted. Now he entered the old coal tunnel that had originally serviced the boiler for Shottum's Cabinet. He took a torch from the side of the barrow, raised and lit it from the last sconce in the tunnel, then held it up. The flaring light revealed the straight passageway ahead, arched in stone and brick, old lumps of coal strewn along its length. Both sides of the tunnel held a series of arched niches, about three feet across and five high, half of which were crudely bricked up. Water glistened on the walls, and he heard a faint, irregular chorus of drips. Otherwise, all was still.

He took another step, pushing the barrow with one hand while holding the torch in the other, and stopped alongside an unbricked alcove. Here, on the tunnel floor, lay a stack of bricks, a bucket of water, a mixing trough, a burlap bag of mortar, a trowel, and a mortar hoe.

Holding the torch before him, he illuminated the interior of the niche. Two bodies were folded inside, shrouded by surgeon's sheets, stiffened by the stains that had crept through before drying. The rats had gotten to them—they always did, Munck thought—and chewed through the shrouds in a number of places. One large piece had fallen away to reveal the decomposing remnants of an arm and shoulder, the purple flesh falling from the bones, a bit of rotted lace from the cuff still circling the wrist.

He fixed the end of the torch into a sconce bolted to the brick wall. Leaning over the barrow, careful not to soil his sleeves further, he picked up the bundle and thrust it into the niche. As it slid in, the sheet partly fell away and the corpse's head flopped to one side, long brown hair spilling. Munck, muttering a curse, wrestled the corpse into the niche, rearranged the shroud around it, and gave it a final shove to wedge it next to its neighbor.

He examined his sleeves and cuffs again with fastidious care, satisfying himself that no additional flesh, fluids, or offal had fouled them. Then he knelt and picked up the burlap bag, measuring out mortar powder into the trough; added water; and began mixing it with the mortar hoe. When it reached the proper consistency, he spread a layer of the fresh mortar along the bottom of the niche and began setting bricks into it, troweling on more mortar to seal the joints and tapping the bricks with the handle to set them in place. Another layer of mortar and bricks went down, then another, and in a short time the alcove was thoroughly bricked up, sealing its contents in permanent darkness.

He rose slowly, plucked the torch from the wall, and turned, wheeling the now-empty barrow—*creak, creak, creak*—back through the maze of tunnels in the direction of the operating chambers, ready to collect the next bundle, which he knew would not be long in coming.

35

Nine-year-old Constance sat in the window seat of her bedroom, her own bedroom, looking out the tall windows of the second floor. "House," it was called by the people who lived here, like Mrs. Palegood the cook, and Mr. Moseley the teacher—but to her it was a palace.

Palaces were not for girls like her. She could remember when her mother and father were still alive, when there was food to eat and warmth from the stove, and their apartment—smaller than this room—smelled like boiled cabbage, and her father, grimy from work on the docks, had patiently showed them card tricks, sign language, and taught them ventriloquism. It had been a small, simple place. There were palaces in a book her father had read to them, a book of fairy tales, dirty and coverless but filled with magic. She remembered every page of that book. On page 37 there was a picture of a white castle on a hill, shining like a diamond, with flags and banners rising above its roofs. On page 44 was a picture of a knight on horseback, and on page 72 was the horrible old witch who'd tried to cook and eat Hansel and Gretel.

Then her father died and they had to move. Their new place was crowded, dark, and very cold, and one of the men there took the book away and tore the pages out to start a fire in the stove. She watched them go up in flames, one by one. And then her mother drowned, and that's when Mary took her and Joe to a dirty place under a staircase, where there were staggering men and loud women and rats. Mary would go out during the day and bring back bits of food at night, while she and Joe hid.

But even that did not last long: Mary was taken, Joe disappeared, and she was left alone. She sorted through garbage for something to eat or wear, always with her heart beating fearfully in her narrow chest, enduring kicks, curses, and names that rained down on her as she did her best to keep from underfoot—"urchin," "guttersnipe," "damned little tramp." *Better you should throw yourself in the river like your mama did*, one leering woman had told her, *and rid the world of an extra mouth.*

But her mother had not jumped into the river on purpose. That was an awful fib. Constance did not understand why that toothless woman said that.

They had put Mary in a big brick building and locked her in there. But she'd still been able to see Mary most evenings—to get a bit of food and words of comfort. And on nights when the cramps of hunger would not let her sleep, and the slimy bricks of her secret hiding places simply refused to get warm, she found herself slipping out into the streets and creeping down to the dark pier where she'd seen her mother winched up in a net, dripping, hair covering her face like black seaweed—and trying to understand why God had put her in a place like this and what she needed to do to make it right.

...And then, this had happened. Sitting in the window seat, she looked around her room again in wonder, at the hanging lace encircling the princess bed, the toys lined up on a shelf, the flowers in the window, the music box on the table, the mountain of soft pillows on the bed. Most of all, the food: roasted chicken with apples, sausages piled with potatoes and gravy, thick slabs of boiled ham, soft warm bread smeared with melting butter, ice cream and cake and candied cherries and chocolates.

And best of all, seeing Joe. But Joe wasn't happy. He wasn't convinced that the kind woman was really their aunt: it was too good to be true. He feared something bad was going to happen. Hearing this, she wondered if maybe they were being fattened up to be cooked and eaten, like Hansel and Gretel.

But what bad things could happen to them? The woman really did seem like a duchess, which after all was *almost* a princess, and she was so kind. The duchess somehow knew her nickname and started calling her Binky. Binky! It was the name her own father called her, because he said it was the word for something small and cute and complicated. The duchess wanted Constance and Joe to call her Aunt. Joe refused, but Constance was trying. She was doing her best to be good. She was trying to deserve all this, even though she was an ungrateful, dirty, good-for-nothing guttersnipe.

She thought back to when Aunt Livia had grabbed her, bundled her into a carriage, and covered her with a thick beaver rug—a real carriage, with soft seats and lamps and a horse with a driver. For a moment she wondered if she was being taken away to some evil place—if she was experiencing one final instance of warmth before the terrible unknown.

But that had been two days ago. She'd arrived at this mansion and been reunited with Joe. No bad things came. What came were toys, and books, and hot baths, and huge breakfasts and lunches and suppers. Everything the lady—Aunt Livia—had promised on the snowy street outside the workhouse had come true. She was warm and dry, and Joe was here—he had his own room on the far side of a bathroom they shared; they were called "Jack and Jill" rooms by their tutor, Mr. Moseley. Joe wouldn't tell her what had happened to him at Blackwell's, but she knew it must have been awful, because he seemed changed. Every now and then, though, the old laughing, teasing Joe surfaced, with his card tricks and pick-a-pocket japes.

Binky didn't know if she'd ever feel at home in her room. It was so grand and warm, and the bedcovers were so soft that she was afraid to go to sleep because she might sink down to the street and wake up back on the cold, wet stones to find it had all been a dream. She spent a lot of her time being careful to move very quietly, not break things, and speak only when spoken to—in short, to be the best little girl a guttersnipe could be—so that she'd never, ever, get put back in that bad place.

Careful not to disturb the child sitting in the window seat, "Aunt" Livia, Duchess of Ironclaw, stood motionless in the carpeted hallway, observing her through the crack of the bedroom door. She found herself fascinated, even obsessed, by the child. Her feelings on seeing her younger self—on calling her by her long-abandoned nickname, Binky, which had once been her own—were too peculiar and inexplicable to be analyzed. And how could there be analysis, without analogue or precedent? She recalled a phrase of H. P. Lovecraft's, when he described the sensations of a truly unique encounter as being "poignant and complex." Those adjectives had always seemed lacking to her. Yet now—in an encounter of her own that could certainly be called unique—she could think of none better. Looking at her tiny self as she went about her day—sitting in a window seat lost in thought, playing with her new toys, whispering with her brother Joe, wolfing down food, her little prayers at bedtime—it was an experience beyond the reach of words.

What came to her mind instead was something most unwelcome: a sudden effluence of her own dark memories, once brutally locked away, now risen again and impossible to resist—three torturing moments in particular, the awful dates of each engraved into her remembrance forever:

Dr. Enoch Leng, June 19, 1881—Come, child; this Mission is no spot for a young waif such as yourself. I'm a physician, let me get you to a place where you'll be cared for, where your ills will be cured. I know you are afraid. But please, do not discompose yourself: resistance is truly unnecessary…

Leng, October 13, 1935—My child, of course it is different! And yes, a certain languorousness is to be expected upon the initial injection; my refinement contains trace amounts of synthetic opiates among other things, but you'll find that even though the formula is different—and rather easier to procure—the benefit is the same…

Leng, January 7, 1951—Foolish, frivolous, thankless girl! After the kindnesses I've shown you: taken you into my care, treated you like my own blood, given you access to books and instruments and paintings so numberless even your mind cannot absorb them all... to now accuse me of using you as a guinea pig those long years ago! Just because you've stumbled over a few papers in those endless basement perambulations of yours doesn't mean you would, or could, understand what I did for you or why. But I shall say this: if you now refuse to take the elixir, if you willfully throw away the bloom of youth in favor of creeping enfeeblement and, finally, worms and dust, you'll not only be sacrificing a priceless intellect, honed by decades of education and my edifying attentions—but in doing so will cause your own sister's death to have been in vain. That's right: in your ignorance you label yourself a guinea pig, but it was Mary who died so that you might live. Your sister, Mary Greene, who died in my laboratory on this very night, exactly seventy years ago, in the vivisection that at last unlocked the final secret of the Arcanum—and allowed you to enjoy a life of the mind not for decades, but centuries. There! I see you are shocked. Well, you have only yourself to blame; I certainly never planned to tell you such details. But when you get over this snit, consider: if you stop taking the arcanum, you'll be sacrificing everything your sister Mary died for. Mary Greene, who died not just for your sins, but for your very life...

Constance stepped back from the doorway, her hand rising to stifle the gasp triggered by these unbidden memories. She'd been so busy with her plans, so pleased by her progress, that she'd let down her guard. She must steel herself mentally, using the *stong pa nyid* meditation technique Pendergast had taught her, to keep such crushing recollections in abeyance.

Pendergast... The thought of him, the memories of him... his eyes, his honeyed voice, his breath caressing her ear... they comprised another mental burden that required ruthless and disciplined suppression. She trembled with the effort necessary to banish these thoughts, telling herself they belonged to another universe, another time, nothing more now than tiny electrical sparks moving among her brain cells, signifying nothing.

As she took a final look at her younger self before moving down the passage, it hit home to Constance that, when she'd seized her younger shade and spirited her off to this house, she had triggered an irreversible fork in time. Up until that point, the two people—the Constance of 1880 and the Constance of the twenty-first century— shared every memory and were effectively one. But now, the girl sitting in the window seat and gazing onto the courtyard below had, through no action of her own, embarked on her own timeline... one to which Constance had no access, one she had no memory of and no way of predicting. Those awful memories of Leng that had assaulted her just now were hers, and hers alone.

She thanked the God of the Universe they would never be memories of little Constance.

36

December 9, 1880
Sunday

YOUR CARRIAGE IS WAITING, ma'am."

"And high time that it is." Carlotta Victoria Cabot-Flint heaved herself out of the drawing room chair where she'd been waiting, walked with dignified step into the front hall, and suffered the parlormaid to drape the heavy beaver coat around her commodious person.

"Have a care, there!" she snapped as the young woman—half her size—did her best to slide the sleeves into place. "I'm not one of those longshoremen you go carousing with on your day off!"

In due time she was out the front door and being assisted down the steps of her Fifth Avenue mansion and out to the carriage standing at the curb. Williams, her coachman, opened the door and, with the help of the maid, assisted Mrs. Cabot-Flint into the conveyance. She paused to wipe a dubious finger along the outside of the gleaming ebony door. It was Williams's duty to make sure that, whenever she made her calls, the brougham was spotless, despite the mud, ice, and filth of the roads.

Once she had been bundled inside, Williams climbed into the driver's seat, took up the reins, and they lurched off with such a jackrabbit start Mrs. Cabot-Flint rapped with annoyance on the front window with her mother-of-pearl cane. Didn't the fellow recall that her liver was acting up, and the doctor had warned her to avoid sudden movement? Actually, perhaps the doctor hadn't specifically mentioned her liver, but she knew that organ was very delicate in a woman of her age and constitution.

She settled back—none too happily—in the seat as they set off down the avenue. Thank heavens, at least the ride would be short. She was due for her private costume fitting—refitting, to be precise, the dressmaker had made wretched work of it the first time around—and none too soon, because the *soirée* was just under two weeks away.

Her thoughts were disturbed by a sudden neighing of horses, followed by a shout, so close it might almost have come from the opposite seat...and then a violent jolt forced her to grab her cane with both hands to avoid slipping forward in the carriage.

What on earth? Of all the intolerable—!

She was about to open the passthrough to excoriate Williams when she saw the cause of her consternation. Just after they had passed Forty-Ninth Street, a carriage—coming out of nowhere—had almost collided with her own, causing her horses to shy and rear against their reins. Williams had nearly been thrown from his seat.

This was outrageous. Mrs. Cabot-Flint had heard tales of the young bloods and dandies who raced gigs through Central Park with all the abandon of Roman charioteers—no doubt emulating Ben-Hur, the ill-bred protagonist of that year's most sensational novel. But this was Fifth Avenue, not some dog track, and such behavior was not to be tolerated. She was of half a mind to tell Williams to call a constable.

She saw he was speaking to the other driver in none-too-friendly terms. This was rather unlike the mild Williams. She noticed that the other vehicle was not some cheap buggy or rockaway such as a cabman would use, but a sumptuous private carriage, whose gigantic, muscular driver was dressed in expensive livery. It appeared no damage had occurred and nobody was hurt—yet. She opened her window partway to order Williams to get back onto his seat, drive on, and leave this gaucherie behind.

Yet now Mrs. Cabot-Flint received a greater surprise. For the door of the other carriage opened and a striking young woman descended and approached the coachmen. It was most shocking that a woman of means should exit her conveyance in the middle of the street, let alone involve herself in an argument among servants. And yet there she was, wearing a visiting dress of striped blue satin, wasp-waisted and worked with white organdy and gold silk. As Mrs. Cabot-Flint stared, the woman removed her bonnet of matching blue satin, revealing glossy dark hair, styled short. The bonnet itself, she couldn't help but notice, was embroidered with pearls and trimmed with an aigrette in pure jet—extremely expensive and of the latest Parisian fashion.

As she watched, Mrs. Cabot-Flint saw the young woman, having defused the altercation, was—merciful heavens!—approaching her own window.

The woman might be wealthy, thought Mrs. Cabot-Flint, but was unknown to her—and, thus, to New York society. Although she resolved to keep a distant *froideur*, she could not very well ignore her completely. She opened her window the rest of the way.

The woman, having replaced her bonnet, stopped outside the carriage and gave an exceedingly graceful curtsy. "I'm terribly sorry if my coachman's error caused you any discomfort or mortification," she said in a cultured European accent. "I hope you will accept my apologies."

Mrs. Cabot-Flint looked down at the woman—whose cool, oddly distant violet eyes held her own—and nodded gravely.

She waited for the young lady to say more, but to her surprise she merely turned and went back to her own carriage, stepping into it without assistance and closing the door. A moment later, her man gave the reins a shake, and the coach began to move away. Mrs. Cabot-Flint noted it was drawn by a matched pair of magnificent gelded black Percherons with white stars on their foreheads, and as the equipage passed by, she saw that it was a clarence coach of the finest workmanship, its dark wood gleaming with yellow-topaz inlay.

On the side of the door was a coat of arms.

A moment later, the carriage was out of sight. Rousing herself, Mrs. Cabot-Flint gave a knock on the passthrough with her cane, urging Williams to stop his loitering. As her own carriage began moving once again, its owner's mind continued to move as well. She had heard that a young European woman of great wealth and high rank—a baroness, or perhaps even a countess—had taken possession of that unusual marble mansion whose construction had exhausted its original owner's fortune. That mansion was close by—on the northwest corner of Forty-Eighth Street. The clarence must have been pulling away from the curb near that very spot.

As she continued down the avenue in her own splendid Victorian coach—rather drab compared to the other vehicle—the thoughts of Mrs. Cabot-Flint fastened on the young woman herself. Everything about her, from the way she had intervened in the coachmen's squabble to the cool and direct manner with which she'd apologized, spoke of a person operating above society's rules. And that gigantic coachman of hers could have passed for one of the Prussian Imperial Guard. Everything about her radiated nobility.

Curiosity among New York's "Four Hundred" about the new resident of the marble mansion was high. If Mrs. Cabot-Flint was the first to make her acquaintance, it would be a social victory of no little consequence.

Settling back again in her seat, she made a mental note to stop on the way back from the dressmaker's and leave her card at the mansion, now receding in the glass panel at the rear of her coach.

37

Vincent D'Agosta was curious to meet the FBI agent from Denver who'd contacted him about the Mancow homicide. The call, coming out of nowhere, was a game changer. Up to that point, he and his team had made little progress. Despite the museum being packed with security cameras and guards, a comprehensive review had revealed nothing out of the ordinary. It was incredible someone had managed to sneak in, lure Mancow into the freezer, lock him in, and depart without being caught on tape—but there seemed no doubt that was what had happened. Dr. Mancow himself seemed above reproach, with no criminal record or history of unethical dealings. The NYPD forensics lab had analyzed the sabotaged freezer door without finding anything promising—no latents beyond the small circle of technicians who used the freezer on a regular basis. The DNA analyses were still pending, but he had little hope they would yield anything useful. The freezer was filthy to begin with, and there was probably well-preserved DNA of people and animals going back a hundred years in there.

Then out of the blue came this call from an agent who identified himself as Coldmoon, regarding a homicide on the Rosebud Indian Reservation. Incredible the two murders could be linked, but as the agent began laying out the progress of his own investigation, there was no doubt they were. The case was breaking open—a huge relief. And it was turning more interesting, at that.

Coldmoon. Odd name. D'Agosta glanced at his watch. He was to meet the agent at the museum in half an hour to give him a walk-through of the crime scene. Unfortunately, they would be joined by what he'd started to think of as the Triumvirate: the museum's meddlesome director, Lowell Cartwright; security chief Martin Archer; and public relations director Louise Pettini. There was no way to avoid their tagging along: the Triumvirate had been in a flutter of anxiety ever since learning the FBI was getting involved.

The museum lay only a couple of blocks from the 20th Precinct, where he was reviewing case files that day, and he decided to walk instead of getting a ride in a squad car. He needed to clear his head and think about how to best liaise with the feds. And it was a beautiful day, a fabulous early summer afternoon, not a cloud in the sky, the air fresh and clean.

He moved briskly down Columbus to Eighty-First, then east toward Central Park West. The museum's security entrance was a circular drive underneath the Great Rotunda. Within ten minutes, he was passing through the metal detector, putting his service piece on the nearby table and picking it up on the other side. Naturally, the Triumvirate was hovering.

"Lieutenant Commander," said Archer, leading him into the large security foyer where Cartwright and Pettini were waiting nervously. "Agent Coldmoon just arrived."

D'Agosta turned to see a surprisingly young agent, dressed in a sharp blue suit, his black hair a bit long by FBI standards and parted in the middle, which along with the knifelike nose served to accentuate the Native American features. He was tall and thin with high cheekbones, black eyes, and looked fit in a rangy way. D'Agosta thought with a twinge of embarrassment of the tire around his own waist. When he was Coldmoon's age, he was...well, also a bit overweight. At least he'd quit smoking those damn cigars.

D'Agosta shook the Special Agent's hand, pleased that the man didn't grip like a gorilla. "Special Agent Armstrong Coldmoon," the man said.

"Lieutenant Commander Vincent D'Agosta." He paused. "That's Vinnie, okay?"

The agent paused for a moment. "Armstrong. Sorry—I'd hoped to be here a couple of days earlier, but with the FBI's worship of red tape back in Denver..." He gave a dismissive wave.

D'Agosta grunted in sympathy. He was only too familiar with that.

"Well," said Cartwright, "shall we take a look at the scene of the incident?" He was clearly in a hurry, eager to get them both out of the museum as quickly as possible.

D'Agosta nodded and the director took off, leading the way with Archer at his side. D'Agosta fell in beside Coldmoon.

"We have," the director was saying, "one of the world's finest collections of nineteenth-century Lakota material culture."

Coldmoon nodded.

"Perhaps, Agent Coldmoon, if you have time, you'd like to see it?"

"Sure," said Coldmoon, "if I have time."

They walked through the Hall of Northwest Coast Indians and past the great Haida war canoe. "That canoe," Cartwright went on, "was carved from the trunk of a cedar tree. It's sixty-three feet long. To get it here, it had to come all the way from British Columbia to New York in 1883—an incredible journey by sea, rail, and finally a team of horses."

"It's magnificent," said Coldmoon.

D'Agosta couldn't tell what the agent was really thinking: his face was a closed book.

They passed through a locked door into the nonpublic area of the museum, then rode a freight elevator to the fifth floor. Another, shorter walk brought them to the freezer.

"Here we are," said the director. "Lieutenant Commander D'Agosta will brief you."

D'Agosta didn't like the way the director was choreographing their walk-through, but he shrugged it off and took out his iPad, on which he had written down the bullet points he wanted to cover. He quickly ran through the most salient information—timeline, position and condition of the body, sabotaging of the freezer door, the results of the autopsy and forensic analysis of the crime scene, a background of the victim, and so on. Coldmoon listened intently, taking no notes. Cartwright and the other two hovered close by, following attentively but thankfully keeping their mouths shut.

It took about forty minutes, and when he was done, D'Agosta asked: "Any questions?"

"As a matter of fact, yes." But he didn't ask anything. Instead, in the momentary silence, Coldmoon turned to Cartwright. "Many thanks to you all for your warm welcome and your escort. Now, I'm sure you'll understand if the commander and I would like to have a few words in private."

Cartwright hesitated. "You mean—you want us to leave?"

"Yes," said Coldmoon, decisively.

"Of course, of course."

They withdrew somewhat reluctantly. As soon as they were gone, Coldmoon let out a long sigh. "Jesus," he said. "Are they always hovering around like that?"

D'Agosta had to stifle a chuckle. "Yeah. They're terrified of bad publicity. I've worked a couple of cases in this place and they're a pain in the fossilized ass. I like the way you got rid of them."

"The museum might in some way be involved," said Coldmoon. "Wouldn't want them meddling."

D'Agosta nodded.

"Anyway, I do have a few questions," Coldmoon went on. "This Mancow, from what I've been able to surmise, must have been involved in some pretty shady dealings to get himself whacked. Have you looked into his finances? His bank account?"

This surprised D'Agosta. "Yes, and there was nothing, unless he's got money stashed in a Grand Cayman account or something."

"Our forensic accountants can look further into that. What about his colleagues here at the museum?"

"They all appear legit."

"Other professional relationships?"

"We're working on those," said D'Agosta. "He has colleagues all over the world—but that's typical of this place."

"Does the museum have a register or log—something to show who visited him recently?"

"Yes. We pulled it. I've got a list, and we're working through it. Now, with this connection to the homicide in South Dakota, we'll have a much better idea who to look for."

Coldmoon nodded. He glanced at his watch. "Five o'clock. Christ, I was up at four AM, had a long drive, a long flight, and then an hour in traffic coming in from Kennedy." He grinned suddenly. "What say you to going off the clock and getting a beer, Lieutenant Commander?"

"I think that's a brilliant idea, Special Agent."

D'Agosta took Coldmoon to the Blarney Stone Tavern, on Columbus behind the museum, nicknamed "The Bones" because of the late owner's crazy affinity for fixing bones to the walls and ceiling. It was none too clean, the kind of place with sawdust on the floor and wooden tables deeply scored by graffiti. Even as the Upper West Side gentrified almost beyond recognition, the Blarney Stone had remained true to its working-class roots. D'Agosta chose it because he sensed in Coldmoon a man who would not appreciate your typical Upper West Side wine bar or bistro.

They settled into an empty booth. "This place is like its own museum," said Coldmoon, looking around at the bones and animal skulls wired to the ceiling and walls. "Where did all this stuff come from?"

"The owner never said," replied D'Agosta. "Rumor was he nicked them from the museum, but that's not likely when you look at those bones—most look like cow or sheep. He died a few years back, so maybe nobody will ever know."

The waiter took their order—a pitcher of Harp, and an order of bubble and squeak to share.

"That museum's quite a place," said Coldmoon. "Never been there before, but I've heard a few snippets from a colleague of mine who handled some big cases there."

"Colleague?"

"Yeah. We just came off two cases in Florida and another in Georgia. God, was I glad to get back west. Now here I am, east again. Just can't get away."

Florida and Georgia. That's where Pendergast had been.

"Your partner," D'Agosta asked slowly. "Is he with you now?"

"No, I was transferred to the Denver FO and got a new partner. This is my first case with them. My new partner's working the case back on the Rez in South Dakota while I follow up here."

"This previous partner..." D'Agosta was almost afraid to ask. "What were the cases he worked on at the museum?"

The pitcher of beer arrived and Coldmoon poured out two pints. "He's sort of a closed-mouth guy, doesn't like to talk about his cases. Bunch of murders is all I could get out of him. Decapitations. He specializes in serial killers."

D'Agosta picked up his beer, took a long draft, then set it down carefully. "Your partner's name wouldn't be Pendergast, would it?"

Coldmoon stared. "You *know* him?"

"I sure do. I worked those cases you're talking about—the museum murders and the one that followed. Others, as well. We've worked together quite a lot. In fact, I recently paid him a visit up at his place on Riverside Drive."

Coldmoon continued to stare. "Jesus. Small world. I left him two weeks ago back in Savannah. He, um, wasn't doing too well." A pause. "So he's home now? Is he okay?"

D'Agosta took another long, thoughtful sip of beer. He wasn't sure how much he should say. "Pendergast..." he replied, "is kind of an odd duck. Hard to read, you know what I mean?" He couldn't believe this young agent had partnered with the legendary Pendergast.

"'Hard to read' is an understatement," said Coldmoon. "The guy plays his cards close. But brilliant—I mean, he's the finest investigator I've ever met. It's almost like he can *read* criminal minds."

D'Agosta released a breath of relief. "That's for sure. The guy's a frigging genius." He stopped himself from saying Pendergast had saved his life more than once.

"So—is he okay? I've been kind of worried."

"Not sure. His ward, Constance, left him and he's pretty cut up about it. You know her?" D'Agosta immediately saw from the expression on the man's face that he did.

"Yeah. I know her." Coldmoon's tone did not imply affection.

"Where'd she go?" D'Agosta asked. "You know what happened?"

Again, D'Agosta could see that Coldmoon did know what happened—but wasn't going to tell him.

After a moment, Coldmoon simply shook his head. "It's a long, crazy story." He sipped his beer.

"Have you been to his mansion?"

"No, we spent all our time down south. He never talked about his personal life—I don't know anything about it. Except for Constance, of course."

"Yeah, he doesn't talk about it because he comes from a...well, kind of a crazy family. Eccentric as all hell. He's got this psycho brother—" He stopped. "I'd better shut up and let him tell you that stuff himself. Is he still your partner?"

"No, that was just for a couple of unusual cases."

"So you're not going to work with him again?"

Coldmoon shook his head. "No idea. He can be pretty challenging to partner with. Maybe you know about that?"

D'Agosta had to laugh. "Oh, yeah. We should pay him a visit—together. That would be something." But even as he said this, he realized it was a bad idea. Pendergast didn't like casual socializing.

"Where are you staying?" he asked, changing the subject.

"The FBI rented me a place on Amsterdam and Ninety-First Street."

"Nice." D'Agosta glanced at his watch. It was past six. "Hey, I better get home to my wife," he said.

Coldmoon finished his beer and forked up the last bit of bubble and squeak from his plate, dropped a twenty on the table, and rose.

"Vinnie, thanks for coming out for a drink. Glad to be working with you."

"That goes double. Your call saved my ass on this case: we weren't making any progress at all."

As D'Agosta walked across the park in the direction of Second Avenue, he marveled at the coincidence. It seemed like a good sign—and he felt, for the first time in a long while, a sense that things might have turned around for him.

38

Dr. Gaspard Ferenc was on his knees, bent over a complicated assembly of wires and integrated circuits, trying to work out a problem in multidimensional internal symmetry, when he heard the soft but unmistakable sound of the zinc-lined door opening.

Keeping his eyes on his work, he cursed under his breath. It had taken him twenty minutes of mental computation to get "in the zone"—what programmers liked to call that heightened state of consciousness during which they wrote their best code. He wasn't going to waste it on an interruption from that goddamned hovering Proctor.

"Go away!" he snapped over his shoulder. "You'll get my report in an hour."

"By all means, finish what you're doing," came the reply. "I'll wait here, if you don't mind."

Ferenc sat up and turned around, in time to see Pendergast flick some dust away from the edge of the soapstone table and perch himself.

This was a surprise. Since their first meeting almost a week earlier, Pendergast hadn't made a single appearance in the basement room that housed the machine, at least when he was there. The two had had dinner together only on his first night, accompanied by wines and cognacs to the point where Ferenc overslept the next day. At that dinner, Pendergast asked many searching questions about the machine, but it had been too early for Ferenc to say anything definite. After that, he had dined alone in the mansion's huge dining room for two nights, which creeped him out sufficiently to ask Mrs. Trask to bring dinner to his room from then on.

It was Proctor who visited the lab twice a day for progress reports and at other, unexpected times. Ferenc did not like Proctor. The more Ferenc saw of him, the more menace the man seemed to radiate, and the more unsettled he felt in his presence. The chauffeur or body-guard or whatever the hell he was never *did* anything threatening or hostile; in fact, he hardly ever spoke—just listened to Ferenc's verbal progress report once in the morning and once in the afternoon, taking no notes.

After that dinner, Ferenc had scarcely seen Pendergast at all. But now here he was, sitting on the edge of the lab table.

Ferenc felt a flicker of pride: the machine looked nothing like it had the week before, with its ruined transistors and scorched oscillators. Now it was surrounded by a delicate scaffolding holding parts and circuit boards and a variety of precision components. From a string run across the ceiling hung pages of diagrams and equations. A power-ful generator hummed away, vented through a pipe in the ceiling, its power cords snaking across the floor.

Pendergast's gaze remained, annoyingly, on Ferenc himself, and he finally gave up trying to concentrate. Ferenc was not one to be micromanaged, even with a paycheck like this one—a characteristic that, along with his habit of looking uninvited into the work of other teams, had helped speed his departure from the Rover project. The reports he'd given Proctor—punctuated by frequent, urgent requests for supplies—had been vague. But he sensed that, with this man, such a tactic might backfire.

"It's annoying, being interrupted," Pendergast said. "But now that almost a week has passed, I'd like a summary of your progress in a rather less piecemeal form than I've been able to glean from Proctor."

"Right," Ferenc said, slapping the machine-tool dust from his knees.

"Although brevity and nontechnical explanations would be appreciated, I find myself curious about some of the items you've asked Proctor to obtain." He extracted a piece of paper from his pocket and unfolded it. "Gallium. Arsenic. Pure, unalloyed gold. A high-precision milling device. Collimation optics, vertically integrated diode laser bars configured for 1060-nanometer wavelengths. Several, ah, AixiZ modules...did I pronounce that properly?"

Ferenc nodded.

"And the item that gave Proctor the greatest difficulty: a nuclear adiabatic demagnetization refrigerator." Pendergast slipped the sheet back into his jacket. "Your shopping expenses now equal the size of your compensation." He lapsed into silence, gazing at Ferenc with those unsettling pale eyes.

"Look, when I began this project, I thought it would cost a lot more than that," Ferenc said. "Consider yourself lucky."

Pendergast gave a nod.

"But to be honest, I was afraid no amount of money could put the machine into working order. Frankly, I didn't even believe this machine could do what you claimed. But I've got to tell you, when I looked it over, and read the notebooks, and finally understood the physics behind it—I was blown away. This machine is...unbelievable." *And worth an absolute frigging fortune,* he didn't add.

"I'm glad to hear it." Pendergast paused. "One reason your fee is so large is because this technology must remain secret."

It was as if the damned man had read his mind. Ferenc nodded obsequiously.

"Naturally, you can imagine the consequences of unleashing this kind of power into a world that is corrupt, venal, brutal, and ignorant."

Ferenc nodded again, maintaining what he hoped was an agreeable smile. Once he realized the machine might actually work, he couldn't help but fantasize about its potential—who wouldn't? Working conditions at the mansion had been great, all his needs attended to. The only thing that bothered him was a feeling of being trapped. Of course, he had not *tried* to leave…but he had sensed it would not go well if he did. Far better to play along, agree enthusiastically with the need for secrecy, take his hefty paycheck, say his goodbyes…and only then consider how best to exploit his newfound knowledge.

And now a thought occurred: They wouldn't be planning to kill him, would they? Wait until he'd finished the job and then finish him off, bury him under the basement floor of this pile? But no, that was crazy. Eccentric though he was, Pendergast seemed to have a strong sense of honor. Besides, if they were going to do *that*, they wouldn't have paid him anything in advance.

He realized that Pendergast was looking at him expectantly.

"Of course," he said hastily. "It would be crazy to share this machine with the world until its potential was understood…for good or evil. In fact," he added, "now that I'm more confident it'll work, I'm sort of wondering how you plan to use the machine—and if that use will be, ah, responsible." He arched his eyebrows.

The look in Pendergast's eyes became so stony that Ferenc shifted nervously and gave a little laugh. "Of course, I have to ask, right? Because, you know, the power of this machine to wreak havoc in the world is almost limitless, as you yourself just now admitted. It would be remiss of me not to ask." Ferenc stopped himself as he began to babble.

Pendergast continued staring at him for a long time. Then his face slowly cleared and he said, mildly: "Continue, Dr. Ferenc, with your narrative."

Ferenc cleared his throat. "As I said, I was skeptical of success— ironically, because several of the components were so outmoded I wondered if they could be found. But as I examined the units more closely—and considered how they functioned as part of a greater whole—I realized many could be replaced and even improved."

Pendergast nodded for him to continue.

"Synthesizing what I learned from the notebooks with my own background in cosmology and string theory, I realized the device worked by breaking through the 'brane' of our universe into other such branes, infinitesimally close but normally unreachable, essentially by shaping magnetic fields into an intricate knot in which various world lines pass around one another to form braids in four-dimensional space-time. These braids make up a kind of topological computational space. You can envision it as a type of toroidal lattice. It's at the center of the lattice—around the hole of the donut, so to speak—where those world lines thread into parallel branes or universes."

He paused to gauge the effect of this. But there seemed to be no effect at all; Pendergast merely waited for him to continue.

"All the simulations I've run are encouraging. Now that I have everything I need, I can move on to assembly and testing. That, in particular—" and he pointed to the large wooden crate containing the recently delivered demagnetization refrigerator— "is crucial to the next phase. The main unit responsible for creating a lattice capable of bringing parallel universes into temporary alignment must be fashioned from special looped circuits of gallium arsenide, held at a temperature near absolute zero while being subjected to rapidly fluctuating magnetic fields."

"Gallium arsenide," Pendergast said.

"GaAs is the element gallium, doped with arsenic. That's why I needed a small furnace and ultraprecision machining device—along with the gold, of course, used in the processing. Now, the secondary 'braiding' unit will be devoted to generating the required magnetic fields. For this, I determined that an 11.3-microjoule main laser, coupled with a smaller laser capable of a 1.9-microjoule frequency-doubled pulse, could activate and deactivate an 8-Tesla field in approximately 50 femtoseconds, initiating the braiding process. A tertiary unit would trap the magnetic fields comprising this braid into a toroidal lattice, at whose center, as I said, will be the...doorway to the multiverse."

He paused to give these last words a little flourish and was rewarded by a small smile from Pendergast. "You make it sound so simple," the agent replied dryly.

"I've left out a lot of workaday stuff: the collimation optics, diode and lens assemblies, heat-sink and cooling systems. With the addition of a few exotic computer chips, I was able to salvage and retask much of the machine's control mechanism to keep the three primary units within safe operating parameters."

Pendergast slid off the soapstone table onto his feet. "So—the device can be made to work, correct?"

"Yes," Ferenc said after a brief hesitation. There were a few rather knotty problems still to be overcome, but he was proud of the progress he'd made and there was still plenty of time.

"And migraines have not been a problem?"

"Nope." The lights in the lab were kept rather low, and Ferenc was always careful to look away from the brilliant glow the device was already capable of generating.

"In that case," Pendergast said, "I congratulate you."

Ferenc demurred even beyond what he thought modesty required.

"And that's why I feel confident in requesting you to accelerate your timetable."

"Whoa. Did you say *accelerate* my timetable? Just because I gave you a simplistic overview of the project doesn't mean there aren't hundreds of steps still to be completed."

"No doubt."

"Mr. Pendergast—"

"I realize this is unexpected, Dr. Ferenc, but nevertheless I believe you underestimate your own abilities. No doubt this will mean a few late nights. But if you're able to complete the project in two weeks instead of three, I'm willing to double your compensation."

"But—" Ferenc fell silent as he did some mental juggling. What Pendergast said was more or less true: he'd assembled the greater part of the device in his head already. And one million dollars had a very nice sound to it.

"A million dollars," Ferenc said. "If the device is completed in two weeks?"

"That's correct."

"*Whether you succeed or fail*—Proctor made that promise the very first day. What if it's completed but doesn't work? I mean, even at this stage there are no guarantees."

"Dr. Ferenc, if you take unnecessary shortcuts, or intentionally build a bogus device simply to make my proposed deadline, I will not respond well."

"Please don't mention 'bogus devices' in the same breath as my name." Ferenc said this with true sincerity. He intended to succeed with this machine, and he hoped his strange employer could see that.

Pendergast, leaning against the soapstone table, looked back at him, arms crossed. "Fair enough. To clarify, the million dollars is yours if you act in sincere good faith and complete the machine in two weeks—*whatever* the outcome. However—" He paused.

"What?"

"We will naturally require your services for a period following the final testing. For an additional remuneration."

"Right. Of course."

Pendergast glanced at his watch. "Now, is there anything you need at present?"

"No, thank you." Ferenc hesitated. "Actually, could you ask Mrs. Trask to bring my meal down here? And would, ah, pepperoni pizza with extra cheese and a six-pack of Coke in a cooler of ice be possible? It's going to be a long night."

"I'm sure that can be managed." And with that, Pendergast turned on his heel and left the improvised laboratory, shutting the zinc door noiselessly behind him.

39

June 2
Friday

Agent Coldmoon entered the vast and echoing Roosevelt Rotunda, with its two giant dinosaur skeletons and screaming hordes of schoolchildren. For all its grandeur, he found the museum unsettling, even a little disturbing: he thought of his ancestors' most sacred belongings, maybe even their bones, stuffed into this temple to...what? Curiosity? Science? There was something about the very concept of a museum like this that offended him: stuff taken from its original owners and sealed up behind glass or locked in storage rooms. On the other hand, it was obviously educational—and he could see the point of preserving such things as that magnificent canoe, which otherwise would have probably been abandoned, burned by trappers or rotted away on some remote British Columbian shoreline.

He spied D'Agosta waiting for him near the information desk, and he made his way over. The homicide commander looked tired and a little put out. Coldmoon briefly wondered if all was right at home.

"Hey, Armstrong," D'Agosta said. "I've got us that appointment you asked for—Security in ten minutes."

"Great."

They walked over to the grand marble staircase and descended to the first floor. Coldmoon instinctively paused again to look at the canoe hanging from the ceiling.

"Impressive, right?" said D'Agosta, noticing his glance. "This place never ceases to amaze."

"I'll say."

They went into the security area. The head of security, Archer, was waiting for them. He didn't look much like a security director to Coldmoon: a small, restless man with a pencil mustache, wearing spit-and-polished pointy-toed shoes, a brown three-piece suit, and a rather flamboyant yellow tie. He led them through the main security lobby to a conference room in the back, with a worktable, whiteboards, and a flat-panel screen. A number of files and a thick visitors' log were arranged with severe precision on the table.

"It's all here, as you requested," said Archer in a high voice. "This is the visitor log to the anthropology area—" he placed his hands on the massive book— "and these files are the credentials presented by those who are allowed entry to the high-security vaults."

"High-security?" Coldmoon repeated.

"The vaults that contain the most valuable objects," Archer explained. "It's quite remarkable how much the value of these collections has escalated in recent years."

Coldmoon nodded.

"It works like this," Archer went on. "To access a vault, a visitor needs to present credentials and must be accompanied by a curator."

"These vaults—how are they accessed, exactly?"

"Via a key code, which each curator is given. Inside each vault is a CCTV camera that records the visit. All footage has been preserved and can be retrieved by date and time. Now—any questions?"

"Much obliged," said Coldmoon, shaking his head.

"Would you like me to stay, in case you need assistance?"

"Not necessary," said D'Agosta, staring at the rows of files.

The head of security left.

After a moment, D'Agosta sighed, crossed his arms over his chest, and said: "Shit on a stick. Maybe we should've sent in some lackeys to do this."

"You mean, so that it takes a week and then has to be redone anyway because someone screwed up?"

D'Agosta gave a knowing chuckle. "This is what I hate about police work—endless piles of paper."

"True," said Coldmoon. "But here's the thing: I'll bet you another pitcher of Harp the killer's name is in one of these files. Think about it: he's probably one of Mancow's professional colleagues or associates. Two people were murdered, in pretty ingenious ways, so that a sophisticated collector could get his hands on Sitting Bull's peace pipe. He's got to be someone who's a collector, maybe even a curator."

D'Agosta sat up. "Let's get to work."

Coldmoon pulled the visitors' log toward him, opened it, and began scanning the pages. The book was organized like a ledger, with the date, name of visitor, signature, institutional affiliation, and the time in and out. On the far right was a space for the initials of the sponsoring curator. Coldmoon quickly figured out which were Mancow's initials—an ECM, ending with a loop—and turned back to page 1. The log started with January 1 of that year and went on from there. He laid his tablet on the table and began copying the entries next to every ECM. After a minute, he stopped.

"Why don't I read off the names and institutions as I write them down," he said, "while you look up their credentials in the files?"

"Good idea," said D'Agosta, without enthusiasm.

The work went more quickly. The files were well organized, and there were not that many ECM entries. In less than an hour, they had compiled a list from January 1 to the date Mancow was murdered. Coldmoon counted up the entries—twenty-six.

"Now we verify their institutional affiliations," he said. "We can start by googling each institution and then searching the website for the name—to make sure they're employed there. If there's no hit, we follow up with a call. That should help us identify anyone who put down a fake name or institution."

"What if they borrowed a real name and institution?" D'Agosta asked.

"If this doesn't work, that's the next step."

D'Agosta nodded. "Good thinking. I'll start at the bottom of the list, you at the top. We'll each take thirteen."

Coldmoon went to work. The first name on the list—which would have been the last person Mancow admitted to the collections before he was murdered—was a Grigory Popescu, professor of anthropology at Babeş-Bolyai University in Romania.

He went to the university website, searched, and the name popped up. Check.

The next visitor's name was Prof. Hans Nachtnebel, professor of anthropology at Heidelberg University. Again it checked out.

The third was a Professor George Smith, University of Central Florida, Sociology Department. Coldmoon searched and it, too, checked out: George Smith, PhD, Adjunct Professor, Department of Social Studies.

Coldmoon was about to go on, but then he hesitated. *George Smith.* The name was just a little too common. A real George Smith would at least use a middle initial—wouldn't he? To distinguish himself from all the others.

He looked over the website of Central Florida University. It billed itself as one of the largest universities in the country, with over sixty thousand students and twelve thousand faculty. An ungoogleable name buried inside a giant university: Coldmoon didn't like it.

In the file, there was a number for George Smith. He called it.

A clipped voice answered. "Social Studies."

"May I speak with Professor Smith?"

"We have several." *Of course*, thought Coldmoon, suspicions further aroused.

"George Smith."

A long pause. "He's adjunct. You can't reach him on the departmental line."

"Could you give me his contact information?"

"We're not allowed to do that."

"Excuse me for not identifying myself," Coldmoon said. "I'm

Special Agent Coldmoon of the Federal Bureau of Investigation, and I'm calling on official business. I really hope I can count on your cooperation, Ms.—?"

A silence. "I'm sorry, but I don't know you from Adam. You'll have to make your request in writing, on official letterhead."

"Your name, please?"

"Phyllis."

"Phyllis what?"

"I'm not going to give you my last name. I don't know if you're really FBI. Like I said, put it in writing. We're very busy here." She hung up.

Coldmoon sat there, fuming. He glanced up and saw D'Agosta looking at him appraisingly.

"George Smith," Coldmoon said. "What do you think of that name?"

"Sounds like bullshit to me." D'Agosta pulled over the file containing Smith's credentials, research interests, and reason for visit, and flipped it open. "Let's see... Mancow took this Smith to view the Hunkpapa collection in one of the vaults." He looked up. "Who's Hunkpapa when he's at home?"

"Hunkpapa," said Coldmoon, "was Sitting Bull's tribe."

"Oh, yeah? Let's get Archer back here." D'Agosta left and returned a few minutes later with Archer in tow.

"What can I do for you?" Archer asked, smiling nervously. He looked more like a maître d' than a security chief.

"You have a camera in the Hunkpapa vault?" D'Agosta asked.

"Hunkpapa?"

"Lakota Sioux," said Coldmoon.

"Oh, yes. Those are valuable collections."

Coldmoon looked at the visitors' log. "We'd like to see footage from the camera in that vault for April sixteenth, between noon and two PM."

"No problem. I'll have it for you in twenty minutes."

Twenty minutes? Coldmoon was impressed.

"We've got a brand-new digital CCTV system here," said Archer proudly, noticing Coldmoon's expression, "with a searchable database and a full petabyte of storage. You just plug in date, time, location, duration—and bingo, the footage is retrieved."

"Very good," said Coldmoon. "Thank you."

Archer bustled out with a little more self-importance than he'd shown on the way in. Coldmoon and D'Agosta continued down the list of names, but none stood out the way George Smith had. Twenty minutes passed, then thirty, then forty. Finally Archer came back in, an expression of chagrin on his face.

"I can't understand it," he said, "but that footage seems to have disappeared."

Coldmoon felt a sudden prickle on the back of his neck. "How?"

"I don't know. The system is highly secure, air-gapped with automatic backups. A malfunction, it seems."

It seems, thought Coldmoon. "I'd like to see that vault."

Archer seemed a little taken aback. "You mean, visit it? When?"

Coldmoon glanced at D'Agosta, then back at Archer. "Now."

Archer looked flummoxed. "Sorry, I can't do that. Because the vault is within the Secure Area, any visits require the permission of the Anthro department head."

"And who would that be?"

"Dr. Britley."

Coldmoon looked at D'Agosta. "Has he been interviewed yet?"

"He's on the list, but he's been evasive."

"Let's go kill two birds with one stone."

40

December 12, 1880
Wednesday

So—can we count on the pleasure of your company, then, Your Grace?"

Mrs. Cabot-Flint sat on the edge of her chair—or as much as her girth permitted while retaining the necessary dignity—both chins quivering ever so slightly in anticipation of the reply.

Constance inclined her head. "You are most kind. I have no fixed engagements on that evening. I should be delighted."

The lady of the mansion clasped her hands together, bejeweled fingers creating a coruscation of parti-colored light. "Excellent! Excellent!" She relaxed in her chair. "Now, may I ask Henrietta to pour you another cup of tea?"

"Please." The Duchess of Ironclaw took a final, fastidious sip from her cup, then replaced it in its china saucer.

As she watched the maid rush over to refill the cup, Constance thought with private amusement what a change the last few days had wrought. She had stuffed poor Murphy into a splendid coachman's livery and directed him to nearly crash into the older woman's carriage with her own on Fifth Avenue. It was perhaps a rather crude way of making someone's acquaintance, but she felt sure that, once the matron realized that Constance was the mysterious new noblewoman everyone in town was suddenly speculating about, she would be putty in her hands. And she was. First came the exchange of cards, followed by notes, and then by an invitation for morning tea at Mrs. Cabot-Flint's Brobdingnagian and philistinish *donjon* a few blocks north along the avenue.

"I'm *so* relieved," Constance's hostess replied. "I mean, you're so obviously a woman of taste despite your tender years, and also...not that I mean to inquire...but I understand New York is your second home, and your title is of European origin?"

What a transparent, ridiculous woman. Of course she meant to inquire. And where would a noble title come from, if not Europe? Perhaps she was thought to be the Duchess of Pittsburgh? But Constance, keeping these thoughts to herself, merely inclined her head with the proper amount of gravitas.

Another sparkly clasping of hands. "It's like a gift from heaven! You saw, Your Grace, our ballroom: one of the largest on the avenue, and perfect for my ball the Saturday after next."

"A most delightful and impressive space." It *was* rather impressive; Lincoln Center would be envious of the sheer cubic footage. Delightful, however, it was not. Like the rest of the mansion, the ballroom was decorated in a mélange of styles, accreted to impress with bulk and cost rather than taste.

Before accepting the tea invitation, Constance had done some research on Carlotta Cabot-Flint and her husband, the industrialist Vandermere Flint. Flint, whom she had yet to meet, was a robber baron of the most villainous sort: he'd amassed his fortune over the past two decades from a series of foundries strung across western Pennsylvania, after shrewdly acquiring an American monopoly on a new crucible process, developed in England, for casting steel in a more mechanized manner. This had led to layoffs and attempted strikes, and he'd put down the labor unrest swiftly and brutally. Flint's origins were obscure, and Constance suspected his father had been a coal miner himself. In any case, the couple were now ensconced on Fifth Avenue, social climbers of the worst sort and intent on drowning any taint of nouveaux riches in floods of money.

"Well, it occurs to me that—if you'd favor me with your thoughts on the matter, I mean—you're in a position to do me a great favor." And once again the woman leaned forward dangerously in her chair.

"How can I be of service?" Constance asked, declining the tea cake offered her by Henrietta with a polite wave of her hand.

"It's..." Cabot-Flint hesitated. "Last month, you know, Caroline held that grand ball—it was at the very start of the season, before you arrived."

Constance nodded. "Caroline" could only be Mrs. Caroline Astor, empress of "the Four Hundred"—the cream of New York society and, reportedly, the number of guests the Astor ballroom could comfortably house.

"I don't know where she got the idea—it couldn't *possibly* have been her own, it was far too clever—but it was a themed ball, based on those stories of the Grimm Brothers and that Offenbach opera. Surely you know the one I'm referring to? It's not premiering until next year, but it's already certain to be *the* concert entertainment of 1881."

Constance understood the reference. *"The Tales of Hoffmann,"* she said. "I'd heard rumors that Monsieur Jacques had begun work on Hoffmann once again."

At the words "Monsieur Jacques," Mrs. Cabot-Flint's eyes widened. "Could it be that you've met the composer?"

"He was a guest at the castle of my parents. It was during the aftermath of the Franco-Prussian War. I was very young, but *Les contes d'Hoffmann* was on his mind even then." She paused. "It was my favorite book of fantastic tales as a child."

"Better and better!" Mrs. Cabot-Flint said exultantly. "You see, my dear—may I take that liberty?—my greatest wish is to hold a ball similar to the one which opened the season, but more...ambitious. Ever since that ball, it seems things *outré* and *macabre* have become the mode this year. I've already called for people to be masked or in costume, but that in itself is *assez de*. Surely you know what I mean?"

"I certainly do," Constance said. Despite the execrable French, the elderly lady's wishes were clear: she wanted to outdo Mrs. Astor, beat her at her own game.

"I've chosen a theme: 'The Red Ball.' You know, after the story by that 'Raven' fellow, what was his name...Poe. I paged through a book of his stories—oh, my dear, my *dear!*—and was lucky enough to find one that, in fact, described a ball. He only mentioned masks, but I wanted to encourage costumes as well."

Constance pressed the woman's hands. "What a fabulous idea! Not only is it au courant, but it builds very cleverly on the novelty of Mrs. Astor's party."

"Thank you *so* much. But the fact is...well, we have no secrets from each other, so I can confide in you that I find myself rather short on...particulars, shall we say, to make the evening unique. I wondered if you might perhaps have some thoughts on the matter?"

This was exactly where Constance hoped she was heading. "So many balls fail in the line of decorations. You cannot just hang draperies on the walls: if you wish to make the event truly memorable, the decorations must be intrinsic to the theme. And your theme is the Red Ball: the vanity of human hopes, the Gothic obsession with ruins and death—borrowed tastefully, of course, from the classics." She paused. "Forgive me if I am taking liberties here; after all, it is your soirée."

"Not in the least, not in the least!"

"Most kind. In that case, we must look beyond superficial touches. I would be happy to lend you some of the surviving articles from my own collection, just recently arrived from Transylvania and currently in storage, to help set the mood. I can have my workmen bring them over."

"You are too kind, Your Grace, too kind...oh, what is it?"

Constance had released the woman's hands and sunk back into her chair, her expression suddenly thoughtful. "It's only that..."

"Do go on."

"Were I to host such an event, I would—and I can't take credit for this idea; it is common in European society—wish to add as many *realistic* effects as possible."

"Exactly to my mind, as well." If the European nobility were doing something, Mrs. Cabot-Flint was only too eager to ape it.

Constance remained silent for another moment. "I find myself hesitant to make recommendations of this sort, because in my limited observations I've found American society to be—how can I say this?—rather conservative in entertainment. But if such a masked ball was to be put on in my country, we would strive for realism. We would, for example, quietly invite persons who could lend a certain *vérité* to the evening."

The elder woman leaned forward, not understanding.

"For example, if we were to hold a masked ball celebrating a military victory such as Waterloo, my family would invite—without telling the other guests—several generals and even a few members of the regular army."

"Why, that's a *capital* idea!" Mrs. Cabot-Flint said. Then she stopped short. "But how would that work with my Red Ball? I can't very well invite murderers, grave robbers, or ghouls." She laughed at her witticism.

"Certainly not!" Constance concealed a brief titter with her fan. "The idea is to amuse, not terrify. In this case, I might suggest—in lieu of the murderers and grave robbers you mention—respectable people whose work perhaps brings them in contact with such creatures, and whose conversation at the ball would thus add a certain *frisson* for the listeners."

"I see!" Mrs. Cabot-Flint's eyes were shining. "There is a judge of my acquaintance who is known for his zeal in prosecuting offenders."

"A 'hanging judge'—excellent. How about . . . ?"

Mrs. Cabot-Flint remained leaning forward expectantly.

"Doctors."

"Specialists, you mean?" asked Mrs. Cabot-Flint.

"Surgeons, in particular. Men of science who are involved with blood."

The hostess stared at Constance. "Is that a step too far?"

"That depends on how memorable, and successful, you wish your entertainment to be." Constance waited.

"One person springs to mind . . . Dr. Featherstone. He's made a fortune treating women's complaints, I believe, but is also known to be a chirurgeon and a specialist in cadavers." Mrs. Cabot-Flint shuddered in delicious horror. "He still supervises dissections for medical students and all that sort of thing."

"Excellent," said Constance. "I'd advise placing him on your private list. But there's another medical specialty you might consider. Psychiatry."

"Psychiatry?" The woman's face wrinkled with puzzlement.

"Mental alienation."

"Ah, yes. I've heard of that. But I don't know anyone who practices it."

"But I do."

"Please tell."

"He's highly esteemed and of good character. Not only is he a skilled surgeon, but he also treats waifs and orphans at the Five Points Mission and the House of Industry *pro bono publico*. I understand he comes from an ancient and distinguished family of the Deep South. He's become well known in Heidelberg for curing madness with surgery." And here she gave Mrs. Cabot-Flint a knowing look guaranteed to provoke another small fit of delicious shuddering.

"Do tell me his name. Oh, *do*." She clasped her hands together.

"Dr. Enoch Leng."

41

Since the door was already partway open, Coldmoon didn't bother to knock. He entered Britley's office unannounced, D'Agosta and Archer following. They found the chairman of the Anthropology Department at his desk, a strikingly elegant man in a beautiful suit, one leg thrown over the other, dictating something to a very attractive woman who was transcribing in shorthand on an old-fashioned steno pad. It was a scene, Coldmoon thought, straight out of the sixties. All that was missing was the beehive hairdo.

Britley eyed them coldly. "What's all this, then?" he asked in an upper-class English drawl.

"So sorry to interrupt," said Archer, "but these gentlemen—"

Coldmoon removed his FBI wallet and let it fall open to display his shield. "Special Agent Coldmoon, and Lieutenant Commander D'Agosta, Borough Homicide. We're investigating the Mancow murder."

"I see," said Britley. He turned to the secretary. "That's all for now, Tenny."

"Yes, Dr. Britley." She gathered up her steno pad, pencil, and portfolio and left.

"They're here to ask you some questions," said Archer.

"Mr. Archer," said Britley, "thank you for bringing these chaps in. I don't think you are needed anymore—I'll take it from here."

As Archer left, Coldmoon said: "We won't take up too much of your time."

Britley looked at them, leaning back his head. "I'm so sorry, gentlemen, but now's not convenient." He rose. "You can make an appointment with my secretary on your way out. Next week should have an opening or two."

"I'm very sorry, Dr. Britley," said Coldmoon, "but we need your time right now."

"Is this in the way of a voluntary interview?"

"Yes."

"Well then, my answer is that I decline to volunteer at the present moment."

"Do you really prefer that we obtain a warrant?" asked Coldmoon.

"That's what will be required to interrupt my busy schedule."

"The interview will be at Federal Plaza."

"You mean, you're going to 'take me downtown'? Ah, that wonderful old B-movie line. Fine: if you can get a warrant, which I doubt, I shall gladly meet you downtown. Now, however, I'm late for an appointment." Britley grabbed his coat and threw it over his arm. "Excuse me, please, gentlemen?"

He began to walk between them, but D'Agosta blocked the exit to the office.

"You, sir, are in my way."

"Who the hell do you think you are, asshole, disrespecting an FBI agent and a lieutenant commander of the NYPD?"

At this outburst, Britley looked at D'Agosta in surprise.

"We're trying to solve a homicide," D'Agosta went on, "in which one of your own people was locked in a freezer and left to die a slow, painful, terrifying death. Can you imagine what the man went through? Right here, in *your* museum. And here you are, Sir Chauncey Dirtbag, on your high horse telling us you're too busy to answer questions? Well, fuck that."

Britley, recovering from his shock, drew himself up in outrage. "I will not tolerate such abusive language from an officer of the law. I feel positively assaulted by it. In fact, this warrants a complaint. You said my cooperation was voluntary."

"Yeah, the interview is totally voluntary." D'Agosta smiled and leaned forward, lowering his voice. "And if you don't *voluntarily fucking cooperate* with us right here, right now, I'll call my pal at the *New York Post,* and tomorrow morning you'll be reading a front-page article about a certain limp-dicked museum department head's inexplicable refusal to cooperate with the FBI and the NYPD in one of the biggest murder cases of the year. The article will pose the question: *what is Dr. Britley hiding?* Oh, yeah, and we'll also make sure Cartwright's name is in there, and maybe those of a couple museum board members most allergic to publicity. And *then* I'll get that warrant and drag your ass downtown—once I've arranged to perp-walk you nice and slow past the entire shouting, screaming, photographing, microphone-waving, videotaping New York press corps."

"I will not be threatened. I'm going to file that complaint immediately," said Britley, but his voice was faltering.

"Oh, yeah! Great! File that complaint! Bring the NYPD *and* the FBI shit-rain down on the museum! I'd guess from that tight-assed accent of yours you haven't been in New York City long enough to know we're *animals* here. We *live* to ream out shitbags like you. We're gonna chew your ass right down to the bone . . . and howl for more. As for threats—." He turned. "Did you hear any threats, Agent Coldmoon?"

Coldmoon could hardly believe D'Agosta's eruption. He gathered his wits enough to shake his head. "All I heard was a polite request for voluntary cooperation."

"Exactly. So whose word is the judge and jury going to believe: that of Dr. Snidely Suckwad, or FBI Special Agent Armstrong Coldmoon and NYPD Lieutenant Commander Vincent D'Agosta?"

Britley stared at D'Agosta, face pale, a thin sheen of sweat on his brow.

D'Agosta removed his cell phone and suddenly changed his tone to one of quiet respect. "Dr. Britley, thank you so much for your offer of cooperation. Mind if I record?"

Britley, after a moment's hesitation, eased himself down in his office chair, his shaking hands gripping the armrests. He nodded.

D'Agosta held the phone forward, quickly activating the microphone. "Please speak your answers aloud and clearly, Dr. Britley."

It was a singularly dull interview, with Britley volunteering no more than minimal information. He described Mancow's research interests, which focused on Lakota culture. He tediously reviewed the dead curator's CV and other background—University of Chicago PhD, Harvard postdoc, museum curator, and adjunct at Columbia. Mancow was, Britley went on, as distinguished as any curator in the field. He had no enemies, was highly respected among his associates, had published numerous papers in peer-reviewed journals, had excellent relations with the Lakota people and Sioux tribal government, and maintained a strong rapport with a network of colleagues across the world. Britley was of the opinion that Mancow had been accidentally locked inside the freezer. What he was doing there in the first place, he had no idea.

Coldmoon asked, "What was Mancow like as a person?"

"Warm. Sincere. Helpful to his peers. A man of integrity."

"Do you know of a colleague of Mancow's by the name of George Smith, of Central Florida University?"

"I can't say I do."

"He visited Dr. Mancow on April 16, and they looked at the Hunkpapa collections in the Secure Area."

"Dr. Mancow did not introduce Professor Smith to me."

"So you don't know the purpose of the visit or what they wanted to see? You didn't meet a visiting colleague of Mancow's on that date: April 16?"

"No to both questions."

"It seems the security footage from that visit is missing. Would you know anything about that?"

"No."

"And Central Florida University, does it have a reputable anthro department?"

"I doubt it has an anthropology department of any note at all."

Coldmoon paused. "May I ask, Dr. Britley, why you were reluctant to speak to us? I would think you'd want to see the killer of your colleague caught."

Britley looked at him for a moment, and Coldmoon sensed a flash of emotion hidden behind that austere face: a deep and enduring detestation of his colleague. "I am of course most anxious to help. It's just that I'm very busy, nothing more. Now...is there anything else?"

"Just one more thing," said Coldmoon. "We'd like to visit the vault containing the Hunkpapa material. We're told you need to authorize it."

"When?"

"Right now."

Britley's face tightened but he didn't protest. He picked up the phone, pressed a button, spoke into it, then hung up. A moment later, a timid knock came at the door. It opened to reveal a young man. "Yes, Dr. Britley?"

"Block," the department head said, "escort these two law officers to the Secure Area. Allow them access to whatever they wish to see."

42

"Do you really have a friend at the *Post* who'll print an article like that?" Coldmoon asked quietly as they followed Block, an assistant curator, down the long corridor.

D'Agosta chuckled. "No. Not anymore, at least."

"You really tore that guy a new one. Maybe I should send him some Depends."

"I'm so fed up with arrogant bastards like that," D'Agosta said. "I've been dealing with them for fifteen years. I guess I lost it—sorry if I shocked you."

"Shocked? I was awed."

The assistant curator was a skinny, earnest kid with a ponytail. They arrived at a large stainless-steel door of the sort found on a bank vault. Block punched in a keypad code, placed his hand on a fingerprint reader, then stepped aside.

"Gentlemen," he said, "please place your right hands on the screen and press lightly until the LED turns green."

Coldmoon went first. "Does this machine keep a record of the fingerprints it registers?"

"I've no idea. You'll have to check with Security."

"Seems like an obvious function to me," murmured D'Agosta.

"Funny no one mentioned it," Coldmoon replied.

The massive door opened and they passed into a stark white

hallway smelling of chemicals and disinfectants. Numbered stainless-steel doors lined each side. It was as silent as a tomb, save for the hush of curated and filtered air.

They followed Block to one of the steel doors, which he unlocked with another code, and they stepped inside a small room, with compact storage in uniform shelving. Block consulted a chart, punched in a setting, turned a crank, and the shelves rolled apart, allowing access to a narrow alleyway between storage cabinets and shelving. They walked down it to a set of flat drawers.

"These three," said Block, pointing to the drawers, "contain the most valuable material from the Hunkpapa band of the Teton Sioux."

"May we take a look?"

"Please put these on." He handed them white cotton gloves and face masks, put on his own set, and they followed his example. Then he pulled out the first drawer and opened the lid, exposing some items of clothing laid flat, covered with a loose sheet of acid-free paper. He drew the paper back. "Ghost Dance shirts," he explained.

Ghost Dance. That was in the final days when Coldmoon's ancestors thought that, by wearing those shirts and dancing and singing, bullets could not harm them, all the white people would sink into the earth and the grass would roll over them, the bison would come back, and their lands would be restored. Everything would return to the way it had been, and the People would be happy again. That crazy and desperate hope ended with the Wounded Knee massacre.

Coldmoon stared at the buckskin shirts laid out in the drawer, painted with Ghost Dance symbols of ravens and magpies flying against a midnight-blue night sky emblazoned with yellow stars. The ever-so-faint smell of woodsmoke and prairie dust rose from them.

"Are they valuable?" asked D'Agosta.

"Oh, yeah. That's why they're in here." After a moment he slid the drawer shut.

"Let's see another." As Block stood back, Coldmoon opened the second drawer and pulled back the paper to expose a row of silver medals.

"What are those?" D'Agosta asked.

"Peace medals," Coldmoon said. "They were given to Native American leaders by the U.S. government."

"These belonged to famous Teton Sioux leaders—Sitting Bull, Gall, Moving Robe Woman, Bear's Rib," Block told them. He picked one up. "Sitting Bull actually scratched his name glyph on his. The medals were treasured by the recipients, who often wore them into battle."

Coldmoon had a cynical thought about that, which he decided not to express. "May I hold it?"

Block handed it to him. The medal, with a hole punched through the rim, was strung on an intricately braided leather thong decorated with beads and eagle feathers. It was well worn, the rim dented. Looking closer, Coldmoon could see the image of a sitting bison scratched into the silver underneath a portrait of Grover Cleveland and the date: 1885.

"He was wearing it," Block said, "on the day he was murdered."

Coldmoon squinted at it. Could this, too, be a fake—like the pipe? But a struck medal would be harder to fake than a hand-carved peace pipe.

Moving on, Block said: "This final drawer is special. It contains Sitting Bull's ceremonial shirt, moccasins, parfleche, and headdress. He gave these to Major Walls during a peace parlay to show his good intentions after the major complimented him on his dress." He hesitated. "Kind of a shame they're locked up in the dark like this."

"I agree," said Coldmoon. "Kind of a shame."

"The goodwill gifts didn't stop the soldiers from shooting him down in cold blood, of course," Block added dryly.

Coldmoon was starting to like this assistant curator.

Block slid open the deep drawer and edged aside the covering sheet of paper to reveal the items. They were indeed magnificent: the shirt, made of buckskin with a collar of bear claws, was decorated with incredibly intricate, brilliantly dyed quillwork. The headdress was not the big, elaborate kind that hung down the back, but a simple and dignified crown of eagle feathers set into a beaded headband, trimmed with dangling ermine tails.

As Coldmoon stared, he had to wonder again: were any of these possibly copies like the pipe, substituted for the real thing? Such a swap would be unlikely to be discovered, at least for many years, given that the collection was locked away and rarely viewed. He thought of the gorgeous quilled shirt Running had been wearing, made by Twoeagle. That murdered artist was certainly capable of making a copy of Sitting Bull's shirt. But had he?

"Mr. Block," he said, "if I wanted to verify these artifacts were genuine, how would I go about doing that?"

"What do you mean?" Block asked. "You think they might be fake? I hardly think that's possible. They were scrupulously collected and curated."

"What I mean is, the original articles might have *recently* been taken and reproductions left in their place. How would you determine that?"

Block thought for a moment. "In the accession file, there usually is a photograph of the object taken when the museum received it. In the old days, those pictures would be from glass-plate negatives taken with a large view camera—extremely sharp and detailed. I think a visual comparison between the accession photo and the item would reveal if it was real or not. You can't really duplicate something like that detailed quillwork, or the eagle feathers in that headdress—there would be subtle differences."

"Could you make that comparison?"

"Um, when?"

"Now."

Block hesitated. "I'd have to get permission from Dr. Britley."

Coldmoon looked at him steadily for a moment. Then he tapped the pocket containing his FBI ID. "I'm going to ask you to do this *without* informing Dr. Britley or anyone else. If there's blowback, I'll have you covered: I'll tell them I expressly ordered you to do this and you were naturally required to cooperate with the FBI."

Block stared, and then after a moment nodded slowly. "But...why do you think these might be counterfeit?"

Coldmoon thought for a moment, wondering if he should take Block into his confidence. The young man seemed intelligent, as well as sympathetic and trustworthy. "We think Dr. Mancow might have been secretly working for a private collector, perhaps someone interested in getting his hands on Sitting Bull's artifacts. They were working in league to steal items from museums by substituting clever fakes. We think that may be the reason Mancow was murdered." He took out his card and gave it to Block. "My private cell phone. Call me as soon as you've done the comparison."

"Jesus," said Block. "That's brazen. Of course I'll help you."

"Thank you."

On their way out of the museum, Coldmoon checked with Martin Archer in Security and discovered that they did indeed keep a record of all the fingerprint data. When asked why he hadn't mentioned that earlier, Archer insisted he'd simply forgotten.

Coldmoon mentally filed that excuse under a simple heading: *Bullshit.*

43

Dr. Ferenc walked through the vaulted reception hall, its display cases packed with bones, gemstones, meteorites, and stuffed animals. It was without a doubt the strangest house he'd ever been in, occupying a big juicy lot right on Riverside Drive overlooking the Hudson—one of the last of the great old mansions along the drive, and no doubt worth a bloody fortune.

He turned toward the library and paused at the open door. Although much of the vast mansion was off-limits to him, he had free access to the guest wing, and there were other rooms in which he was welcome—perhaps *tolerated* was a better word—including this one.

The library was a fine room, paneled in dark wood, whose shelves were full of old books bound in calf grain or buckram and stamped in gold—rare volumes in languages both alive and dead, embracing literature, mathematics, philosophy, astrology, and more exotic disciplines. There was often a low fire flickering in the hearth, and the air carried the pleasant scent of leather, smoke, and furniture polish. With a harpsichord in one corner and old-master paintings here and there among the books, the entire room hearkened back to a long-vanished era. Ferenc wished he could have a library of his own like this someday. With a million dollars, maybe he could.

He stepped through the door. Pendergast was not in his usual seat before the fire, and—conscious of a freedom conferred on him by the man's absence—Ferenc walked over to examine more closely the curious objets d'art displayed within a small glass-fronted shadow box. The whole house was like a museum.

"Dr. Ferenc," came the cultured voice from behind him. "I hope this evening finds you well."

It was all Ferenc could do not to whirl around in surprise. He turned, suppressing an unreasonable feeling of guilt. Pendergast had apparently been standing near the harpsichord, but Ferenc could have sworn that corner of the library—the entire room, for that matter— had been empty when he entered.

"I'm fine," he said. "And I've come with good news."

"I'm all ears."

"The machine is complete," he said, proudly.

Pendergast did not show any outward emotion except for a sudden stillness, accompanied by—Ferenc thought in the firelight—a faint contraction of his pupils. "Does it work?"

"Well, I believe so. It has to be, ah, field-tested, of course."

"Of course."

"I just want to point out that I made the deadline. I mean, for the extra half million."

Pendergast inclined his head.

"But there's something I need to explain," Ferenc said, taking a breath. "It's not a problem, really, so much as a . . . warning label."

Pendergast remained still.

"I don't believe the risk of operating this machine can ever be fully mitigated."

"And why is that?"

"Well, you know it takes two people to run the restored machine. I've trained Proctor on how to assist me. But it's a really complex device. Proctor and I have tested it as far as we can. If it works at all, it might work perfectly a hundred times. Or it might malfunction on the second try. It's quite possible that the more times it's used, the greater the chance of something going wrong, a failure that might . . ." He stopped.

"Might strand the user in a parallel universe?"

"Exactly."

"Permanently?"

"Yes. If the machine fails while someone is away, well, there are so many parallel universes, constantly shifting in space-time, that it might not be possible to find the right one again."

For a moment, Pendergast's face remained unreadable. Then he nodded. "Congratulations. And thank you. Caveat duly noted."

"Would you like to see it? The workroom is in rather a mess still, but I can go over the operational principles with you, show you the main differences from the original device. And we can discuss how to complete the 'shake and bake' process, as we called it during the Rover assembly."

"I will meet you in the lab in half an hour."

"Half an hour?" Ferenc was surprised. He'd assumed Pendergast would be in a hurry to see it immediately.

"Yes. I want to take care of a few matters. The half million will be given to you in cash by Proctor, once you have operated the machine." He raised a hand, anticipating Ferenc's objection. "Whether or not it functions properly—as we agreed. And you will receive another quarter million once you've finished, ah, tending it for a certain period to come."

And, with a brief motion of his hand, he indicated the library exit.

44

Fᴇʀᴇɴᴄ sᴘᴇɴᴛ ᴛʜᴇ ɴᴇxᴛ fifteen minutes getting the laboratory into some kind of order, dismantling the temporary scaffolding, then running down a long, written checklist, ticking off each element of the device and all the settings and sequences required to open the portal to another universe.

He was more or less an atheist—"more or less" because he preferred studying the *how* versus the *why*. He'd worked on projects involving everything from nuclear weapons to the exploration of the planets. But somehow, this device was different. Nonbeliever though he was, he nevertheless felt that he had some unspoken agreement with Creation that there were certain boundaries beyond which science should not go...and by resurrecting this device, he was testing that agreement.

Reading and rereading the old notebooks and folders, watching Proctor's video frame by frame, he'd learned some of the history of the machine and how its earlier incarnations worked. The machine was no longer meant to *glimpse* a few minutes or more into the future; instead, in its final form it had *sent* a person into the past—to a very specific date and place: November 27, 1880, Longacre Square, New York City. To achieve this, the machine had to safely drill through several other parallel universes, including the one that had caused such mayhem in Savannah.

That had caused such mayhem. Maybe that was what gave him the funny feeling in the pit of his stomach. The many-worlds theory had been proposed almost three-quarters of a century earlier and was now a cornerstone of quantum mechanics. Still, it was one thing to study such theories, or poke at their outer fringes with supercolliders or near-absolute-zero magnetic fields and superconductivity—it was quite another to actually vault somebody into a place straight out of *The Twilight Zone.* He knew he could be curious, even too curious, about projects he'd been assigned to in the past...but nevertheless he'd always known the *reason* they were necessary.

Pendergast was already rich, and he wouldn't need to go to a specific time and place to make a financial killing of some kind. And he was no fool: he was clearly aware of the dangers involved. But just a few minutes ago, he'd brushed aside Ferenc's mention of those dangers. Whatever the motivation, it was of supreme importance to the man.

Putting aside for the moment toying with the universe in this fashion, it was the secrecy Pendergast insisted upon that annoyed him. Pendergast refused to discuss anything about his plans. Ferenc felt certain the subject was discussed in detail with Proctor when the two were alone, but his own questions along these lines had been met with near hostility: *Your business is to get this machine operational again. My business involves the question of why. No curiosity or inquiries in that direction will be entertained.*

Although he had no proof, he sensed the final use of the original machine—an act which caused its destruction—had not been authorized, or perhaps even anticipated, by Pendergast.

The door opened and Proctor stepped in, interrupting his thoughts. He carried a shabby briefcase, which he placed in a corner, then shut the door and glanced around wordlessly. Ferenc had worked with the man night and day for the past two weeks, and while it was true he'd been a godsend, the guy nevertheless oozed distrust and suppressed violence. But Proctor knew Ferenc had poured his heart and soul into the machine. No one could doubt that. The finished apparatus was more complex and refined than its predecessor, because it now had to connect to a specific universe at a specific place in time. This complexity meant two operators rather than one. The delicacy of calibration required, and the constant monitoring of the super-cold temperatures of the main assembly to ensure everything remained within a tight range, kept Proctor fully occupied—while at the same time Ferenc was busy guiding the lasers in the secondary assembly to initiate and maintain the braiding process and regulate the magnetic flux whose lattice formed the portal...

The door opened once again and Pendergast came in. Ferenc was surprised to see his employer not dressed in his usual black suit. Instead he was wearing a tailored jacket of brown twill, with lapels so narrow the necktie at his throat was scarcely visible. The jacket was cut away below, allowing a vest of the same material and a gold watch chain to be visible. The trousers were equally narrow, tapered, and patterned with a stripe. He wore a bowler hat and held a large bag, similar to a Gladstone, over which a heavy broadcloth overcoat had been draped. In short, he looked like a man who had just stepped out of the nineteenth century—or, Ferenc thought, was about to step back into it. He realized with a chill that the man was going to "test" the machine right here, right now—on himself.

Pendergast's silvery eyes took in the machine. The menacing, Frankenstein-like electrodes of polished steel and copper that made up the business end of the original device had been replaced by next-generation lasers and optics. It was not the same machine that had been destroyed: it was better. But not infallible.

Now Pendergast turned his eyes toward Ferenc. "Ready when you are, Dr. Ferenc."

"I thought we were going to test it first? Best practices: shake and bake, remember?"

"No time."

"Surely we should at least try it on, say, a mouse, or a Pomeranian?"

"No."

He stared. The man certainly had cojones. Ferenc turned to Proctor. "Um, are you ready?"

Instead of replying, Proctor took his position at the console on the far side of the machine.

"Jesus, Mr. Pendergast, I really don't think this is a good idea."

The resulting stare unnerved him. "You *do* believe the machine will work?"

"Yes, of course. But you know, as I implied earlier, it's a bit like Russian roulette."

"And I *will* be able to return to this universe—this place, and this time—by retreating to the precise spot where I entered that parallel universe?"

"Yes. It worked for the old machine, and I've got the coordinates dialed in. Just remember: the *precise* spot. And—" he tried to chuckle— "let's hope some hapless passerby doesn't loiter over the same place."

Pendergast's eyebrows rose. "Is that a possibility?"

"We've used the new machine to look into the parallel universe at the date and location last used by the old device, and we've synced the timeline accordingly. It's a foul cul-de-sac off Longacre Square, and it seems more or less deserted. If you want to come back you have to be in the exact spot and remain there for at least ten, fifteen seconds. So is it a possibility? Yes—but admittedly remote. One thing to remember, however: time passes along the same continuum. If you're gone a day there, a day will pass here."

A curt nod. And then, in a sudden, odd gesture of affection, Pendergast strode over to Proctor and extended his hand. The man took it and they shook gravely.

"Carry on as discussed, if I don't return," Pendergast told him.

"Yes, sir."

He turned to Ferenc. "Proceed."

Shaking his head, Ferenc pointed to two marks he'd made on the floor with spray paint and stencil: a large X in red, and an equally large circle—about three feet away from it—in green.

"If you could stand on the red X, Mr. Pendergast?"

Pendergast took up the position. From the way he carried the Gladstone bag, it was obviously heavy. Ferenc placed his hands on the master control panel and began going through the sequence to fire up the machine, one knob and lever at a time. Proctor did his own part, monitoring and finely adjusting numerous dials, oscilloscopes, and touch screens. A hum, low but discernible, came from the machine as it powered up.

"Braiding underway," Ferenc said. "Lattice forming. Proctor, how is the semiconductor temperature?"

"Within tolerances."

Pendergast remained on the indicated spot, motionless. He looked silly with his bowler hat and carpet bag, but the expression on his face was forbidding.

Watching the controls for any unexpected spikes or warning messages, Ferenc moved on to the next step. "Main laser online," he said. "Secondary laser now coming on."

A second hum sounded, slightly higher in pitch than the first. Ferenc paused for a moment, listening for any interruptions or deviations that could signal a malfunction. He realized his heart was pounding.

"Proctor? Diagnostics on the lattice?"

"Primary and secondary both flat."

"Okay. The lattice is stable. I'm going to begin shaping the magnetic fields. Ten seconds until portal generation."

He glanced at Pendergast, who nodded his understanding.

"Careful of the light," Ferenc told him.

The original machine, he knew, had been full of sound and fury, shuddering and groaning with effort, especially when overdriven during its last few uses. Beyond the low humming and a smooth whirring of gears, this new device couldn't have been more different. Ferenc counted down the seconds. Three, two, one...

The empty space above the green-painted circle shimmered briefly—and then, as it had done in all the tests, a circle of blinding light appeared, with what looked like a vertical pool of agitated water within. It enlarged before stabilizing.

"Step into and through the circle," Ferenc said, careful not to stare at it himself.

Pendergast—after the briefest of hesitations—stepped forward.

The secondary humming leapt in volume. Quickly, Ferenc looked over his instrumentation. There had been a spike in the magnetic field, but already it was receding. He should have expected that, in fact. The circle of light, which had distorted slightly as Pendergast passed through it, stabilized again, then dimmed somewhat. Beyond the agitated surface, Ferenc glimpsed a brick wall, some trash, and a wedge of sky.

Ferenc returned his attention to the control panel. Everything was nominal.

"Status?"

"All stable," said Proctor.

"Power down to maintenance level."

Slowly, Ferenc dialed back his own power assemblies in reverse order, and then—after a brief set of diagnostics turned up no issues—lowered it to baseline power. The unit would have to be held in station-keeping mode 24/7 in order for Pendergast to return at will. This was one of the many risks involved—if the machine somehow failed while he was away, they might be unable to dial it back to the same spot in the same universe—and Pendergast would be lost forever.

The humming sounds faded, and the portal of light became hazy and transparent, almost invisible.

Pendergast had vanished.

Ferenc let out a long, slow breath. He glanced around the makeshift lab, as if to reassure himself that the device had, in fact, worked—and that Pendergast was now in another, parallel timeline, close by yet infinitely far away. Of course, there was no way of knowing for sure what had happened. Maybe he was a pile of steaming meat in that alleyway. But the greatest chance for failure had come and gone without a hitch—without even a test. He felt a surge of triumph.

"Fuckin' A, *yeah!*" he cried, punching the air.

He glanced over at Proctor. The man stood at the console, expressionless as a stone. Then he pointed toward the shabby briefcase sitting in a corner.

"Your payment," he said.

Ferenc, still tingling from the experience of the last quarter hour, walked over and picked it up.

"As Mr. Pendergast explained to you," Proctor said, "we will continue to require your services while the machine is operational."

"Right," Ferenc replied. He barely heard. He had opened the briefcase and was now staring at half a million dollars in cash.

45

June 8
Thursday

COLDMOON'S CELL RANG AT ten minutes to seven. He had just sat down at the breakfast table in his tiny Ninety-First Street apartment, a mug of burnt coffee in his hand and a bowl of Corn Pops in front of him. With a muttered curse he reached for his phone, but the expression on his face changed quickly when he saw the call was from Block.

Even before he could say anything, Block blurted out: "The shirt and headdress are fake."

"Whoa, hold on." He fumbled with the phone, putting down the coffee cup. "Okay. Let's have it."

"They're both fake. No question about it," came the breathless voice. "The headdress feathers aren't quite the same, and the beadwork has small but absolutely unmistakable differences. There are several light stains on the original that aren't on the forgery. As for the shirt, the quillwork doesn't match."

"You're sure?"

"*They aren't the same.* The peace medal, the moccasins, and leggings on the other hand are real."

"Jesus. When did you figure this out?"

"Around three this morning, but it was too late to call."

"And you've told nobody?"

"Nobody. But I was going to ask—what do I do now?"

Coldmoon thought about that. The fingerprints of "George Smith" had been collected from the museum's palm reader and sent to

Quantico. He would hear later that day if there was a match. In the meantime, they'd have to get a warrant to seize the fake shirt and headdress. There might be DNA and other forensic evidence recoverable from them—maybe even Twoeagle's.

"What you do right now is nothing," said Coldmoon. "Don't tell anyone and leave the artifacts sealed up. Nobody should be allowed to access them—they're evidence in a homicide investigation. You got it?"

"Yes."

"So just keep it to yourself and go about your day as usual. We'll get a warrant to take those two items as soon as we can. We don't need to involve you in it—at least, not now."

"I understand."

"Good work. Thank you."

"I just hope you can get the originals back. This really burns me up—it's bad enough these things are kept locked in the dark, but now they've probably gone off to some rich bastard's private collection in Dubai or wherever."

"We'll get them back," said Coldmoon, and hung up, surprised at how the young man's pointed comments provoked his own surge of outrage.

He considered this remarkable turn of events. There was someone out there with big bucks and an obsession with Sitting Bull—and ruthless enough to kill for it. He hoped to hell they'd get a hit on those fingerprints.

He dialed D'Agosta.

Later that day, as D'Agosta drove Coldmoon to the museum to serve a warrant for the two fake items, Coldmoon received a ding on his cell phone, indicating an email from Quantico. He pulled out his phone and looked. It was from Latent Print Operations: the report he'd been waiting for all day.

"Holy shit," he murmured, opening the email and scanning it.

D'Agosta was just turning the squad car into the museum's security entrance. "What you got there?"

"The report from Quantico."

"Yeah?"

"They got a hit on those prints."

"Tell me."

"They belong to a Venezuelan named Ramón Armendariz y Urias. We've got his prints on file because he passes through U.S. customs several times a year—where, of course, they collect fingerprints of foreign nationals."

"So who is he?"

"We don't have a file on him, but International Operations slapped together some info. Armendariz left Venezuela years ago, during the Chávez regime. It seems he made a lot of money in oil before the Venezuelan petroleum industry collapsed, got the dough out of the country and well hidden in overseas accounts. A quiet guy, but..." He grinned. "He frequents the auction houses. And guess what he buys?"

"Native American artifacts?"

"Bingo."

"So where do we pick this scumbag up?"

"That's a problem. He lives in Ecuador."

"Oh yeah? Do we have an extradition treaty with Ecuador?"

"We do, but the extradition of an Ecuadorian citizen is forbidden by their constitution."

"You said he was Venezuelan."

"He was. But with all his money, he finagled Ecuadorian citizenship."

"So—are you saying we're shit out of luck?"

As the squad car came to a halt at the security entrance, Coldmoon leaned toward D'Agosta. "No."

"I'm all ears."

"The guy doesn't know he's a suspect. He doesn't have any reason to fear coming to the States. So what we do is lure the bastard back to the U.S. and nab his ass when he steps off the plane."

"And just how are we going to do that?"

Coldmoon smiled. "Leave that to the FBI—*amigo.*"

46

December 22, 1880
Saturday

AT AROUND EIGHT THIRTY PM, a series of gleaming carriages began to arrive at the encrusted-limestone mansion occupying the entire frontage of Fifth Avenue from Fiftieth to Fifty-First Streets. The carriages stopped at the mansion's grand entrance, illuminated by hundreds of candles within brass lanterns, their wicks specially treated to emit a reddish flame. The occupants of the carriages descended onto a blood-colored carpet that led past the entrance columns into the house itself. They were dressed in costumes that ranged from the eccentric to the ghoulish, loosely based on the Gothic theme of the Red Ball. As the hour of nine approached, the number of carriages swelled, until half the avenue had become a traffic jam, as coachmen and valets scrambled to escort the gaudily clad heiresses, captains of industry, and men of finance into the mansion.

Inside, Carlotta Cabot-Flint stood at the top of the twin set of marble stairs curving up from the reception hall to the second floor. She was surrounded by a gaggle of women of a certain age, talking avidly as the guests arrived, guessing who they were and what they were dressed as. Jeweled bracelets and rings flashed in the lights as they gestured this way and that with their plump arms. One woman was dressed as Eurydice, with the viper that killed her, fashioned of dyed foxtails, draped over her shoulder. Another was costumed as Salome, carrying a Venetian-style mask in the likeness of John the Baptist, set on a golden stick. The rest were clad in similarly macabre fashion, depicting figures from history or characters from the novels of Horace Walpole and Matthew Gregory Lewis. The group of women at the top of the stairs were beyond excited. Even at this early hour, they could sense the Red Ball was destined to be *the* diversion of the season.

Mrs. Cabot-Flint inwardly rejoiced. At just this moment, none other than Evangeline Rhinelander was pressing her hand in two white gloves and singing her praises—the same Mrs. Rhinelander who, two years ago, had not even deigned to recognize her at the Brunswick.

A hush fell over the group as Caroline Astor, doyenne of New York society, entered the reception hall on the arm of her husband. She was dressed head to toe in white satin, with traceries of rubies forming elegant patterns through the material. She, too, held a Venetian mask before her face, but she was nevertheless identifiable by the unique coiffure no other woman dared imitate. The mask she held was also white, and the hush in the room grew as they saw it was the face of Janus, the two-faced Roman god, mouth drooping in the universal visage of tragedy.

Mrs. Astor stopped in the middle of the reception room. She raised her head and mask, looking up through the eyeholes at her hostess. For a moment, all was still, as she lowered the mask and curtsied to Mrs. Cabot-Flint. Then, with a light movement, she raised the mask and twirled it around to reveal the other—the merry—face of Janus.

A gasp of admiration rippled through the crowd, followed by a scattering of applause. Once again conversation rose, and the orchestra in the adjoining salon struck up another Hungarian waltz.

Carlotta Cabot-Flint stood quite still as what had just happened sank in. Caroline Astor had come dressed as the Woman in White from the famous Wilkie Collins novel. By pausing to recognize her hostess in such a public manner, she'd just bestowed on Mrs. Cabot-Flint the very highest acknowledgment of social approval possible in the glittering firmament of Gilded Age New York.

As her mind once again returned to the buzz of excitement around her, she thought for a moment of the duchess. She had to admit the young woman was responsible for much of the evening's success. She had promised to supply decorations for the ball, and that morning, workmen dressed in outfits bearing the Ironclaw coat of arms began bringing in some select ornaments, several fire braziers, gigantic clocks, and as a centerpiece, two massive, muscular legs of sculpted stone—as if from a ruined statue of antiquity—made of papier-mâché but looking strikingly real.

Directing this procession of fabulous things, in French-accented English, had been a woman named Féline, in the employ of the duchess. Mrs. Cabot-Flint, though surprised at the rather brusque arrival of workmen, felt too astonished to object, and her momentary aggravation melted away as the finished space took form. Within six hours, her vast ballroom had been transformed into an exotic palace in scarlet and crimson. Féline had also changed the musical program. Handel, Beethoven, and Brahms were tossed out in favor of the thunderings of Liszt and music from various composers she had never heard of—Fauré, Saint-Saëns, Dvořák.

The duchess had suggested—quite cleverly—that although this was to be a costume ball, each guest should be asked to wear a fourragère— a braided cord of the military fashion—of a particular, assigned color around their left shoulder. This would allow the duchess and Mrs. Cabot-Flint to identify who each guest was, without them being able to identify each other. The duchess had explained that when she finally revealed the reason for these colored fourragères, it would be seen as a clever *beau geste*, to be no doubt imitated at parties for the rest of the season. Lastly, the duchess had persuaded her to hire male and female dancers from La Scala, who happened to be in town preparing for holiday performances: a troupe that included the prima ballerina Alessandra Legnani. They were dressed as figures both arabesque and grotesque, and they danced pas de deux among the masqueraders, their gossamer-thin costumes and supple, muscular bodies adding a frisson of sensuality to the fête.

As the hostess looked down over her entertainment with enormous satisfaction, she saw—among the masked and costumed revelers laughing, drinking, and dancing—the duchess herself, dressed, she could see, as Lucrezia Borgia, the poisoner. She stood in a corner near the entrance to the ballroom, speaking to a young woman. Mrs. Cabot-Flint peered more closely and was able to identify the girl as Edith Jones, who'd been introduced into society the year before. She came from an old patroon family and was Mrs. Astor's niece. What a shame, Mrs. Cabot-Flint thought, that the girl should be of such plain appearance. Nevertheless, with her breeding and background, she was sure to make a good match despite her looks. She wondered what on earth the duchess was doing, half-hidden at the entryway instead of mingling with the guests—and why she was speaking to the girl.

Constance stood in a discreet location that afforded a view of the arrivals without herself being seen by them. She couldn't help but relish the outrageous spectacle she and the sharp-witted Féline had helped create. Had circumstances been different, she might have allowed herself to savor fully the grotesque cavalcade of expense and vulgarity that was passing before her eyes. But there was a reason for her to be where she was, and she had to remain watchful and guarded.

As she scanned the crowd, glass of champagne in one hand, a man caught her eye. He was dressed as a harlequin, with a sequined mask and the obligatory cap and bells and no fourragère to indicate his identity. She hadn't seen him come in. He was in earnest conversation with a portly gentleman in the garb of a medieval executioner, and they were about to move into the second chamber and out of her sight. She felt a chill of horror: something about him—the height, build, or was it the way he moved?—reminded her of her quarry. Could Enoch Leng have somehow crept in while she wasn't looking? That seemed impossible. Not everyone had followed the instructions to wear a fourragère. But on closer examination, the man was too tall to be Leng, and she returned her gaze to the entrance.

A high voice intruded on her thoughts. She turned to see a girl of about eighteen approaching. Her hair was put up in the fashion of young ladies newly introduced to society. The *robe de gaulle* she wore, identical to the one in Vigée le Brun's 1783 portrait, made it clear she was costumed as Marie Antoinette. The girl had added a gruesome touch: a white silk ribbon tied around her neck, dotted with crimson.

"We are both like Mr. Huxley," the girl said archly, a hand straying to the ribbon around her throat, "observing a savage ritual and hoping we won't be boiled in a pot for dinner."

Constance stared at the girl, dismayed that her watchful stance was so obvious but surprised at the observation. "I should be careful not to untie that ribbon if I were you."

The girl laughed and held out her kid-gloved hand. "My name is Edith. Edith Jones."

Constance took the hand with amused gravity. "And I am the Duchess of Ironclaw."

"Ah, the famous duchess. Is it really so? A title such as Iron Claw, I mean?"

Constance was perturbed by a note of skepticism in the girl's voice. Her eye strayed back to the entryway as another knot of guests arrived. "Ironclaw is an Americanism. It's actually *Inowroclaw.*"

The expressive eyebrows rose, and the girl's penetrating brown eyes widened with interest. "The town's been abuzz about your arrival. How pleasant to meet you."

"Likewise."

"My apologies—I should be addressing you as Your Grace, of course."

"It's America. We might as well dispense with such formalities."

Edith laughed in relief. "We are a rather primitive bunch. Allow me to offer a collective apology."

"No need. I actually felt relief when I disembarked from the liner— I'd been told people were still going about in loincloths."

"That was last season. So tell me—who are you waiting for with such keen interest?"

Now Constance felt another twinge of alarm, mingled with annoyance at this meddlesome, all-too-perceptive girl. "I'm not waiting

for anyone in particular. I'm enjoying the spectacle, like your Mr.
Huxley."

"I see. May I be so forward as to ask where in Europe you're from?"

"Transylvania. But my ancestral home is Galicia. I'm of the House
of Piast."

"Transylvania: home of Vampirismus. Have you read the story?"

"I have," said Constance.

"So frightfully Gothic! I'd love to go there someday. I had a friend
from Transylvania, whom I met while convalescing in the Black
Forest. She spoke Romanian. Is that also your native tongue?"

Now the conversation was edging onto dangerous ground. Constance spoke six languages, but none of them was Romanian. She
smiled and redirected the subject. "Convalescing in the Black Forest?
So you've lived abroad, Miss Jones?"

"Oh, yes. My parents trundled me everywhere. France, Italy,
Germany, Spain. We're *terribly* well bred." She made a disrespectful
gesture, flicking her fingers as if shooing away a fly. "I find it all quite
absurd. Don't you? I could see it in your face as I walked over."

Constance felt exasperation and admiration at the same time. Could
this callow, pimply-faced girl possibly see through her? She tried to
laugh it off. "Are my feelings really so obvious?"

"I suppose you think me very forward."

"You'll find it serves you rather well in life."

"Thank you for saying that. I never *mean* to offend, yet I seem to,
again and again. I made a hash of my coming out last year. My mother
has spent the last five months in Newport reminding me of the poor
impression I made. Newport, so full of *amour propre* they make the
milkmen shoe their horses with rubber! She forbade me from reading
novels—until I am married."

"Do you have suitors?"

"Yes, but they're *so* dull—New York's dullness is 'through all the
realms of Nonsense, absolute.'"

At this quotation from Dryden, Constance had a sudden premoni-
tion of the young woman's future: enduring trivial conversations with

superficial men who were attracted only to her money, culminating in a loveless, stifling marriage. She would be lost unless she could find some consuming interest or diversion to occupy herself. "No novels until you're married?"

Edith flushed. "What do you think?"

"*Je pense que c'est stupide!*" said Constance with sudden fierceness. "I've been reading novels since I was nine." She lowered her voice. "Steal them from your house library and read them under the covers or in the closet. Hide them under your mattress. If caught, lie, and then steal more. That is my advice to you, Miss Jones. Read, read, and never stop: it's what will save you."

Edith laughed again, this time in mixed surprise and relief. Constance was about to join in when she half-glimpsed a man lingering at the mansion's entrance. Her heart literally stopped for a single, terrible moment.

"I must take my leave," she said.

The girl's face fell. "Just as we'd become acquainted!"

But Constance was already slipping away, leaving the girl standing alone near the ballroom entrance, staring after her, a confused and hurt expression on her face.

47

Dr. Enoch Leng paused at the entryway to take in the full sweep of the grand reception room. Very little impressed Leng, but as his eye roamed about the marble and limestone expanse, festooned in crimson and scarlet, with Chinese screens, draperies, giant masks—and two statuesque legs, arranged as a centerpiece—he found himself unexpectedly surprised and amused. It was impossible to believe that a vacuous woman like Mrs. Cabot-Flint and her swine of a husband could have pulled this off. Leng almost hadn't come, but the truth was he'd needed reminding of his life's great work and why he'd embarked on it. Lurid exhibitions such as this were vitally necessary, from time to time, in extinguishing any spark of empathy and rekindling his hatred of mankind and all its grotesqueries.

He had brought no one to the ball; there was no one to bring. Munck was in the carriage, no doubt enjoying the spectacle through the tall windows much as a feral dog might enjoy the guillotine, excited by the noise and movement, understanding nothing save the blood.

Professor Leng resumed strolling to the end of the carpet, his black monk's robes sweeping the floor behind him, and made his way to the trunkless legs of stone. They were remarkably well made out of papier-mâché, fauxed to look like granite.

He read the inscription on the pedestal below.

My name is Ozymandias, King of Kings;
Look on my Works, ye Mighty, and despair!

"Ozymandias" happened to be his favorite poem. Someone—surely not the Cabot-Flints—had supervised the fantastical decorations, and he should like to find out who.

He strolled around the legs of stone. To his right, he could see through a grand archway into the ballroom itself. He paused to watch an almost naked dancer flit past him—one of the La Scala company, according to the invitation he had received—and a magnificent specimen of pulchritude she was. Briefly he mused on the delectable image of her body splayed on the table of his operating chamber. But such was not to be; he had to make do with lesser specimens, although he was in fact trying the "fatted calf" approach on the most recent experimental subjects, hoping for better results.

Leng had just finished his slow turn around the reception hall when he felt a presence next to him. A woman—a most striking young woman—was also admiring the centerpiece. She was cloaked in white, with an exotic white turban decorated with laurel leaves, a jeweled headband, and flowers pinned to her breast.

She spoke in a low, contralto voice:

Two vast and trunkless legs of stone
Stand in the desert... Near them, on the sand,
Half sunk a shattered visage lies...

And at this, Leng gently interrupted and continued:

whose frown,
And wrinkled lip, and sneer of cold command,
Tell that its sculptor well those passions read

He bowed and took her hand. "Professor Enoch Leng."

As he raised her hand to his lips, the woman said: "Be careful of the ring."

Leng paused. "Ah. Of course. You're wearing the infamous hollow ring with which Lucrezia Borgia administered her poisons."

"The very same."

He held the hand for a moment, examining the ring on her index finger. It was of thick gold, heavily granulated and set with tiny diamonds and rubies. He turned her hand slightly and noted, on the inside part of the band, a tiny hole, currently covered, and next to it a diamond button, evidently used to open the hole with a spring in order to release the poisoned powder.

"Ingenious," he said. "Where did you get it?"

"From my father."

"And your father is—?"

The woman gently withdrew her hand. "I am the Duchess of Ironclaw," she said. "My father, God rest his soul, was Duke Casimir VIII. But he was more than a duke: he was an ardent chemist and a passionate collector. He had the most admired cabinet of curiosities in Transylvania, where we lived in exile from the family duchy."

Leng raised his head. Her eyes were a most extraordinary violet. "Pleased to meet you, Your Grace."

"Likewise, Dr. Leng. Or would you rather I called you Savonarola?"

"Ah yes, my costume: the mad monk of San Marco."

"How curious," said the duchess. "Our lives are linked. My 'father,' Pope Alexander VI, ordered you burned at the stake."

"What a charming coincidence, *Lucrezia*," said Leng. He paused and gave a little bow. "May I ask for the honor of your presence at the next dance?"

She curtsied. "You may."

He held out his arm and she took it. He felt her light touch as he led her into the grand ballroom, ablaze in light, where the small orchestra was playing what he recognized as a Valse-Caprice by Gabriel Fauré, a young French composer Leng found particularly entrancing. He was again struck by the originality and brilliance of the ball's organization. As a second Valse-Caprice began, Leng took the young duchess in his arms.

"Duchess, I'm most intrigued by who conceived this ball," he said, as he turned her about the floor. "Surely not the Cabot-Flints?"

"Well," she said, "I had a small hand in it."

"It is most original. My compliments." Leng digested this remarkable bit of information. Who *was* this duchess? There must be a great deal of gossip going around about her, but not being connected in these social circles, he had not heard it.

He would have to look into all that.

"I'm curious about your father, the duke," he said. "What sort of chemical research did he do?"

"He had eccentric ideas and interests—chemically, that is."

She seemed reluctant to discuss it. "I myself am interested in chemistry," he said, "specifically what Berzelius termed 'organic chemistry,' the study of compounds derived from biological sources."

"How curious! So was my father."

But still she did not explain further.

The waltz ended and they came to a rest, separating and lowering their arms. The flush of activity had pinked the duchess's cheeks.

"May I have the honor of the next one?" Leng asked.

"You may."

To Leng's surprise, a Dvořák string quartet began to play. It was hardly dance music, being slow and of a *tempo rubato* nature, and Leng could see many of the dancing partners around them puzzled as to how to follow it. But not the duchess, who stepped up to him, ready to be turned about the floor again. And encouraging everyone to dance to this ultramodern music came the La Scala dancers, weaving among those on the ballroom floor in their scantily clad state. He found the rhythm of the piece and began to lead.

"And your father's cabinet of curiosities," asked Leng, "what did it consist of?"

"It was also of a chemical nature. Quite esoteric. Bottles and bottles, all of different colors. He collected organic compounds from insects, flowers, roots and leaves, inner organs of beasts and fowls, glands of snakes and spiders and toads, that sort of thing." She hesitated. "His primary focus was on the biological activity of poisons."

At this, Leng almost lost the rhythm of the dance. He quickly recovered. "Ah. Perhaps that explains your interest in Lucrezia Borgia?"

"I've long felt that poor Lucrezia was a woman surrounded by cruel and overbearing men. With that little hollow ring of hers, she took power back from them and quite literally put it into her own hands, to be administered as needed."

"One could look at it that way," said Leng, amused. "And this cabinet of your father's—may I ask where it is now?"

"At the bottom of the Atlantic, alas. But I still have his papers and formulae."

Leng had to bite his tongue to stop himself from further questions. *Doucement*, he said to himself. *Doucement*.

"And what gave you the idea of coming as Savonarola?" she asked.

"I confess I'm attracted to his dark view of mankind. I should love to have witnessed his bonfire of the vanities—what a horrifying spectacle that must have been."

"You might say this ball itself is a sort of bonfire of the vanities, wouldn't you agree, Doctor?"

"I would indeed, Your Grace," said Leng, struck anew by the acuteness of her observations.

The quartet came to its coda, the dancing ended, and they separated again. Leng was tempted to ask for the next dance as well, but another, he knew, would be a violation of etiquette. He was not done with the duchess, however; no, indeed. This ball was not, however, the place and time to continue such an interesting conversation.

"I'm afraid, Your Grace," he said, "that I have another engagement. But I hope our acquaintance is just beginning. I wonder if I could ask you to luncheon, at your convenience?"

The duchess gazed at him with those purple eyes. Then she slipped a linen-hued calling card out of the folds of her costume and proffered it to him with a gloved hand. "Like Belinda, I tend to spend my mornings wrapped in the arms of Morpheus."

"I'm sure Pope would approve. Perhaps tea, then?" he said, bowing and offering his own card. "These holidays do tend to scatter one's schedule to the four winds. Would you care to set a date?"

"Perhaps sometime next week?"

Leng thought a moment as a guest dressed as a harlequin passed by, leaving the entertainment early as well. "Perhaps tomorrow?"

"You're a rather forward fellow."

"It's only tea—and I promise not to cut off any locks of your hair. Besides, I think we'll find we have much to talk about."

"In that case, I shall accept, while doing my best to ignore the unseemly haste."

"Most excellent. Shall we say Delmonico's? At half past two?"

"We shall." And as she offered him her glove, Leng felt a shudder—whether of anticipation or something else—course through her limbs.

48

Dʀ. Leng walked briskly down the carpeted stairs and away from the mansion, the elegant music and chatter of conversation fading slowly behind him. Most of the partygoers' carriages would be waiting in stables and other places nearby, but a few stood here at the Fifth Avenue curb, horses snorting vapor into the chill air. Leng knew his would be among them: Munck enjoyed gaping at people almost as much as he liked cutting them open.

Leng had little patience with therapeutic nihilism, the approach he'd encountered at medical schools in Heidelberg, Salpêtrière, and elsewhere. He believed in a more aggressive approach to illnesses of the mind, surgical whenever practicable, and he dismissed iatrogenic injuries as a necessary risk of the curative process. Many lunatics, maniacs, and victims of so-called melancholia had passed beneath his hands—and scalpel. When he at last came upon Munck in a Turkish prison, he knew he had found his ideal chargé d'affaires. Like many Circassians, Munck had been forced to flee his homeland in 1864 during the Russian genocide, but for a different reason than the rest— he was sought by the authorities for mutilating and eviscerating dogs, cats, and farm animals. The man was not homicidal or a sexual deviant; he was a *hämophile* in the word's original sense, possessed of an uncontrolled urge to see, and spill, blood. Leng had saved him, educated him, and given him a place in life—and in return received the man's hound-like devotion, quite remarkable in a man otherwise free of anything like empathy or conscience. And finally, even though he had been confined in a prison for idiots, Munck was of above-average intelligence. With his urges properly channeled, the Circassian had the cleverness and cunning of an apex predator. And, like said predator, he was oblivious to the suffering of his prey.

As Leng walked toward the avenue, pulling on his gloves, he saw his gleaming black carriage pull away from the curb to pick him up in front of the mansion. One of the numerous valets waiting nearby rushed over to help Leng up the steps while Munck held the carriage door open, small eyes shining out of the darkness: he had shuttered the interior lantern in order to see better.

"Well, Munck," Leng said as he took his seat, "did you enjoy yourself as much as I did?"

"Lots of people, there was," Munck replied, wiping his mouth with the back of his hand. "Lots of *ladies*." This was true: at affairs like this one, women showed rather more flesh than Munck was used to seeing—other than on the operating table.

"Yes, there was one lady in particular that made the evening worthwhile," Leng said.

"The lady you was dancing with?" Munck asked eagerly.

Leng couldn't help but chuckle. The clever Munck must have snuck out of the cab to peer inside the mansion—and he had enjoyed his ogling. "The same. I found her most intriguing—*too* intriguing, somehow. I had the strangest feeling I'd met her somewhere before." He thought a moment. "Munck, I believe I have a task for you."

The short man leaned closer, eyes dewy, forehead damp despite the chill. "Yes?"

"Tomorrow, I want you to go to the public library, and—" He stopped. "Let's discuss it back at the residence. Just now, I'd like a moment to arrange my thoughts."

"Very good, sir." Munck rapped for the driver to move on, and the carriage slid out into traffic and began fading into the night—watched, at a distance, by a guest wearing the cap and bells, and the red spangled mask, of a harlequin.

49

December 23, 1880
Sunday

CONSTANCE GREENE, SELF-STYLED Duchess of Ironclaw, awakened to light streaming through the silk curtains of the bedroom. Rising, she went to the window and drew the drapes back, to see snow blanketing Fifth Avenue, lying softly on the rooftops and outlining the branches of the sycamore trees. Everything looked clean, renewed, after the unexpected snowfall. She realized that, among other twenty-first-century conveniences, she had left behind accurate weather predictions.

As she gazed out at the magical scene, the bells of St. Patrick's, three blocks away, began tolling the hour. She counted the bells: nine o'clock. Today was the day her plans would launch; today at tea with Leng.

As she stood at the window, sounds of life reached her from below: the bustling of Mrs. Palegood in the kitchen, the two children playing a game in their rooms, and from outside, the clopping of hooves on the avenue and the call of a lone newsboy hawking the morning's papers. A scent of coffee wafted up, mingling with the smell of freshly baked hot cross buns: one of Mrs. Palegood's specialties. It was a moment of domestic bliss...but she quickly stopped herself from sinking any further into it. She must never forget that Mary was in great danger. She had business to conclude—an ugly business—before she could gain the ease necessary to truly accustom herself to her new life.

Constance washed, dressed, then went down the hall to Binky's room. She listened at the door for a moment, hearing chatter and giggles. She knocked and then opened.

The children were playing cards—Old Maid, or more precisely its predecessor, known as Black Peter—and upon her entry, Binky jumped to her feet and gave a clumsy curtsy. Joe looked up silently. It was upsetting to see the little girl so submissive, so eager to please. These were not qualities Constance admired. But she knew the child was nervous and uncertain and feared making a mistake. All too understandable, given what the girl had been through—and she told herself Binky would soon adjust to her new life and become more...herself.

Joe's adjustment, on the other hand, seemed problematic. He remained aloof and—despite everything, including the regular lessons with Moseley and all her personal kindnesses—still suspicious. His Blackwell's Island ordeal had affected him even more deeply than she'd feared. He would need time.

"Children," she said, "how would you like to go on an outing?"

"Where?" cried Binky, clapping her hands.

"To the Museum of Natural History." The museum had opened three years before, a Gothic Revival building erected in the uptown wasteland known as Manhattan Square.

At this, little Constance clapped her hands again in excitement, eyes shining.

"Dress warmly for the carriage ride. We'll leave in half an hour." She hesitated, glancing at Joe. "We're going to see...dinosaurs."

At this, a flash of interest crossed Joe's face before it shut down again.

Murphy brought the carriage around and helped them in, the horses steaming and stamping in the cold sunlight. The light mantle of snow was still virgin on the sidewalks, but in the streets it was already churning up into a mess of slush, wheel marks, and horse manure. They set off uptown, the matched Percherons clip-clopping up the avenue to Fifty-Ninth Street, then heading crosstown to the West Side and continuing up Eighth Avenue. Binky had her nose pressed to the glass, drinking everything in with childish fascination. Constance, recalling her own early memories of the Five Points, had never seen fresh snow—it turned to filthy, frozen soot almost before reaching the ground.

Beyond Sixty-Sixth Street, the city seemed to halt. The roadways had been laid out, but there were very few buildings, mostly vacant lots in the process of being cleared and leveled. At Seventy-Second Street, the hulking form of the Dakota—at present it was only half constructed, and it would not get the moniker for another eighteen months—loomed up, occupying the block to Seventy-Third. Now it was Constance's turn to stare fixedly out the window, unable fully to shake off the many memories and emotions that came to mind of the vast structure—and Pendergast's rambling apartments within.

To the north, another expanse of vacant lots stretched ahead to the museum, grim and severe despite its newness, surrounded by a wilderness of rubble, stagnant ponds, a scattering of small goat farms, and the wooden shacks of squatters in the process of being evicted as the city marched inexorably northward. To their right stretched the expanse of Central Park, vast but still relatively wild and undeveloped.

The carriage turned into the museum's drive, then halted at the entrance. Murphy helped them down. Constance, taking the children's hands, ushered them past a pair of stern-looking guards and into the grand gallery that soared upward two stories and ran half the length of the building. Its walls were lined with glass cases full of mounted and stuffed animals, fossils, and skeletons. Binky gasped and squeezed Constance's hand more tightly. Even Joe's eyes widened.

The place was thronging with all manner of humanity: top-hatted gentlemen, workers in overalls, popinjay dandies, scruffy boys staring slack-jawed, and nannies on outings with their young charges. Constance released the hands of Joe and Binky to let them explore. She was pleased to see how fascinated little Constance was by the exhibits: a giant mammoth skeleton with curved tusks; a fanciful reconstruction of a dinosaur; endless cabinets stuffed to the gills. Some of the labels, she noted from the perspective of a twenty-first-century education, were wildly inaccurate. Not only that, but the tusks on the mammoth had been mounted in reversed position, so that they curved outward instead of in, and the reconstructed dinosaur looked nothing like any that had actually walked the earth. But of course, none of this mattered to the two children, who were entranced.

They reached the end of the central gallery and climbed a set of cast-iron stairs to the second floor, displaying dioramas full of stuffed animals, artificial wax plants, and painted backgrounds. The children devoured the exhibits, one after another, until at last Constance decided she'd best reserve some of that childish interest for a future visit.

"It's such a beautiful day," she said at last, gathering them to her. "Why don't we take a ride around the park?"

50

ONCE AGAIN THEY ENTERED the carriage; Murphy picked up the reins and then guided them southward. Compared to the Central Park that Constance was familiar with, this stretch looked unkempt, with half-built roads, piles of dirt and rocks, downed trees, and other signs of a landscape under construction. Once they passed the remains of the Old Reservoir, however, a degree of orderliness began to impose itself. There were carriage paths and walkways winding among the bare trees, and the Mall and Bethesda Fountain had been completed. Murphy turned in at a transverse lane, circling the north end of the parade ground. The lane itself was already packed and scored with innumerable wheel ruts, but the meadows to either side were mantled with snow, the tree limbs and bushes covered in white icing.

Binky looked out the carriage window, eyes wide. "It's so *beautiful!*"

Joe, too, was clearly astonished by the vista, although—as in the museum—he kept his emotions and thoughts to himself. She wondered what it would take for him to let down his guard and finally accept the reality of his new life in a Fifth Avenue mansion. Her memories of Joe before he'd been arrested were hazy at best, but she recalled how guarded and withdrawn he'd been after his release...in that brief space of time before he was killed in the pickpocketing attempt gone wrong. She glanced at him privately as he scanned the fields of snow and lines of trees. She had always thought the challenge would be freeing him from imprisonment—but that had turned out to be just the first step.

Binky was pulling at her sleeve and speaking excitedly. "May we stop, Aunt Livia? Just for a minute?"

Out the carriage window, Constance could see young people cavorting at a distance, but the snow nearby remained virgin and she noticed a turnout just ahead. She directed Murphy to pull into it.

"Make sure you keep your mittens on," she said to the children. "Caps, as well. If you're good, I'll show you how to make snow angels."

She opened the carriage door and Binky was out in two bounds. Immediately she dipped her mittened hands in the snow—gently, as if it were delicate gossamer that would disappear with rough handling. Then—seeing the furrows her hands had made—she began scooping up great handfuls of snow, tossing them in the air, clapping them between her mittens and sticking out her tongue to catch the flakes as they streamed back down.

Joe had descended more slowly from the coach. Constance watched as he stopped and looked out over the vast expanse. He crouched and slid a mittened hand across the unbroken snow, as if conducting an experiment.

Binky's shrieks of delight were a stark contrast to his silence. She traced figures, laughing at the images she made. The sun had warmed and softened the snow, and Binky began packing and forming it into what, no doubt, would be the base of a snowman. Getting out of the coach, Constance knelt and showed her how to roll the snow into a ball, pushing it along to make it bigger, exposing the dead grass beneath. Joe watched, and she hoped he might join in.

When the base was finished, she started another ball for the snowman's body. Suddenly, she heard Murphy's warning shout. At the same time, she saw a flash of movement and looked up to see Joe bolting away from them, running toward a distant stand of trees.

Disbelief and rage mingled within her. After all the kindnesses and proofs of fidelity she'd demonstrated, he'd still run away, as untamable as a wild animal. Murphy was down off his seat now, beginning to lumber after the boy, but he was big and slow.

The same, however, could not be said of Constance.

She took off, hand clutching the snowball she had started to make, and—with aim long perfected by training with a stiletto—she launched the missile at him, shouting furiously: "Oi! *Half Jigger!*"

Hearing the epithet nobody save his father had ever called him, Joe turned and looked back—just in time to get the speeding snowball full in the face. He staggered back in astonishment, slipping in the snow, but even as he righted himself, Constance came at him with a cry of "Ungrateful *bastard!*" as she scooped up another handful of snow and rocketed it toward him, again making a direct hit, this time on the side of his head as he tried to duck.

"Criminy!" Joe yelped, stumbling back once more in reaction to the unexpected onslaught.

As he regained his balance, his eyes met Constance's over the playing field of snow. Their gazes locked...and something that could not be put into words passed between them.

His flight forgotten at this assault on his person, Joe abruptly reached down, grabbed a fistful of snow, packed it, and threw it hard at Constance, missing her. He'd hurled plenty of stones in his young life, but the weight and arc of a snowball were new to him. His second snowball did better, connecting with her shoulder, but meanwhile Constance—not holding back—had already launched another missile that hit him square in the stomach. He lobbed off a third, and this one caught her in the neck, spattering her bare skin. Joe laughed despite himself as he watched her try to shake off the snow in discomfort. Binky joined in, tossing a snowball at Joe, who returned it, and soon they were all throwing snow at each other with abandon. Even Murphy, instead of hoisting himself back into his seat, joined in. Several passing carriages, filled with well-to-do couples taking the air, slowed to stare at the highly improper free-for-all among the woman, her children, and the coachman.

As suddenly as it erupted, the contest came to an end. Constance busied herself with brushing the snow from Binky's coat and hair, careful not to take any notice of Joe, who was approaching—first with hesitation, then with a freer step. As he came up, she turned and brushed the snow from him as well, allowing herself a gentle sweep of the fingers across the face she had so recently struck in anger…with a snowball.

Then, with a brisk "up you go," she bundled the children back into the coach and Murphy urged Rascal toward home. Binky talked almost nonstop, excited beyond description by the experience, but both Joe and Constance were content to ride in silence. Until moments before, she had forgotten the name, Half Jigger, by which her father called Joe on those occasions he misbehaved—it had surged up out of her memory unbidden. She did not know what Joe himself might be thinking, but one thing she now felt confident of: her relationship with him had rounded a corner. Though Joe might not yet fully trust her, he *accepted* her…and she no longer needed to fear his running off from this, the only family he knew.

51

MARY GREENE SWAM SLOWLY back into consciousness from a dream. It was a dream that seemed to have been going on a long time, days or even weeks, one that she'd occasionally felt she was half awakening from—like a diver rising toward the water's surface—before slipping back into what seemed like a fairy tale. In the endless dream, she was reclining in the pergola of a castle above a bay: shimmering in the summer's light, cool breezes stirring the hanging silks. Now and then, a handsome man in white armor had appeared—no doubt a prince. And, as in most fairy tales, there were frightening creatures, too…one in particular who occasionally approached out of the mists…a misshapen figure, who she assumed was a servant. Usually when he intruded upon her dream he was carrying a silver platter of some sort or other. And now, as the veil of unconsciousness began to part, the figure returned once again, carrying his silver platter, which held something that—as the veil parted still further—revealed itself to be a bloody knife.

This image of a knife swept away more fragments of hazy dreaminess. She looked around and, to her amazement, found herself half buried in a princess bed, enclosed in the same hanging silk curtains that had been in her dream. She tried to sit up and was immediately seized by dizziness. She closed her eyes for a moment; the dizziness began to clear—and then she opened them again, content for the time being to look around. Instead of a castle pergola overlooking the sea, she found herself in a small but sumptuous room with red velvet wallpaper, paintings in gilt frames, shelves of books, a writing desk, velvet chairs, and a floor covered with a Persian carpet. Globes of cut glass on the walls cast a yellow light from the gas flames within.

Wherever could she be?

Vague recollections darted like minnows through the depths of her memory; it was all she could do to occasionally catch hold of one. There had been the workhouse, of course. And then, suddenly, the great doctor, singling her out for treatment. This had been followed by a ride in a magnificent carriage...but after that, all her memories slipped into the endless dream as the carriage continued on its way to the magic castle.

She continued looking around the room. It had two doors but no windows. Something had been troubling her, not only during the dream but even before—at the workhouse—but everything had been so rushed and she'd had no chance to tell the doctor...

Binky. Her little sister. Where was she? If she, Mary, was here in this strange magical room, how was Binky getting enough to eat?

She tried again to sit up, intending to get out of bed, only to find herself overwhelmed once again by dizziness and—instead of rising—half collapsed on the side of the bed with a cry of confusion.

A moment later, one of the doors opened. She saw a slender man standing in it, backlit by a bright light. This must be the prince of her dreams, because he was dressed in white—but, rather than white mail, it was the coat of a doctor. He paused a moment at the threshold, then stepped into the dim light of the room. Now she recognized the keen, aquiline face, the deep-set eyes, the wet red lips, the pale-blond hair combed back—and the small, oval, gold-rimmed glasses. He was not as handsome as the prince of her dreams, but he was elegant, and neat, and now she managed to remember his name: Dr. Leng, who had taken her from the Five Points House of Industry. But when had that been? Everything was in such confusion.

"Ah, Mary, I'm so glad to see you're awake," said the doctor in a gentle voice, stepping into the room and coming over to her bedside. "You've been rather ill these past few weeks, but luckily with the resources of my private clinic, you're over the worst of it now and well on the road to recovery. You've been sedated, though, and I expect you're a trifle confused."

Mary nodded mutely.

"Of course you are. Please do not discompose yourself. You're safe here in my house, and you'll continue to be well taken care of. I got you out of that workhouse just in time. I don't want to frighten you while you're still on the mend, but given your illness, you would not have fared well had you remained there—not fared well at all."

He held out his hand and grasped hers, then gently raised her up and helped her sit back on the bed.

"But..." Mary stopped, trying to focus her thoughts. "But what about my little sister, Constance? Who's looking after her?"

At this, Leng tilted his head. "Ah. A sister?"

"Yes, yes. Our parents are dead, she was living in the streets. I gave her food through the window of the workhouse."

"I see."

"And Joe, my brother." She sobbed at this additional, sudden, unexpected recollection. "He's on Blackwell's Island."

"A brother, too? Dear me."

She tightened her grip on his gloved hands. "Oh, Doctor—can you help them?"

He returned her tearful look with a kindly gaze. "Of *course* I can help them. I'm so sorry to hear about this. I didn't realize, when I took you from the workhouse, that you had any family at all."

"I'm so worried. How...?" She tried to organize her thoughts once more, but the confusion and fog just made her feel weary all over again.

"How long have you been ill? I don't know when exactly you first contracted it, but you've been under my care now for—oh, almost a month."

"That long? Oh! Constance is only nine years old and...and it's wintertime!"

He released her hands, only to pat them again comfortingly. "I'll find her. You have my word. Of course, you'll have to tell me all about her: where she lives or hides, what she looks like, and that sort of thing. As for—Joe, was it?—I have some acquaintances at Blackwell's; I can certainly find out how he's faring, and perhaps manage to do something for him as well."

"Oh, thank you, *thank* you!" She tried to grasp his hand again, as a drowning person might, but even as she did she felt her strength giving way.

He rose. "I will have Munck, my manservant, bring you something to eat and drink. Do not be alarmed—nature was unkind when forming his appearance, but he is an excellent nurse and as obedient as a puppy. But please remember, Mary: you've had a close call, and we have to be careful. For the time being, you'll have to stay here until you recover a little more of your strength." He strolled to the door and turned. "I'm so glad to see you better, my dear, and I shall undertake a search for your siblings forthwith."

He departed and Mary, her head feeling a little clearer, was able to stand up and, one hand on the frame of the canopy, look around the room. The doctor must be very rich, that was clear, to have a private clinic like this in his very own house. Everything was of the richest quality: the spines of the books stamped with gold; the thick writing paper on the desk, with a gold fountain pen and inkwell ready to use; the old pictures of horses and dogs on the walls. And she'd never seen anything like the bed, with its carved wooden frame below a shining canopy of embroidered silk, creating a sort of cocoon, and within it a feather bed covered with a peach-colored satin puff. Just looking at it made her feel sleepy all over again.

A timid knock came at the door, then it opened and a small man came in. It was the misshapen servant of her dreams, with a knobbly face and two bright green eyes, dressed in simple but clean clothes. He bowed several times as he approached, in a crabwise scuttle, carrying a silver tray with a cup of sherbet, a tall glass of juice, and a platter of meats and other delicious-looking tidbits. He set it down on a small table beside her bed, still bowing incessantly, an unctuous smile on his lips.

"'Ere you go, miss," he said. "The doctor's special order. Lemon sherbet, juice, and some Eyetalian delicacies. 'E's one for the meats and cheeses, miss! Please now, eat hearty—doctor's orders, as they say!"

He retreated backward out the open door with more bowing, shutting it quietly behind him.

Mary realized she was quite thirsty, and drank down the juice quickly—it was orange juice, or at least she thought it was; she'd never tasted anything so fresh and delicious. Her appetite sharpened, she gobbled up the sherbet with a silver spoon. She glanced at the meats and cheeses set around the platter, then began plucking up first one and then another, wolfing them down with slices of bread. She felt famished.

A small basin of water sat on one side of the platter, with a linen napkin beside it. She had some faint recollection of what this must be: a finger bowl, she thought it was called. She dipped her fingers in the cool, faintly scented water, dried them on the napkin and dabbed her lips with it. The dizziness was stealing over her again—strange that she would feel sleepy so soon after waking—but it was a delicious kind of sleepiness, and one after the other she let her cares and uncertainties fall away. The doctor would see to Binky and Joe. The doctor would see to everything. As the languorousness continued to steal over her, she lay back down on the feather bed, sinking in deeply, and immediately fell asleep.

52

THEIR TABLE STOOD IN the center of Delmonico's dining room. On one wall, a flickering gas fireplace gave the ornate chamber a cozy feel. Against the opposite wall, a veritable army of waiters in white ties, black coats, and white aprons stood at attention, backs ramrod straight, their eyes roving the room for the barest raising of a finger or glance of an eye. Behind the table, a magnificent flower arrangement conferred a sense of privacy, as well as scenting the air with the fragrance of roses and peonies.

It was half past two, and Delmonico's was serving tea to a busy room full of Fifth Avenue ladies. There was a low murmur of conversation, the tinkling of cups and spoons, and the hushed comings and goings of waiters bearing pots of tea and magnificent silver tiers of teacakes and sandwiches.

Leng had insisted on holding Constance's chair, taking the duties of their waiter upon himself. He then took the seat opposite her and whisked his napkin into his lap as the waiter hovered to take their order.

"May I ask what you will have, sir?"

"The high tea," said Leng crisply. "Earl Grey. With sandwiches, teacakes, and petits fours."

"Yes, sir, coming forthwith." The waiter scurried off.

Leng turned to Constance. "I'm so glad we were able to arrange this *rencontre*, Your Grace." He gave her a slow, sensual smile. "The tea and cakes here are good, but the petits fours are *sublime*."

Constance did not respond immediately. Now that they were free from the mania of the ball, she had a chance to study his face more closely. He looked exactly as she remembered: the colorless skin, the eyes set like pallid sapphires in an oddly delicate face, the white-blond hair and the slender frame that nevertheless radiated strength. It unnerved her to see so clearly the Pendergast family resemblance in this face, with a habitual expression of icy indifference that reminded her of Diogenes.

Leng's charming, probing conversation as they danced—and in particular, his invitation to tea the very next day—had alarmed her. Once again, she was reminded just how clever and dangerous he could be. But it was that very fact, she'd decided, that made it necessary for her to act. January 7 was close—closer than it seemed. There was no way of knowing for sure what Leng would do or how he'd react. She had no choice but to put him off-balance and seize the initiative, aiming for his most vulnerable spot—the thing he coveted most.

And yet she had to be careful—exceedingly careful—not to overplay her hand. Not with Leng. She covered her internal disquiet and revulsion at his person, keeping her face light and insouciant.

"Dr. Leng, you mentioned you're interested in poisons. I find that curious. To what end?"

"Just one interest among many," said Leng, with an offhand wave. "My primary training is in psychiatric surgery—by that I mean surgery of the brain to alter behavior in patients suffering from psychosis."

"That sounds rather alarming."

"Not at all!" He chuckled. "I was lucky enough to study with a young, iconoclastic, and brilliant German doctor, Emil Kraepelin, who believes dementia praecox is a clinical disorder, deserving of treatment rather than imprisonment. As for the surgical aspect, penetration of the skull—for beneficial reasons—is one of the oldest medical operations for which we have evidence... although of course the early practitioners were woefully misguided. Today, it's a gift to be able to permanently relieve the dreadful and sometimes violent symptoms of mental alienation."

"I know, of course, about trepanning. But I didn't know surgery involving the brain was possible."

"In that sense, it *is* new. But progress has been remarkable."

"And where are you consulting?"

"At Bellevue Hospital."

"Nowhere else?"

"I also offer my services to the poor and unfortunate."

"How lovely for them—and how generous of you. But getting back to your interest in poisons... You didn't answer my question."

"I'm interested in the action of compounds that interfere with normal biological processes. The study of biological toxins can help illuminate life's fundamental secrets."

"Do you conduct experiments with poisons? I mean on animals, of course."

"Your Grace! You are certainly a curious young woman." He chuckled again. "No, all my work is done *in vitro*—that is, in cell cultures."

"I should think the temptation to experiment *in vivo* would be strong."

Constance saw, finally, a faint look of displeasure, possibly even suspicion, pass like a ripple across his face. "Your Grace, shall we speak of more pleasant subjects? Here is our tea."

The waiter busied himself placing the pot on the table, while a second waiter arranged two silver tiers, one resplendent with petits fours, the other with assorted finger sandwiches from which the crusts had been removed.

"Shall I pour, sir?" he asked Leng.

"We'll pour for ourselves."

"As you wish." The two waiters departed.

Leng paused a moment before speaking again. "Now: do tell me more about your illustrious family and how you came to leave your native land. I must confess I've never met a duchess before."

Constance forced a knowing smile. "And you still haven't."

He looked at her inquisitively. "How so?"

"Because I'm no duchess—as you no doubt already surmised."

His eyebrows rose. "No?"

"And while we're about it, let's clear up another misconception: I am not here at your invitation. You are here at mine."

At this, Leng looked momentarily flummoxed. Constance went on. "I've engineered this meeting from the start. *I* was the one who suggested you be invited to the ball. *I* was the one who intercepted you. *I* was the one who arranged for the Ozymandias sculpture, knowing your fondness for that poem."

She took great satisfaction in seeing his pale face grow paler. But it took him only a moment to recover.

"Allow me to serve you, *Your Grace*." An ironic tone crept into his voice as he tipped the teapot toward her cup.

"Thank you." Constance put a cube of sugar and a little milk into her cup, and Leng poured out the steaming beverage. With tongs he placed an assortment of sandwiches on a plate for her, then served himself.

"Now: tell me why you were so anxious to meet me."

"Who wouldn't want to meet the celebrated Enoch Leng, Surgeon, Mental Alienist, and Consulting Psychiatrist at Bellevue?"

He waited for her to go on, his face remaining studiously neutral.

She sipped the tea—perfectly steeped, rich with the fragrance of bergamot: one sip, two, and then a third—before she put the cup down. "I have taken an interest in you, Dr. Leng."

"I shall consider myself flattered." A smile played about his lips.

Constance had the sudden urge to remove it—but at the same time, that smile reminded her to keep to her plan and not push things too far. "I know quite a bit about you."

Another leisurely sip.

"I'm aware, for example, that you are expending enormous sums on acquiring exotic chemical poisons, reagents, and laboratory equipment."

"Perfectly normal; I'm a scientist engaged in important research."

"Perhaps. You have also extracted rare and fearful poisons not only from vipers and spiders; you've scoured the world to collect poisons that are untraceable, that are slow acting as well as instantaneous; poisons that are tasteless, colorless, and odorless. You have found these poisons in the skins of frogs in the Amazon, in the bladders of fishes in Japan, in the tentacles of jellyfish in the Austral regions, in the deadly fungi of Africa and the giant hornets of Indochina. You have in fact built up a remarkable arsenal of poisons, and you are analyzing these toxins and teasing out their chemical formulae and structures. You have even been able to synthesize and, shall we say, *improve* on some of them. Which returns us to the question I asked earlier: to what end?"

"To what end indeed?" Leng continued smiling, although the look on his face had become as frozen as a winter pond.

Constance, seeing that look, knew this was the moment to strike. "Since you insist on being coy, I will answer the question myself. You have a project. A project that will take many decades, possibly even a century, to complete."

"And what project might this be?"

"To destroy the human race, which you consider the most vile, brutish, and malevolent plague ever to infect the earth. And that isn't the extent of my knowledge—*Antoine*."

The man now went so still, he could have been a wax figure. And then, finally, a reaction broke through Leng's frozen façade. His features seemed to contract, betraying an astonishment and dismay so powerful there was no holding it back.

"I see you are shocked. No doubt I would be, were I in your position. The problem is, your quest to find the universal poison, disease, or other means capable of extincting Homo sapiens will likely take more than your lifespan. You already know that. So you are engaged in a *second* research effort: to extend your life."

She paused while the flower display behind them rustled. An underwaiter, back to the table, circled the arrangement, plumping the flowers, sorting through them, removing dead stems and adding fresh flowers from a hamper. As she waited for him to leave, Constance enjoyed watching Leng struggle to control the expression on his face.

When the man moved away, Leng spoke. "But how..." he began in a strangled voice, then stopped himself.

"*How* do I know all this?" She leaned forward and lowered her voice. "That is something I will never tell, and you will only waste your time trying to investigate. But do not fear: I'm not here to expose you." Constance calmly took a sandwich from her plate, giving it a little nibble. "Ham and minted pea. Delicious." She took another bite and followed it with a sip of tea. She nodded toward Leng's cup. "Dr. Leng, your tea is getting cold."

Leng drained the cup, then set it down with an unseemly rattle of china. "What do you want?" he managed to ask.

"Let us enjoy our tea for the moment, shall we?" Constance dropped in a sugar cube with a pair of tongs, added some milk, and poured another cup. She stirred slowly, set down the spoon, and took a leisurely sip. Then she selected another finger sandwich and held it daintily between thumb and forefinger. "Roast beef, tomato, and horseradish, I believe." She took a bite.

After a moment, Leng also poured another cup. Was his hand trembling?

She had struck. Now it was time to take a step back—and make sure the provocation was not too great. "I come with a proposition," she said.

"A proposition." Leng tried to smile. "I should have guessed. If we are to be in business together, may I at least know your name?"

"No, you may not," said Constance. "And as for what I want, we'll leave that aside for the time being. The important thing is, I have what *you* want."

"And, pray tell, what is that?" She could only admire at how quickly sarcasm was creeping back into his voice.

"The Arcanum."

He stared, thunderstruck all over again.

"Your research in psychiatric surgery has pointed the way. To develop this 'Arcanum,' this elixir to extend your lifespan, you require living human subjects."

"This is...quite absurd," he said.

"Let us, please, dispense with useless protestations of ignorance. The fact of the matter is, I have the complete sequence needed to synthesize the Arcanum you seek. I will give it to you as my part of an exchange."

"An exchange." He stared at her, his pupils mere pinpoints. "For what?"

"As I said: we'll leave that aside for the time being." Constance reached into her reticule and took out a small, leatherbound notebook and gold pencil. Opening the notebook, she began to write. For several minutes, there was only the sound of a pencil scratching on paper. Then she turned the notebook around and pushed it toward him.

He picked it up and stared.

"Do you know what that is?" she asked.

Still Leng stared.

She had, long ago, searched out and memorized the long and complex chemical synthesis hidden within Leng's own notebooks—from a date that was still many years in the future. Even Pendergast was unaware she possessed knowledge of the original Arcanum. She suspected that he, too, had discovered it when he first took possession of the Riverside Drive mansion...but they had never spoken of it.

"It's impossible," he said at last, voice strained.

"So you do recognize it. That makes things much simpler. Those chemical equations and reactions," she said, nodding at the notebook, "outline the first twelve steps in the synthesis of the Arcanum. There is of course a great deal more to it: the initiating factors, catalysts, enzymes, substrates, intermediate steps, equations and formulae—everything necessary. I have it all."

She watched closely as Leng stared at the pages. "This is extraordinary," he finally said. "I can hardly believe it. How on earth did you accomplish this?" He was so absorbed in the formula itself that everything else paled beside it. This was what she had hoped for—what she had counted on.

"I might add," Constance said, "that I am not claiming to have developed this synthesis on my own. Did you assume yourself to be the only one searching for the fountain of youth? Now, as to what I want: it will be revealed to you at the time of our transaction."

Leng looked puzzled afresh. "How can I be sure to have what you want, at a moment's notice?"

"Listen carefully: I *know* you have what I desire. We will meet at noon, on December twenty-seventh, in the public square at the intersection of Chambers and Center Streets. I will be accompanied by one, perhaps two acquaintances of mine, whose sole purpose will be to guarantee my safety. Then, and only then, will I name my price. At that point, you will directly fetch it and bring it to me in that public square...and I will give you a notebook containing the complete synthesis of the Arcanum."

She watched as he briefly considered this. "You put me in an uncomfortable position. What happens if I refuse the, ah, price?"

"You'll find the price to be within your means and, indeed, quite reasonable under the circumstances. If you refuse, you'll never see me, or the Arcanum, again. There will, naturally, be no negotiation."

"Why can't you just tell me the price now? Then I could be sure of complying."

"The matter is not open for further discussion. You have my terms and conditions. Now: do you agree, or not?"

"Today is Sunday," he said after a moment. "To be followed by Christmas Eve, Christmas, and Boxing Day. My, ah, bank won't be open for business again until December twenty-seventh. Assuming it is money you want?"

"Do not try my patience with more questions. I need your answer now."

Once more, Leng went silent. Constance was fairly sure she knew what he was thinking. The public square she had suggested as a meeting place was mere blocks from the private banking house where

Leng transacted all his financial business: this was, in fact, critical to her choice of December 27 as a diversion. She had been careful to say nothing about Leng's laboratory or where he performed his work. Shottum's Cabinet, and the tunnels beneath it where Mary was hidden somewhere, were equally close to that same public square—in the *opposite* direction. Leng would assume she wanted money; hence, her frequent repetition of the word "price." Or perhaps, he would speculate, she wanted something he was storing in a bank vault: some other prized possession of his. It was natural for him to speculate. But the last thing she'd want was one of his victims. That was her belief— and the gamble that had precipitated this exchange.

She'd misled Leng, thrown him off-balance, as much as she dared. She had no intention of giving him the actual Arcanum—she would never further his murderous project, in this universe or any other. A few select changes would nullify it, while still convincing him it was real. But in point of fact, this was academic: because in a few days, a week, perhaps a month, he would be dead by her hand.

"I agree to your proposition," said Leng.

She reached out a hand for the notebook. After an insolent delay, Leng returned it. She placed it back in her reticule. Then she plucked a petit four from the tier and took a dainty bite, savoring its sweetness. "Just as you promised, Dr. Leng—sublime. And now, I really must be going. Thank you so much for tea."

The fussy flower plumper, an under-waiter in the requisite black suit and white tie, finished freshening the displays and, his hamper filled with wilted blooms, turned to exit the elegant confines of Delmonico's through the staff doors. He paused briefly in the doorway and glanced back, his silvery eyes fixating on the man and woman just now finishing their tea. Then he turned and vanished catlike through the door—headed for Longacre Square.

53

June 9
Friday

Vincent D'Agosta was only too glad to get out of Borough Homicide and hail a cab uptown to Riverside Drive. Agent Coldmoon's arrival had been a breath of fresh air, and he couldn't deny a lot of progress had been made, but at the same time, it had sent the case spinning off in a totally new direction—a direction that didn't seem to involve D'Agosta much except in keeping up with paperwork and maintaining the pretense of continuing an unsuccessful investigation.

As the cab left the West Side Highway and merged onto Riverside Drive, Pendergast's mansion loomed up. "Nice crib!" the driver said as he pulled over. "Who lives here—some Colombian drug lord?"

"Yeah," said D'Agosta, getting out. "And his *guardias* have itchy trigger fingers."

Even before he could knock, the door was opened by Proctor, who stepped to one side as D'Agosta walked into the dim entryway.

"He's waiting for you in the library, sir," said Proctor. "You know the way." He turned and disappeared down some dim passageway off the refectory. D'Agosta watched him go. The man would always remain a cipher—not unlike his boss. He headed toward the library. As he crossed the vast reception hall, he wondered what Pendergast wanted. Over the phone, the agent's voice had retained little of its usual polished suavity.

Pendergast was in his usual chair. A carafe of green liquid stood on the side table next to him, along with a slotted silver spoon, a lighter, and the other paraphernalia of the man's absinthe habit.

Pendergast glanced over. "Ah, Vincent, how good of you to come on such short notice. Forgive me if I don't rise."

"No worries, stay where you are."

"May I offer you a—what is it—Budweiser Light? What I have to tell you may require mental fortification."

"Sure, thanks."

Mrs. Trask had materialized in the doorway, and now she disappeared once again to fetch his beer.

D'Agosta gave Pendergast a closer look. His face was still pale as death, of course, and the usual gleam in his eyes remained a hard, icy-blue flame. He wondered again what the hell was going on.

"My dear friend, before we go any further, I must ask you about this current case of yours. I understand it has drawn in my temporary FBI partner. How is it going?"

"Great," said D'Agosta sarcastically. "Just great."

"Has he not proved congenial?"

"Coldmoon's a most congenial, stand-up guy, smart and no-nonsense and easy to work with."

Pendergast inclined his head. "What's the problem?"

Mrs. Trask set the beer in front of him, along with a frosty glass. D'Agosta poured it out while Pendergast took a sip of absinthe.

"The problem is, he's taking over the meat of the case. In a day or two, he'll be off to Ecuador on an undercover operation while I stay back here, running interference and basically twiddling my thumbs."

Pendergast shifted in his seat. "Ecuador? Operation? You mystify me."

"Coldmoon linked the museum murder to a homicide out in South Dakota and the theft of Indian artifacts. Looks like the two killings, his and mine, were part of a mopping-up process, and we've got a suspect—a really solid one. Problem is, he lives in Ecuador, apparently some hacienda way the hell up in the Andes. We've got to lure him back to the U.S. on some pretense in order to arrest him, because we can't extradite. So the plan is for your pal Coldmoon to fly to Ecuador on a fishing expedition, while I cool my heels in New York, pretending we're totally baffled. That might make the guy in Ecuador relax, but meanwhile my job will consist of taking abuse from all sides for not making any obvious progress."

"I see. And you have no other cases of particular import at present?"

"We've always got other cases, but they're all pieces of shit."

"So you could potentially take some time off?"

"Well...workwise, it's not a problem. But, I mean, Laura wants us to go somewhere, take a vacation. We really haven't discussed it in detail." He took another gulp of beer and waited for Pendergast to explain why he had summoned him.

A long silence as Pendergast stared into the fire. "I'm involved in something that I simply can't do alone, and I require someone I can trust implicitly: someone who is utterly capable and reliable, and that I've worked with enough to know well. That is, of course, you. It— involves a journey."

"Where?"

Another long silence. "Vincent, is it fair to say you've witnessed many strange things during our long and fruitful association?"

"That's putting it mildly."

"You are about to experience by far the strangest. I'm not quite sure how to explain this to you, so I'll be as direct as possible. I only ask that you suspend your disbelief until I provide proof."

"Okay," said D'Agosta, lifting his beer for another sip.

"In the basement, I have a time machine."

D'Agosta almost choked on his beer. He put the glass down, coughing.

"Constance used this machine without my knowledge or permission, and has gone back to 1880 to save her sister from death and, I believe, to kill her old guardian and nemesis, Dr. Leng."

He looked steadily at D'Agosta, as if challenging him to doubt his words. D'Agosta could find no words.

"You *do* recall Dr. Leng, my dear Vincent?"

D'Agosta felt his skin crawl. "Jesus. Of course." How could he forget the Surgeon, whose mass murders had terrorized New York? That was before the death of Bill Smithback, the reporter who covered the killings both new...and old. He stared at his beer as the details came back to him: Leng was an ancestor of Pendergast's, and he'd discovered an elixir for prolonging life that required harvesting human body parts. Leng had lived in this very mansion before Pendergast inherited it following his death—and, in a cruel twist of fate, Leng had taken the innocent young Constance, first as a guinea pig, then as his ward, keeping her sequestered in the house and greatly slowing her aging process along with his own. It was only much later she'd learned that her older sister, Mary, had been a victim of the very experiments that kept her young.

Pendergast, he realized, was speaking again. "As you know better than almost anyone, Leng is exceedingly, *supremely* dangerous. Constance has already taken him on, alone, and I fear she will ultimately fail—and perish—in the attempt."

It had finally happened, D'Agosta decided: Pendergast had snapped. He always knew genius and madness went hand in hand. It had been the same with his younger, implacably evil brother, Diogenes. Wherever Constance had actually gone, whatever had really taken place here—and it was obvious something *had* taken place—had pushed the FBI agent over the edge.

Pendergast rose. "Let me show you. It's in the basement."

"Uh, sure." D'Agosta gulped down the rest of his Bud. If Pendergast had gone insane, there was no way to guess how he'd react if crossed—and D'Agosta didn't want to step down into that basement without one last taste of beer.

The agent walked to a dim corner of the library, where the press of a concealed button caused a bookcase to swing outward. Beyond was a stone staircase descending into darkness. At the bottom, D'Agosta followed Pendergast through the mansion's basement until they reached a large door, lined in metal, with a keypad beside it. Pendergast rapped on the door and it was immediately opened by Proctor. Another man was in the room, D'Agosta saw, wearing a white lab coat and standing beside a very large machine—if the word *machine* could be used for the most outlandish contraption D'Agosta had ever seen, a monstrous contrivance that resembled something out of a sci-fi movie, joined in unholy alliance with the work of H. R. Giger.

Pendergast turned to the man in the lab coat. "Dr. Ferenc, you may begin."

"Now, wait," said D'Agosta as the man started messing with the dials and a low humming sound gradually filled the room. "What are you going to do?"

"Not me, *we*," said Pendergast. "I am going to take you on a brief field trip into the past."

"No," said D'Agosta. "No way." He wasn't getting anywhere near that crazy device, which would surely electrocute them all—if not worse.

"It's the only way to prove I haven't lost my mind—as you no doubt are thinking—and to persuade you just how critical the situation is." He raised an arm. "Proctor? The frock coat, hat, and hobnail boots, please."

"Just wait a damn minute," D'Agosta protested as Proctor draped the articles over his head and shoulders, swapped out his footwear, then returned to a monitoring station at the far end of the machine. The pitch was rising quietly; the man in the white coat was murmuring something; and then D'Agosta saw a ring of light begin to form in front of the machine.

"Oh no," D'Agosta said. "*Hell*, no."

As Pendergast donned a top hat of his own, the ring of light grew larger and brighter—and then a wavering, intangible meniscus formed inside it, beyond which D'Agosta could see vague outlines of what looked like buildings.

"Slow down!" he said. "We've got to talk this out first."

Pendergast came over quickly and grasped D'Agosta's shoulders, leaning in and fixing him with his gaze. D'Agosta had never seen the man like this. He felt Pendergast's fingers clamp against his shoulders like steel. *"I must have your help, old friend,"* he said, *"or I shall be lost."*

When Pendergast continued to hold his gaze, D'Agosta found he could do nothing but nod in assent.

"Leave your sidearm and cell phone on that table."

D'Agosta removed his weapon and phone and did as instructed. Pendergast helped him on with the heavy coat. Then—with a warning to not look directly at the circle of light—he gently guided D'Agosta toward the shimmering surface and walked through along with him.

54

D'Agosta became aware of a sudden lurching sensation in his gut, then felt himself falling. He was about to give a shout of alarm when he realized he was lying on a cobbled surface, dirty with trash and something worse.

"My dear Vincent." He heard the familiar voice, felt a strong arm slipping under his shoulder. "Let me help you up."

After a moment, D'Agosta managed to stagger to his feet. He felt Pendergast brushing his coat. "Let's get some of this filth off you," he heard the agent say, "or we're liable to be arrested as vagrants."

D'Agosta looked about, the world swimming back into view. They were standing in a narrow alleyway. Solid brick walls rose on either side, and a rotten wooden fence blocked the far end. The air smelled of smoke, horseshit, and piss. At the opening to the alleyway, he could see what looked like a bustling boulevard on a winter's evening.

"There, I think you're presentable," said Pendergast, stepping back and handing him his top hat.

D'Agosta took it and stared at him, still stunned.

"Shall we?" Pendergast gestured toward the end of the alleyway.

Still D'Agosta stared. He was trying to process what was happening, but couldn't quite manage it.

"Come," said Pendergast, linking his arm with his. "Let us go then, you and I."

D'Agosta walked with him out of the alleyway, then stopped again, looking about. He was at one edge of a vast, open square of hard-packed dirt. Horses and carts were going this way and that, while pedestrians streamed along cobbled sidewalks on all sides. A racket of clopping hooves, shouts, and whistles cut through the air. Low brick buildings stretched ahead as far as the eye could see. The lamps were just being lit.

"Welcome to Longacre Square, December twenty-third, 1880," Pendergast said. "Or, as it will later be known, Times Square."

D'Agosta stared, scarcely able to think. "It's June, not December," he said stupidly.

"Pull yourself together, my friend," Pendergast replied sharply. "This is going to be a brief visit: just a tour of the city in a hansom cab. Ah—here comes one now."

Pendergast whistled and a horse-drawn carriage came clattering over, its driver perched on a seat behind the cab and holding a long whip in one hand. With Pendergast's urging, D'Agosta climbed in and onto the bench seat, Pendergast joining him a moment later. The front of the cab was open to the air, with two glass windows on either side.

"Let us keep our voices low, shall we?" Pendergast said. "Now, Vincent: are you warm enough?"

D'Agosta pulled his coat closer around him. It was very chilly, and patches of dirty snow lay here and there. "This is...so *bizarre*."

Instead of answering, Pendergast turned to their driver. "Head over to Fifth Avenue and turn north, if you please."

"Yes, sir." The man flicked his whip and the horse took off at a steady trot.

Pendergast glanced back at D'Agosta. "Bizarreness, like salt, gives flavor to existence. Without it, life would be as long and tedious as an opera by Wagner."

"But...how did you manage this...I mean, what the *hell* is going on?"

"You already know where we are. I'll explain everything else when we return to our own timeline—the how, what, and most importantly, *why.* The purpose of this jaunt is to, first, convince you I'm not insane and that I actually have a device that can transport us to an alternate time…and second, to give you a taste of 1880s New York, so that when we return you'll have had the chance to accept the reality of the situation, get over your surprise, and be able to act more naturally. One has to be careful here: after all, no matter what we do, we will never look quite right or speak quite normally."

The cab turned onto Fifth Avenue and began making its way uptown, revealing a parade of large, gorgeously ornamented mansions on either side of the broad avenue, the windows glowing softly in the gathering dark.

"Welcome to the Gilded Age," said Pendergast.

D'Agosta stared at the structures of stone and brick, rising four and five stories, in a motley display of architectural styles, with turrets and towers, gables and gargoyles. A few looked faintly familiar, but most were completely unknown to him.

"The Appletons," said Pendergast. "The Tookers on your left, the Rhinelanders to your right, the Havemeyers, the Stuyvesant Fishes…" His languid fingers flicked left and right as they passed mansion after mansion. Then Pendergast turned to the driver once more.

"Slow down at the next block, please, but don't stop." He leaned toward D'Agosta. "Vincent, please direct your attention to that town house there."

The driver brought the horse into a walk as Pendergast indicated a tall, somewhat narrow mansion of pink marble whose taste and elegance made it stand out from the rest. It was still in the last stages of completion, with a steam hoist raising a block of stone to the roof and workmen scurrying about.

"Who lives there?" D'Agosta asked.

"It belongs to a woman calling herself the Duchess of Ironclaw. Known to you and me as Constance Greene."

"You're shitting me."

"Careful, my dear Vincent—this era is quite intolerant of such language."

D'Agosta could hardly believe what he was hearing. He peered at the house with renewed interest. "I see a child in a second-floor window. Who's that?"

"That is also Constance Greene."

"What the—?"

"There are now two of them, you see—the Constance of the 1880s, who is just a child, and the Constance that we know, who has returned to the past with violence on her mind."

D'Agosta shook his head wordlessly.

"I learned these facts, and much more, on the first two occasions I used the machine to return to this place. But I'll spare you those details. The point is, she is playing a most dangerous game, and already she's in deep—very deep. Her life is at risk—as, my dear Vincent, yours will be, too, should you agree to assist me. But all shall be explained once we're back in more familiar surroundings." Pendergast rapped on the roof. "Driver, return us to Longacre Square, if you please."

55

For D'Agosta, the next half hour passed in a blur: another sensory overload of unfamiliar sights and sounds; another jolting trip in a darkened carriage; and, strangest of all, that feeling of hurtling through a limitless void, ending with the nightmarish sensation of falling. And then they were back in Pendergast's basement lab, Pendergast standing, D'Agosta lying flat on the floor. He could hear voices as the whine of the machine ran down. He closed his eyes and took several deep breaths, opened them, and rose unsteadily to his feet.

"You may leave us, Proctor," he heard Pendergast say. "And Dr. Ferenc, once you've completed the post-shutdown assessment, you may consider your work done for the evening."

"The machine registered some unusual readings on this trip," said the man named Ferenc. "It's probably due to operating with two persons rather than one, but I'd better stick around to make sure it's nominal."

Proctor left. Pendergast helped D'Agosta off with the heavy coat and hat, gave him back his weapon, cell phone, and shoes, then gestured at the still-open door. "Vincent, shall we retire to the library?"

D'Agosta stepped forward, staggered, righted himself. He tried to speak, but his voice came out a croak. "I'm not going anywhere until you explain—no bullshit, no ten-dollar words—what the *fuck* just happened."

For a moment, Pendergast was still. Then he seemed to relent. "Earlier, I told you that I needed your help. But in order to truly make you understand the magnitude of what I'm asking of you, I had to take you back in time: to the place where your help is needed."

"Back in time," D'Agosta echoed.

"Actually, that's not precisely correct. This machine creates a portal to a parallel universe, providing a bridge of sorts to an alternate New York City in an alternate 1880. I'll spare you the technical details, save to assure you that nothing we do there will alter our own timeline. You could shoot my ancestor in that alternate 1880—which would, in fact, simplify matters considerably—but that would not in any way impact my existence in our own world."

D'Agosta took another deep breath, got his voice back. "If it doesn't make any difference, if that world doesn't intersect with our own...then why should we give a shit?"

"Constance is there. *My* Constance."

"And the other Constance? The little girl I saw?"

"She is a part of the other timeline." Pendergast hesitated. "It's complicated, but my Constance felt that using this machine offered her a way to right past wrongs, redress grievances...and perhaps provide a more suitable home for her and her siblings. I used the machine to make sure she was...flourishing."

"And to let her know she had a way home, in case she'd changed her mind," D'Agosta said before he could stop himself.

Pendergast did not answer directly. "What I discovered confirmed my worst fears: Constance would not be content with saving her brother and sister. She intends to wreak vengeance on her former guardian."

"You mean...Leng?"

"Yes, I do. She is so blinded by her desire for vengeance that she's not thinking clearly. She cannot prevail over that man—not alone. If I don't interfere, it will end in a way so awful I fear to imagine it. But I can't do this by myself—certainly not without giving away my presence to Constance. I need you, old partner."

"But..." D'Agosta began. Then he halted. His mind was in turmoil. If Constance had made this choice, who was Pendergast to interfere? Surely she'd reject his meddling if she knew.

He felt Pendergast take his elbow. "Let's proceed to the library. We can talk more freely there—and I'll do my best to answer the other questions I know you must have."

And they left. For a moment, the lab was silent. Then Ferenc emerged from behind the housing of the machine's secondary assembly, where he'd been running postoperative diagnostics. He stretched a moment, massaging his lower back. And then he stood motionless for several minutes, staring speculatively at the closed door, before returning his attention to the equipment.

56

Dr. Enoch Leng strode out of the chapel, converted to a foul-smelling dormitory, and into the antechamber of the Five Points House of Industry, snugging his thin leather gloves tight. He had finished ministering to the patients confined to the corner of the chapel that served as an infirmary: three consumptives, two cases of grippe, and one girl afflicted with gonorrhea. But before taking his leave, he had also examined a half-dozen young women as possible candidates. While he was disappointed to find that none was an ideal specimen for his needs, there were two that might be suitable, should he find no others on his next visit. To prepare for this possibility, he pronounced the two girls anemic and prescribed "vitamins"—actually, low doses of arsenic coated in sugar—so that, should he end up requiring them by the time of his next visit, they would present with sufficient nausea, abdominal distress, and neuropathy to justify transferal to his private sanatorium.

At the sound of his footsteps on the wide pine boards, Miss Crean, the nurse in residence at the workhouse, came forward, moving with all the appearance of a reanimated cadaver, wearing a long dark dress buttoned from neck to waist that served as a uniform.

"Are your rounds complete, Doctor?" she asked, her air of frosty authority checked by the presence of the eminent surgeon.

"They are indeed, Nurse."

"And may I inquire whether our residents are all fit to work?"

"For the most part, yes. There are two, however, who bear watching. I've given them both medication for anemia. If they don't improve, they may need further attention on my next visit."

"Very good. And the five patients in isolation?"

Isolation, Dr. Leng reflected, was a relative term. "The consumptive Irish girl is poorly. The pestilence has spread throughout both lungs, and I don't expect it to improve—especially in this damp and chilly weather. You might consider removing her to an, ah, even more isolated location; consumption is a disease of the vapors, you know, and proximity to others encourages transmission."

He realized that, by saying this, he was in all likelihood condemning the small, red-haired girl to an even quicker death—Miss Crean would probably have her ejected, kicked onto the street, where in her current condition she would rapidly expire—but quickening the inevitable, he thought, might almost be considered humane.

Leng watched as the thin woman's piercing eyes took this in, revealing nothing.

"I do have a request to make," he said.

"Of course, Doctor."

"You will remember the girl I admitted to my private sanatorium at the end of November—Mary Greene?"

Miss Crean nodded.

"You'll be pleased to hear that she is much improved."

Miss Crean nodded again. No doubt all of Dr. Leng's patients improved...because none of them had ever come back.

"It has come to my attention that she has a sister—a younger sister. Her name is..." He made a show of taking a notebook from his breast pocket and consulting it. "Constance. Is she a resident of the work-house? I inquire because her older sister, Mary, turns out to have a rare kind of disease which passes from mother to daughter, due to an imbalance in bilious humors—a superabundance of black bile at the expense of yellow bile. The sister will develop the same ailment as Mary, and it would be better to treat her now, at an age when it is still preventable."

Leng had read Mendel's articles on biological factors years before, as well as the lectures Louis Pasteur had presented to the French Academy of Sciences just that month under the title *Sur les maladies virulentes et en particulier sur la maladie appelée vulgairement choléra des poules*. But he knew most ignorant people, even doctors and nurses, still stubbornly clung to a belief in humorism.

"We have no such person at the House of Industry, Doctor," she said. "I'm not aware that Mary Greene had a sister."

"No? The Mission, perhaps?"

The nurse shook her head. "Is there any particular reason for your interest?"

"Yes." And in fact, there was. As his shock at the confrontation over tea had eased, he'd become aware of a different feeling: familiarity. Specifically, the facial features of the duchess. But he was not going to tell this to Miss Crean. Instead, he said: "It's because, while this disease is usually passed on within families, it also occasionally manifests with great virulence among the elderly—of the fairer sex, in particular."

Miss Crean's face did not change when she replied: "I did once see Mary Greene in furtive conversation with an urchin girl."

"Ah," said Dr. Leng.

"The bookkeeper here has a rather unhealthy interest in the comings and goings of people in the Points," the woman said. "Perhaps he knows more of this." Turning, she called out: "Mr. Royds!"

There was an odd rustling sound, like a nest of disturbed rats, and then a filthy-looking man with sleeve garters emerged from a dark corner of the entrance room. He approached them from the far side of the divider, then halted, touching his cap in the direction of Leng. He approached Miss Crean, who exchanged a few low words with him. He nodded once; listened some more; nodded again; then came around the divider and—with another touch of his cap—he exited the heavy front door into the night.

"He may know of the person in question," the woman told Leng. "At least, he's seen a waif that fits the description. He's off now, to ask around."

Fifteen minutes later, the vile fellow returned. And not long after that, Dr. Leng exited the House of Industry, after having given Royds several coins for his trouble. On the front steps he stopped and took a moment to look around at the nocturnal scene. The squalor and noisome air bothered him not in the least.

Royds's investigations had borne fruit. Almost two weeks ago to the day, a young girl bearing a similarity to Mary Greene had been abducted from Mission Place sometime during the early hours of the evening. Although *abducted* might not be the right word—the girl had been chased and seized by a lady, some witnesses said, but after struggling had allowed herself to be led off of her own accord. The woman was quite young, and her eyes, according to a witness to this bizarre abduction, were a most unusual shade of violet.

Dr. Leng pulled off a glove, put two fingers to his lips, and emitted a piercing whistle. A few moments later, his carriage—glossy black and elegantly appointed, one of very few that could travel through the Five Points unmolested—came around the nearby corner.

As he stepped in and closed the door, and the carriage moved away, Leng considered the developments. Joe Greene, a young pickpocket, had escaped Blackwell's Island in the general riot that had taken place there on the night of December 1, and was now presumed drowned. And roughly a week later, his younger sister, Constance, had been spirited away from this place . . . by a young woman with violet eyes.

Interesting, Leng mused as his carriage moved toward cleaner, grander streets to the north and west. *Most interesting indeed.*

57

It was past ten pm when Laura got back to their condo. D'Agosta was sitting on the living room couch, where he'd flung himself down three hours before and hadn't moved from since, his mind working nonstop.

"Hi, baby!" Laura said as she hung up her coat.

"Long day?" D'Agosta replied. He was aware she'd stopped asking him how his own work was going—a subject likely to lead in a depressing direction. But this day was different: how could he explain to her, or anyone, what had happened?

"Oh my God," Laura said. She'd walked into the bathroom to freshen up, leaving the door ajar. "I thought I'd seen everything," she continued, over the sound of running water. "But the things this second unit is asking for just keep getting more outrageous. They can do so much with digital effects and green screen now, you know, that they want to make sure every *real* location shot counts. And I mean *counts*."

D'Agosta half-listened.

"...So for this remake of *Side Street*, they wanted to head north and set up this long establishing boom shot, where the camera pans down from the skyline all the way to the pavement. The kind you just can't duplicate on a soundstage or with a workstation. The AD wants the camera to linger over the Fifth Avenue intersection, looking straight down, so there's no question it's the real thing. The *intersection*, right? Outside the main branch of the library. At *rush* hour."

Hearing this, D'Agosta felt a curious sensation of unreality. That meant Fifth Avenue in the lower Forties. He'd been there himself a few hours earlier—but it sure as hell hadn't been any Fifth Avenue he'd ever seen before. He wondered if the whole thing was some kind of trick, or if he'd had some sort of mental breakdown or maybe just dreamed it. But he knew that couldn't be right. It had been all too real: the cries; the gaslit dimness that settled over the city as evening drew near; the smell of horseshit and soot; the old buildings and carriages and plumes of coal smoke rising into the sky. If he hadn't left the heavy cloak, hobnail boots, and top hat back in Pendergast's basement, he knew their apartment would now be full of that very same stink.

"...Just that setup alone would have taken hours and at least two dozen uniforms. But that was only the beginning, because next they planned to show the outer wall of a bank vaporize, with gold bars spilling out into the street." Laura's voice had taken on an artificially bright edge. "While most of it would be CG, it still meant closing the block for hours, a bitch of a setup, and no less than four cameras. It was a day with bad going to worse."

Bad going to worse. That's what Pendergast had said, too. "*If I don't interfere, it will end in a way so awful I fear to imagine it. But I can't do this myself. I need you, old partner.*"

He came out of his brooding with another jolt, only to see Laura standing before him. Her hair was damp, her arms crossed in front of her. "Okay, Vinnie. What's up?"

"Sorry." Laura was too sharp to be put off with an evasive answer. "It's not work," he said, certain that's what she was thinking. "That's mostly in the hands of the feds now. I've decided to hand it over to Wybrand anyway. The investigation's going overseas, and there isn't much for us to do until they get their man back to the States."

Her brows knitted. "Wybrand? You've done all the footwork so far—what's the point of letting him take the credit?"

"I wouldn't get much credit for mopping up. Just the opposite:

we've got to pretend we're making no headway on the case, or the target in Ecuador might get spooked. So there's nothing to do, essentially, except take heat for not making progress."

"I see." Laura seemed dissatisfied. She could tell there was more. D'Agosta took a deep breath. He wasn't ready to talk about anything that had happened to him today—it was too strange, too sudden, too new. And Laura wouldn't believe it. Nobody would. It would scare the shit out of her, make her think he was having a breakdown. But he had to tell her something...unless, that is, he decided to turn down his friend's request.

"I went by Pendergast's place again," he said.

"Really?" she asked, taking a seat beside him. Her question was carefully neutral. Laura hadn't mentioned Pendergast since his name came up at the restaurant.

"Yes. He wanted to see me."

"And did you finally find out what's been troubling him?"

"Yeah. I did."

A pause. "So? What is it?"

D'Agosta took in another deep breath. "Laura, I can't tell you."

It was almost as if he'd slapped her. She flinched, drew back on the couch. "Can't? Or won't?"

Both. How can I explain what I don't understand myself? You've already put up with so much—how can I lay this on you, too? Aloud, he said: "Laura, you're the best thing that ever happened to me. I mean that."

"Save that shit for the Hallmark Channel."

"He needs my help."

"Oh God, no—again?"

D'Agosta could see in her eyes that her long patience with him was nearing an end.

"And just how does he want to try getting you killed this time?" she asked.

"It's...complicated."

"In other words, you *won't* tell me."

"Laura—"

"You know, Vinnie, I just don't get you. Here you are, shutting me out for weeks, while I've been trying every damned way I can think of to reach *you*, help *you*, find out what's wrong—and then Pendergast lifts a finger and you come running to him like some lapdog."

There was nothing D'Agosta could say to refute this, so he just shook his head.

"Can you at least tell me what's involved? I mean, do you have to go away? Is it some secret a police captain can't know? Is it an FBI case, or something personal?"

"Personal. I...I haven't decided what to do. And I can't tell you because I promised him—and anyway, you wouldn't believe me."

"I'll tell you what I don't believe," she said, standing up. "I don't believe we're having this conversation." And she strode to the closet, got out her coat, and left, closing the front door quietly behind her.

58

December 24, 1880
Monday

Christmas Eve, and the sidewalks of Fifth Avenue were crowded with shoppers gazing into store windows, buying presents, and ordering geese, figgy puddings, and sweetmeats for the feast that would take place the next day.

A little farther north, as the shopping district gave way to the elegant houses of the rich, a black carriage had pulled over and was standing on the eastern side of the avenue, just north of Forty-Eighth Street. The coachman had descended from his seat, taken off his coat despite the chilly weather, rolled up his sleeves, and was industriously repairing what appeared to be some mechanical problem with the undercarriage.

Inside the coach itself, Dr. Enoch Leng had taken from its case a beautifully machined brass telescope, made by Dollond of London. He extended the eyepiece and, holding the device by the primary barrel, aimed it through the smoked glass of his carriage window at the building directly across the street: a private town house, whose beautiful marble façade exuded a cool pinkish-white glow.

Raising the eyepiece into view, he slowly extended the secondary barrel of the refracting telescope—careful not to rotate it—until a magnified portion of the façade of the mansion came into sharp focus. Slowly, very slowly, he panned over the façade, taking mental note of the architectural features, the windows, the various decorations and carved stone embellishments, paying particular attention to possible means of ingress. He noted its corner location, and the fact that the mansion's roof was in the final stages of completion, the work now suspended due to Christmas Eve.

As he was completing his observations, there was a commotion from behind the house. A minute or two later, the duchess's coach, drawn by magnificent matched Percherons, its doors embellished with a coat of arms, emerged from a private carriageway onto Forty-Eighth Street. It turned onto the avenue and bore north. Leaning back from the window of his own conveyance and adjusting the telescope's field of view, he caught a momentary glimpse of the Countess of Ironclaw as the carriage passed him.

So the woman was going out. Under normal circumstances, he might have followed her. However, this unexpected departure offered him another and perhaps more fruitful option.

Leng raised the telescope, giving the mansion a final pass with the objective lens. As he did so, he saw a boy pass by one of the upstairs windows, books under his arm.

He lowered the instrument, slipping on the lens cover, then retracting first the eyepiece, then the secondary extension, into the primary barrel, and placed it in its leather case.

Leng gave a quiet rap on the door, signaling the coachman that he could cease feigning to work on the carriage. Once the driver was back in position on his seat, Leng instructed him to go around the block and pull over on Forty-Eighth Street, fifty yards or so back from the intersection with Fifth Avenue. As the carriage began to move, Leng opened a cabinet hidden in the forward seat and selected certain articles of clothing from it. The lid of the cabinet held a mirror on its inside face, along with cosmetics and business cards. He rifled through the cards until he found the one he was looking for.

When the black carriage pulled up to the curb of Forty-Eighth Street, the man who descended from it bore little resemblance to the brilliant surgeon Dr. Enoch Leng. While many men of the time still affected a cane, the one Leng now grasped was no mere accessory of fashion: he leaned upon it with a pronounced limp. The frock coat had been replaced by more common, but clearly well-tailored, business attire such as a commercial banker might wear. Most altered, however, was the face: Leng now sported muttonchop sideburns, faintly blue-smoked pince-nez that made his eyes difficult to see, and a jaundiced complexion. This was crowned, literally, by a top hat that, by the very sheen of its expensive, glossy beaver felt, drew the eye to it rather than the wearer. More than any of this, however, was an overall change in Leng's mannerisms, tics, and all the little eccentricities that make up a person, so nuanced they remain recognized only subconsciously.

He made his way, slowly but with dignity, around the corner onto Fifth Avenue and up to the attractive marble mansion. He paused for a moment, taking note once again of the unfinished work high above. Then he made his way up the steps and knocked firmly on the front door.

It was answered by a woman in a maid's uniform. "May I help you, sir?" she asked.

Leng touched his hat with the slight degree of deference required when meeting the lower classes. "Yes, thank you," he said in an accent more common in the states of Missouri and Kentucky than New York. "Might I inquire if the mistress of the house is in? I would appreciate having a brief word with her." As he spoke, he took a single, polite step inside out of the weather, and though his head was inclined downward while addressing the shorter woman, his eyes were every-where, taking in every angle, dimension, and architectural feature in sight with the precision of a camera. They were standing in a front hall, which had an inner door as well as an outer one, and through the open inner door Leng could see that the house appeared to be well organized, tight, and secure.

He put his weight on his cane, turned his face, and emitted a wheezy, consumptive cough.

The woman was well trained. "I'm afraid the duchess is out," she said, standing in front of him and refusing to give up ground, despite the unpleasant cough. "If you would care to leave your card—"

This was interrupted by the appearance of another figure, approaching out of the dimness of a far gallery. Seeing the new person arrive, the maid fell silent and took a step back—an action Leng took as an opportunity to close the front door and take another discreet step forward.

As the figure approached, Leng saw it was a woman, very different from the housemaid. She had an erect carriage and was young and discreetly beautiful. As she came up to Leng, she looked directly at him and spoke politely, but with neither deference nor intimidation.

"As you've just heard, the mistress of the house is out," she said in English made all the more exquisite by a pronounced French accent. "I am Her Grace's personal assistant. May I inquire as to the nature of your visit?"

While she spoke, she shut the stout inner door through which she had come, confining the three of them to the front hallway.

Observing this, Leng knew he would not be let any farther into the mansion. It was here he would have to conduct his business.

"I am indeed sorry to trouble you on Christmas Eve," he said, with another cough. "Please allow me to introduce myself: Wilberforce Hale, Juris Doctor, here on behalf of a client who lives in an abode very near your own." While he spoke, he removed a card, which he held up briefly and then laid in a silver salver on a tiny table placed there for that purpose.

The personal assistant nodded her acknowledgment, but made no effort to identify herself. Leng, while taking note of this breach of decorum, was unconcerned: he already knew she was named Féline, as he had learned many other things about the mansion and its occupants.

"Since the duchess is out, I shall make my business as brief as possible," he went on. "My client is a man of wealth and probity. He understands that—how shall I put this?—accommodation must be made to fit circumstance. Hence, he has not up to now complained at the lengthy hours—from early in the morning until late at night— or the attendant noise involved with the completion of this residence.

However, my client is also a religious man, and if I may say so, one who respects long-standing tradition. He has noted that work has been proceeding here on the Sabbath as it does on all other days, continuing into the Christmas Season. The celebration of Christmas has always loomed large among his family's traditions. Many relatives and friends will be gathered there in festivity and the contemplation of the true meaning of the holiday. In that spirit, and in light of the patience he has extended so far, he has asked me to request that you cease all work on the residence from now until the first day of the New Year. And he further asks that, thereafter, work ceases at seven in the evening and does not commence until seven the next morning."

He halted and gave the woman a stern look.

She said nothing in reply to this, and in the brief silence Leng heard a childish laugh, and then a voice—faint and far above, but obviously that of a young girl.

The sound of this voice answered the final question Leng had about the composition of the house's occupants. When the woman still didn't answer, he said, "If I may be blunt, mademoiselle, my client had hoped this visit would not be necessary. And, if I may be blunt just a moment longer, he hopes this request will be understood as both fair and rational under the circumstances, and that your employer will honor it...in which case she will not need to hear from me again, and this visit can serve only to welcome Her Grace to this splendid neighborhood."

He had shown his steel, but only in the politest of ways, following it up with another cough.

Finally, the woman responded. "I thank you for your visit, Mr. Hale," she said. "I will see that Her Grace receives both your card and your message."

"I can ask no more. And upon that note, allow me to wish you, and all who occupy this beautiful dwelling, the best of the season." And, with a bow and a slight doffing of his top hat, Leng turned, exited the outer door, and made his way down the steps, hearing the door close firmly behind him.

As he made his way back to his carriage, Leng had not the slightest concern about any inquiries the duchess might make. He had not identified his client, and it could be any of half a dozen who lived in the nearby palaces. Beyond that, he had gone so far as to hire the real lawyer, Wilberforce Hale, for this express purpose under an assumed name. Should the duchess contact him directly, which was unlikely, the lawyer might be surprised his client had taken such a step in his name, but was bound by privilege to say nothing more.

As his carriage proceeded down Fifth Avenue, Leng carefully arranged all the little details in his mind that he had observed about the mansion and its occupants. As he expected, the house was the residence not only of the duchess, but of the missing Joe Greene and his younger sister, Constance.

If only Mary Greene were at home, he reflected, the trio of siblings would have been complete.

59

June 10
Saturday

COLDMOON APPROACHED THE SAME booth in "The Bones" where
Vinnie D'Agosta had taken him the day they first met. The lieutenant
was already seated, back to the front door—a professional courtesy
to Coldmoon as a fellow law enforcement officer—and the pitcher of
Harp sat beading up on the worn wooden table, two empty glasses
beside it.

"This place again?" Coldmoon asked as he slid into the booth,
hoping his trousers wouldn't stick to the seat. He nodded at the bones
nailed to the walls. "Don't you see enough of this shit during your day
job?" He laughed.

"It's a time-honored tradition," said D'Agosta. "And it seemed
easier, since you know where it is."

As D'Agosta poured out the beers, Coldmoon took a closer look
at his haggard face. "Jesus," he said. "You look like ten miles of bad
road."

"That's good, because I feel more like fifty."

"Let's hear about it."

D'Agosta just shook his head. "Just some personal shit in my life.
Tell me instead about this plan of yours to nail that bastard Armendariz. When you feds suddenly clam up, that means you're making
progress."

Coldmoon couldn't help but grin: this was often the case. "You're right. As I told you, Ecuador won't extradite one of their own...even one who bought his citizenship. So I'm going down there to dangle something he won't be able to resist."

"And just what is this article you'll be dangling? Sitting Bull's condom?"

Coldmoon looked at D'Agosta askance. "We know the guy collects only the best. So the plan is to tease him with an artifact so valuable, so unique, he'll be like a harpooned fish, and we'll just pull him in." Coldmoon reached into his jacket pocket, took out a laminated color photograph, and laid it on the table. It showed the tanned hide of a buffalo, leather side up. Painted on the leather were over a hundred pictures and pictographs in a spiral pattern, starting from the center and traveling round and round outward to the edges.

"What is it?"

"It's called a Winter Count. Shortly before you white devils wiped out most of our cultural heritage, this is how we Lakota recorded our history. We painted it on buffalo skins like this one. Each picture represents the most important event of the year—one per year. The Winter Count buffalo hide belonged to a visionary medicine man who also served as the tribe's historian, and he used the pictures as a kind of mnemonic device. It was his responsibility to memorize the tribal history and recite bits and pieces of it to anyone who asked. It was called a Winter Count because we considered the year to run from first snow to first snow."

"That's impressive."

"It sure is." He pointed to the first drawing, in the center of the buffalo hide: a dramatic streak of red and yellow, with sparks coming off. "That evidently represents a big fireball in the sky—an asteroid. And the last picture, all those horses crowded together with men in blue lying on the ground, records the Battle of Greasy Grass—aka the Little Bighorn. That happened in 1876. Counting back from that known date, the first drawing was made in 1775, before the Lakota even knew the Wasichus existed. Incredible, isn't it? One hundred and one years of Lakota history. The reason it stops in 1876 is because the owner of this Winter Count was killed—bayoneted by a soldier."

"Who *was* the owner?"

At this, Coldmoon smiled. "Crazy Horse."

"Crazy Horse...wow. Can't say I know much about him."

"Unlike most Lakota, Crazy Horse rejected every single thing related to the whites. Even when he was dying, he refused to be put into a white man's bed and died on the floor. Crazy Horse was never defeated in battle and never captured. He surrendered of his own free will. He never allowed himself to be photographed, so we don't even know what he looked like."

"Whatever he looked like, it sounds like he had a real pair on him."

Coldmoon smiled. "Oh, yeah." He tapped the photo. "Crazy Horse inherited the Winter Count from his father, also called Crazy Horse, but it had been started by his great-grandfather. The agent of the Red Cloud Agency in Nebraska, who befriended him after he came in, saw it and described it as a buffalo pelt that must have come from a massive bull. He also described many of the pictures. Crazy Horse kept it rolled up in the corner of his tipi but he would unroll it on request and tell stories of the tribe's history. After he was killed, the Winter Count disappeared—taken probably by his agent friend. That's when it vanished. Today it's like the Holy Grail: lost to history, never found but believed by many to still exist."

"And you found it?"

"*Waslolyesni!* Nobody's found it. An artist in the FBI lab back in Quantico ginned this up, based on historical descriptions." He put the picture back, patted his pocket. "It's a very clever fake."

"Pretty juicy bait, I'd say."

"This is the true rara avis of Native American artifacts. I'm going down there right away—tonight."

"*What?*"

"Yeah. It seems Armendariz is really hot to trot, so I'm taking a red-eye."

"Jesus."

"I'll be undercover, posing as the descendant of Crazy Horse. That Winter Count was secretly passed down through the generations to me, and I'm going to sell it—and be a traitor to my people. I've got a lot of photos to show him. Problem is, I'll tell him, the original weighs two hundred pounds and is eight feet long, rolled up. If he wants it—and he will—he'll have to come back to the States in person. With a shitload of money."

D'Agosta shook his head. "And just when were you planning to tell me all this?"

"Hey, I've been cooling my heels for almost two days. I didn't want to say anything until the operation was approved. I can't take much credit for it, actually, besides coming up with the bait that would lure him back to the States. Our International Operations Division took care of the rest—deepfaking these photos, making contact with Armendariz on the down low, in a way that wouldn't spook him. I just got the green light two hours ago—and now, suddenly, things have gone from station-keeping to general quarters." He paused to sip his beer. "I'm glad we got a chance to talk face-to-face. Sorry to leave you here while I'm down in South America having all the fun."

"Don't be sorry. Something unexpected has come up. I'm tapping a lieutenant commander in the homicide division downtown, a guy named Wybrand, to take over the case. He's a pro at that kind of stuff."

Coldmoon frowned. "Yeah? And just when were *you* planning to tell *me* this?"

"Right now. That's why I asked you here."

Coldmoon watched as D'Agosta toyed with his half-empty glass. He couldn't claim to know the man well, but he'd seen enough to know he was a stand-up cop. He put in the time and, most importantly, he *cared*. Coldmoon knew D'Agosta was catching the ass end of this assignment, but he was still a professional—so why was he transferring the case?

"What's this unexpected thing?" he asked.

"A friend needs my help."

A friend. Unexpected. Suddenly he knew.

"Pendergast," he said. "Is that it?"

D'Agosta stared at him. "How the hell—?"

Coldmoon laughed. "I worked three cases with him, remember? *Something unexpected has come up.* Sounds exactly like Pendergast. So— what are you doing for him? Is it official or a side hustle?"

D'Agosta licked his lips. "Side hustle."

Coldmoon settled back to listen.

"I'm pretty sure you know that Pendergast is upset and why. And you know where Constance disappeared to. You called it a 'long, crazy story.'"

Coldmoon didn't answer. He felt a tightening in his gut.

D'Agosta drained his glass. "Well, you were right about that. Crazy as a sprayed cockroach. And it's not over yet."

"What are you saying?"

Now it was D'Agosta's turn to lean forward in confidence. "You're a good man, Armstrong. So why don't we share what we know? You tell me what happened to Constance and I'll tell you what Pendergast is up to."

Coldmoon waited before replying, then finally broke into a smile. "Well, it's like this: Constance used that machine in the basement of a Savannah hotel to send herself back in time to a parallel universe, to prevent the deaths of her two siblings."

D'Agosta poured himself a fresh glass. "Pendergast had that machine transported from Savannah to his mansion here in town."

Coldmoon stiffened in shock. He knew Pendergast had been hit hard by what happened—that he was mourning the loss of Constance, or feeling guilty, or maybe both—but he'd never expected this. "But it was fried all to hell!"

"Not fried enough."

"So what's he doing with it?"

"Opening a portal to New York—in 1880."

This was crazier than anything Coldmoon could have imagined.

"Son of a bitch." He looked back at D'Agosta. "You're sure it's really working?"

"I'm sure. Because we used it. Together."

"*What?*"

"I didn't believe him. I told him he was stone nuts. He has Proctor and some propeller-head down in that basement operating it for him—so he took me back to 1880 to make me a believer."

"Don't get me wrong, but are you sure it wasn't just some hallucination?"

"If I was still wearing the boots from that field trip, I'd prove it to you by scraping off some vintage horseshit and garnishing your beer."

Coldmoon paused to let this fresh surprise settle in. Now that he thought about it, it shouldn't have been that much of a surprise at all. It was pure Pendergast.

"How can I help?" he asked simply.

D'Agosta shook his head. "I don't think you can help. You know, this relationship between Pendergast and Constance, I just don't know what the deal is there..."

"Neither do I."

"He's using the machine to shadow Constance, try to keep her out of trouble. He doesn't dare show himself for fear of how she'd react. You know she's kind of..." D'Agosta didn't say it.

"Crazy? She's one scary—well, let's leave it at that."

D'Agosta couldn't help but laugh. "Armstrong, I went back to 1880. *I saw Constance.* She lives in a mansion and she's running around posing as a goddamned duchess."

Coldmoon swallowed. His mouth had gone dry, and he moistened it with some beer. "So what does he want you to do?"

"There's this doctor named Leng. Enoch Leng. He's the one who kidnapped and killed Constance's older sister. You know Constance—she probably plans to rip the balls off Leng and feed them back to him with a little beurre blanc."

Coldmoon grimaced. He'd never been able to shake the image of Constance, covered in dirt and blood, walking calmly out of a haze of machine-gun smoke, leaving behind a charnel house of dead bodies. "Yeah. I can see that. So he wants to stop her?"

"No," said D'Agosta. "He wants to make sure she's successful. Leng's the one man in the world, *any* world, you don't want to cross swords with. So Pendergast is trying to help her without her knowing about it—and he asked me to be his partner."

"*Jesus.* How much does your wife know about this?"

"Nothing. All she knows is I'm taking time off to help Pendergast with some private problem. She wanted to go on a vacation with me...we're having kind of a rough patch. And she doesn't much like Pendergast, thinks he's a bad influence, that helping him is liable to get me killed. I wouldn't tell her what we're up to, so she got really pissed off and went to her mother's."

"She's got good reasons."

D'Agosta smiled mirthlessly. "The thing is, I owe Pendergast. But I owe Laura, too. The idea of going back there..." He paused. "Pendergast didn't mince words. There's a decent chance we won't make it back. I just don't know what to do. I still haven't decided."

There was a silence that stretched on before Coldmoon spoke. "This is one problem nobody can advise you on. You know that, right?"

"Yeah," D'Agosta said. "Shit."

"Pendergast hates relying on others. He'd never ask such a thing unless it was truly necessary."

D'Agosta nodded slowly.

In the long silence, Coldmoon realized something: for all his show of agonized indecision, deep down D'Agosta had already made up his mind. And that meant, as a friend, the best thing he could do was reassure him and speed him on his way.

"I should also point out," Coldmoon said slowly, "Pendergast asked *you*. Not me. Not anyone else. It's a big ask...but how can you turn him down?"

"Right."

Coldmoon stood up to leave. "I gotta go pack."

"Watch your ass in Ecuador," D'Agosta replied. "And don't worry about this end—I've got Wybrand up to speed already."

"Next round's on me," Coldmoon said. "We should both have some interesting stories to tell."

D'Agosta nodded.

"I'm headed uptown," said Coldmoon. "Walk you to the subway station?"

"No. Thanks," D'Agosta said. He pulled out his phone. "I've got to compose an email to Laura, telling her I'm gonna be out of range for a bit. Piss her off even more."

Coldmoon paused to rest a firm hand on D'Agosta's shoulder. "*Taŋyáŋ ománi*, partner," he said. Then he turned and made his way out of the bar and into the warmth of the evening.

60

Mary sat at the writing table and drew a creamy sheet of paper to her. Taking up the gold fountain pen lying to one side, she dipped it into a pot of blue ink and, with great care, began penning a letter to Constance. Her tongue pressed against her upper lip in concentration as she formed the cursive letters, one by one, trying not to make a blot, and agonizing over her spelling. She wanted the letter to be perfect, for the doctor to be proud of it, and for little Constance to be inspired by her big sister, so that one day the girl would write far more beautifully than she could.

Was it really just yesterday that she'd at last awakened—awakened fully—to find herself in Dr. Leng's care? She still had periods of drowsiness, but she was able to get up and move around the room now without dizzy spells. Mary felt a rush of gratitude to the doctor, who just that day had told her he'd managed to place Constance and Joe—whom a judge of his acquaintance had ordered released from Blackwell's—in the home of a childless couple blessed with wealth, and that they could go back to school. She was disappointed she couldn't see them right away, but of course she understood they had to settle into their new lives first. And naturally, she had to get well. But it wouldn't be long, the doctor had promised. None of it would take long.

Dearest Binky,

I was So Happey to hear You & Joe are safe & Off the Streets. The Doctor has been so kind he is an Angle sent from Hevven. I am feeling beter but for Faintness the Doctor says will go way soon.

The Doctor treets me very well & gave me a Nice Room in his own hous only on acct of my illness I cant have any windows for feer of the city air. But I am mending every day. Meen while it is warm & the Bed is Soft. The wall-papper is red velvet & there are pichurs of horses and dogs.

O Binkie I cant wait to see You & I am cownting days to Janry 7—when the Doctor thinks that I can come visit You & Joe.

The Food O my good ness Meets & Cheeses and Bread, with juice from reel Oranges. I asked for choklit onct but the Doctor laft & said the diet was so I get better & then I get all the Kandy I want affter. I am geting plump Youll not even know Me!!!

Please rite & tell me abt your new Family. From what the Doctor tells me They sound ever so nice. Do You have a fether Bed like wht I have?

Hugs from Your loving Sister,
Mary

She laid the letter out, carefully rolling the blotter back and forth as her father had taught her, and looked at the results. It was disappointing. There were blots, the lines weren't as straight as they should be, and there were some words that didn't look right. But she wanted to get it off as quickly as possible, so she carefully folded the letter, inserted it into an envelope, and wrote *For Constance Greene* on the cover. Then she sealed and gummed it for Munck to take away later.

She wanted to write a letter to Joe as well, but she felt lassitude slowly enveloping her limbs once again. Instead, she let herself fall into a daydream about the future. The filthy streets with their leering men, the cold dirty ice in the gutters—everything was already so far away that it seemed like a receding nightmare. First she'd awoken to this beautiful room, and now her greatest wish had come true: the doctor had not only rescued Joe and Constance, but had managed to find a good family where they could be happy and taken care of. After so much deprivation and tragedy, it seemed as if God had finally taken notice of them. She felt another upwelling of gratitude to the doctor, and even a touch of affection for his funny manservant Munck, with his knobbly face and bowing, scraping ways.

January 7. The doctor had promised. She could scarcely wait for that day when they would—at last—all be reunited once again.

61

June 11
Sunday

Aʀᴍsᴛʀᴏɴɢ Cᴏʟᴅᴍᴏᴏɴ sᴀᴛ ɪɴ the black chauffeured Jeep that had picked him up at the Quito airport in the middle of the night—while Tom Torres, the FBI's International Operations Division "legat" in Ecuador, watched from a place of concealment to ensure nothing went wrong. Now he was headed northward into the mountainous province of Imbabura. Coldmoon used the drive to mentally rehearse one last time the details of his undercover identity.

Torres had briefed him over the phone before he'd left New York. The legal attaché explained the confusing situation as best he could. Ecuador would not extradite Ramón Armendariz y Urias to the United States, as he had recently acquired Ecuadorian citizenship. On top of that, Armendariz was extremely wealthy and had friends in high places. But Armendariz was a brash, outspoken fellow, and he had pissed off the comandante general of the Policía Nacional by meddling in Ecuadorian politics, weeping crocodile tears about the repressive hand of the state. So the police had seemed willing enough to assist the American FBI in setting up a sting operation to lure Armendariz back to the States.

It was Coldmoon's assignment to be the wasp delivering the sting.

He had never been to Ecuador before. Perhaps more importantly, this was his first overseas assignment, and now he felt both excited and apprehensive, staring out the back window of the Jeep as the vehicle climbed up a winding highway ever deeper into the Cordillera, the backbone of mountains that ran through the heart of Ecuador. Even though Coldmoon had arrived with a cover identity worked out back in the U.S., Torres had been helpful with details, telling him to arrive in an off-the-rack suit and polyester tie. His undercover name was Armstrong Witko, a direct descendant of Crazy Horse and a registered member of the Oglala Sioux Tribe. The FBI had created an online trail for him, including a Facebook page with posts going back ten years, a genealogy easily accessible online, employment history, credit score, and even a minor criminal record. Coldmoon had been shocked at how quickly and cleverly the FBI could create, out of whole cloth, a multiyear existence of someone. This, along with the International Operations Division as a whole, was an aspect of FBI work he'd been entirely unaware of. It seemed a lot had changed, and changed quickly, in the undercover field since he'd graduated from the academy.

It was a given that the item had to be heavy enough to lure Armendariz back to America in order to evaluate it. It also had to be fabulously valuable—and have an ironclad history that would satisfy the well-educated collector. Ultimately, Coldmoon's own original idea—the so-called Crazy Horse Winter Count—had won out.

Coldmoon, clutching a file of cleverly produced pictures of the (fake) Crazy Horse Winter Count, along with forged papers documenting the provenance of the robe, pondered all this as the Jeep departed the highway and continued up a series of ever smaller roads into the highlands of Ecuador. From what little he could see in the 4 AM light, it was wild and spectacular country, the horizon dominated by a row of towering volcanoes covered with glaciers and snow. They passed through a number of tiny villages with whitewashed houses and red tile roofs.

Under other circumstances he would have enjoyed the drive. But despite his excitement, he could not shake a feeling of unease. Armendariz was no fool, and if he saw through the deception, Coldmoon's life wouldn't be worth a plugged nickel. Up in the high Andes, on the remote seven-thousand-acre hacienda where Armendariz lived like a feudal lord, Coldmoon would be disappeared without a trace at the first scent of anything fishy. But Coldmoon knew this wasn't the real reason he was nervous. He was used to running his own cases from beginning to end—enlisting help where necessary, but always on his terms. This operation was much bigger than he was used to, and it was being run in a different way entirely. International Operations had taken his notion for how to nail Armendariz and turned it into a reality—with minimal input from him. Now all he had to do was carry out the sting. But if he screwed up, he wouldn't just be letting himself down—he'd be letting down the whole platoon of faceless FBI spooks who'd toiled to put everything together.

Just as the sun broke over the horizon, the road turned from asphalt to cobblestones and continued up a long, beautiful valley, dotted with pastures of grazing cows and horses. A final turn brought them to a mossy wall of whitewashed stone extending across the narrow valley, into which was set a heavy wrought iron gate, guarded by two men with automatic rifles. One of them leaned in and the driver presented his credentials along with Coldmoon's passport. The guard examined them and nodded, opening the gates and waving them through.

The car drove into a cobbled courtyard, as large as a village square, beyond which stretched an ancient and magnificent hacienda. Long, arched portals on three sides opened to a second courtyard, then a third, each edged with rose gardens and featuring a central, massive flowering tree laden with blossoms. Coldmoon had imagined something quite different—vulgar and modern, with a pool, scantily clad women, loud music, and lots of booze. Instead, entering this smuggler's hacienda was like stepping back into a more genteel, simpler, nineteenth-century way of life. Woodsmoke coiled from countless chimneys rising from tiled roofs. Nestled at the far end of the main hacienda stood a stone chapel gleaming with stained glass, and beyond that a stable with horses, a vineyard, vegetable and herb gardens, an apiary, orchards, and a dairy with cows, all enclosed by stone walls. The mountains rose up to the great slopes of Volcán Imbabura, its summit now socked in by gathering storm clouds.

The driver parked the vehicle, then rushed around to open the door for Coldmoon. He stepped out to see an exceedingly tall man, dressed in an old-fashioned, tight-fitting Spanish suit with silver buttons, come striding down the colonnaded portal, flashing a smile, followed by several uniformed employees. He, too, looked as if he'd stepped from another age.

"Armstrong Witko!" He grasped Coldmoon's hand in his own and gave it a shake. "Welcome to Hacienda Angochagua! I apologize for the unseemly hour. Did you get any sleep on the plane? My men will show you to your quarters: I imagine you must be fatigued after your long journey." He had long, flowing black hair and spoke English almost perfectly, with just the trace of an accent, his voice hearty and emphatic.

Coldmoon was too nervous to be fatigued. He mustered a smile. "Thank you, Ramón—if I may."

"Of course! We're going to be good friends, I am sure." Armendariz turned and spoke to his employees in Spanish, ordering them to collect his bag and take it to the Diego Suite. He turned back to Coldmoon. "Do you speak Spanish? Not that it matters—we will conduct our business in English."

"I don't speak it, and thank you, I appreciate that." Coldmoon did in fact speak Spanish fluently, but it was thought that it might be useful for him to hide that fact.

Armendariz paused and said: "*Aŋpétu wašté.*"

"*Taŋyáŋ waŋčhíyaŋke,*" Coldmoon answered, startled.

"So glad to see you speak Lakota, however."

"Of course," said Coldmoon, realizing he had just passed his first test. "Spoken it since I was a kid. And you? How did you learn that greeting?"

Armendariz laughed. "I have a deep interest in all things Native American—as you must have assumed. But don't test me, it's about all I can say." He hesitated a moment. "Sorry, but I have to ask: what is it like to be descended from Crazy Horse? You, standing right here...I can hardly believe it."

"It's not so great. I wake up angry every morning."

Armendariz laughed again, then smacked his hands together. "Jorge here will show you to your quarters. We'll meet in the great hall at noon, and after lunch—we have roasted a suckling pig, one of our specialties here—we'll talk business. That should be interesting—no?" After a moment, he added, his voice dropping an octave in tone: "Very interesting indeed."

62

Ferenc walked down the basement hall, whistling a tune from *Oklahoma!*—probably the most boring musical ever performed on stage. But he was in a good mood, and he'd grown used to the gloom and damp of his surroundings. He thought with satisfaction about the fat stack of money—unexpectedly large at this point, yet unquestionably deserved—now accumulating interest in an offshore account. Even more satisfying was the fact that, now that the difficult part of his task was basically done—the machine had been repaired to realistic tolerances and, just as important, Pendergast had successfully used it four times—he just had to maintain the thing until the man returned, when he'd get another hefty compensation.

Along with a good possibility of more where that came from.

As he rounded the corner and approached the heavy door leading to the machine, his whistling broke into full-throated voice:

Oh, what a beautiful mornin'
Oh, what a beautiful day
I've got a—

What the hell? Something was wrong with the security keypad beside the door. He'd typed in the code and pressed his hand against the fingerprint screen, but the authenticator light remained red. He tried again, with the same result.

As he was about to try a third time, he heard an all-too-familiar voice behind him: "Don't bother."

Annoyed, he turned to see Proctor coming down the passage. He was dressed in the usual monochromatic palette: gray mock turtleneck, black sports jacket, dark trousers, black cap-toe Oxfords with extra-thick soles—all purchased, no doubt, in the mercenary department of Brooks Brothers.

"Stop singing," he said by way of welcome. "I just finished my breakfast."

"This damn keypad is broken," Ferenc said.

"It's not broken." Stepping in front of Ferenc and shielding his movements from view, he pressed a code into the keypad—more digits than before, from the sound of it—and then used the fingerprint scanner beside it. Now the light turned green and Ferenc heard the lock snap open.

Proctor indicated Ferenc to precede him inside.

"What's going on?" Ferenc asked as he opened the door.

"Change of protocol."

Ferenc was about to reply, then stopped. Along the wall nearest the door—the one spot in the makeshift lab that had always remained more or less empty—there was now a small table, with a plain wooden chair beside it. What might be on the table Ferenc didn't know, because it was completely covered by an olive-green drop cloth. Above this table, close to where the wall met the ceiling, three small devices of unknown function had been installed.

Wordlessly, Ferenc walked over to the machine, picked up the tablet that lay beside his own worktable, and brought the tablet to life with the press of a button. He wasn't going to give Proctor the satisfaction of asking questions. He didn't like Proctor—he hadn't from the first moment he saw him walking up his driveway, and the passing weeks had only deepened that impression. The man was humorless, sarcastic, terse, almost sleepy in his movements even while radiating a cool, lethal ferocity. The fact was, Proctor scared the hell out of Ferenc—but he'd never admit it.

Today's business was fairly simple. The machine, currently idling, had to be exercised at half power on a regular schedule, like a generator—which, Ferenc thought, it more or less was. Since running the machine was a two-person job, he'd need Proctor for that. Assuming all went well, that only left an hour or two of checking the various components, looking for anything that might be trending toward failure or showing signs of stress or fatigue. This was something he could do on his own—thank God. But it was something the engineer in him knew had to be done: the last two times Pendergast had used the machine, he'd taken along a sidekick of some kind—a cop, Ferenc figured. The present trip was expected to last at least a week. From what he'd gathered—and overheard—this current trip was the main event. Once they emerged from the portal, he'd get the rest of his dough...and the job would be complete.

At this thought, he stole a glance at Proctor. It unnerved him to see the man standing by the door, arms folded, staring back at him.

"Well, what are you waiting for?" Ferenc said, put out by the eye contact. "Let's run this test cycle—while we're still young."

Wordlessly, Proctor stepped forward and took up a position at his station, while Ferenc ran through the primary checklist he'd designed. Then they went through the activation sequence, bringing first the main laser, then the secondary laser online.

"Talk to me," Ferenc said in his best commander's voice.

"Flatline," came the equally flatline response.

Ferenc glanced at his set of controls as the familiar humming sound grew louder. "Lattice stable. I'm bringing the fields up to 50 percent."

More humming. Proctor was staring at his control panel, apparently seeing no abnormalities. Ferenc listened as well as watched. He noticed no glitches, no spikes.

"Thirty seconds," he said. "Prepare for baseline."

They went through the power-down sequence until they were

once again at idle; Ferenc completed the post-op checklist, and then he readied himself for the tedious process of examining the three main assemblies and their ancillary components. Grabbing a few tools off his worktable, he prepared to duck behind the machine without bothering to wish that bastard Proctor a nice day.

But there was no sound of a door opening and closing. Ferenc waited a minute, then looked over. To his surprise, Proctor—instead of leaving the lab as usual at this point—had taken a seat in the chair by the door and was looking back at him.

"What are you doing?" Ferenc asked.

Proctor didn't reply.

Ferenc straightened up. "We've exercised the machine. I don't need you anymore."

"Change of protocol," Proctor repeated.

"Okay. Maybe you'd better tell me all about this new protocol of yours."

"From now on, access to this room is restricted. I'll admit you for scheduled tests and maintenance; assist or monitor you as necessary; then let you out again. Should there be any problems with the device, or additional servicing is required, you will alert me, and we'll proceed along similar lines."

"Well, what's the new door code? I may need to get in here for emergency repairs or something. What if there's an electrical fire?"

"Smoke, temperature, and movement monitors have been installed and are operational. I will be present in this room at all times when you are here. If you need access to the machine at any time of the day or night, you will call me and I'll provide it within ten minutes—and stay with you until your work is completed."

Ferenc couldn't believe what he was hearing. After all the time he'd put in on this project—the labor, the brilliant shortcuts, the brainstorms that had turned unfixable problems into fixable triumphs—they were rewarding him with this kind of treatment?

Like many arrogant, egotistical geniuses, Ferenc grew short-tempered when he wasn't praised and pampered, and now his ego overcame his better instincts. "Really? And just when did you get the brilliant idea to institute this *protocol*?"

"I'm merely following the instructions of Agent Pendergast," came the cool reply.

Agent Pendergast. Suddenly, Ferenc visualized how it must have played out. He'd been allowed to work on the machine under minimal supervision while trying to restore it to working order. But now that it was operational, and his job here had entered a second and final phase—maintenance—the supervision was no longer minimal. What before had felt like a silken thread was now more of a choke collar.

"So Pendergast doesn't trust me—is that what you're saying?"

Proctor stood up slowly. "Agent Pendergast is suspicious, but inclined to give you the benefit of the doubt. I, on the other hand, haven't trusted you since I drove up to your shack."

Ferenc wasn't sure what infuriated him more—this dismissive, distrustful treatment or the fact Pendergast had been thinking one step ahead of him. He stepped forward quickly, rashly. "I've delivered what nobody else could—and now I'm being treated like a galley slave? You can take this machine and shove it up your ass."

Proctor came forward, too—he didn't run, not exactly, but within the space of two seconds he was standing in front of Ferenc, leaning well into his personal space. Despite Ferenc's petulant outburst, some instinct for survival cautioned him to stay perfectly still.

"My employer gave you a gift—the chance to work on something extraordinary. Something better than a go-kart picking up and sniffing rocks on Mars. You took that gift, knowing full well what it entailed. You'll see the mission through—to the end. And when it's done, you won't say a single word about it. To *anybody*."

Ferenc tried to respond but found that, though his mouth worked, no sound came out.

"Not only do I not trust you," Proctor said in that same, awful, weirdly calm tone, "but I don't *like* you. Step out of line, and you'll vanish. Just like that."

While these words sank in, Proctor remained as still as if he were made of marble. Silence descended on the lab. After perhaps thirty seconds, Ferenc gave a faint nod of acknowledgment. Proctor took one step back, and another, then walked to his chair by the door and sat down while Ferenc returned to work, blazing with rage and shame.

The minutes passed as Proctor sat in the chair, watching him work. Ferenc discovered he wasn't getting much done: the unexpected confrontation had left him so upset it was hard to concentrate. At last—just as he was finally getting into the rhythm of the inspection—he heard the rasp of a chair upon the floor, followed by the sound of footsteps.

He looked up from where he was crouching behind the device. Proctor had moved the chair behind the mysterious table. As Ferenc watched, he pulled away the tarp, exposing several items: a small pile of sturdy plastic containers with locking tops; a weighing scale such as you'd use for diamonds or gold dust; some hammers and other tools; a miniature burlap sack—and some machine, bolted to the table, that reminded Ferenc of the device his mother had used to force ground pork into sausage casings.

As he watched, Proctor began arranging the plastic boxes and tools in front of him. When he opened the burlap sack and spilled its shiny brass contents onto the table, Ferenc—who'd rubbed elbows with plenty of survivalists, hunters, and nut jobs in the backwoods of West Virginia—realized what he was doing: reloading spent shells with new bullets.

Naturally the guy would roll his own. Why leave it to someone else when you can tailor bespoke ammo to your own murderous specifications? Muttering to himself, Ferenc ducked down again to continue his inspection. As he did so, he tried unsuccessfully to tune out the sounds of the operation taking place across the room. He could hear Proctor rubbing down the brass cartridges with a lube pad, cleaning out the burnt powder, and inserting new primers with a hand priming tool. For some reason, this process—just the thought of the man getting something accomplished, instead of wasting time watching him—irritated him even more. A sound like the scattering of tiny pebbles informed him Proctor was now measuring out gunpowder in the scale. He figured the cold-blooded sadist would probably load his bullets heavy, 150 or even 160 grains for a 9mm hollow-point. Next, he heard the low *whump* of the reloading press. He'd test one round for weight, then run the rest through.

Sure enough: as Ferenc tried once again to get on with his work, he heard the press being cranked, again and again and again. Then a brief silence, followed by a series of short, sharp volleys: *crack, crack, crack* ...

Goaded beyond endurance, he stood up. Proctor had lined up the shells—at least a hundred—in neat rows, and was now crimping down the bullets to the proper depth. He *was* making hollow-points—the fucker. Not only that, he was using tweezers to seat some kind of rubber or polymer into the dimples, making sure the bullets wouldn't clog on clothing but rather penetrate through to flesh before mushrooming.

"I could just walk out of here, you know," he said.

Proctor had put down the tweezers and picked up a caliper, no doubt to measure the Parabellums for correct length. He raised his eyebrows in mute inquiry.

"Today, for instance. I could walk on out of here—and just keep walking. Screw you and your 'protocols.' I'd lose a lot of money, sure, but I've made a shitload already, and it just might be worth it, seeing you left in the lurch. What happens when you can't exercise the machine by yourself? Or if, maybe, it blows a gasket?" He barked a laugh. "I'd like to see what you'd do then."

As Proctor sat staring back at him, caliper in hand, Ferenc heard his own last words echo a few times, then die away: *I'd like to see what you'd do then.*

"You know," Proctor said at last, "they did a study in England a few years ago. On cats. Not the wild kind, but the domesticated ones: house cats who know where their next meal is coming from. They discovered that when hunting prey—mice, birds, rabbits—80 percent of the time, the cats intentionally gave their victims a brief warning before they sprang. And when later these same cats played with the captured mice, one time in ten the victim got away as a result. Why would cats do this, they asked—take a chance on losing their prey after a long, slow stalk? Tease them instead of killing them outright? The answer they arrived at was simple: the house cats were bored. Seeing fear in your victim's eyes, it turns out, is an excellent way to relieve monotony. So—do you really want to leave, Dr. Ferenc? Because, to be honest, part of me is hoping you'll do just that. You see, it's not only cats that experience monotony from time to time."

This was the longest speech Ferenc had ever heard the man make. Throughout, he had maintained a light grip on the caliper. After a moment, he let his gaze drop back to the table and began measuring the finished rounds.

After another moment, Ferenc returned silently to his inspection.

63

December 25, 1880
Christmas Day

THE HANSOM CAB LET them off in front of the Hotel Normandie, at the corner of Broadway and Thirty-Eighth Street. After the horse and cab clattered away, and a bellhop had rushed down the stairs to carry up their luggage, Pendergast halted to look up at the grand edifice. He stopped D'Agosta with his hand and held up his cane.

"A moment, my dear Vincent," he said, leaning in close to be heard over a group of carolers singing on the nearest street corner.

"Sure thing." Since he'd shown up the night before on Pendergast's doorstep, telling him, in effect, to send them back to 1880 before he changed his mind, D'Agosta had been doing as little thinking as possible, content for now to follow Pendergast's lead.

"The Hotel Normandie is not the most expensive hotel in New York, but it is a place frequented by wealthy Europeans who are careful with their money—a perfect place for an idle English dandy like myself, a remittance man as it were, traveling on an extended pleasure tour of the States."

"Is that the rationale behind your ridiculous accent?"

"Not ridiculous. It is a late-Victorian British upper-class drawl, entirely suited to my character."

"You sound like you have a pebble in your mouth."

Pendergast pointed again with his cane. "Pay attention, please—recall that you're a visitor here in more ways than one. Now: this hotel has the very latest amenities. That includes steam heat, speaking tubes, water closets on each floor, and fire bells in every room."

"Water closets? You mean bathrooms?" D'Agosta looked up at the giant hotel, which must have fifty rooms to each floor.

"Yes, indeed. Such luxury. Two for the gentlemen, two for the ladies."

"Jesus." D'Agosta followed Pendergast in, walking behind as he'd been instructed. The guy certainly looked like an English dandy in his morning suit, tailored waistcoat draped with a gold watch chain, fancy silk cravat, and neck-choking collar, swinging a Malacca cane with a lion of carved ivory on its head. D'Agosta suspected he enjoyed the role. He, on the other hand, had been forced into the dress of a manservant, which was stiff, hot, scratchy, and altogether too tight. Lucky it was wintertime: an outfit like this in summer would be deadly.

"Shall we go in, Vincent?"

"Why the hell not?"

"You must get used to addressing me as *sir*," Pendergast said in a lowered voice. "Always remember that you are my American manservant, somewhat slow of mind and awkward of speech." He gazed at D'Agosta, one eyebrow raised. "I shall have to be quite rude to you, as that is the way of the English with their servants."

D'Agosta heard himself laugh. "Right. *Sir.*"

They strode up the steps into the lobby, which was garlanded with seasonal decorations and thronging with well-to-do travelers. They went up to the marbled counter.

"Room 323, if you please."

"Yes, sir," said the clerk, "and Merry Christmas." The man handed him the keys to their suite and they walked over to the elevator, where a young man dressed in burgundy velvet with gold piping held open the cage doors.

D'Agosta halted, staring at the rickety-looking cage. "Um, maybe we should take the stairs."

"Sir, I can personally vouch for its safety," said the operator, in a speech that was clearly rehearsed. "This is the very latest in steam-powered elevators, absolutely guaranteed by Mr. Otis himself to be safe—even if the cables do break."

"Break?" said D'Agosta.

Pendergast entered the elevator, then turned. "Are you coming, Vincent?" he said in the peremptory tone of a master addressing his inferior. "You heard the man. Get cracking!"

D'Agosta got in. With a hiss, the elevator began its creaking, swaying, wheezing progress to the third floor.

A minute or two later, they entered their suite—two bedrooms and a sitting room. The two suitcases Pendergast had brought with them, and which D'Agosta had temporarily been forced in his position as servant to carry, had preceded them and were stowed near the door. Pendergast took off his cape while D'Agosta dumped his greatcoat across a massive Victorian armchair and collapsed on top of it. "Not bad for a hundred and forty years old," he said, looking around. "How much was it?"

"Three dollars and fifty cents a night. American plan."

"How did you pay for it? You bring some old money with you or something?"

"I did indeed. On my initial journey, I carried with me fifty pounds of Morgan silver dollars that I picked up at an auction. Well worn and of little numismatic value, with a total face value of one thousand dollars."

"A thousand dollars? What's the equivalent in today's money—that is, yesterday's money?"

"Given that a thousand dollars equals two years' salary for a working man, and you can buy a house for a few hundred, I would estimate its buying power at perhaps one hundred thousand dollars."

D'Agosta whistled. "You could make a business out of that. You bring money back here, invest it, and because you know the future market movements, make a quick killing."

"And then?"

"You bury it and dig it up in the present."

Pendergast said, "You're forgetting: this isn't our timeline or our universe. You would dig where it was buried and find nothing."

"Oh. Right." Pendergast had explained how "time travel" was a simplistic term for what the machine actually did—a process involving parallel universes—but D'Agosta hadn't really understood. "Well, we could make a killing in *this* 1880, turn it into gold bars or diamonds, then carry them back using the machine."

"We could. But we won't."

"Why not?"

Pendergast shook his head. "It would be wrong. And dangerous. Such a project might involve months, and the longer we stay here, the more chance there is for the machine to develop a fault."

The idea of being stuck here forever sent a shiver through D'Agosta. Oddly enough, being separated from Laura by space as well as time had eased his worst feelings of depression and guilt—it was too late to turn back, and he had other things to worry about now. But he was still counting on helping Pendergast, keeping undercover, and then getting back to his own world—in one piece.

"So what's in those?" he said, nodding at the suitcases. "More silver dollars? Or gold bullion, maybe? They certainly weighed enough."

"This is now my fourth trip to this place—I've had plenty of time to assemble a list of items that our business may require...before we can return."

Our business may require. D'Agosta shuddered. "I need to use the bathroom," he said. "What should I do, *sir*?"

"It is down the hall, to the left I believe. Or you can make use of the chamber pot under your bed. Conveniently emptied twice a day."

D'Agosta groaned. "I'll wait."

"As long as we're on the subject, the maid will draw you a bath, if you so wish, on twenty-four hours' notice. The bathing rooms are also just down the hall. Hot water for shaving and washing will be supplied every morning to our rooms." Pendergast tilted his head. "In the Normandie, we enjoy the very summit of comfort and luxury."

"Yeah. Right. As long as there's free Wi-Fi, I'm happy." He looked around. "What time is it, by the way?"

"Six o'clock. What I might suggest, Vincent, is a cold bottle of champagne and some caviar aux blinis while we discuss the next steps. I'm afraid a can of your usual pedestrian beverage is out of the question, although I am sure they can provide a tankard of Manhattan Ale . . . at room temperature."

"Champagne will do just fine."

"As my manservant, you shall have to order it. Just ring the bell on the wall over there and put your ear to the speaking tube. When you hear a voice, bellow our order."

D'Agosta heaved himself out of the chair and went over to the indicated contraption. He pressed the bell and waited, and then a voice sounded, hollow and distorted in the tube. D'Agosta moved the tube from his ear to his lips. "Bottle of champagne, caviar and blinis, to room 323, please."

He heard a muffled affirmative and returned to his chair.

Meanwhile, Pendergast had taken a chair of his own, and he leaned forward, elbows on his knees, clasping his hands. The bemused air with which he'd entered the hotel was now gone, replaced with an expression of the utmost seriousness. "Vincent, it is impossible for me to thank you enough for making this sacrifice on my behalf. So, if you don't mind, I won't even try—for now, at least. Now we must talk strategy. Time is of the essence."

"Go ahead."

"In our own timeline, we know Leng killed Mary on his operating table on January 7, 1881. But here is the problem: *we are no longer in our own timeline.* By intruding into this parallel universe, we have disturbed it like a rock thrown into the surface of a pond. And even now, our disturbance—or more to the point, Constance's disturbance—is rippling outward in ways we can't predict."

"If we can't predict the consequences, what does that mean?"

"Well, specifically, it means that Mary may not be killed on January 7. In this timeline, she might be killed later. Worse, she might be killed earlier. While I cannot be sure, of course, I believe Constance has made one fatal error: she thinks she has two weeks in which to complete her plan of action. We can't make that assumption. Mary, and everyone else for that matter, is in danger, because now that this time-pond has been so thoroughly disturbed, there is simply no way to predict what will happen."

D'Agosta shook his head. "Constance is no dope. What do you think Leng suspects?"

"He can't possibly suspect that Constance comes from the future—if he ever learned that, we would be lost. But here's what I believe he *does* know." Pendergast held up his hand, spidery fingers rising one by one.

"One: He knows she's no Duchess of Ironclaw.

"Two: He knows she's prying into his life and already knows a great deal about it.

"Three: He will eventually notice, if he hasn't already, the resemblance between Constance and Mary.

"Four: He will conclude that, because of her wealth and position in society—not to mention high intelligence—he must assume her interest in him is a threat, perhaps a grave one. Remember, Leng is pitiless and insouciantly destroys lives in ways you can't imagine. If he feels threatened, his response will be ruthless and efficient."

"What kind of response?"

"He is consummately clever, Vincent—there is no way to know how he'll strike, or where, or when. That's why I need your help. He might cripple or even kill Constance. Then again, he might just as well decide that this is a sporting proposition and allow her to play out her hand...for his own amusement, before striking her down." Pendergast shook his head. "We simply do not know."

"So where do I come in?"

"I need you to watch the house with minute attention. He'll want to learn more about the mansion and its occupants, if he hasn't already. He might even attempt a break-in to gain information. I want you to report back what you see—of him, or more likely his devilish assistant, Munck—without making yourself obvious."

"That's easy enough to say, but how are we going to get 24/7 coverage of her house? I can't watch the place for days on end—and neither one of us has a cell phone."

"I fear things are rushing to a head...and that we won't have 'days on end.'"

A knock came at the door and D'Agosta got up to answer it. A bellboy rolled in a trolley with a bottle of champagne stuffed into a silver bucket and a large tray of blinis piled with sour cream and caviar.

"Over here," said Pendergast, gesturing.

The bellboy wheeled it over next to his chair, and Pendergast slid a hand into his pocket and extracted a silver dollar, languidly holding it out to the bellboy between two fingers.

"Thank you, sir!" the boy said, taking it with a smart bow and leaving.

"You may serve me," said Pendergast. "It will give you good practice."

With a chuckle, D'Agosta poured out two glasses of champagne, then slid a half-dozen blinis onto a small plate, retreating to his seat to leave Pendergast to get his own caviar. He stuffed two blinis in his mouth and took a swig of champagne. Damn, it was good—better than he remembered champagne ever tasting. Could there be something in the water, or the grapes, or even the soil they grew in, that had changed for the worse over the last century and a half?

Finally, D'Agosta broke the silence. "Do you know what Constance is planning to do?"

"I know what she told me, in the note she left behind. And I overheard her making a most unwise proposition to Leng. If she can manage to rescue Mary, her next act will be to kill Leng."

D'Agosta stared. "*Kill* the man? Really? She'd go that far?"

Pendergast lowered his voice. "You know her almost as well as I do."

D'Agosta nodded. He was right: of course she would want to kill him—and there'd be no stopping her.

"How is she going to do it?"

"She offered Leng some chemical formulae he's desperate to

acquire. She didn't say what she wanted in return, but obviously she will demand that he turn over Mary, immediately—without giving him time to plan an effective countermove."

"And then she'll kill him?" D'Agosta repeated. "How?"

"She lacks a volcano to throw him into," Pendergast said dryly. "But that stiletto of hers strikes as fast as a black mamba and is just as deadly if the victim is taken by surprise. But you see, Vincent, this time the victim will *not* be taken by surprise. Leng might well be one, even two steps ahead of her, and she'll never get the opportunity to strike."

"So what's your plan?"

"I plan to—what is that useful baseball term?—*shortstop* her. Since Constance cannot be deterred, our only course of action is to rescue Mary ourselves."

"And Leng?"

"*We* will kill him."

"You and me?"

"Yes."

"Can't we just rescue Mary and leave the man alone?"

"As long as Leng remains alive, Constance and her siblings will never be safe in this world. And we know, from the mass grave uncovered in lower Manhattan that sparked the Surgeon murders, that he will go on to kill dozens of other young girls. So you see, Vincent, it is *not enough* that we rescue Mary."

"We also have to do Leng," D'Agosta muttered. "It's murder, plain and simple."

"Indeed." Pendergast smiled and reached once again for his champagne glass.

64

June 12
Monday

GASPARD FERENC HOPPED IMPATIENTLY from foot to foot as he waited for Proctor to open the lab door. The lock clicked open and Ferenc pushed his way in first, ahead of Proctor. The fear of Pendergast's henchman and his threats hadn't dissipated—but it now competed in Ferenc's mind with the ongoing sense of outrage, backed by humiliation.

He took a slow turn around the idling machine, glancing here and there, opening the occasional panel to ensure the instrumentation within showed no signs of failure, wiggling leads and running resistance tests to make sure everything was optimal. "Okay, let's get this over with," he said at last, walking over to the master control panel. Proctor, who'd been watching silently, took up his own position. The man's worktable, Ferenc noticed, was once again covered by a tarp. Maybe Proctor hadn't yet had a chance to expend all the rounds he'd made for himself the day before.

Ferenc woke the machine from its idle state, one section at a time, nodding to Proctor, who followed him in lockstep.

"Checklist complete, lattice forming," Ferenc murmured.

"Semiconductor temperature stable," Proctor said.

"Bringing the main laser online," Ferenc told him. "Braiding should commence in five seconds."

The familiar low hum rose slightly as both men adjusted their instrumentation. Ferenc waited, watching his panel closely, then engaged the second laser. "Lattice forming. Bringing the power up to 50 percent."

As he followed through, the slow crescendo of humming was interrupted by a brief stutter. The two men looked at each other.

"Holding at 40," Ferenc said. "Diagnostics show anything unusual?"

Proctor shook his head, and Ferenc waited another few seconds. The humming remained stable. "Taking it up to 50."

As he began increasing the power, the stuttering returned. "I've got a spike in the secondary," Proctor told him. "There's a red light."

"OK. Let's bring it back down to idle—slowly."

Once the lasers were offline and the main power was down to 5 percent, Ferenc stepped back from the master control panel.

"What is it?" Proctor said.

Ferenc rubbed his chin thoughtfully. "Don't know. A thorough check would mean shutting it down and running every component through an analyzer or oscilloscope."

"We can't shut it down. It has to remain in idle, or Pendergast can't return."

"Don't teach your grandmother how to suck eggs, all right? That's what we'd do *ideally*. Since it isn't an option, I'll need to test it at idle."

"Can it still be inspected thoroughly?"

"Yes. I think. But it will take longer." Ferenc paused, still rubbing his chin. "Look: we'll switch places. You take up a position here at the master console. I'm going to send some pulses through the secondary and tertiary units, and I want you to read the indications back to me."

Ferenc got a few pieces of equipment from his workbench and returned to the rear of the machine, while Proctor took over the master console. Ferenc made a slow, thorough inspection, occasionally stopping to run current through a component or subject a subassembly to an abrupt change in temperature, each time asking Proctor for the results.

"I think I've found the problem," he said after about twenty minutes. "There's a series of variable resistors back here that are getting too much juice." A few moments of silence passed. "I want you to turn the rotary potentiometer—marked 'SEC 2-C' on the master console—to the twelve-o'clock position... *slowly*."

Proctor turned the knob.

"Hold it!" Ferenc said. Then: "Okay, dial it back down." Ferenc peered at the back side of the device, fiddled with it, and then called out: "Try it again."

Proctor repeated the process. A moment later, Ferenc rose from behind the central section of the machine. "Got it," he said, dusting off his lab coat.

"Problem's resolved?" Proctor asked.

"There was a unit that simply wasn't intended to remain in idle all the time, with current passing through it constantly. I adjusted an inbound capacitor to compensate. But we'll need to run a full test to make sure—as well as keeping an eye on those resistors, going forward. Wouldn't want them to fail while the machine is idling some night when nobody's here to notice."

"If that's a possibility, you should install a warning system to alert us to such a failure."

Proctor suggested this as if such an undertaking was as simple as rubbing two sticks together. "All in good time. First, we need to complete our test cycle... and make sure I'm right."

Once again, they took up their respective positions on opposite ends of the machine. Ferenc brought the fields up to 50 percent. This time, the humming remained stable. There was no stuttering.

"All right," he said. "Prepare to go to 100 percent."

"Full power?" Proctor asked. "Why?"

"You're damn right. Didn't you hear me say we had to run a 'full test'?"

Proctor didn't reply, but he looked a little doubtful.

"Look. It's not enough to exercise this thing at 50 percent. What would happen if it failed while Pendergast was returning? Christ, he'd be sent off who knows when or where, and you'd never see your boss again. If that abnormality was symptomatic of something worse, we need to know about it now—while there's time to fix it."

After a moment, Proctor nodded.

Ferenc exhaled audibly over the constant hum. "All right: primary and secondary readouts on the lattice still good?"

Proctor nodded.

Ferenc brought the power up to 75 percent, watching the master control panel carefully. "Braiding complete," he said. "Lattice stable. Keep a close eye on your readouts—I'm going to bring it up to 100 percent."

"Understood." Proctor leaned closer to his instrumentation panel.

Slowly, slowly, Ferenc brought the power up to full, working the magnetic fields in the process as a potter might shape clay on a wheel. The humming increased in intensity but remained steady. Suddenly, the air above the green-painted circle on the floor seemed to fold in on itself—and then the portal appeared, wavering ever so slightly, intensely bright.

"Don't look at it," Ferenc warned. "Keep your eyes glued to the instrumentation, let me know if you see the slightest fluctuation. We'll hold for ten seconds, then dial it back to idle and check for any irregularities. I'll count down."

"Understood," Proctor said.

"Here we go. Ten, nine, eight..."

Ferenc reached beneath his console and triggered a tiny switch. "Seven."

There was a barely audible puff, and then a mist—launched, it seemed, from somewhere directly above the secondary console—suddenly enveloped Proctor's head and shoulders.

"Oops!" Ferenc said.

Proctor, concentrating on his panel, took a millisecond to react. He leaned forward, then back.

"Take deep breaths," Ferenc suggested. "That way, the stinging in your lungs won't last as long."

Proctor moved away from his console, staggering slightly. The mist around his head was clearing, but his face and the front of his shirt remained wet and beaded with droplets. He turned toward Ferenc and began to approach him, face black with rage, then paused. He took another step—breathing shallowly. Ferenc began to fear Proctor might actually be a superman instead of just a man. But then Proctor stopped; swayed unsteadily; then fell forward, crashing face-first against the concrete floor.

Ferenc, who'd done nothing to arrest the fall, clucked in sympathy. "That must have hurt."

He waited a moment longer, checking the machine's operation, then setting it to dial back remotely to station-keeping mode in five minutes. He glanced up at the clock, took note of the time. Then he pulled off the white lab coat that had covered his clothes, checked his pockets, and gingerly circled the wavering circle of brilliant light, eyes averted, until he stood directly in front of it. "Geronimo," he whispered.

He stepped through the circle, his image rippling slightly before first growing faint, and then disappearing altogether.

65

December 26, 1880
Wednesday

Ferenc staggered, experiencing the sensation of falling that occurs in dreams. Just as he was bracing for a violent impact, he felt a hard, cobbled surface materialize under his feet. He swayed, regaining his balance, and looked around. He was in a crooked, filthy alley, the brick walls pasted over with vintage advertisements in script straight out of a Civil War broadsheet. Except the ads weren't vintage at all—they looked brand new, the glue so fresh he could practically smell the horse collagen…if it wasn't for another, stronger horsey odor invading his senses. He stumbled forward, out of the alley and into a big open square.

He looked first left, then right. The square was busy with traffic made up entirely of horse carriages. The air was hazy with coal smoke.

He'd prepared himself for this, of course—looked at pictures while figuring out how to dress, making sure he was ready both mentally and emotionally for the shock of going back in time—but in fact, looking around, he realized nothing could have truly prepared him for the reality. It was like a movie set, only noisier, dirtier—and endless. He stood still a moment, taking deep breaths, slowing his heart and letting the realization sink in. He'd done it.

"Fuckin' *A!*" he whooped, pumping his fist in exultation.

A woman in a bustle, walking past with two young children, stopped to glare at him in shock and horror.

"Excuse me," he said, adding "ma'am" as he turned quickly away. Damn it, he had to be careful, say as little as possible, not attract any attention. He converted the fist-pumping gesture into a vigorous rubbing of his arms and shoulders, as if warding off a fit of shivering. In truth, it *was* cold—colder than a witch's tit. He'd forgotten that, in the 1880 he had arrived in, it was December rather than June.

Enough of this: he could reflect on this amazing journey, and its sights and sounds, once he was safely back home. He took a moment to get his bearings and then, ducking his head, he started making his way south on Broadway, careful to blend in with the crowds whenever possible.

They shouldn't have been so goddamned secretive; they should have trusted him more. They must have known that, in the course of rebuilding the machine, he'd learn its function. Proctor knew it was his pushy inquisitiveness, in part, that got Ferenc thrown out of the Rover project: but, Jesus Christ, all good scientists were curious. Every single time the subject got around to what exactly Pendergast planned to do with the machine, the man shifted the conversation elsewhere. Ferenc had voiced his concerns about its ethics, and Pendergast had ignored him. They had kept him in the dark, treating him like a child, ignoring his concerns—so it was only natural he would hide a miniature voice-activated recorder with SSD storage in the guts of the machine. The morality, the safety protocols of science, practically demanded it.

Fucking Proctor. He hated the stone-faced bastard. The man had actually threatened to kill him. This after he'd done the impossible—and in a mere two weeks at that. After that threat Ferenc lost any last vestiges of scientific misgivings—and he covertly removed his recording device, for review in his rooms later that evening.

Of course, by that time he'd already finalized a plan...but he still wanted to find out whether there was something he didn't know about, something weird or dangerous waiting back in that particular parallel timeline, something he *wouldn't like*—which was perhaps what they'd been keeping from him. And to think, once he had listened to enough of their taped conversation, he realized it was nothing more than ancestral bullshit! Just some drama about saving a girl and killing a doctor. To use a device of this power and potential on such a trivial thing was a crime. Pendergast's mission sounded like a ten-cent bodice ripper, when—with a machine like that at hand—billions could be made, worlds changed, history remade.

He crossed Fortieth Street with a crowd reeking of sweat despite the chill. He'd done his best to dress the part, with a flannel lumber-jack shirt of red-and-black plaid from L.L.Bean, black cargo pants, and Doc Martens lace-up leather boots in the original style, 1460. Even so, he noticed he was on the receiving end of more than one sidelong glance, as if he'd just gotten off the boat from Timbuktu or something. He paused a moment to scuff up his boots, rub a little horseshit on them to take the shine off. He probably could have used a little more research on the clothing. But that didn't matter—he'd researched what counted most.

Ferenc had always been paranoid and secretive by nature, and years spent working on scientific projects both classified and other-wise had only exacerbated that tendency. But it wasn't paranoia that told him Proctor was a major problem. He'd despised the man from the start—with his terse, Zen-like irony, his tougher-than-thou Special Forces manner, his lack of respect for Ferenc's genius: *You have a reputation for being meddlesome, difficult, and prickly.* But that little speech he'd made yesterday, after Pendergast traveled back here for the main event, had surprised and alarmed him. *Step out of line and you'll vanish. Just like that.* Ferenc didn't know what Pendergast had planned after this little sortie of his was finished, but he was now convinced Proctor meant to tie up the loose ends...including him.

When it's done, you won't say a single word about it. To anybody.

During the last week, as the machine underwent its final tests and appeared functional, he'd had an idea. A rather brilliant one, actually, that could quickly be put in place. He was working almost full-time in the lab, anyway; he had the parts he needed; and an extra hour here and there on top of all the moonlighting didn't matter.

Proctor had frightened him—but also angered him. Ferenc had decided to use that anger before he had the chance to lose his nerve. And it had worked perfectly. He had refilled his current prescription for bihydrodiozipene nasal spray, used for severe migraine auras, and the order had gone unremarked. He'd greatly concentrated the spray before placing it in an atomizer bulb and valve, which he'd planted behind Proctor's control panel during that day's preliminary checklist. The machine's stuttering, accomplished by a clever but harmless misalignment, created the pretext to run it at 100 percent. And then—from his own control panel—he'd sprayed a nice, thick cloud of sleepy-bye all over Proctor as he stood at the far end. The man would be out for at least five but probably more like ten hours. What Ferenc needed to do would take three or four at the max, and he'd be back in the twenty-first century, out of that creepy house…and gone, baby, gone. Proctor could cram that extra quarter million up his ass—with Special Force—because compared to what Ferenc would bring back with him, the $250,000 they were paying him for "maintenance" was chicken feed.

Christ, it was cold.

When he got to Thirty-Sixth Street, he paused to look ahead at Herald Square. There they were, on the right, exactly where they should be: three spheres of golden brass—at present quite dull and tarnished—suspended on a bar above a shop front half a block ahead.

Ferenc had to stop himself from pumping a fist again in triumph.

The one problem that had really stumped him was, ironically, what should have been the most trivial: money. For his scheme to work, he needed a hundred dollars, give or take.

A hundred dollars in 1880s currency.

Under normal circumstances, he could have headed downtown and bought the old money from a dealer in rare coins. But he couldn't just head downtown—Proctor would have had issues with him exercising such a freedom. Neither could he purchase the old money by mail, like he had some of the equipment and his extra dose of migraine medication: it would have been spotted and his intentions instantly revealed. How could such a simple thing be such an impediment?

The answer came to him as he was browsing the internet, researching the other elements of his plan: the approach, the transaction, the return. He'd been looking at an old photograph of Broadway in 1881...and there it was, right in front of him. A pawnshop.

As soon as he saw that, he knew he had the answer. Ten more minutes of scrolling confirmed it. In the 1880s, China was a mysterious and exotic place. The few Chinese artifacts that made their way to America—jade, in particular—were rare and highly coveted.

As it happened, Pendergast's endless display cases circling the reception hall had more than their share of jade objects: Ferenc had seen them. Size, he learned, mattered less than the delicacy and complexity of the carving, as well as the hue of the mineral itself. And so it had been the work of sixty seconds—with Pendergast off on his strange trip and Proctor in the back kitchen with Mrs. Trask—for Ferenc to slip one of the cases open, pocket two small but highly figured ornaments of cicadas and lotus flowers, rearrange the rest of the "Jades of the Six Ceremonial Periods" display so it looked untouched, and slide the case closed.

Now, smiling at his own cleverness, he crossed the street and entered the pawnshop. Ten minutes later he was back outside again, with a hundred and twenty dollars in period-accurate gold certificates in his pocket, along with a used hat and cape to help him blend into the crowd.

The rest of his short journey was uneventful.

The New York Federal Bank of Commerce was a hulking structure on Twenty-Sixth Street and Fifth Avenue, with a formidable colonnaded façade of Corinthian marble. Ferenc stopped for a moment across the street, readying himself, as he watched people—mostly men—come and go from the bank. Many were dressed in heavy coats of what looked like beaver or buffalo or something, and all wore hats. As did he.

You've got this. Get in there, make the transaction, and get your ass back to that portal.

Squaring his shoulders, he walked across the street, climbed the wide steps, and entered the building.

66

THE MAIN FLOOR OF the bank was warm, thank God. It had a high, vaulted ceiling, decorated with frescoes, and the vast space rang with footsteps, coughs, and the echo of voices. To the left and right were low, rail-like dividers such as one found in a courtroom, behind which sat men working at desks. Beyond them were rows of offices with doors of frosted glass. The tellers—Ferenc supposed that's what they were called, even in the 1880s—lay straight ahead of him, ensconced behind a huge brass partition. Uniformed guards armed with truncheons were everywhere.

He walked up to the nearby desk used to fill out slips. It had glass inkwells set into it, and its wooden surface was stained with splotches of blue-black ink. As the patrons around him greeted each other, wishing one another a happy Boxing Day, he took a sheet from the open glass drawer beneath and pretended to fill it out as he prepared himself.

Ferenc's father had been a frosty, distant mathematician with little time or love for his children. He had left his wife when Ferenc was fifteen, shortly after which Ferenc himself departed his native Hungary, along with his mother and younger brother, for an aunt's house in Reading, Pennsylvania. Although Ferenc had absorbed very little math from his father, he'd come away with a rather impressive knowledge of the man's two hobbies: stamp and coin collecting. His father had talked—the only times when his voice sounded eager—

about U.S. coins, in particular the three rarest: the 1794 "silver plug" dollar, the 1849 Coronet double eagle . . . and the Stella.

The Stella was a strange $4 gold piece created in hopes of furthering international trade, but the idea was abandoned before many coins had been struck. The two types of Stellas—one showing a profile of Lady Liberty with flowing tresses, the other with coiled hair—were made for only two years. Ferenc's father had spoken reverentially about this unicorn of a coin, called the "superstar" because of the large five-pointed star on its reverse—but also because of the prices it commanded when it came up for auction.

Ferenc had retained this interest of his father's, after a fashion, and had followed those auctions into adult life. The coin was so rare that it didn't show up often. A coiled-hair, PF67-graded "Cameo"—so termed because the coin sported a deeply recessed field that showed off the facial features in fine detail—had sold in 2013 for $2,500,000.

Two and a half *million*. And that was a decade ago. But the main reason Ferenc had taken his chance with the machine was because the only two years the Stella had been minted *were 1879 and 1880*. And his research had shown that the New York Federal Bank of Commerce habitually received the first, and largest, deliveries of new coinage coming from the Philadelphia mint. They were certain to have a sizable inventory of fresh, uncirculated Stellas, sharply mirrored and unblemished, with only the tiniest handling imperfections: sure to fetch a numismatic grade of PF68 or even higher. He had a hundred dollars to exchange for 25 of these coins.

He took a deep breath, surveyed the lines of waiting customers, and then—careful not to look nervous or stand out more than he could help—chose the shortest line and fell into it. There were only two people before him—and already the first of them was leaving.

He rehearsed in his mind what he was going to say. The transaction was an ordinary one, and it shouldn't take more than five minutes. Then he'd leave the bank, return through the portal, give the unconscious Proctor a good kick in the nutsack . . . and disappear with a roll of perfect $4 gold pieces that he could sell, discreetly and at long intervals, for a hundred times the amount of money Pendergast had already paid him.

His luck was holding: the only man now in front of him was already concluding his business, and he'd gotten in line just in time—a number of people had come into the bank, and there was now someone behind him, an overweight woman in a ridiculous bonnet who, when they made eye contact, quickly looked away with a moue of distaste.

"Sir?" A voice was speaking, and Ferenc realized it was directed at him. He turned to see the teller—a birdlike man with a visor and dun-colored vest, sporting a ludicrous number of buttons—looking back at him through the opening in the brass portcullis.

"Yes," Ferenc said. "Yes. Apologies." He fumbled in his pocket and brought out the money the pawnbroker had given him, smoothing the gold certificates on the cool marble counter. "I'd like to exchange these for twenty-five four-dollar gold pieces. New ones, if you please." The *only* ones, of course—there were no old ones. He could barely keep from rubbing his hands together in anticipation: specimens straight from the mint, with that lovely, straw-colored hue of gold still unsullied by greasy hands. He'd pick out only the most gemlike specimens, with high relief and maximum eye appeal, sharply struck with no visible imperfections: after all, the slightest spot or mark could mean the difference between a grading of PF68 and PF69 . . .

He was roused from these thoughts by the teller, who had not moved and was speaking to him again. "I'm sorry?" Ferenc said.

"Sir, I said that we don't have any such coins available."

Ferenc looked in disbelief. This was impossible—the coins had been minted just that year. "What? Are you sure?"

"There are none in my cash drawer. In fact, I can only recall seeing one—and that was three, perhaps four months ago."

"Well, what about the other cash drawers? That coin was only made for . . . I mean, it's brand new. *Somebody* here must have some!"

The teller was silent for a moment. "Just a moment, please," he said, stepping back from his crenellation and walking out of view. The woman behind him sighed with impatience.

Within two minutes, the teller had returned. "I'm very sorry, sir, but I've checked with my associates here at the windows, and none of them have the coin you're interested in, either."

This had to be a nightmare: Ferenc had done all the research, and he knew that if any, *any* bank, in any year, had those coins on hand, it would be this one and this year. He felt frustration and anger rising within him...but with them an acute awareness that he was a stranger in a very strange land. It would not do to make a scene. The teller was just lazy, the coins were there in the bank somewhere, and he just had to fucking *look* for them.

"I appreciate your taking the trouble," Ferenc said, leaning forward slightly. "Now, I would very much like to speak to your manager, if you would be so kind as to summon him for me."

The teller let his gaze flit over Ferenc's shoulder, where three people were now waiting behind him. "Certainly," he said, and disappeared once again.

The woman sighed again, more audibly. Ferenc bit his lip and kept his eyes forward.

Another few minutes, and the teller returned with an older gentleman, who wore no visor and was considerably better dressed. He had a salt-and-pepper beard, carefully trimmed. "Now," the man said to Ferenc, the teller standing to one side. "How exactly can I be of service?"

"It's quite simple," Ferenc said. "I wish to exchange these notes for an equal value of four-dollar gold pieces."

The manager nodded, as if affirming this request for himself. "I'm sorry to disappoint you, sir, but as my colleague here indicated, we have no such specie on hand."

The man's tone was polite but not nearly as solicitous as the teller's. Ferenc hardly noticed. "That's not possible. How can you have *none*? They're here, somewhere."

"My land!" said the fat woman behind him.

Now the manager paused to take in the entirety of Ferenc's appearance—from the hat to the cape to the lumberjack shirt. "Do you have an account with us, Mister...?"

Ferenc thought fast. This was rapidly going south, and he had to salvage the mission somehow. Fast. He drew himself up. "No, I have no account here. My name is...Murrow. Edward R. Murrow. I'm a reporter with the *New York Herald*, and I'm writing an article on the beauty of these new coins and...and their importance for foreign trade. My editors might become alarmed if your bank, given its federal affiliations, can't even provide a sampling! In fact, such an anomaly might prompt them to investigate—" he thought for a second— "the fractional reserves you maintain at this site."

The manager flinched slightly, no doubt imagining the run on the bank such an article might cause. "Wait here, please, Mr. Murrow," he said. Then he walked away, leaving the teller standing awkwardly on the far side of the marble counter.

The line behind Ferenc grew more restless, but he didn't care. Now, at last, he'd get some results.

The manager—after a more protracted delay—returned with a box covered in velvet. He placed the box on the counter. "Before we proceed, Mr. Murrow, I want to assure you, and your newspaper, that the New York Federal has more than enough cash and other assets on hand to cover any exigency. I'd like to emphasize that fact: *more than enough.*"

"I'm glad to hear it," Ferenc said, eyes on the box. "Let's complete the transaction, and I will write an article that is, ah, satisfactory to all concerned."

The manager paused in the middle of removing the velvet. "I think you misunderstand," he said. "We have plenty of gold specie on hand— twenty-dollar Libertys, ten-dollar Eagles—but the coin you speak of is a special case." He removed the velvet, placed both hands on the polished wooden lid beneath. "Nevertheless, under the circumstances, I've been authorized to release these to you." And he opened the box.

Ferenc bent forward eagerly—and couldn't believe his eyes. Nestled within two pockets of red silk were a pair of gold Stellas. He stared in hideous disappointment. One, an 1879 Flowing Hair Stella, was nicked and covered with bag marks. And the other—an 1880 Coiled

Hair, the rarest of the lot—was defaced by roller marks and planchet blemishes, strikes of the variety least prized by coin collectors.

He stared at the manager. "This is it? Just these two?" He knew that even shitty Stellas would still sell for a couple hundred thousand. But he'd been expecting to return with twenty-five Cameo-condition, even Ultra Cameo coins...these probably wouldn't score higher than PF62.

Now it was the manager's turn to lean forward. "You must understand, Mr. Murrow," he said, still clearly worried about negative publicity. "We have thousands of gold coins in our vault. But this particular oddity...well, the fact is we only received a dozen of the 1879 strike, and this year we only received four, including this one, too damaged to be considered anywhere near proof..."

But Ferenc was no longer listening. Because at last he understood— and the revelation crushed him. All this time, he'd been counting on the fact he could be *there*, in the very year the coins were minted, and easily get his hands on them...not realizing that contemporary collectors, or preferred customers, or bank presidents, would have been there before him. The rarest Stellas had been minted in tiny numbers...and he'd overlooked the fact that people had been collecting rare coins, even contemporaneous ones, for centuries. In 1931, people had even hoarded rolls of uncirculated Lincoln *pennies* because of the year's low mintage. Too, too late, it was obvious that grabbing a fistful of proof-quality Stellas in 1880 was no more likely than grabbing a fistful of tickets to the 2007 Led Zeppelin reunion, where 20 million fans vied for 20,000 seats.

As he felt himself bowing beneath this awful realization, there came an irruption from the woman behind him. "If you are quite done pawing those coins, *sir*, the rest of us have important business to attend to."

Something inside Ferenc snapped. "Shut up, bitch," he said, wheeling around, then turning back. "I'll take these two," he said, stretching his hands forward. He'd be lucky to get half a million for them, but he could kick himself later; it was time to get his ass back to...

"You, sir!" sounded a rough voice to one side. It was a bank guard who'd been watching—and listening. "What did you just say to this lady?"

A heavy hand clapped itself onto Ferenc's shoulder, just as he heard the bank manager utter, "Good *Lord!*" The manager was staring at Ferenc's wrist...and Ferenc, following the gaze, saw that the man was gaping at his cheap Japanese watch. A Casio G-Shock, black and beat up, that he hadn't taken off in five years and never gave a thought to.

"What the devil have you got there?" demanded the guard, as he wheeled Ferenc around and forced back his sleeve. His eyes widened, too, as he saw the LED numbers, glowing like magic against the clear background...numbers that changed every second.

Ferenc made a sudden move, taking advantage of the guard's surprise to twist out of his grasp and run for the door—only to find his way blocked by two more guards and half a dozen citizen do-gooders.

"You're not going anywhere!" one of them said, grabbing at the watch he had seen the guard examining. As he did so, the man inadvertently pressed one of the buttons on its bezel.

A beeping noise sounded.

"It's a *bomb!*" somebody cried.

"Insurrectionist!" cried another.

"Anarchist!" They surged into him, and Ferenc was spun around. Two articles he'd brought along for protection, a folding knife and a Taser, clattered to the floor. An angry gasp rippled through the group. One kicked the knife into a corner. Another grabbed the Taser and fumbled with it, accidentally pulling the trigger. There was a loud *clack* as the dual electrodes shot out, arcing toward a woman pushing a perambulator, striking her in the side. She fell with a piercing scream and writhed on the floor, amid an eruption of shrieks and shouts and a wail from the baby.

"*Agitator!*" Somebody punched him in the side of the head and he went down, the mob kicking and grabbing at him. He tried crawling out from under the rain of blows, but whistles sounded as the cops arrived. Moments later, he was dragged to his feet by uniformed constables of the Metropolitan Police, his arms clapped in handcuffs.

They began dragging him out of the bank. "Hey, no!" he cried. "Let me go! I haven't done anything!"

"Hear that foreign accent, Jonesey?" said one cop, giving Ferenc a wicked shove out the door.

"I heard enough," said another.

And now, out of nowhere, appeared a paddy wagon, nineteenth-century style, drawn by horses with leather blinders. A crowd was gathering outside, chattering and pointing. Ferenc, realizing just how crazy and desperate his position was, began to struggle as he was hauled down the steps. "I didn't do anything! Listen, just let me go, please!"

He felt an overwhelming panic—if he didn't get back before Proctor woke up, he'd be up shit creek. Or, even worse, he might never get back at all. He might be stuck in this universe forever, rotting in a jail cell. He had to stop this, now.

"I'm from the future! You saw the watch! There's proof! Just let me go, *please!* I'll leave, I'll just go back! I didn't hurt anybody!"

"You hear that, Jonesey? Says he's from the future."

"Move it, pal!"

They half dragged, half pushed him into the back of the paddy wagon. And now Ferenc realized there was only one person on earth—on *this* earth—who could save him, one person who had the presence of mind and the gift of articulation to sort this out...and quickly.

"Listen to me, please!" he said, voice rising in desperation. "I told you, I'm from the future. Listen, *listen!!* Let me find Pendergast. He'll explain everything, he'll make this right!"

And his cries continued, even as they grew muffled by the clanging of the steel doors at the back of the wagon. "Pendergast! Get Pendergast! *Get Pendergast...!"*

67

D<small>R. E</small>NOCH L<small>ENG</small> STEPPED into the massive shadow of Bellevue Hospital, the expression on his face preoccupied and distant as he made his way inside. Potential patients at the Five Points had recently proven unsatisfactory, due to spreading typhoid, even as his accelerating research was requiring more subjects than ever. He had planned to confine his rounds today to the young women's infirmary, his attention focused on the new arrivals.

But he'd barely set foot inside the building when he was accosted by the medical resident, Norcross, who would soon qualify as a specialist in afflictions of the mind. He had considered, briefly, taking the man into his confidence, but then he realized that while brilliant and of a subservient disposition, Norcross did not have the requisite elasticity of moral judgment. A shame.

"Dr. Leng!" the student resident said, coming up to him. "I thought you might come by today."

"Why is that, Norcross? What is special about today?"

"Well..." Norcross hesitated. "I'd assumed you'd heard about the anarchist bank robber who's been admitted. The police brought him in. The entire hospital is aflutter."

"Is that so?" Leng was interested in neither anarchists nor bank robbers. He continued to walk toward the women's ward while Norcross fell into step beside him.

"He's a special case," Norcross went on. "They asked me to examine him, and I did, but..." He hesitated. "I found the presentation of his illness rather outside my experience. The police asked the hospital for a judgment of confinement as a criminal lunatic, but of course I wasn't qualified to provide it and Dr. Stamm doesn't arrive on the premises until this afternoon."

"What exactly is the presentation of symptoms?"

"For one thing, he claims to be from the future. He was hysterical, struggling and raving, and yet...he didn't seem fulminant."

"Not fulminant," echoed Leng, slowing his step. This mildly stimulated his curiosity. "And claims he's from the future. Well, Norcross, let us take a look at him."

"Very good, doctor." They turned down a flight of stairs and through the two doors of banded iron, then along the passageway leading to the ward for the criminally insane.

"He quieted down when the orderlies threatened him with a straitjacket. But he's remained in an agitated state, continually demanding to see a particular person."

"I see," Leng replied as he followed the student in residence. There were in fact standing orders for him to be notified whenever a particularly unusual patient was committed, and this one seemed more than a little curious. "Where was he apprehended and what were the circumstances?"

"At the Federal Bank of Commerce, where he started a fracas. After he was subdued, several strange devices were found on his person. The police confiscated a knife and some other kind of weapon that accidentally discharged, wounding a bystander...The other two items are here, under lock and key."

"What are they?"

"It's hard to say. He claims one is a timepiece and the other he claims is a kind of voice telegraph."

"A timepiece from the future?" This grade of psychosis might be unusual enough to merit a note in the *Lancet*.

They stopped outside a cell, locked and barred like the others.

Inside, a man was pacing back and forth in great agitation, talking to himself and showing other signs of emotional distress. He was dressed in a red-and-black plaid shirt, dark trousers, and boots. Seeing Norcross, he stopped pacing and hurried toward the bars.

"Have you brought him?" the man asked. His eyes were red-rimmed, and sweat beaded his face. "Have you brought Pendergast?"

On hearing this name, a shock like a bolt of electricity passed through Leng's body.

"Listen, you've got to find Pendergast—he'll clear everything up." The man's voice was trembling, on the verge of hysteria.

Leng recovered his presence of mind. "Pendergast? May I have a first name, please?"

At this, the man hesitated. "I don't know it."

"And you claim to come from the future?"

"Yes, *yes!* Look, just find Pendergast, he'll explain everything!"

Leng took a step away from the cell and turned to Norcross. "May I see his possessions?" he murmured.

Norcross led the way back along the corridor to a tenantless cell that served as a storage area. He unlocked a metal drawer, slid it out, placed it on a table in the center of the room, and opened it. He handed Leng a pair of white cotton gloves, then stepped away.

Leng glanced at the two items inside the tray. Then he reached in and removed one of them, holding it in his hand. A very queer feeling came over him as he gazed at the object. A glowing rectangle was set in a black frame, backlit as if by a candle. But there was no candle or even the sensation of heat, and the source of the light was mysterious. Within this illuminated rectangle, black numbers in an ugly font were blinking. The biggest set of numbers read **2:01 27**, with the last two incrementing every second. He watched until these two numbers reached **59**, and then they reset to **00**, and the time changed from **2:01** to **2:02**.

He reached into his pocket and pulled out his heavy gold pocket watch, which told him the time was six minutes after two. *It always did run a little fast*, he thought to himself as he slipped it back into his waistcoat pocket.

The object was held by a wrist strap that resembled gutta-percha or India rubber, but of marvelous flexibility and strength. Leng was reminded of the "wristlet watches" currently in vogue on the Continent: women's bracelets with small clocks attached, instead of the far more sensible and reliable pocket watch.

The silence lengthened as Leng pondered the blinking numbers.

Then he laid the object aside and took out the other one. It was much less impressive, but finely made, a thin rectangle of glass on one side, set into a case of brushed metal like aluminum. The glass surface on one face was blank. There were a few buttons on the side, which did not respond when he pushed them. The metal back had several round pieces of glass in one corner and, bizarrely, the image of an apple in the middle, polished to a high gloss. The object was entirely inert, appearing to have no function whatsoever.

He put both devices back in the tray and indicated for Norcross to lock it up once again. Then he followed the resident down the hall a second time.

"Are you getting Pendergast?" the man in the cell asked eagerly as they once more came into view.

"May I have your name?" asked Leng.

"Ferenc. Gaspard Ferenc."

"Thank you, Mr. Ferenc. I should like to ask you a few questions."

The man wiped sweat from his forehead with the butt of his wrist. "Can you please make it quick? It's been at least four hours. I have to get back, *right away...*" His voice started to rise again.

"I shall be quick." Already—from years of observation—Leng sensed this man was not insane. But he kept this to himself. "Now, Mr. Ferenc, would you please repeat for me the information you've given to others? Especially about this man you seek—Pendergast."

The man fought back another spasm of panic and impatience. "I know it sounds crazy, but I'm from the future. Well, not the future in a literal sense, but an alternate timeline."

Leng was careful to betray no expression. "What was your purpose in coming here?"

The man hesitated. "I didn't do anything wrong."

"Then tell me what you *did* do."

The man hung his head. "I came back to purchase some coins. Coins that would be very valuable in...the future."

"And how, exactly, did you 'come back'?"

"I used Pendergast's machine."

"Tell me about this machine."

"It's complicated. It involves a lot of quantum theory, and...forget it." He fetched a long, shuddering sigh. "Pendergast hired me to fix it. You see, I worked on the Mars Perseverance mission—but of course you'd know nothing about that. I used the machine to come here and exchange some money. Nothing wrong about that." He was babbling.

The Mars Perseverance mission, Leng repeated in his mind. "And this man Pendergast? What is his role in this situation?" He spoke in a calm, coaxing voice.

Ferenc suddenly fell silent. Then he said calmly, "Doctor, I don't believe I caught your name."

Leng ignored the question. "Are you saying that this man you're looking for, Pendergast, also used the machine to come back here?"

Ferenc hesitated, as if warned by some sixth sense. "I've answered your questions."

"I am not done asking, Mr. Ferenc. Now tell me: what is this man Pendergast doing here?"

Again, Ferenc went silent. The only noise was the gibbering and muttering from other cells down the passage.

"Speak up!" Norcross said sharply. "Dr. Leng is trying to help you."

"Leng!" Ferenc repeated in alarm, jumping back from the bars as if shocked.

Leng gazed upon the man's face, now white as a sheet. He was sorry that Norcross had spoken his name. But no matter; he could find out everything he needed to know despite that.

"Thank you, Mr. Ferenc." He nodded to Norcross, signaling he was done. They both departed, leaving the prisoner in his cell.

Down the hall, Leng turned to Norcross. "A most interesting case indeed. I'm much obliged to you for calling my attention to it."

"I had hoped as much," said Norcross, a glow of pleasure on his face.

"Definitely worthy of further study. We shall file the paperwork to have him immediately discharged into my care. There is much to be learned from this rare presentation."

"An excellent idea, Dr. Leng."

"Please inform Dr. Cawley and complete the paperwork posthaste."

It was the work of thirty minutes. Leng exercised his standing authority to transfer any patient at Bellevue under his purview to his own facility. Norcross took care of the paperwork with his usual efficiency and dispatch, glowing inside with the great interest Leng had taken in the case as well as his own role in it. As he watched Dr. Leng proceed down the hallway with the patient, now heavily sedated and gentle as a kitten, Norcross realized something: He had seen the good doctor remove many female patients to his private sanatorium in the past. But this was the first time Dr. Leng had taken a man.

68

VINCENT D'AGOSTA, DRESSED in a shabby greatcoat and gloves, watch cap pulled down and collar turned up against the chill, stood in the little newsstand on the south side of Forty-Eighth Street, around the corner from Fifth Avenue. The owner of the newsstand, which in addition to newspapers sold broadsheets and penny novels, had been given a handsome fee to take a few days off, no questions asked. D'Agosta had taken his place that morning. The newsstand gave him a clear view of the marble town house Constance Greene now owned. It was a beautiful building, but D'Agosta could see the place was well fortified against unauthorized entry. The front door was massive and banded with iron. Around the corner on Forty-Eighth Street was the entrance to the carriage driveway, leading to the stables and stone garage where the three horses and carriage were kept. All the first-floor windows had iron bars across them—bars that looked freshly installed. An eight-foot wrought iron fence topped by spikes screened the building on two sides, and the dark service alleyway that ran behind it parallel to the avenue was barred by an even taller fence. It was a marvel of urban design that all these precautionary measures still allowed the place to resemble a mansion instead of a fortress.

As the afternoon wore on, he kept a constant eye on the residence, occasionally interrupted by buyers of papers but always remaining hyperalert.

The only weakness in his position was that he had no direct view of the mansion's front façade. There was no way to surveil that without loitering on Fifth Avenue and making oneself conspicuous. In this well-policed Gilded Age neighborhood, anyone hanging around for any length of time would arouse suspicion. For the same reason, it seemed unlikely that Leng or one of his henchmen would choose to spy on the town house from the avenue. D'Agosta was pretty confident anyone watching the house would likely approach from the bustling Forty-Eighth Street corner—a corner busy with traffic and, in addition to his newsstand, hosting a bootblack and a peddler selling roasted chestnuts from a cart.

He clapped his gloved hands together and took a small turn around the space, trying to keep warm. Horses and carriages clattered by on the cobbled street, the sound of hooves echoing off the building façades, and he could smell the chestnuts roasting nearby. He tried not to think about the still-staggering fact that this was 1880. He'd seen some crazy shit working with Pendergast, but this was one thing he still couldn't wrap his mind around. And how the hell was he ever going to explain it to Laura? He kept returning to his argument with Laura and the way she'd walked out. *Sorry I vanished like that—you see, Pendergast and I went back in time to 1880 to rescue crazy Constance Greene, who was living on Fifth Avenue, passing herself off as a duchess and preparing to murder someone.* He could just see Laura's face as he tried to explain.

He made an effort to banish thoughts of Laura from his mind—there was nothing he could do about it now.

"The *Herald*," came a crisp request from a gentleman, interrupting his thoughts. The man placed a nickel on the counter and D'Agosta handed him the paper. He dropped the nickel into the cash box and watched the man walk off toward Madison Avenue. Nothing suspicious there.

D'Agosta had taken up his position at ten that morning, less than twenty-four hours after he and Pendergast had returned to Longacre Square. Pendergast had previously arranged for him to take over

at the newsstand, and as soon as D'Agosta was installed, Pendergast had rushed away in a God-awful hurry on some mysterious
mission.

Not long after he'd manned the kiosk, he spied one of the children
in an upstairs window. It was the girl, Constance, her dark hair cut in
a short bob and tied with a ribbon on one side, playing with a deck of
cards. And then he had seen the other Constance—the Constance he
knew—approaching the town house by hansom cab and being let in
by a maid. The same person, but of two different ages: coexisting not
only in the same world, but in the same *house*. It was like no science
fiction story he'd ever read—going back in the past and meeting yourself was a logical no-no. Yet it was happening before his eyes...and not
only that: Constance had set herself up in a veritable palace. Where
had she gotten the damn money? But he reminded himself that if
anyone could pull it off, she could. D'Agosta had never met a more
formidable woman. Scary and, quite possibly, not completely sane.
He'd heard about her escapades—getting revenge on her seducer by
hurling him into a live volcano in Sicily, spraying acid on the bastards
trying to kill Pendergast at the Brooklyn Botanic Garden—and he'd
sure as hell seen the results.

Even though it was only four o'clock, the winter night was already
falling. No daylight saving in 1880. A man came by with a long rod,
lighting the gas lamps one by one. A horse and carriage clopped past.
The bootblack packed up his kit and left. Soft lights went on in the
marble mansion, and the shades were drawn.

And then an old man came down the street, walking slowly with a
cane. D'Agosta watched him suspiciously. The man paused in front of
the kiosk and fished a nickel from his pocket with a grubby hand and
placed it on the counter.

"The *Sun*," he said in a cracked voice.

D'Agosta turned to get the paper from the stack behind him.
When he turned around again, he was startled to see the man had
taken off his hat and Pendergast was standing before him, pale and
agitated. "Sorry to surprise you, my friend," he said in a low voice.

"I've done a little more probing and I'm more concerned than ever. I fear Constance is overplaying her hand."

"What does that mean?"

"It means things may come to a head even sooner than I expected. We must not make the mistake of underestimating how dangerous Leng is. It may no longer be a question of days anymore—it may be less. I fear for Mary, and I *must* find her." He took up the newspaper.

"What's your plan, then?" D'Agosta asked in an undertone as he dropped the nickel in the cash box.

"Through a combination of research, memory, and observation, I am reasonably confident of Mary's location. I intend to rescue her tonight. I also have reason to believe his man Munck might appear after dark, to shadow Constance or provide Leng with intelligence on her activities, so keep an eye out for him."

"How will I know this Munck guy?"

"He's small, five foot four, very solid, and has a peculiar limp, a sort of hitch while lifting his right leg. It's subtle, and he makes an effort to hide it, but you will see it if you look. He's very good at blending into shadows."

D'Agosta nodded.

"Remember: under no circumstances whatsoever are you to reveal yourself to Constance. If that happened, our entire mission here would be for naught. Constance believes herself to be free now, in control of her own destiny, without worrying about me or...our private relationship. If she learned I were here, meddling in her life—it would unhinge her."

D'Agosta had seen Constance unhinged before, and he hoped never to see it again. "I understand."

"When you close up the newsstand at five, remain behind its shutters and continue watching the house. If Munck appears and, unexpectedly, does more than simply reconnoiter—in the unlikely event, say, he tries to enter—stop him. You may have to kill him—otherwise he will kill you. He is a brutally evil man who takes pleasure in opening people up to watch their lifeblood flow into the gutter. By ridding the world of him you will be saving lives."

D'Agosta swallowed.

"Can you do that, my friend? We will escape to our own time quickly enough, and you'll not have to face the law."

D'Agosta finally nodded. "What if Leng shows up instead?"

"He would not expose himself in such a fashion—he will want more intelligence about the house first." Pendergast removed a heavy object from his coat and passed it over: a revolver. D'Agosta took it and tucked it away.

And then Pendergast turned and walked off with his paper, vanishing into the darkening winter evening, as D'Agosta resumed his long watch.

69

A. X. L. Pendergast paused halfway down lower Manhattan's Catherine Street, running his eye along the foul succession of grog-shops, cheap lodging houses, and oyster cellars. The winter night was feebly illuminated by flickering gas lamps. A smell of rotten fish, urine, and boiling mutton permeated the air, and the noise was continuous: the clattering of hooves, the snatches of music from the taverns, the bellowing and singing of drunken sailors staggering along the street. From the waterfront two blocks away, he heard the clanging of a ship's bell and the drawn-out reverberation of a steam whistle.

His attention finally settled at the far end of the block, specifically on a three-story brick building in the Gothic Revival style, streaked with soot. A small crowd was queueing up at an entrance, while a barker paced back and forth, crying out: "See the preserved body of the Ancient Mermaid of Mandalay!" Occasionally, he would alternate that invitation with another: "View the bones of the Countess de Brissac, executed by guillotine, and touch the blade that ended her life!"

Pendergast's eye traveled upward to a wooden sign in gold letters that arched over the entrance, announcing the name of the establishment:

J.C. Shottum's Cabinet
OF
Natural Productions & Curiosities

Observations complete, Pendergast continued down the block and got into the queue filing into Shottum's. He paid two pennies to a fat man in a greasy stovepipe hat and entered the building. He found himself in a large foyer, with a mammoth skull on one side and a badly stuffed Kodiak bear on the other. A miscellany of objects dominated the center, including a petrified log, a dinosaur thighbone, and a giant ammonite, crowded willy-nilly next to a totem pole and a meteorite.

Most of the crowd were streaming through the foyer to the entrance of the "Dinosaur Cyclorama," which promised to put the viewer inside a 360-degree depiction of the "Savage Age of the Terrible Lizards." The visitors to Shottum's Cabinet, he noticed, were a mixture of young dandies in derby hats, working toughs, and longshoremen coming off work. To the left and right were doorways to further exhibits.

While he had, of course, never been inside this building—it had burned many decades before his birth—he had re-created it very carefully as an intellectual construct. He took a moment to inspect how the real thing compared to the Cabinet of his imagination and—where it differed—made a mental note for future consideration and refinement.

Then he moved across the hall to a doorway at the far end marked "The Gallery of Unnatural Monstrosities." He slipped through the entrance into a dark passageway. This, he knew, was the oldest and least-visited part of Shottum's Cabinet, its exhibits grown stale. He passed by a table displaying a sealed jar containing a human baby floating in yellow liquid, with two arms sticking out of its forehead. Beyond was a stuffed dog with a cat's head sewn onto it. The exhibits were dusty and unkempt, and a faint smell of rot drifted through the air.

Moving swiftly down the dim passageway, he passed more grotesque exhibits in various alcoves—a giant rat from Sumatra; the alleged liver of a woolly mammoth found frozen in Siberia; a misshapen human skull labeled "The Rhinoceros Man of Cincinnati." Several turns of the passageway brought him to the exhibit he was searching for. In a dead-end alcove big enough for only one person stood a glass case containing a desiccated human head, tongue still protruding from its mouth, with an identifying placard.

THE HEAD OF THE NOTORIOUS MURDERER AND
ROBBER WILSON ONE-HANDED
HUNG BY THE NECK UNTIL DEAD
DAKOTA TERRITORY JULY 4 1868

Next to it was another item, labeled:

THE NOOSE FROM WHICH HE SWUNG

and beside that:

THE FOREARM STUMP AND HOOK OF
WILSON ONE-HANDED WHICH
BROUGHT IN A BOUNTY OF ONE THOUSAND DOLLARS

Behind, at the rear of the exhibit, at the far end of the alcove, hung a heavy drapery. Pendergast drew this aside to reveal a wall of bare wooden boards. He inspected the boards, pressed a small knothole, then the entire wall. It opened inward to reveal a small but deep closet with a padlocked metal door in the back. Closing the wooden partition behind him, he approached the padlock, removed his set of picks, worked on the simple lock for a moment, and then discarded it. Pulling open the door, he exposed a staircase going down into a blackness that exhaled dust, mold, and chemicals.

He paused. He had already deduced, from old building plans and his own mental re-creation, where this secret entrance must be. If his chain of deductions continued to be accurate, it was down this stairway that Mary Greene would be found—not in Leng's mansion on Riverside Drive, but somewhere in this warren of subterranean tunnels.

The mansion on Riverside would be a dangerously inconvenient prison. Pendergast also knew that, in his own timeline, Leng had disposed of Mary's body in the coal tunnel below Shottum's Cabinet of Curiosities, along with many other victims. Therefore, she must have been kept alive down here before her vivisection: transporting her dead body from the uptown mansion would not only be an annoyance, it would involve unacceptable risk. She was likely at this very moment imprisoned in some fetid cell, while Leng fattened her up on a special diet necessary for the successful surgical extraction of her cauda equina—essential for the production of the Arcanum that would, when perfected, prolong his life.

He slipped out of his pocket a 1,000-lumen tactical flashlight, while with the other hand he drew his single most accurate and dependable sidearm: a Jim Hoag Master Grade Colt 1911. He probed the stygian darkness with his flashlight and ventured down the staircase.

70

At the bottom of the stairs, Pendergast's bright beam revealed a circular chamber forming the hub for three stone tunnels, crudely cut and mortared, streaming with damp. He switched off the light and waited, listening intently. He could hear the faint dripping of water and the distant, muffled hum of machinery, but there was no sound of human presence.

These tunnels had been constructed almost a century before beneath what had been Cow Bay, to serve as part of the city's waterworks. In the intervening years, Cow Bay had been filled in and become part of the Five Points. The waterworks eventually could not keep up with the growth of the city and was shut down in 1879 after the opening of the Central Park Reservoir. The Cow Bay Waterworks and its service tunnels were then bricked up and sealed.

But not for long. Leng had secretly reopened the tunnels and converted them to his own use. He had connected the waterworks passageways to the abandoned coal tunnel underneath Shottum's Cabinet, which in turn was linked to the secure basement staircase Pendergast had just descended—a connection Leng had discovered from perusing old plans, unknown to even Shottum himself. It had become Leng's private entryway into a self-contained world underneath the slums of the Five Points.

The old coal tunnel, with its numerous storage alcoves, proved the perfect place for Leng to seal up the deceased victims of his surgical experiments. In the adjacent waterworks tunnels, he had retrofitted a laboratory and—Pendergast surmised—also created cells for victims he or Munck seized from the out-of-the-way alcove in Shottum's Cabinet. Pendergast also knew that a number of these victims had proven unsatisfactory. Some had relatives who inquired into their disappearance; others were tubercular or otherwise diseased. Leng needed healthy young stock, with no prying family . . . and so in 1880, as he prepared to move all surgical work from his upstairs digs at Shottum's to these subterranean spaces, he also turned to a new source of victims: the Five Points Mission and nearby House of Industry. There, he had set himself up as a consulting physician and alienist *pro bono publico*, where he had his pick of orphaned girls without families, selecting those who both met his requirements and would never be missed.

In Pendergast's own timeline, Leng—after taking Mary—had learned to his surprise that she *did* have a family: a sister, Constance, and a brother named Joe. This was why Leng had hunted down and captured Constance after he had vivisected her sister. Joe had by then been killed and no longer posed a threat. But that was in their parallel multiverse; here, his own Constance had arrived and disturbed the timeline, intent on saving her siblings and revenging herself on Leng. As a result, he could no longer count on history unfolding as he expected.

He turned his Defender flashlight back on at its low, 5-lumen setting, allowing only the tiniest ray to illuminate the way forward. He knew that, while Munck may or may not be busy elsewhere, Leng could have other assistants lurking down here as well. And it was entirely possible Leng himself might be in his secret laboratory or someplace within these corridors. He had to proceed with the utmost caution.

As he moved, spiders and centipedes, disturbed by his presence, scurried away from the light, sometimes dropping to the floor with a soft pattering noise and skittering about his feet. Puddles of fetid water lay here and there among the stones, some wriggling with tiny albino eels. The sound of distant machinery grew louder, groaning and echoing through the damp spaces.

The first tunnel he took wandered about before terminating in an old iron headgate, left over from the obsolete waterworks and rusted shut. He backtracked. A second tunnel soon brought him to a riveted iron door, also padlocked. He extinguished his light and listened at the door, but there was no sound from beyond. Both lock and hinge were free of rust and well oiled—perhaps this was the entry he hoped to find. He silently picked the lock and set it aside. Then he thrust open the door with his foot and panned back and forth with both flashlight and weapon.

His beam revealed a short stretch of tunnel ending in a brick wall, which had itself been broken through, the bricks neatly stacked to one side. He crept up to the opening and shone the light in, gun at the ready. He started with recognition as the beam illuminated what lay ahead—the infamous coal tunnel beneath Shottum's.

Of the dozen alcoves on either side of the tunnel, two-thirds had been freshly bricked up, while stacks of bricks and bags of mortar beside the ones that remained open indicated work ready to be done when fresh victims arrived.

He knew that each bricked-up alcove contained three victims, which made a total of twenty-four killings so far in Leng's ghastly series of experiments—he knew, because he had seen all this before, in his own timeline in New York, excavated and exposed to daylight more than a hundred years *after* it had been used as a catacomb.

Twelve more bodies were to come before the niches were fully occupied—if Leng were allowed to continue.

But he would not be allowed to continue.

The alcove that had, in his own timeline, contained Mary's body was still empty.

As revealing as all this was, it was not his goal. Pendergast backed out of the tunnel and retraced his steps, taking the third and final tunnel. It, too, ended at a padlocked iron door, again with well-oiled hinges and lock. On the dirty floor, Pendergast saw evidence of recent comings and goings—tracks of shoes and the wheels of a cart.

Once again, he picked the lock and threw the door open, panning his weapon from right to left. The air in this tunnel was fresher than in the others, and past the locked doorway the walls and floor were relatively dry and clean. He paused to listen, but again could pick up no sound of human presence beyond the wheezing machinery, which he now surmised might be a primitive airflow system.

He sensed he was nearing his goal. Strange that he had seen no evidence of activity or a guard on watch; but then again, Leng could have no suspicion that he, Pendergast, was here—or that he even existed. Just as he had no reason to think anyone would stumble across this hidden lair beneath the Five Points. While Leng was preternaturally intelligent and suspicious, he could not possibly deduce that people from the future, his own descendant Pendergast among them, had come to stop his experiments—and kill him.

As he moved down the tunnel, Pendergast came across a prison cell with a barred door; directing the light within, he saw a stone bench for sleeping, a chamber pot, and a single book, swollen from the damp. A tin plate of old food lay on the floor, and his beam, sweeping over it, disturbed a pack of rats who backed off with bared teeth. Next to this was another cell, and then another: a row of them, all empty but showing signs of recent occupation. Obviously, they had been holding areas for Leng's victims—in the days or weeks before they had perished under his blade.

…But where was Mary? She *had* to be imprisoned somewhere down here. It was inconceivable Leng was keeping her at his Riverside Drive mansion—and surely she wasn't yet on the operating table, being vivisected…

He quickened his pace. The very last cell in the corridor had a solid iron door instead of bars, and again it was padlocked. This door was newer than the others and looked recently installed. The padlock quickly yielded and he eased open the door, surprised to find light shining out from the widening crack.

He glanced in—then froze in surprise.

Hardly able to believe his eyes, Pendergast advanced into a room unlike any other in this foul abattoir: a richly furnished chamber with velvet wallpaper; globes burning brightly with gas; a table and chairs with writing paper, pens, and ink; a sofa covered in silk; a bookcase of fine editions; and sporting prints of horses and dogs on the walls. The rumble of fresh air came from a grate in the ceiling. At the far end stood a canopy bed draped in silk—and the shape of a person, presently sleeping under the covers.

So *this* was where Leng was keeping Mary while he fattened her up for his next harvesting. A clever kind of concealment, indeed.

Not wishing to alarm, Pendergast advanced noiselessly to the bed where Mary lay asleep, covered by a silk coverlet. A glass of orange juice, half drunk, stood on the bedside table. He stuck in the tip of a finger and tasted it, not surprised to find it laced with laudanum.

Now he leaned over the bed, not wanting her to cry out at the sight of a stranger. Despite his reconnoiter, Munck or some other villain might nevertheless be nearby.

"Mary," he whispered, gently touching the body covered by silk brocade.

Instantly, he knew something was wrong. The body did not yield to the press of his finger; it was oddly stiff. He gave a harder nudge, surprise and horror rising as he felt the familiar rigidity of a corpse in the early stages of rigor mortis. With an involuntary curse he reached over, grasped the edge of the blanket, and pulled it back to reveal the face of the corpse: lying on its back, eyes wide open, mouth distorted in pain and terror.

71

A FEW MINUTES BEFORE eight o'clock, D'Agosta noted a small, dark figure approaching east on Forty-Eighth Street, walking at an even pace, derby hat pulled down low, upper body swathed in a heavy black cape. D'Agosta squinted into the darkness: was that a limp? The man moved almost invisibly along the sidewalk, as if he were most at home in the shadows. It was the dinner hour, and the street had quieted down, the clip-clop of horses and the bustling of pedestrians much reduced and the peddlers gone home. The gaslights on the street threw out what, to D'Agosta, was surprisingly little light. In fact, the darkness of the city amazed him. There wasn't an electric light on the entire damn island, the night interrupted only feebly by the gleam of fire. For the first time in his life, he could see stars above the city—a vast glittering bowl of them, arching over the dark buildings—something no New Yorker had seen in over a century, even during blackouts.

Watching the man through the slats, he tensed up: there did seem to be an odd little hitch in the man's gait, subtle but apparent nevertheless. It *was* Munck. He was taking full advantage of the dimness of the lights, instinctively slipping in and out of the pools of darkness as he made his way toward Fifth Avenue.

As he approached the rear of the mansion, D'Agosta felt his tension ratchet upward. His job was to protect the inhabitants of the house. But Munck was just there to observe the house and its inhabitants...wasn't he? What if he attempted a break-in? The mansion was well hardened for a building whose construction was not quite complete. But Pendergast's words rang in his mind: *Under no circumstances whatsoever are you to reveal yourself to Constance.*

From inside the shuttered newsstand, he watched as Munck slowed his gait, then paused in the darkness at the back of the town house, near the locked and barred entrance to the carriage entryway. Ostensibly it was to light a cigarette: D'Agosta made out the flaring of a match and the brief glow of the tip. Munck was clearly observing the house, staring upward at the lighted windows on the second floor.

D'Agosta began to relax. The man was only spying; he would be crazy to force entry. Besides, what good would that do? He peered through the slats as the figure lingered in the dimness. He tossed away his cigarette and strolled several yards back to the narrow service alleyway behind the town house...with its twelve-foot wrought iron barrier and cruel-looking spikes. No way was this short, gimpy fellow going to get over *that.* D'Agosta reassured himself further by feeling for the lump of the revolver in his pocket.

Minutes passed. It was freezing cold in the confines of the shuttered newsstand, made all the more uncomfortable by the tight space and the inability to move about, and D'Agosta felt increasingly stiff. He flexed his shoulders and rubbed his gloved hands together, wiggled his toes in the heavy hobnail boots. Still Munck loitered next to the alleyway, now smoking a second cigarette.

Suddenly, he dropped the cigarette and leapt up onto the iron bars, climbing up the barrier like a damned monkey, scrambling hand over hand with remarkable strength and rapidity. At the top, he vaulted over the spikes, shimmied back down the far side, then disappeared silently into the darkness behind the house. This remarkable display of physical agility had taken all of thirty seconds.

"What the *hell?*" D'Agosta muttered, staring at the empty spot where the discarded cigarette still burned. Was Munck set on the kind of close surveillance that could not be done from beyond the fence?

Or, against all odds, was he attempting to break in from the rear alleyway?

After a moment of agonizing indecision, D'Agosta threw open the kiosk door and darted across the street, head down so he wouldn't be recognized by a chance look from inside, then flattened himself against the wall next to the alleyway. A gaslight at the far end illuminated its length, and cautiously he looked around.

Munck was nowhere to be seen.

Where had the bastard gone? D'Agosta glanced over at the mansion, where the building met the ground. Then he looked up—and caught his breath in dismay.

From his vantage point inside the newsstand, he'd noticed hours before that all the windows of the structure had been securely shut. But now, a single second-floor window was open, its curtain billowing. He could see that the back side of the town house was composed of dark, unevenly shaped blocks. Higher up, evidence of roof work could be seen in the form of pulleys and hooks, dangling here and there.

The fact the man had decided to do it—that he'd been *able* to do it—hit D'Agosta like a blow. But there was no doubt in his mind: Munck had managed to climb the wall...and was now already inside the house.

72

Munck looked across the empty room to the only door, which gave onto the second-floor hall. This room, he knew from earlier observation, was almost never entered. He would be safe here as he prepared for what the professor wanted him to do.

I shall need the female child intact. Her room shares a water closet with her brother's. You will need to pay heed to the coachman and avoid rousing him if at all possible. There is also a tutor who lives on the third floor, but he is far less dangerous. The housemaid, cook, butler, and the rest live belowstairs— there is no egress from the basement save in the back kitchen, so if you are discovered you should have no difficulty barring the door and keeping them in the basement. However, it is my hope you will be able to take the child quietly, without waking the house. The security measures I saw during my brief visit were formidable. However, there was a second-story window off the stairway that looked easy enough to force—and I know you have no problem making that kind of entrance.

The professor had been right—the window locks were well made but no match for his expertise or the small set of tools he carried with him.

He placed his ear to the door and listened intently. As in every house, there were many small noises, which he now began to individuate. The two children were in a room down the hall, playing some sort of game...cards, judging from the few words he caught. He could hear the high, piping voice of his target, quarreling good-naturedly with her brother.

The tutor had, indeed, retired to his room on the third floor—Munck had seen his shadow briefly pass by a window—where he was no doubt settling down for the evening with a glass of port, his work done. The coachman was safely on the ground floor, in his apartment next to the carriage station, drinking beer—on the far side of the mansion, unable to arrive upstairs in time to render any aid.

Again, Munck, it is my strong desire that you effect this removal without alarming or awaking anyone. But I realize this may not be possible. Not counting the coachman, there are two people who reside in the house you will need to exercise the utmost caution with. They reside on the second floor, with the children. The Frenchwoman who acts as a private secretary is more than she seems: a snake to be dealt with quickly and mercilessly. And the duchess herself is even more formidable, perhaps exceptionally so; however, under no circumstances can she be killed. Damaged, rendered temporarily powerless, yes; killed, and I fear your own life will be forfeit.

Munck shuddered at this warning. If he failed, he wondered how the professor would choose to kill him, and whether it would involve a great deal of blood.

His ears, sharpened by years of precisely this kind of work, told him a great deal about the house: the Frenchwoman was busy on the first floor, supervising the clearing of the table from dinner, while the cook was in the kitchen kneading dough for next morning's sweet rolls. The butler and the rest were in their rooms belowstairs.

Munck's heart beat faster at the anticipation of what was to come. The achievements of his previous life, of which he was justly proud, had been due to his keen senses and animal cunning. These same qualities also served him well acquiring patients for the professor.

The only person whose location he did not know was the duchess herself. She was the most unpredictable member of the household, but he would hear her eventually: she couldn't remain silent forever. He let his mind relax, allowing the little sounds to come to him, along with snippets of conversation carrying vital information about the household. He inhaled, taking in the scents.

If, despite your best efforts, an alarum is raised in the household, it would be best if you treat everyone, save the duchess and the young boy, with the greatest prejudice; the sensationalism of murder will misdirect the authorities. If this is the path things must take, then you may reward yourself with a short but sweet playtime of bloodletting, before bringing the girl to me.

Munck shuddered again, this time in the grip of an entirely different emotion.

He could now hear the boy's voice raised in protest over some point or another of cards. As he listened, he heard a step down the hall—there she was: the duchess. Her step was very light indeed. She entered the room and he heard the murmur of her voice, the slight protest of the boy Joe, and then more soft footsteps and murmurings, followed by the opening and closing of a door.

Joe had gone to his own room. It was past eight o'clock: bedtime. The duchess remained in the girl's room, speaking softly. It took several minutes, but finally that door closed as well: the duchess had left the girl in her room for the night.

He waited.

The duchess's footsteps passed by his door, went down the carpeted stair, and vanished. Silence settled over the household. Now was the time to act.

He eased the door open a crack and peered down the hall. Empty. Two doors down, he knew, was the girl's room. He slipped out into the passage and moved carefully to her door. He paused at the threshold— then, silently and with great rapidity, he opened the door, strode over to the bed, and clapped his hand over the girl's mouth before she even knew what was happening. She struggled, eyes wide.

"Do what I say or I'll kill your brother," he told her in a whisper.

She stopped struggling.

"I'm going to remove my hand. You make a sound, your brother dies. Nod if you understand."

She nodded, her violet eyes wide with fear. But there was no panic in them: Munck knew she had spent all her life in the Five Points, and the sight and sound of violence was not new to her.

He removed his hand. She continued staring at him. "You're coming with me. Nice and quiet, like."

He pulled back the covers and yanked her out of bed. She was in her nightdress. That would not do. He crept to her closet, pulled out a sweater, coat, and shoes.

"Put these on. Real quiet, now."

She began putting the clothes on over the nightdress. As she did, Munck moved back to the door, listened a moment, and then cracked it. The hall was still empty. Then, suddenly, the door leading to the third floor opened and the tutor emerged. Munck was startled: this was not part of the expected routine.

The tutor closed the door to the stairway and began approaching along the hall. Munck instinctively realized he must be coming to the girl's room to say goodnight. That, of course, could not be permitted. Munck felt the gratifying thrill of what was about to happen course over him as he slipped out the door—and, all in a silent rush, met the surprised tutor and slit his throat from ear to ear before he could utter a sound.

The man collapsed, twisting slightly as he did so, blood jetting like a fire hose. Munck skipped back to avoid the spray, allowing himself to just douse his hands in it, exulting in the glossy gorgeousness of the blood painting the wall as the man knelt, hand fumbling at his throat, the look of surprise in his eyes fading to blankness as he toppled over.

Munck slipped back into the bedroom, then stopped. The girl was gone. He was unconcerned: the door to the water closet remained in the same position it had been before. The little vixen was hiding. He would find her soon enough.

He looked under the bed—nothing. Then he yanked open the

closet door, swept aside the clothes—and there she was, the little mademoiselle bitch. He jerked her out into the room, pulled out a silk handkerchief, gagged her—and then slapped her hard across the face. The little guttersnipe hardly flinched, staring back at him with such hatred it gave him a queer sensation in his gut.

Then he grabbed her by the neck and pushed her out the door and down the hall, in the direction of the stairs.

73

Pendergast, frozen with horror, could do nothing but stare at the face exposed by the coverlet. The body in the bed was not asleep, but dead and growing stiff: but it was not the corpse of Mary. It was Gaspard Ferenc.

As Pendergast stared, the awful revelation sank in. Ferenc had somehow escaped Proctor's supervision and managed to use the machine himself. Somehow, he had been captured by Leng; tortured; and killed.

Following immediately upon this revelation was another, even more terrible: Leng now knew everything.

No wonder he had attained this underground room so easily, with no resistance. He had been practically lured here by Leng. From the depths of his horror, Pendergast felt a surge of self-loathing at being outmaneuvered.

But there was no time to think about that. He must get back to Constance's mansion—because that was surely where Leng would strike while he wasted his time down here.

He turned and sprinted from the room, down the corridor, through the doors, and—at last reaching the staircase—raced up it two steps at a time. A moment later, he burst through the door into the alcove and ran from Shottum's Cabinet, scattering the patrons in his headlong rush. Once in the open air again, he dashed northward up Catherine

Street. There were no cabs to be found in the slums, but there would surely be some along the Bowery.

And there was one: waiting at a cab stand, the driver dozing in his high perch. Pendergast leapt up on his horse and pulled out his knife, slashing off the traces and reins and freeing the animal. The cabbie, roused, began shouting and trying to strike at Pendergast with his whip, but it was too late: Pendergast dug his heels into the horse's flanks and, with a shrill whistle, sent the animal galloping up the Bowery toward Union Square and beyond.

74

D'AGOSTA STOOD OUTSIDE the iron bars, staring up at the open window and its curtain, fluttering almost like a distress signal in the cold December wind.

Munck had climbed up there and gotten in. There was no other possibility. What was the bastard doing? Making a nocturnal recon... or something worse?

More to the point: what should *he* do?

Pendergast's dire warning about alerting Constance or no, one thing was clear: he had to get inside. He couldn't let that brute roam free.

Yet he couldn't just go pound on the front door and demand to be let in. That was lunacy—and besides, raising the alarm like that would let Munck know they were on to him. He could do a lot of damage in the household before D'Agosta could even talk his way inside.

For that matter, the bastard could be doing a lot of damage *now*.

There was only one option: to get into the house the same way Munck had.

He looked up at the iron bars, topped with curved spikes. He was out of shape and approaching the far end of middle age, with a tire around his middle and no climbing experience. But he immediately shed his heavy coat, feeling the sudden, bracing cold—which if nothing else, energized him—grabbed two wrought iron bars, and hoisted himself up. Thank God the bars were spaced just wide enough so he could wedge his hobnailed boots between them.

One hoist, two, three, boots slipping a little, four...and then he was high enough to grasp the curve of one of the iron spikes. Pulling himself up, he grabbed the adjoining spike. Scrabbling with his boots, the hobnails digging into the iron, he hauled himself up with a groan of effort, his face hovering just below the tips of the spikes, pitted with rust and pointing downward. Facing *him.*

What now?

Without giving himself time either to rest or think, he braced his feet and pushed off, swinging his body out and up, landing hard atop the recurved spikes. One leg didn't quite clear the spikes, and a point tore through his pants and scored a gash along his thigh. But at least he was lying on top. Looking down twelve feet. It seemed more like a thousand.

He paused, breathing hard. Then, keeping himself balanced, he swung his legs over the spikes, and—gripping maniacally at the bars— scrabbled with his feet until he managed to wedge them once again between the bars, this time on the other side. He began working his way back down, releasing first one hand, then one foot, allowing his body to slide a little each time. But just as he was getting the rhythm, one of his boots slipped out of position; a hand slid down the rusty bar, filling the meat of his palm with sharp flakes of iron. He lost purchase with the other boot—and he fell.

A split second of terror and then he hit the ground, rolling instinctively. He ended up lying on his side, the wind knocked from his lungs, desperately trying to suck in air. Christ, did he break something? Or, more likely, everything?

After a minute he struggled to his knees, then hauled himself to his feet, using the nearby bars as a crutch. He moved his limbs gingerly, one at a time. Nothing broken. Just half a dozen hematomas.

He reminded himself that the longer he delayed, the more time Munck had to spend in the house.

He walked beneath the open window. From his position, with the ground floor sloping gently into a rise of land, the second floor might as well have been the penthouse. Mother*fucker*, was he really going to climb that?

Naturally, the mansion didn't have the nice, low, nine-foot ceilings of twenty-first-century apartments. This would make the second-story climb even longer.

He noticed a series of decorative stone lintels, or whatever the hell they were called. Above each of them, the rear wall of the house was built of pudding-stone blocks that afforded a number of small, protruding horizontal ledges.

He stared upward for a moment in clean, cold fear. Then he said savagely to himself: *Get your fat ass moving.*

He grabbed a lintel with both hands, raised one leg to put a boot on it, and hoisted himself up. Then he repeated this with another lintel: another hand, another foot, pulling himself up to the next decorative ledge. As long as he kept his hobnailed boots sideways, he seemed to get a pretty good purchase. But already the muscles of his arms and legs were protesting from the effort.

Unconsciously, he glanced down and felt the sudden choke of panic. *It's only ten feet*, he told himself. *It's going to get worse. Keep going, and don't look down.* But he *had* to look down, if only to make sure of the placement of his boots—and each time, as he ascended farther and farther from the ground, the sight seized his gut with terror.

Reaching the main ledge of the first floor, he stopped to rest, holding gratefully on to a window bar as he caught his breath. He went on; there was no time to waste. He started up the next story, using a lintel first as a handhold, a foothold, and then he climbed a section where only the rough projecting stones and sloppy mortar offered purchase. Trying not to think of how small these improvised ledges were, he pulled himself up, found a fresh purchase, then pulled himself up yet again, keeping his eyes fixed on the second-floor window above.

And then he stopped. What now? The final five feet were smoother, the stone blocks offering little opportunity for a grab or a hoist.

He felt his thigh muscles burning, and both arms were trembling with the effort of simply holding himself in place. He had to keep going—or he'd run out of muscle power and fall. Instinctively, he glanced down.

Shit. Big mistake.

He would have to edge sideways a bit. To his right, there was a ring driven into the stone, an artifact from when the builders had used a pulley to finish the surfacing of the house. But it was almost out of reach—he'd have to edge sideways from his already precarious perch. Without giving himself time to think better of the idea, he stretched, mustered the strength for a tiny hop, and managed to grasp it.

Now his legs were fully extended, thigh muscles screaming.

He grabbed a projecting stone, got his foot on the ring, pushed up, and finally grasped the lower edge of the open window. He groped blindly at the sloping sill and, reaching in farther, managed to get a good hold on the wooden casement. He got his other hand on it, then raised one boot to a piece of projecting mortar. He put his weight on it, slowly, then released his other foot. The mortar broke off, his boot slipped—and suddenly he found himself dangling by his hands, feet scrabbling wildly for a purchase, heart in his throat. With a surge of panic, he chinned up with brute force, hauling himself over the threshold with his arms, and fell headfirst into the darkened room. He lay on the floor, gasping for breath, his heart pounding like a tom-tom, his muscles jerking, his palms and fingers and knees scraped and stinging.

He gave himself sixty seconds to recover, no more. A quick look around showed the room was empty. He pulled the revolver from his pocket and rotated the barrel—a six-shot Colt .45, fully loaded—and then got to his feet and tiptoed painfully to the door.

He could hear no sound. He eased the door open and looked out—and was stunned to see a man crumpled on the floor, his head resting at an unnatural angle, blood dripping down the wall and soaking the carpet.

Munck had already been at work. *Dear God, what if...*

And now a door closer to him opened and a cloaked figure emerged—Munck—and he was holding the little girl by her neck. He looked over, saw D'Agosta—and raised a six-inch knife to her throat.

She was gagged, her eyes wide.

"Drop the gun now," he told D'Agosta in a whisper. *"Not a sound. Or I do to her like what I did the schoolteacher."*

75

D'AGOSTA FROZE. HE might be able to get off a shot with the revolver, just possibly, before Munck cut the girl's throat—but the Colt .45 was not an accurate weapon, and the man was using the girl as a shield.

Under no circumstances whatsoever are you to reveal yourself to Constance...

"*Now*," said Munck, the tip of his knife just pricking the girl's flesh, a drop of blood welling up at the point of contact.

D'Agosta held out his arm and let the gun swing by the trigger guard.

"On the carpet," the man said.

He did as instructed, mind going a mile a minute. This was no mere recon: the schoolteacher was dead. But not the girl. D'Agosta realized she was not so much a hostage as a kidnap victim. That meant Leng wanted her alive. Munck *might* not kill her—it all depended on how strict Leng's orders had been.

"I'm going to leave," Munck said. "If you raise any alarm before we're out the front door, I cut her throat."

The man lowered the knife from the girl's throat as he began backing toward the staircase. And in that moment, D'Agosta knew that—whatever orders he'd been given, and as unexpected as this situation was—he had no option but to act.

He leapt forward and rushed the bastard, who in turn jumped to one side and lashed out with the knife, slashing his forearm as

D'Agosta warded off the blow. But his forward momentum was so strong that he body-slammed the man. Surprisingly, Munck didn't go down, merely staggered—short as he was, he was as massive as a rock—and he swung his knife back around with the intention of sinking it in D'Agosta's back. But he was encumbered by the girl, and this allowed D'Agosta to punch his own arm upward, striking the descending forearm, which—following through on the punch—he slammed against the wall, the knife flying.

Again, Munck backed toward the stairway, dragging the girl with him. Just then, decorative drapery was flung aside from one wall, and out of a hidden door a woman appeared. She advanced on Munck with a poker.

"*Meurs, salaud!*" she cried.

Munck, clasping the girl to him, abruptly raised his left hand in an odd, martial salute, twisting his wrist as he did so. There was a clang of ringing steel—and suddenly three long, thin blades slid out from below his fingers: a giant, spring-loaded claw, hidden beneath his forearm.

D'Agosta skipped back in surprise as the foreign woman swung the poker, but Munck ducked and swept his arm in a wide angle, slashing her brutally across the midsection. As she fell back, Munck lunged with animal swiftness toward D'Agosta, aiming for his eyes; D'Agosta pivoted, in a desperate attempt to dodge the blow, but Munck twisted his own wrist simultaneously and—though the bloodied claw just missed D'Agosta—its metal enclosure impacted violently with his temple. D'Agosta staggered back, bright lights filling his vision, the sudden warmth of syncope beginning to envelop him. The man raced down the stairs, hauling the girl roughly along with him, even as D'Agosta—struggling to recover his wits—grabbed his gun from the floor, almost collapsing in the effort.

As he lurched down the stairs, he saw that Munck, moving like lightning, had already vanished from the landing below. D'Agosta could hear the house coming to life. Reaching the bottom landing, he saw Munck make a beeline across the entryway and through the first of two doors leading to the street. He raised his gun, but staggered, unable to get a bead on the man.

Suddenly, flying out of a darkened parlor, came a figure—Constance—stiletto raised, terrible in the silence of her attack. Munck reached the outer door and grasped the handle, yanking it open, but Constance slammed it closed again; D'Agosta saw a flash of steel and Munck lurched back immediately, cut badly across the face. Quickly collecting himself, he sprang at Constance, his nightmare device catching her knife arm; then he yanked the door open again and leapt out with the girl into the cold December night.

Constance, sleeve torn wide and blood welling, took up the pursuit. D'Agosta tried to follow. But as he reached the threshold, a wave of dizziness forced him to stop...even as he saw the man—Munck—clambering into the compartment of a sleek trap that had just pulled up in front of the mansion, evidently loitering nearby and expecting his emergence. A glossy thoroughbred was in the traces. A gloved hand from within helped Munck inside, the girl clutched close...and then the horse took off, galloping at high speed down Fifth Avenue and vanishing into the winter darkness. D'Agosta began to raise his gun again, but his chances of hitting the target were nonexistent—all he'd do was alert the neighborhood and draw the police.

Constance ran down the steps, sprinted to the corner...then sank to her knees in the dirty snow, letting forth an incoherent cry of rage and pain, stretching out her bloody hands into the night.

The scene began to whirl around him, and D'Agosta half sat, half collapsed onto the marble floor of the entryway. A darkness that had nothing to do with the time of night closed in from the sides of his vision and he lost the struggle to maintain consciousness.

76

D'Agosta wasn't sure how much time passed until he recovered his senses, but it could not have been long. He found himself lying on the floor of the parlor, looking up at Constance, who stood over him, her face contorted, violet eyes raging.

The coachman arrived with a thud of heavy boots and quickly took in the scene. "Your Grace, you're injured!" he cried in a coarse Irish accent. "What bitch's bastard—?"

Constance was heedless, staring down at D'Agosta.

The coachman looked down at him. "Is this the one what done it?" He took a step forward, face darkening.

"Murphy, attend to Féline," Constance said. "Upstairs. Find Joe and keep him safe. Instruct the other servants to lock down the house."

"Do you not want me to bring the carriage round—"

"You'll never catch them," said Constance. "Now, see to Féline and Joe—I fear that beast killed Moseley."

Murphy backed away, then went up the stairs. Other staff began arriving, but Constance was still staring at D'Agosta, her eyes burning right through him, the terrible look making him forget his pounding head, the dire situation...everything.

D'Agosta wanted to say something, wanted to explain, but he couldn't think clearly enough to speak. Instead, he struggled to a sitting position, head swimming from the blow.

A maid was attending to Constance's injured arm, wrapping it in linen cloth, but she had recovered her stiletto and was now pointing it at D'Agosta with her other hand. "Before I kill you," she said in a low, trembling voice, "I want an explanation."

D'Agosta still couldn't find the words. As Constance moved closer, he wondered, with strange detachment, if she was about to cut his throat. He heard, as if from very far away, the clatter of a galloping horse—and then, much louder, an abrupt pounding on the door.

"Open the door!" came a cry. "Now!"

It was the voice of Pendergast.

Still staring at D'Agosta, Constance rose, walked across the reception hall, and threw open the front door.

Pendergast stood there, heaving with fatigue.

"*You!*" was all she said.

Pendergast brushed past her, saw D'Agosta, then quickly came over and knelt beside him.

"Did they get Binky?" he asked.

D'Agosta managed to nod.

As Pendergast patted him gently from head to toe, examining him for wounds, he spoke to Constance through clenched teeth. "You and I were never supposed to meet in this world," he said. "But since we have, it's best you hear all—and quickly. Leng knows about the machine. He knows who you are. He knows you've come from the future to kill him. He knows *everything.*"

Constance stared. "Impossible."

"*Absolutely* possible," Pendergast said. "We must prepare ourselves. There's no time to lose."

"He kidnapped Binky—"

"He's been one step ahead of you at every turn. At the ball, at tea— and believe me: this is just the beginning."

Silence filled the marble foyer as Constance, surrounded by a semicircle of house servants, went very pale. She stared at Pendergast, unmoving, while the agent rose and stepped away from D'Agosta. She said nothing, but the expression on her face made it clear she was veering from one unfathomable emotion to the next.

"We'll have to watch you for signs of subdural bleeding," Pendergast told D'Agosta. He turned and held his hand out to Constance, who slapped it away.

"You don't have the luxury of anger right now," Pendergast told her. "We've got to prepare. Your sister is at immensely grave risk. We must—"

He was interrupted by a knock at the door, polite and tentative.

Everyone turned toward the sound.

"It appears to be a delivery, Your Grace," the butler—who had recovered his composure—said, peering through the eyehole.

Pendergast drew his weapon and stood to one side, aiming at the door. He nodded to the butler. "Open it."

A young messenger in beautiful livery stood in the doorway, holding a handsomely wrapped gift box, tied up and garnished with fragrant white lilies. "Delivery for Her Grace, the Duchess of Ironclaw," he said.

Constance stared at the man. "What the devil is this?"

"There's a note, madam," said the delivery person, his eyes widening as he took in the scene: Constance bandaged, D'Agosta lying prone on the floor.

She snatched the package from him as he turned and made for the street. Holding it under one arm, she plucked away the envelope that was tucked beneath a gold ribbon, tore it open, and extracted a card, engraved with a black border. As she stared at it, her face drained of all color. Then she dropped the card and tore the gold wrapping from the package, strewing the flowers about the floor and exposing a small mahogany box. She seized the lid and pulled it off. Inside, D'Agosta saw a flash of silver. Reaching in, Constance extracted a silver urn, then let the box fall to the floor. Taking the urn in both hands, she held it in front of her face, staring at the engraved label on its belly. For a moment all was still...and then the urn, too, slipped through her nerveless fingers and struck the floor with a crash, its top flying off and the urn rolling across the floor, spilling a stream of gray ashes behind it.

The urn finally came to rest against D'Agosta's leg, the engraved label on its upper side. He squinted to read it, his vision still cloudy—but the words etched into the silver were nevertheless deep and clear:

MARY GREENE
DIED DECEMBER 26TH 1880
AGED 19 YEARS
ASHES TO ASHES
DUST TO DUST

77

June 13
Tuesday

SPECIAL AGENT ARMSTRONG COLDMOON rested on a couch in the security office of Miami International Airport's north terminal, his eyes half-closed. Outside, it was still dark: the sun wouldn't rise for another hour. The five-o'clock arrival would ensure, he had hoped, a quiet setting for the arrest. But the idea wasn't working out. The mile-long concourse of the north terminal, with its nearly fifty boarding gates—the central hub for international tourists coming into Florida—was already filling up. He listened to the sounds of passenger chatter from beyond the closed door with rising apprehension. The man couldn't be armed, but he still might cause a ruckus.

When Coldmoon had suggested they meet at a remote airfield in South Dakota—the guy had a private plane, and this would keep the arrest low profile—Armendariz had pushed back. Why not take an American Airlines flight into Miami, as his private jet was not overseas rated? He didn't mind flying commercial, he said. Perhaps he felt safer in a crowd. Coldmoon wasn't thrilled to make the arrest in such a public place, but Tom Torres had lent him two plainclothes agents who'd taken the same flight, just in case Armendariz had some trick up his sleeve. And again, by arresting him in the secure portion of the terminal, it was guaranteed he and any bodyguards with him wouldn't be armed.

But that was ultimately of little importance. It was his first big-time international case, and it had gone perfectly. The sting operation worked better than he'd anticipated. Coldmoon had figured he'd have to remain in character, undercover, for a couple of days, schmoozing with Armendariz while the wealthy antiquities collector took his measure as they enjoyed horseback rides, tasting wine from his winery, and whatever else billionaires did for entertainment. But what he hadn't anticipated was just how eager Armendariz had been to acquire the Winter Count. They'd talked over lunch, had a few drinks...and then they'd shaken hands. Armendariz wanted to see the Winter Count right away—he was practically salivating over it. He told Coldmoon to fly back to the States to prepare for the transaction, and he would follow in two days—after pulling together the $2 million purchase price. If it was as promised, the money would be wired and he'd fly the artifact back to the hacienda to join the rest of his collection.

The beauty of it all was that this transaction, at least, would be legal. Witko was the legal owner, there was a clear (if phony) provenance from Crazy Horse himself, and there were no export restrictions. And Armendariz was so eager to acquire it, he showed no qualms about flying to the States—the most crucial part of Coldmoon's plan.

Coldmoon was astonished at how little Armendariz fit his mental picture of a murdering, grasping, billionaire collector. The sense of menace Coldmoon had felt when he arrived at the palatial hacienda was, he soon realized, mostly in his own mind. Beyond the armed men at the gates, he'd seen no other weapons and few bodyguards. Armendariz himself had been the opposite of crude or intimidating. He was garrulous, hospitable, and carried himself with a kind of Old-World dignity and charm. If anything, the man reminded Coldmoon more of an intellectual—a professor, maybe, or a journalist—than a wealthy, ruthless criminal. He apologized for his eagerness to see their transaction concluded. He didn't drag Coldmoon to visit a garage full of gleaming supercars, or show off rooms stuffed with gilt furniture, and there were no blonde bimbos hanging around a pool. He did take Coldmoon to his museum and showed him a number of truly splendid Lakota artifacts—but Coldmoon had been disappointed not to see the famous pipe or Ghost Dance shirt. The man was clearly being cautious that way.

One of the local FBI agents, sitting at a nearby desk, interrupted his thoughts. "Landing in ten."

"All units in place?"

A pause. "Six airside, four more beyond the security perimeter, just in case."

"Good." Coldmoon reached for the cup of coffee beside the couch, then thought better of it. He'd ingested enough caffeine over the last seventy-two hours to give a tree sloth tachycardia. But, given the target's eagerness, this had been the only way to work it: straight flight back to Miami and spend the next twenty hours with the local field office coordinating the grab.

It was on the flight back to Miami that he'd figured it out. Armendariz *was* an intellectual. Would some bloodthirsty cartel boss be likely to collect Native American artifacts? And, other than raising some political hackles in his adopted country, he seemed to keep a low profile—at least, that's what International Operations had told him, which was where Coldmoon got almost all of his intel. He'd asked Coldmoon many questions about his family, his great-great-grandfather, and his life growing up on the Rez. He seemed genuinely interested. Coldmoon found it hard not to like the guy... until he reminded himself he was a murderer, thief, and cultural expropriator.

Cultural expropriator. Coldmoon himself understood the collecting impulse. As a kid, he'd accumulated every Madball he could find—just about the only toy you could buy on the Rez because they doubled as baseballs, sick-looking things that hurt like a motherfucker if you got hit with one. There were a dozen or so different kinds, and he vividly remembered a time he would have done just about anything, legal or otherwise, to get his hands on the Oculus Orbus. But these people like Armendariz...intellectual or not, he didn't care about finally honoring the treaties and returning the Black Hills to the Lakota, or helping bring jobs to the Rez. No, his type was all about spending millions on things they didn't create, had no connection to, and that rightfully belonged back with the Lakota themselves.

He checked his watch. "Flight status?" he asked the guy at the desk.

"Wheels down, taxiing."

"All right." He looked around the rest of the room. "Let's get busy."

He stood, put on his jacket, snugged his Browning into the small of his back, then headed for the door and out into the fresher air of the terminal. Thank God: as was usually the case, the security office smelled like old socks, BO, and scorched microwave popcorn.

The concourse was even busier than he'd feared. Coldmoon followed the small procession—two local agents, two TSA security officers, and two Miami plainclothes police—down the wide concourse, through security control, past the duty-free shops and the Skytrain access, to an unmarked door. Opening this, they descended one flight to the international arrivals and customs zone for Concourse D.

Multiple voices were sounding over the airport's speakers, and ahead in the distance Coldmoon could see large bunches of people coming in their direction—just deplaned and headed for customs. His own small group made its way around the customs barrier, then took up a three-point position at the spot where pedestrian traffic slowed to form lines. Coldmoon looked around, satisfying himself with the layout. Not far away stood the two ICE agents who would be making the actual collar. He'd have plenty of time himself with Armenderiz—later.

He took a deep breath and tried to savor the moment. This was a big op—and he was in charge. His overwhelming feeling was an eagerness to get his man in the bag.

...And then, just like that, he turned and saw Armendariz, his tall, elegant figure clearly visible among the crowd. He was wearing another formal Spanish suit, black hair still immaculate after the long flight. In one hand was a leather carry-on, a dark coat slung over his forearm. He did not appear to have bodyguards with him, but if he did they were the responsibility of Torres's people, not Coldmoon.

Armendariz, approaching now, saw Coldmoon, and his face lit up in a smile. "Mr. Witko!" he said, holding out his hand in greeting. "*Buenos días!*"

Coldmoon stepped forward, smiling and grasping the hand that was offered. He held it firm as the two ICE agents came up. When he saw the rest taking backup positions, he let go.

"Ramón Armendariz y Urias," said one of the agents, a Hispanic woman with short mahogany hair, "you are under arrest for homicide and grand larceny, among other felonious offenses." As she spoke, the other ICE agent smoothly slipped a pair of cuffs on the astonished man and snugged them tight.

Armendariz blinked in complete surprise, looking oddly vulnerable, like a sleeper who'd just had his bedcovers ripped violently away.

"Specifically," Coldmoon added, "for the suspected murders of Grayson Twoeagle and Eugene Mancow."

For a moment, Armendariz looked at the small circle of somber faces surrounding him. Then they returned to Coldmoon. "Armstrong?" he asked. "What is this?"

"Take him away," Coldmoon said.

Each taking an arm, the ICE agents began steering Armendariz toward a door leading from the concourse to customs security. It was only then, as he was forced into motion, that the billionaire seemed to awaken from his daze. "No!" he said, beginning to struggle. "What is this? What are you doing to me?"

Inwardly, Coldmoon cringed. This was just the kind of scene he'd hoped to avoid.

Seeing resistance, more officers rushed over. Gasps arose from the people in line for customs, there was a surge backward in the crowd, and a dozen phones were quickly held up.

"This is a mistake!" Armendariz said. "Did you say homicide? Grand larceny? This is insane, a colossal mistake. Why are you doing this? *Where are you taking me?*"

And then suddenly—to Coldmoon's dismay—the man began resisting, trying to tear his arms away from the agents, swinging them to and fro, all pretense of sophistication and civility gone. As still more law officers came over to help subdue him, and as one body they half pushed, half dragged Armendariz toward the door, his voice turned into a yell as he struggled against his captors. "Help! *Help!* Armstrong! I'm innocent! *Don't let them take me! Don't let—!"*

But the rant was abruptly muffled by the closing of the security door—and soon, even that faded away. As the excited chattering around him subsided and people once again turned their attention to getting out of the airport, Coldmoon was struck by how much he still had to learn when it came to reading people. Here he'd spent hours preparing a mental dossier on Armendariz's personality—but this spectacle took him by surprise. He'd never expected such an outcry, such melodrama, the man trying so feverishly to maintain his innocence and free himself.

This musing was interrupted by one of the Miami FBI agents. "Good job, Coldmoon," the man told him. "ICE and DHS will take a while processing him—that was the deal. I doubt we'll get custody for at least three, maybe four hours. Want to head back to the office?"

"No. Sleep is what I want." Automatically, Coldmoon began to turn in the direction of the official parking lot, then stopped. "Call me when they've released him to us, okay?"

"Sure thing."

"Thanks." Coldmoon walked away.

The case was over. They had their man. Of course, there would be mopping up to do, accomplices to arrest, interrogations, evidence gathering—but the key to everything had been getting Armendariz on U.S. soil, and they'd done that without a hitch. It was like a dream, how willingly the man had walked into their sting. Now that it was all over, Coldmoon was surprised to find he really didn't feel all that different. He did wish that D'Agosta could have been here to see the collar. He was curious whether the NYPD lieutenant commander had ever witnessed such an Oscar-winning performance as Armendariz gave when they'd slapped the cuffs on him.

78

December 27, 1880
Thursday

D'AGOSTA RESTED IN A wing chair, watching the rising sun work in vain to penetrate the shutters that wreathed the parlor in gloom. His head pounded in time to the beat of his heart.

In the hours that had crawled by since the assault, the house had settled into a frozen state of shock. Féline, slashed by Munck, had been sutured and dressed by Pendergast, and given an injection of antibiotics Pendergast had carried in his pocket from the twenty-first century. Murphy had taken Moseley's body to the basement, where it had been secretly interred under a newly laid brick floor. Joe was upstairs, asleep, being looked after by a maid. The rest of the servants had retreated to their rooms save for Gosnold, the butler, who insisted on remaining at his position in the parlor.

The urn and spilled ashes had been swept up and taken away. The card that had come with it, however, remained where Pendergast had placed it after reading the contents: on a side table near D'Agosta. All the long night, D'Agosta had been unable to bring himself to read it. But as the sky outside continued to brighten, he finally turned his head painfully toward the table, reached out, and took it up.

My dearest Constance,

I present, with condolences, the ashes of your older sister. They come with my thanks. The surgery was most successful.

Your plan was a desperate one from the start. I sensed you would double-cross me; it was just the mechanics of your betrayal that puzzled me. And then, mirabile dictu, *the instrument that could lay bare the precise scheme was delivered to Bellevue . . . and from there into my hands.*

You have the Arcanum; I have you: or rather, your younger self. Give me the formula, true and complete, and the girl will be returned to you intact. And then our business will be concluded . . . save for one thing. This is not your world to meddle in; it is mine. You, and those who followed you, will return to your own forthwith. Leave mine— or suffer the consequences.

You will signal your agreement by placing a candle inside a blue lantern and hanging it in the southeastern bedroom window of the third floor. I will then contact you with further instructions.

If I do not receive this signal within 48 hours, young Constance will suffer the fate of her older sister.

Until our next correspondence, I remain,

Your devoted, etc.
Dr. Enoch Leng

D'Agosta cursed under his breath and laid the note aside.

In the moments after the liveried messenger departed, Constance had been incandescent with rage and—D'Agosta was certain—at the very brink of madness. Her feral hysteria had been the most unsettling thing he'd ever witnessed. Pendergast had said nothing, his face an expressionless mask of pale marble. He had listened to her imprecations and recriminations without response. And then he had risen and taken care of Féline, examined D'Agosta's head wound, and silently supervised the cleanup of the murder scene and Murphy's disposal of the body. Everyone appeared to be in unspoken agreement not to involve the authorities in any way—which, D'Agosta knew, would surely lead to disaster.

And now the three of them remained in the parlor, silent as statues, sunk in a mixture of grief, guilt, and shock as a new and uncertain day crept into life outside the shuttered windows.

It was Constance who finally disturbed the uneasy stasis. She rose and disappeared upstairs. After ten minutes she reappeared, holding a small, well-worn leather notebook. She turned to the butler, who was still waiting at the parlor entrance. "Light a taper in a blue lantern and place it in the window of the last bedroom on the right, third floor."

"Yes, Your Grace." Gosnold disappeared to fulfill the request.

"Just a moment," said Pendergast. He turned to Constance. "Is that the Arcanum?"

"Did you think you were the only one who had a copy? You forget: I was there while he developed it."

"So you intend to comply with Leng's instructions? You'll give him the Arcanum—which will allow him to carry out his plan?"

"Do you have a better proposal?"

Pendergast shut his eyes, then opened them again without replying.

"It won't matter that he has the Arcanum," she said. "Because he won't live long enough to use it—I will see to that."

Once again, the parlor was silent for a moment. Pendergast shifted in his chair. "Don't you think Leng has already anticipated this intention of yours?"

Constance stared at him. "It doesn't matter."

"It does matter. Leng knows everything and anticipates everything. Whether you care to admit it or not, he is far cleverer than either of us. Not only that—he knows I'm here. He will be prepared for whatever you do—whatever *we* do."

"He will not," said a sudden, soft voice from the darkness, "be prepared for *me*."

A match flared in a rear doorway of the parlor.

And then a figure stepped forward, lighting a salmon-colored Lorillard cigarette set into an ebony holder. The flare illuminated the pale face, the aquiline nose and high smooth forehead, the ginger-colored beard, and the two eyes—one hazel, the other a milky blue—of Diogenes Pendergast.

"I am come," he said, "as your Angel of Vengeance." Then the match was shaken out and the figure returned to silhouette as a low, quiet laugh filled the room before dying away, leaving the parlor once again in shadow and silence.

TO BE CONCLUDED . . .

To the Reader

First: thank you for reading this book. Second: our apologies for what is, at least in part, an inconclusive ending.

When we began *Bloodless*, the Pendergast novel preceding this, we did not realize the story would grow and spread until it encompassed a narrative that we began in our earlier novel, *The Cabinet of Curiosities*— a narrative that you now know is not over yet.

Ideally, this novel fits into a sequence one might call the Leng Quartet: *The Cabinet of Curiosities*, *Bloodless*, *The Cabinet of Dr. Leng*, and a fourth, concluding novel which we are writing as fast as possible. And we promise to make up for leaving the story hanging fire by ultimately bringing it to a most satisfying finish.

We thank you again for your interest in our work.

ABOUT THE AUTHORS

The thrillers of **DOUGLAS PRESTON** and **LINCOLN CHILD** "stand head and shoulders above their rivals" (*Publishers Weekly*). Preston and Child's *Relic* and *The Cabinet of Curiosities* were chosen by readers in a National Public Radio poll as being among the one hundred greatest thrillers ever written, and *Relic* was made into a number-one box office hit movie. They are coauthors of the famed Pendergast series, and their recent novels include *Bloodless*, *The Scorpion's Tail*, *Crooked River*, *Old Bones*, and *Verses for the Dead*. In addition to his novels, Preston writes about archaeology for *The New Yorker* and *Smithsonian* magazines. Child is a Florida resident and former book editor who has published seven novels of his own, including such bestsellers as *Chrysalis* and *Deep Storm*.

Readers can sign up for The Pendergast File, a monthly "strangely entertaining note" from the authors, at their website, PrestonChild.com. The authors welcome visitors to their Facebook page, where they post regularly.

Water damage   cml/circ 2024